George Fleming

Rabies and Hydrophobia

Anatiposi

George Fleming

Rabies and Hydrophobia

Reprint of the original, first published in 1872.

1st Edition 2023 | ISBN: 978-3-38213-325-2

Anatiposi Verlag is an imprint of Outlook Verlagsgesellschaft mbH.

Verlag (Publisher): Outlook Verlag GmbH, Zeilweg 44, 60439 Frankfurt, Deutschland
Vertretungsberechtigt (Authorized to represent): E. Roepke, Zeilweg 44, 60439 Frankfurt, Deutschland
Druck (Print): Books on Demand GmbH, In de Tarpen 42, 22848 Norderstedt, Deutschland

TO MY ESTEEMED FRIEND,

MONSIEUR HENRI BOULEY,

Member of the Institute of France, the Academy of Medicine, and other learned Societies; Inspector of the French Veterinary Schools, and Officer of the Legion of Honour;

This Treatise is Dedicated,

IN RECOGNITION OF THE DISTINGUISHED AND VALUABLE SERVICES HE HAS RENDERED TO COMPARATIVE ANATOMY AND PATHOLOGY, AS WELL AS TO HUMAN MEDICINE, DURING A LIFETIME DEVOTED TO THE STUDY AND PERFECTING OF VETERINARY SCIENCE.

BROMPTON BARRACKS, CHATHAM,
March 7, 1872.

of the book, but to adopt that which I have chosen ; though it is much to be desired that comparative pathologists should desist from employing a term which has led to serious mistakes, and is based on a single symptom not invariably present in even only one of the many creatures susceptible of the disease.

CONTENTS.

exudations in various regions, but more particularly towa cardiac origin of the large vessels and the thoracic por the trachea. When the course of the disease has no rapid, there may be tumefaction, infiltration, and even tion of Peyer's glands in the intestines. In the other of anthrax—the apoplectic, erysipelatous, and carbunc there can be no difficulty in arriving at a diagnosis.

RABIES AND HYDROPHOBIA:

THEIR HISTORY, NATURE, CAUSES, SYMPTOMS, AND PREVENTION.

BY GEORGE FLEMING, F.R.G.S., M.A.I.,

PRESIDENT OF THE CENTRAL VETERINARY MEDICAL SOCIETY; MEMBER OF COUNCIL OF THE ROYAL COLLEGE OF VETERINARY SURGEONS; VETERINARY SURGEON, ROYAL ENGINEERS; AUTHOR OF "TRAVELS ON HORSEBACK IN MANTCHU TARTARY," "HORSE-SHOES AND HORSE-SHOEING," "ANIMAL PLAGUES," "PRACTICAL HORSE-SHOEING," ETC.

WITH EIGHT ILLUSTRATIONS.

LONDON:

CHAPMAN AND HALL, 193, PICCADILLY.

1872.

PREFACE.

In 1866, while engaged in preparing a work on Animal Plagues in general, my attention was more particularly directed to the extension of Rabies, within a certain period, to countries in which it had been previously unknown; and also to the unusual number of deaths occurring in this country, and especially in Lancashire, in that year: no fewer than thirty-six persons having been reported as dead in England from hydrophobia. In 1868 the disease was assuming greater proportions among the canine species, and West Lancashire appeared to have become a centre from which it spread in various directions, until it became widely disseminated, and had attained the dimensions of a serious epizoöty—formidable alike to mankind, as well as to the other domesticated animals. There can scarcely be any doubt that this prevalence and extension of rabies is largely due to the ignorance prevailing with regard to its nature, the symptoms which precede its more violent stage, and the almost total absence of efficient veterinary police measures to suppress it; as well as to the existence of dangerous errors, which have become so deep-rooted in the popular mind through their transmission from generation to generation, that it would seem an almost hopeless task to attempt their eradication.

Since the death of the distinguished English veterinarians, Blaine and Youatt, it may be said that in this country nothing has been added to our knowledge of the disease as it manifests itself in the dog; while, so far as the other domesticated animals are concerned, I am not aware that anything of any note has been done to elucidate the malady in them; and I believe no proposal has yet been made with a view to limiting or suppressing it by well-devised legislative measures, founded on an intimate knowledge of its nature.

I have endeavoured, therefore, in the following pages to offer a complete treatise on the subject from a sanitary, and also from a comparative pathologist's, point of view; for I believed that my labours would be incomplete, and would lose much of their value, did I omit to include mankind in the list while treating of every other creature that suffers from its effects. In this instance, as in so many others, it is almost impossible to divorce human pathology from its twin, and by no means to be despised, sister—comparative pathology. For many years the student of disease has had ample reason to regret the neglect with which the latter science has been treated in this country, and to wonder why human and veterinary medicine should be so strangely isolated from each other, instead of affording mutual aid in the advancement of medical knowledge. There cannot be a doubt that it will be better for society and humanity in general when the healer of disease in mankind knows something of the maladies of the inferior animals, and when the veterinarian receives that training which will enable him better to understand the morbid conditions of his own species; for he will then be more fitted to comprehend those of the creatures for which he is to prescribe. It is to be sincerely hoped that both branches of medical science will ultimately be looked upon as one, and that the benefits to be derived from their union may be fully realised.

In the historical portion of the work, I have endeavoured to make this first attempt to trace the progress of rabies from the earliest up to the most recent times as complete as possible; and I only regret that the limits to which I had bound myself precluded the possibility of entering more fully into details. The geographical extent of this strange malady has also been elucidated as amply as circumstances would permit, and everything available connected with the etiology, incubation, statistics, and other points related to it has been utilised. The symptoms, particularly in the dog, have received the most careful attention; for on these being thoroughly understood depends, in a great degree, the prevention of the disease in other animals and in mankind. The proposed remedial, preservative, and preventive measures have been also most carefully considered.

The legislative measures suggested for adoption may appear to some lovers of the dog as unnecessarily severe, and inimical to the comfort of that animal; but any one who has had experience of rabies in man or the lower creatures will, I feel certain, agree with me that severity is absolutely necessary if the terrors of a terrible disorder are to be averted. I yield to no one in my admiration of, and regard for, the most faithful and affectionate animal man has domesticated, and I am convinced that the enforcement of these measures will not only benefit it, but will also spare its companions, human and otherwise, much serious risk and annoyance, pain, disease, and death.

In explanation of the title of this work, I may state that my reason for giving two designations for the same disease arose from my anxiety not to mislead or be misunderstood: *hydrophobia*, though in general used to designate the malady now under consideration, and particularly among medical writers, is altogether inapplicable when applied to the disease in the dog or other animals, and has been a source of confusion and danger; while *rabies*, though the better term of the two, and not so likely to cause confusion or misapprehension, is yet not sufficiently well known to warrant its being applied solely to the affection in man and all other creatures. I had no other course, therefore, in seeking for a title by which to indicate the scope

RABIES AND HYDROPHOBIA.

INTRODUCTION.

Of all the maladies that are transmissible from the lower animals to man, there is perhaps not one which possesses so much interest, nor a knowledge of which is so important for the human species, as that which is popularly, though erroneously, designated *Hydrophobia.* It is even to be doubted whether any of the many diseases which afflict humanity, and are a source of dread, either because of their painfulness, their mortality, or the circumstances attending their advent and progress, can equal this in the terror it inspires in the minds of those who are cognisant of its effects, or who chance to be exposed to the risk of its attack, as well as in the uniform fatality which terminates the distressing and hideous symptoms that characterise the disorder.

And what renders the story of this malady still more sad and alarming is the fact, that it is generally derived from the most faithful and numerous of our domestic pets and servants—the dog—whose attachment to—I had almost said "veneration" for—man brings this animal at all times and everywhere to share his company, to join with him in sport, pastime, toil, or hardship, and whose motto justly deserves to be *semper fidelis.*

Probably long before arrows were invented, the dog aided man in obtaining the means wherewith to live by the chase. And it is pre-eminently, among all the domestic animals, the self-constituted friend of man, because more than all other creatures it comes nearest to him in its gregarious instincts and degree of intelligence. From its remarkable sociable qualities, its highly-developed intellect, and its affection for mankind, it is able to follow and live with him, sharing his fortunes, in all the various conditions and occupations of life.

This very companionship invests the disease with greater danger and alarm; for the animal which is the solace of many a lonely hour, our friend in countless emergencies, which is never more pleased than when we are happy, and never so sad as when we are absent, which would willingly sacrifice its life for us, and would certainly be the last to cause us pain or anxiety—may, at any moment, when seized with the disorder, unwittingly and unwillingly become directly instrumental in bringing upon us a cruel death. Noxious creatures we may either avoid or exterminate, and their being generally in a wild state greatly diminishes the chances of receiving injury from them; but with the dog—and also the cat—it may be said that we are always incurring the risk of becoming affected with a disease which is more painful and agonising, and as certainly fatal, as that due to the most poisonous wound inflicted by any other creature. The pet that in an apparently playful mood has licked our face or accidentally scratched our hand while fondling it, may have inoculated us with a more tormenting venom than that of the cobra, and whose effects, if less prompt, are no less destructive to life.

The mystery that attends the action of the inoculated virus is another cause for the dread which attaches to the very name of the disease. A man is bitten by a dog which is to all appearance quite healthy. The injury is so trifling as to be left unheeded, or treated like an ordinary wound. After a certain period—sometimes even after several months, and when the accident had been almost or quite forgotten—strange and distressing symptoms of illness suddenly become manifest, and in a brief space the victim expires in a terrible agony, which remedial measures can scarcely alleviate.

And man is not the only victim to this mysterious infection; for there is every reason to believe that all creatures are susceptible of its influence, though all are not alike capable of disseminating the virus when they themselves have become inoculated and offer evidences of its presence. This tendency of the disease to become panzöotic—*i.e.*, to affect every species of animal (*παν, all, ζῶον, an animal*)—renders it a still more dangerous and destructive malady; for in addition to the loss it occasions by causing the death of valuable domestic creatures—such as the horse, ox, and sheep—it exposes our own species to the attacks of animals which do not generate the infecting element, and these attacks may bring about results as serious as if they had been due to inoculation from the dog or cat.

Owing to the transmissibility of the disease in this manner, we often have it widely spread and of long duration; as though it is rapidly fatal, yet a contaminated animal may live long enough to inoculate several others, and some of these may again become as active agents in the propagation of the poison, and, wandering into different localities, extend the malady to a great distance from the place where it first appeared. In this way is destruction and alarm greatly augmented.

Unlike all other animal diseases, this is usually—in fact, almost invariably—propagated by the *bite* of a beast already suffering from it; and however harmless and inoffensive the creature may be while in health, yet no sooner do the more marked symptoms show themselves than it appears to be irresistibly impelled to attack all other animals with which it may happen to come into contact, and inflict those wounds with its teeth by which the saliva, the infecting medium, obtains access to the blood of the creatures so injured.

We have said that the disease is popularly, but erroneously, designated *Hydrophobia*. This term, which literally means "dread of water" (*ὕδωρ, water*, and *φόβος, fear*), is only applicable to what is sometimes a symptom of the malady in mankind—the aversion to water or other liquids being but seldom, if ever, observed in any of the animals affected, and it is even rare in man; besides, it is not a special or characteristic symptom when present, as a repugnance to fluids is occasionally witnessed in various affections, such as phrenitis, hysteria, gastritis, and other disorders of the human species.

The apparent dread of liquids in general is merely the result of an instinctive dislike induced by difficult and painful attempts to swallow, and this dislike is exaggerated in man—in which the symptom is most marked—by the imagination when fluids are attempted to be swallowed, or at the sight or even thought of these, which causes spasms of the pharynx, œsophagus, and adjacent organs. The designation is, therefore, and particularly with regard to the lower animals, inappropriate, and is liable to mislead and prove most dangerous if its literal meaning be alone relied upon to distinguish the disease from other maladies. And even the dread, when present, is not confined to water, but to all fluids indiscriminately—a circumstance which has led to the term *hygrophobia* being proposed, instead of hydrophobia. The condition of intense terror and the fear of everything—animate as well as inanimate—which so painfully marks the course of the disease, has induced others to name it *pantephobia;* while the peculiar nervous excitability which is developed, even by a current of cold air passing over the patient, caused the ancient medical writers to particularise it as *aërophobia.*

From a morbid supposition sometimes present in the mind of the suffering individual that he was personally identified with the dog, the malady was at one time named *cynanthropia,* and at another period *cynolyssa,* from the fact that the bite of a venomous animal tormented or harassed. By others it has been proposed to name it *dyscataposis*—a difficulty in swallowing with symptoms of choking; also *phobodipsia, erethismus hydrophobia, clonos hydrophobia,* and *lyssa canina.*

The ancient Greeks termed it *lyssa* (λύσσα), or *lytta* (λύττα), and the Romans *rabies.* Pliny speaks of it as the *rabidus canis;* Cicero says, "Hecubampatant propter animi acerbitatem et *rabiem in canem* esse conversam;" and elsewhere, "Iracundie et rabie se facere aliquid." Horace alludes to it as the *canis rabiosa*, and the "dog-days" as the *rabiosa tempora signi;* and Ovid has the expression "rabiem collegit dolor." The term "rabies" strictly implies fury, madness, fierceness, &c., but it has also been employed to denote poison. Thus Seneca says, "Sparge intentam rabiem draconis." Other authors at this early period employed the term "rabies" to designate this particular disease of dogs and other creatures, and in recent years it has been generally adopted by veterinary writers. It is certainly a much better appellation than that of "hydrophobia," inasmuch as, if not absolutely correct in its definition of the nature or character of the affection, it does not mislead, nor is it likely to give rise to serious blunders. Besides, it most closely corresponds with the term "mad" we usually apply to the animal suffering from the malady, and which finds its equivalent in the French *rage;* the German *hundswuth, tollwuth, wuthkrankheit, hundtollheit;* the *arrabiato* or *rabbia* of the Italians; the Spanish *rabioso*, or *mal de rabia;* and the *turbarea* of the Roumanians.

Linnæus divided the disease into two distinct genera, if we may use the expression: viz., "rabies" and "hydrophobia." The first he defined in these words: *Desiderium mordendi lacerandique innocuos;* and the second: *Aversatio potulentorum cum rigore et sardiasi*, adding *sæpius præcedenti maritata.*

Hydrophobia may, without risk, be applied to the disease in mankind, and serve to distinguish it; but it would be most injudicious to retain it as a designation for the madness or rabies of the lower animals.

The term "rabies" should be applied to the disease when transmitted to man. "Hydrophobia" is not even a proper designation for the malady in him, inasmuch as authors have described a spontaneous hydrophobia in the human species, or certain symptoms resembling those of hydrophobia, which certainly were not the same as those produced by the bite of a rabid animal, neither was the presence of a transmissible virus proved to exist.

We shall, however, when not applying to the disease the common designation of "madness," use the term "rabies" with respect to the lower animals, not only because it is almost the oldest and the ordinary technical term, but also because it is the most correct, the simplest, and the safest. "Hydrophobia" we shall generally employ, in conformity with medical custom, when speaking of the disease in mankind.

The dog is not the only animal in which the malady is believed to be primarily manifested, for the cat, fox, jackal, hyæna, and wolf are each supposed to be capable of developing it; and hence, in addition to "canine," we have "feline," "vulpine," "lupine," and other kinds of rabies. The disease can also be transferred from these creatures to all other warm-blooded animals, by means of the virus generated during its development or progress.

HISTORY.

Canine rabies can lay claim to a long and an interesting history, for among the ancient peoples who were cognisant of the disease, it appears to have been held in no less dread than among ourselves at the present day. Its great antiquity is undoubted. Plutarch asserts that, according to Athenodorus, it was first observed in mankind in the days of the Asclepiadæ, the descendants of the god of medicine, Æsculapius, by his sons Podalirius and Machaon, who spread through Greece and Asia Minor as an order of priests, prophets, and physicians, preserving the results of the medical experience acquired in the temples as a hereditary secret. They were the earliest physicians known to us, and it is not unlikely that they may have been the first to observe the madness of dogs transmitted to mankind. And Pausanias, in his "Travels in Greece" (book ix. 2), alluding to the story of Actæon, the son of Aristæus and Autonoë, who was torn to pieces by his own fifty hounds because he had surprised Diana and her attendants at the bath, was of opinion that the only foundation for the myth arose from the circumstance that the famous hunter was destroyed by the dogs when they were rabid.* In the "Iliad," Homer is thought to refer to it when he mentions the dog-star, or Orion's dog, as exerting a malignant influence upon the health of mankind; and the epithets he makes Teucer apply to Hector, in which the latter is compared to a raging or enraged dog, have led some writers to imagine that Homer was acquainted with the malady, which I think is more than

* See also Euripides, Bacch., v. 335. Apollodor., lib. iii. cap. 4.

probable, from the terms he employs.* Aristotle, in the fourth century before our era, alludes to it, and, strangely enough, asserts that the human species is exempted from its attacks: "Dogs suffer from these diseases, which have received different names: *lytta, cynanchè, podagra.* The 'lytta' produces madness, and they infect every creature which they bite, *except mankind*, with the disease. This disease is fatal to dogs and to any other animal they may bite, except man. . . . Camels also are seized with lytta."† Hippocrates is supposed to refer to it when he says that persons in a frenzy drink very little, are disturbed and frightened, tremble at the least noise, or are seized with convulsions.‡ He appears to have recommended the tree-box as a preventive.

Andreas of Caryste, a physician of the Alexandrian School, has left a work on this disease, which he designated κυνόλυσσος.

Artemidorus of Sida, another physician of this school, in describing the malady, located it in the stomach, as it was accompanied by sighs and vomiting. Herophilus Gajus, who lived about the same period and belonged to the same sect, believed hydrophobia to be seated in the membranes of the brain.

Celsus, three centuries after Aristotle, appears to have made the malady his particular study, though he was of opinion that the bites of all animals were dangerous, from the presence of a virus. Indeed, it was fully recognised by this celebrated physician, and seems to have been generally known in ancient times, that the saliva alone contained the morbific principle. In his description of wounds, he says: "I have spoken concerning those wounds which are mostly inflicted by weapons; so it follows that I may speak concerning those which are made by the bite, sometimes of a man, sometimes of an ape,

* Κυνα λυσσητηρα.—*Iliad*, viii. 299. Κρατερη δε ἱ λυσσα δεδυχεν.—*Ibid.*, ix. 39. Ο λυσσωδης.—*Ibid.*, xiii. 53 Λυσσα δε οἱ χηρ.—*Ibid.*, xxi. 542.

† "Historia Animalium," lib. viii. cap. 22.

‡ Hippocrates a Fœsio, lib. i. Prædict., p. 68. Coacarum prænotionum, 98. Van Swieten, Commentar., vol. iii. p. 536. "Phrenitici parùm bibunt, ex levibus strepitibus facile irritantur, tremuli sunt, aut convulsionibus tentantur."

often of a dog, and sometimes of wild animals or of serpents. But every bite has mostly some venom" (*autem omnis morsus habet fere quoddam virus*).

Of the malady itself, he writes: "The Greeks call it ὑδροφοβίαν (*hudrophobian*)—a most wretched disease, in which the sick person is tormented at the same time with thirst and the fear of water, and in which there is but little hope."

He earnestly recommends the practice of resorting to caustics, burning, cupping, and also sucking the wounds of those bitten by rabid dogs, and endeavours to show that there is no danger attending the latter operation, by referring to the family of Psylli, who, with the Marii, another African tribe or family practising at Rome, enjoyed the special privilege of abstracting the poison by suction with the mouth.* In sucking the wound, it appears to have been recognised that it was most essential for the safety of the operator that no sores or abrasions should be on his lips or in his mouth. "If the wound is violent, the cupping instrument (*cucurbitula*) is to be applied; if very slight, a plaster is to be immediately put on, and particularly that of Diogenes. . . . If the dog was rabid (*si canis fuit rabiosus*), the venom of it is especially to be drawn out with the cupping instrument. Afterwards, if the part is neither nervy nor muscular (*neque nervosus, neque musculosus*), the wound is to be cauterized; if it cannot be burnt, it is not unfit for blood-letting. Then those applications suitable for other wounds are to be put over the burnt wound; but if not burnt, then those medicines which violently corrode. After which the ulcer will be healed in the usual way."

* "De Medicina," book v. chap. 27. "Venenum non gustu, sed vulnere nocent . . . Ergo quisquis exemplum Psylii secutus, id vulnus exsuxerit, et ipse tutus erit, et tutum hominem præstabit." Lucan, in his "Pharsalia" (book ix. 891), speaks of the Marmarian Psylli, inhabitants of Libya, as being "unhurt by the cruel sting of the serpents; their tongues are equal to powerful drugs, their very blood is safe, and can admit no venom." He describes one of these people abstracting the poison from a bitten individual, after incantations and other formulæ. "Lying down upon the pallid wounds, he licks them, sucking the poison with his mouth, and squeezes the limbs with his teeth, and holding the deadly poison drawn forth from the cold body, spits it out."

These sagacious precautions not only show that the disease was well understood, but that it must have been more or less prevalent in those early times, and that the skill of the fathers of medicine was severely tested in devising preventive measures. Hot, and also cold, bathing, especially in the sea, was another measure recommended by Celsus,* though he must have been convinced that it was far less efficacious than suction. As a curative measure, however, he appears to have had confidence in it, and gives instances of its success when the disease had appeared. "The only remedy is to throw the patient unexpectedly into a pond, and if he has not a knowledge of swimming, to allow him to sink, in order that he may drink, and to raise and again depress him, so that, though unwillingly, he may be satiated with water; for thus at the same time both the thirst and the dread of water is removed.† But another

* "De Medicina," book v. chap. 47. "Protinus in Balneum immittunt, eumque ibi desudare, dum vires corporis sinant, vulnere aperto quo magis ex eo quoque virus distillet."

† This formidable treatment has been continued up to a recent period, and Van Helmont gives us a curious illustration of its application and success in his day. "There is a castle situated by the sea-side, four leagues from Ghent, which they call Cataracta. I saw a ship passing by it, and therein an old man, naked, bound with cords, having a weight on his feet; under his arm-pits he was encompassed with a girdle, wherewith he was bound to the sail-yard. I asked what they meant by that spectacle? One of the mariners said that the old man was an hydrophobid, or had the disease causing the fear of water, and had lately been bitten by a mad dog. I asked toward what part of the sea they wished to carry him? Did they intend his death? 'Nay, rather,' said the mariner, 'he shall presently return whole: and such is the blessing of the sea, that such a kind of madness it will presently cure.' I offered them some money to take me along with them, as a companion and witness. When we had sailed about an Italian mile, the mariners did open a hole in the bottom, whereby the whole ship was almost sunk, even to the brim: indeed, they used the brine to recoct Spanish salt. And when as that hole was now again exactly shut, two men withdrawing the end of the sail-yard, lifted up the top thereof, and bore the old man on high; but thence they let him down headlong into the sea: and he was under the water about the space of a *miserere*, whom afterwards they twice more plunged, about the space of an *angelical salutation*. But they then placed him on a smooth vessel, with his back upwards, covered with a short cloak. I did think that he was dead; but the mariners derided my fear, for his bonds being loosened, he began to cast up all the brine which he had breathed in, and presently he revived. He was a cooper of Ghent, who being thenceforth freed from his madness, lived safe and sound. Also the mariners did relate that the Dutch,

danger arises, lest distention of the nerves may destroy the enfeebled body, being harassed in cold water; should this happen, the patient is to be taken from the pond immediately, and put into hot oil." "Some, after the bite of a rabid dog, immediately send the patient into a bath, and suffer him to sweat there while the strength of the body permits. In doing this, the wound is also opened, and the poison distils all the more out of it. They afterwards follow the bath up with large quantities of pure wine, which is antagonistic to all poisons; and when this has been done for three days, the man appears to be free from danger. But fear of water usually arises from that wound which has not been properly attended to." Celsus also recommends salt as an application to wounds caused by the bites of dogs. Euripides, the Greek tragic poet, who lived in the fifth century before our era, is reported to have been cured by bathing. Virgil, in his "Georgics," classes rabies among the diseases of cattle and sheep, induced by a pestilential state of the air.* Scribonius-Largus, a Roman physician in the time of Claudius (early in the first century), briefly notices the disease, and asserts that no person was ever cured of it.†

Gratius Faliscus, a poet and contemporary of Ovid, who lived in the first century of our era, in a work entitled, "The Cynegeticon," has described some diseases of dogs, and among them he mentions rabies. He knew the fable of the worm in the dog's tongue as the cause of the malady, a myth rendered popular by Pliny, and which is commonly believed by ignorant people even in our own time. Indeed, the belief in the presence of an abnormal condition of the tongue, and the deve-

by a raw herring salted, applied to the bite of a mad dog for three days' space and renewed, do take away all fear of madness. When this has been neglected, at least by the beheld manner of plunging they are all cured."—*Helmontii*, Ad Not. Oper. Phys., p. 62.

* "Georgics," book iii. 496. "Hinc canibus blandis rabies venit."

† "De Comp. Med.," book c. 45. "Nemo adhuc, correptum hoc malo expeditus est."

lopment of what have been designated the "sublingual lyssi" in connection with that organ, as influencing the production of madness in the dog, is very ancient, and no doubt may be referred to a period long anterior to Faliscus. Pliny but re-echoed this belief when, in a passage of his famous work, he says that there is situated beneath the dog's tongue a worm, which the Greeks named "lytta." * Elsewhere this writer speaks of a sediment from the saliva being found beneath the tongue.† And he mentions Belladonna as a remedy for the disease. There is so much that is curious and interesting in Pliny's references to the malady, as well as so much truth derived from observation, though mixed up with superstition and silly hearsay, that we will reproduce his remarks: "There is a small worm in a dog's tongue known as 'lytta' (*rage* or *madness*) of the Greeks. If this is removed from the animal while a pup, it will never become mad or lose its appetite.‡ This worm, after being carried thrice round a fire, is given to persons who have been bitten by a mad dog, to prevent

* "Historia Naturalis," book xxix. chap. 32. "Est verniculus in lingua canum qui vocatur a Græcis *lytta*."

† Ibid. "Est limus salivæ sub lingua rabiosi canis."

‡ This removal of the worm from the dog's tongue, or "worming" as it is popularly termed, has been practised from the days of Pliny to our own time, and is, as might be expected, a perfectly useless, nay, injurious and painful operation. Beneath the organ, in the middle, is a somewhat loose, tendinous looking fold of membrane, which constitutes what in technical language is called the "frænum," or bridle of the tongue, and is designed to assist the animal in lapping. When in its ordinary relaxed condition, this frænum looks like a small worm, and the resemblance is perhaps even more complete when it has been torn out; hence the name of the operation, which is a cruel one, and gives the poor dog a very sore mouth for several days, in addition to rendering the tongue less capable of performing its important functions. The supposition that this procedure will prevent a dog from becoming spontaneously rabid, or liable to infection if bitten, is excessively absurd, as the presence of the imaginary worm has no influence whatever in the production of the malady, while its absence must be a source of inconvenience to the dog, and far more likely to induce rabies than to prevent its occurrence. The operators justly deserve the punishment which will be awarded them, should they come within the cognizance of the Royal Society for the Prevention of Cruelty to Animals. Dr. Samuel Johnson, who was never at a loss for a definition, when alluding to the opinion prevalent in his time with regard to this worm, called it "a substance, nobody knows what, extracted nobody knows why."

their becoming mad. This madness, too, is prevented by eating a cock's brains; but the virtue of these brains lasts for one year only and no more. They say, too, that a cock's comb, pounded, is highly efficacious as an application to the wound; as also goose-grease mixed with honey. The flesh also of a mad dog is sometimes salted, and taken with the food, as a remedy for this disease. In addition to this, young puppies of the same sex as the dog that has inflicted the injury, are drowned in water, and the person who has been bitten eats their liver raw," &c. "So virulent is the poison of the mad dog, that its very urine even, if trod upon, is injurious, more particularly if the person has any ulcerous sores about him. The proper remedy to apply in such a case is horse-dung, sprinkled with vinegar, and warmed in a fig. These marvellous properties of the poison will occasion the less surprise when we remember that 'a stone bitten by a dog' has become a proverbial expression for discord and variance."* The dog, in Pliny's time, must have been looked upon as a more curious animal than we are accustomed to regard it nowadays, and to have been possessed of some mysterious influences which we cannot now perceive; for he remarks, "Whoever makes water where a dog has previously watered, will be sensible of numbness in the loins, they say." Some of his preventive measures are on a par with those of a later age. "When a person has been bitten by a mad dog, he may be preserved from hydrophobia by applying the ashes of a dog's head to the wound. These ashes are very good, too, taken in drink, and hence some recommend the head itself to be eaten in such cases. Others, again, attach to the body of the patient a maggot taken from the carcase of a dead dog; or else place the menstruous blood of a bitch, in a linen cloth, beneath his cup, or insert in the wound ashes of hairs from the tail of the dog that inflicted the

* "For the manner of a dog is to bee angrie with the stone that is thrown at him, without regard to the partie that flung it, whereupon grew the proverb in Greek, *κύων εἰς τὸν λίθον ἀγανακτοῦσα* (a dog venting his rage upon a stone)." —*Holland's* Plinie.

bite.* Dogs will fly from any one who has a dog's heart about him, and they will never bark at a person who carries a dog's tongue in his shoe, beneath the great toe, or the tail of a weasel which has been set at liberty after being deprived of it. There is beneath the tongue of a mad dog a certain slimy saliva which, taken in drink, is a preventive of hydrophobia. But much the most useful plan, is to take the liver of the dog that has inflicted the injury, and eat it raw, if possible. Should that not be the case, it must be cooked in some way or other, or else a broth must be taken prepared from the flesh. When a person has been bitten by a mad dog, it is the practice to make an incision round the wound to the quick, and then to apply raw veal to it, and to make the patient take either veal broth or hog's lard, mixed with lime, internally. Some persons recommend a he-goat's liver, and maintain that if it is applied to the wound the patient will never be attacked with hydrophobia." † Cauterization is lauded as a cure. "Some affections are cured by cauterization with red-hot iron, the bite of the mad dog more particularly; for even if the malady has been fully developed, and hydrophobia has made its appearance, the patient is instantly relieved on the wound being cauterized." ‡ The root of horse-parsley taken in drink and applied topically, he vaunts as a remedy for the disease; but he particularly recommends the dog-rose or eglantine, the supposed virtues of which had only been discovered in his own time, and of course in a remarkable way. "Down to our own times, the bite of a mad dog, the symptoms of which are a dread of water and an aversion to every kind of beverage, was incurable; and it was only recently that the mother of a soldier who was serving in the prætorian guard received a warning in a dream

* This recommendation may have given rise to the advice so frequently tendered by the bacchanals of modern days to those suffering from the effects of unpleasant potations, that "they should take a hair of the dog that had bitten them;" meaning that to set themselves right again they ought to become homœopaths, and resort to the tipple that had made them so uncomfortable.

† Book xxvi. chap. 43.

‡ Book xxxiv. chap. 44.

to send her son the root of the wild rose, known as the cynorrhodos, a plant the beauty of which had attracted her attention in a shrubbery the day before, and to request him to drink the extract of it. The army was then serving in Lacetania, the part of Spain which lies nearest to Italy; and it so happened that the soldier, having been bitten by a dog, was just beginning to manifest a horror of water when his mother's letter reached him, in which she entreated him to obey the words of this divine warning. He accordingly complied with her request, and, against all hope or expectation, his life was saved, a result which has been experienced by all who have since availed themselves of the same resource."* "Canine madness," he also says, "is fatal to man during the heat of Sirius, and proves so in consequence of those who are bitten having a deadly horror of water. For this reason, during the thirty days that this star exerts its influence, we try to prevent the disease by mixing dung from the poultry-yard with the dog's food, or else if they are already attacked with the disease, by giving them hellebore." †

M. Artorius, an Asclepiade of Bithynia, and the friend and physician of Augustus, has left a treatise on the disease, in which he seeks to prove that it is seated in the stomach, as evidenced by the hiccoughs and bilious vomiting usually accompanying it.

Eumedes, celebrated for his *amours* with Sivilla, the daughter-in-law of Tiberius, and a physician of the Methodic School, makes some interesting observations on hydrophobia; among others, that even the shedding of tears is sufficient to excite the spasms of the pharynx, and also that it is rare that those attacked are saved.

Ovid states that hydrophobia and gout were in his day reckoned among the incurable maladies.‡

* Book xxv. chap. 6. † Book viii. chap. 63.

‡ "Ep. ex Ponto.," lib. i. el. iii. 23, 24.

"Tollere nodosam nescit medicina podagram,
Nec formidatis auxiliatur aquis."

Magnus of Ephesus, who lived in the time of Galen, located the disease in the stomach and diaphragm.

Columella, whose writings were well known to Pliny, and who lived about the same period as that distinguished naturalist, notices rabies, and informs us it was believed among the shepherds that if, on the fortieth day after the birth of a pup, the last bone of the tail is *bitten off* the sinew will follow with it; after which the tail will not grow (*fœdum incrementum*—foul increase), *and, as many shepherds say, this operation secures the dog from the disease.*" *

One of the best of the ancient authorities on the disease was Cælius Aurelianus, a physician, who was born at Sicca Venerea, in Numidia, but at what period he flourished is not established, some writers contending it was during the reigns of Trajan and Adrian, and others in the fifth century. His knowledge of the malady appears to have been chiefly obtained from the writings of Eudemius, Soranus, and others, of whom but little or nothing is now known. He appears to have studied the history of the disease with much attention, as he has appropriated an entire chapter to the discussion then carried on among physicians as to whether hydrophobia was a new disease, which he, of course, answers in the negative. Of the places where it most prevailed he mentions Caria and Crete. The latter island, he says, was particularly free from poisonous animals, but the canine disease was very common. "The hydrophobia in man," he adds, "is preceded by extreme irritability, unusual motions of the body, disturbed sleep, or absolute wakefulness, indigestion, stretchings, yawning, nausea, imaginary notions of bad weather, and no appetite for drink. To these symptoms succeed, when the hydrophobia begins, a desire to

* "De Re Rustica." It is curious to find this barbarous, useless, and disfiguring operation carried down to our own day and practised by the ignorant and brutal, frequently for the same reason that was given by Columella's shepherds; and it is also satisfactory to know that the disgusting performance is recognised in our courts of justice as cruelty to the dog, convictions having been obtained against perpetrators by the Royal Society for the Prevention of Cruelty to Animals.

drink (*appetentia bibendi*—a violent thirst), with terror at the sight, sound, or name of water. The patient is even afraid of fomentations with oil; his pulse is dense (hard), small, and irregular; there is sometimes a small degree of fever, convulsive motions of the stomach, spasms in the precordia, numbness of the joints, and torpor of the bowels; frequent inclination to micturate; trembling and catching of the limbs; voice hoarse, resembling the barking of a dog; spiral posture of the body, like that of a dog lying on the ground; anxiety when any person enters the room, as if apprehensive that he should bring water; redness of the face and eyes; body emaciated, the upper parts pale and perspiring; *cerebri frequens tensio cum seminis involuntario jactu.*" He speaks of hydrophobia being also spontaneous, or rather a symptom in other diseases.* In the chapter devoted to the remedies (*Quomodo curandi sunt hydrophobi*), he details the measures adopted by his predecessors; how Artorius advised his patient to be plunged into cold water; while Niger and Eudemius bled their patients and gave hellebore; that some gave castor, some oil of roses, others scammony, and others again snow instead of water, thinking the patient might gratify his thirst in that form when he could not do so with water; some made use of stratagems to induce

* "Acutis Morbis," book iii. chap. 9. "Est præterea possibile, sine manifesta causa, hanc passionem corporibus innasci, cum talis fuerit strictio, sponte generata qualis a veneno." It is curious to note that the Greeks suffered greatly from rabies, if we are to judge by the frequent mention of the disease by medical and other writers, and also by the number of superstitious, remedies, and antidotes it gave rise to. These are too numerous to allude to here; but we may notice that Pausanias, in his account of ancient Greece, speaks of a fountain of very cold water, which being drunk, *instantly* cured persons bitten by a rabid dog.—*Arcadia sive*, book viii. p. 637. Edit. Kuhnii. Leipsic, 1696. And Scribonius, a pupil of Apuleius Celsus, referring to the antidote prepared against hydrophobia by his master every year, and sent into Sicily, where rabies was very common, mentions an amulet used in Crete, by Zopyrus, even when the disease became manifest; this was a piece of a hyæna's skin bound on the left arm of the person bitten.—*De Comp. Med.*, chap. 45. Galen also speaks of the antidote which Mithridates is said to have received from this Zopyrus the Cretan; and he gives a multitude of preparations and antidotes recommended by Cratippus, Hiras, Belchionius, Zeno Laodicæi, Claudius Apollonius, Menippus, and Menelaus.

the victim to drink, which would make the most serious smile; but after all it was found that the disease was a deadly one. The treatment prescribed was as follows: "Let the patient's chamber be tolerably warm and light, and have the part that was bitten covered with a piece of clean warm flannel. If it be necessary to bleed him, let the blood be received in the hand of the assistant, lest the noise of its falling into the basin should affect the patient. Talk to him about washing and drinking, and if he hears this without alarm, you may then give him something to drink; if not, you may let him suck through the spout of a pot, covering his eyes or darkening the room. Let his nurses be discreet and not loquacious, and have him exercised in a stretcher or sedan chair. If he refuses to take any liquid by the mouth give it him by enema," &c.

Pedanius Dioscorides of Anazarbeus, Cilicia, about this period alludes to the disease in his work on *Materia Medica*. He gives an exact description of it, mentions its transmissibility to mankind, and its fatality when once it really manifests itself; and adds that it is possible to prevent it by cauterising the bitten part.

Apuleius Celsus follows Pliny in recommending Belladonna as a remedy.

In the third century Claudius Ælianus of Præneste, and Claudius Galenus of Pergamus, give a fair description of the malady; and in the same century Olympius Nemesianus, a poet of Carthage, among some other diseases of dogs, describes rabies. In the fourth century Oribasius of Pergamus, physician to Julian the Apostate, describes hydrophobia, and alludes to its being generally fatal;* but he also speaks of a curable form of the disease as due to other causes than the bite of a dog. Vegetius Renatus also enumerates rabies among the other maladies to which the lower animals are disposed, and recommends, as an antidote for cattle that have been

* "Synopsis," book viii. chap. 13. "Ex is verò qui a cane rabioso morso fuissent, servatum esse neminem."

wounded by a mad dog, "to give them the boiled liver of the dog to eat; or to make it into balls, and force it down as a medicine."* In the sixth century Theomnestus, in his "Geoponica," devotes some attention to it. Ætius, a physician of Mesopotamia, who flourished in this century, has left us a more accurate account of the disease in the dog than any of the ancient writers. He says that "dogs are naturally hot and dry. That the increase of temperature which the air acquires in the summer months causes them to go mad, and that this madness is called rabies." He also attributes the disease to sudden mutations and variations of the atmosphere, such as take place when the summer and winter are extreme. Dogs also become mad, he adds, from thirst when deprived of water, and that then the malignity of the venom is greatest. The symptoms of the malady were first manifested by the dogs becoming mute, then delirious, and incapable of knowing those to whom they have been most accustomed—not even recognising their masters. They refuse food, are thirsty, but do not drink, and usually pant. They breathe with difficulty, keep the mouth open with the tongue hanging out, and discharge abundance of frothy saliva. Their ears and tail hang down, they move slowly, and are dull and sleepy. When they run, it is faster than usual, and in an irregular and uncommon manner.† A century later Paulus Ægineta, a physician, offers a good account of hydrophobia. He follows previous authors in enumerating the symptoms, and distinguishes between the disease as due to the bite of a dog, and that remediable, simply nervous hydrophobia arising from other causes. The inoculated hydrophobia was always mortal.‡ It may be here noted, that though we have no mention of any general outbreaks of rabies, such as have occurred in more recent times, yet the

* "Artis Veterinariæ," book iii. chap. 48. *Vide* Scriptores Rei Rusticæ, vol. ii. p. 1152.

† Aetii Tetr., ii. serm. 2, chap. 24.

‡ "De Re Medicinæ," book v. chap. 3. "Cæterum eorum qui in hanc affectionem inciderunt, nullum sanatum esse."

literature of the subject is by no means scanty, and we generally have much truth mixed up with a great quantity of fiction and superstition, due to imperfect observation and credulity.

In our own country, it is probable that the disease was present from the earliest times, though it is not until two or three centuries subsequent to Paulus Ægineta that we find any special indication of its presence. The first mention of it in our early records would tend to show that it at times prevailed as an epizoöty,* and in such a formidable manner as to become memorable. For instance, the earliest mention I can find of the disease is in the laws of Howel the Good, of Wales, which were revised about A.D. 1026. In them an outbreak is alluded to as a most noteworthy event. Speaking of the legal worth of a brock or badger, it is stated that "*during the year there was a madness among the dogs*, it obtained the privilege of a sow." †

That the malady was a frequent and a serious one in England, we have also conclusive evidence in certain Anglo-Saxon manuscripts which have been preserved to us, and which contain remedies and incantations wherewith to cure or exorcise the disease. In one of these—a Saxon "Herbarium," supposed to belong to the tenth century—are the following recipes: "For bite of dog, take galli crus (*Panicum crus galli*), pound it with grease, and with a hearth-baked loaf lay it to the wound, and soon it will be healed." "For bite of mad dog, bishopwort (*Betonia officinalis*)." "The plant 'waybread' (*Plantago major*) for rend of mad dog." "The herb vermenaca or ashthroat (*Verbena officinalis*) for bite of mad dog." "The

* The term *epizoöty*, or *epizotia*, is that employed in veterinary science to designate a disease which, about the same time and over a wide extent of country, attacks a large number of animals of the same species. Though usually applied to maladies which depend upon, or owe their origin to, general and, most frequently, obscure causes, yet it has also been given to those whose extension is due to the presence of an infecting element. It is derived from ἐπί, upon, and ζῶον, an animal. A malady of this kind is also sometimes termed an *epizoötic*, but this is not commendable; still less is *epidemic*, which is frequently applied, even by medical writers, to diseases in the lower animals, whereas it refers only to those of mankind (being derived from ἐπί, upon, and δῆμος, the people).

† "Gwentian Code," book ii. chap. 23.

herb personacia beet, or *beeta*, for tear by mad dog." The herb 'millefolium' or 'yarrow' (*Achillea millefolium*) is lauded for bite of mad hound. "The herb 'spreritis' (*Anagallis arvensis*) against bite of wood hound" (mad dog). "The herb eryngium for bite of mad dog." *

In another manuscript—a Læce or Leech Book of about the same date—there is a remedy for "rending of hound." "Pound ribwort, lay it on the wound, and boil rue in butter; tend the wound therewith," &c. The same book has other equally simple remedies for "bite of mad dog." But the most interesting fact in connection with rabies in England at this early date is to be found in another Anglo-Saxon manuscript on medicine, entitled the "Medicina de Quadrupedibus" of Sextus Placitus (in all probability a fictitious name), written, it is presumed, at the commencement of the eleventh century. Amongst a farrago of fantastic recipes for all kinds of maladies—real or imaginary—is one for "tear of mad hound," which contains a notice of the ancient superstition of the worm in the dog's tongue. "Take the worms (*thymas*) which be under a mad hound's tongue (*under thede hundes cunzan*), snip them away, lead them round about a fig-tree, give them to him who hath been rent; he will soon be whole."†

* "Leechdoms, Wortcunning, and Starcraft of Early England," vol. i. pp. 3, 7, 21, 37, 53, 65, 149.

† It is remarkable to find Pliny's prescriptions, particularly the one just referred to, almost word for word, in this Anglo-Saxon leech-book, the fig-tree only being substituted for the fire; and it is still more remarkable to find the tradition of the worm beneath the dog's tongue, and the supposed benefit attending its removal, yet existing, and in countries far beyond the limits of Ancient Greece or Rome. In the first-named country, according to Dr. Xanthos (*Archives Général de Médecine*, 1824), the lysses, or worm, has been believed in from time immemorial, and an operation has been resorted to similar to that mentioned by Pliny and recommended in the Leech-book. Armand has reported to the Paris Academy of Sciences that such a tradition and practice is yet prevalent in Thrace. Auzias-Turenne asserts that a similar tradition is popular in Turkey and Moldo-Wallachia (*Recueil de Méd. Vétérinaire*, January, 1869). It is common in Roumania. According to Ramon de Sagra, it is also popular in Galicia, in Spain. Even in the Brazils, the existence of the sublingual worm is deep-rooted in the public mind. In 1819, Karamsin informed the Medical Society of Moscow that he knew of a man who pretended to cure people who had been

Elsewhere in the same medical treatise is a recipe "for a laceration by a mad dog." "A hound's head burnt to ashes and thereon applied, casteth out all the venom and the foulness, and healeth the maddening bites." Again, "A mad dog's head and his liver sodden, and given to be eaten to him who has been torn, wonderfully healeth him."

But the mad dog was employed, it would appear, to cure other maladies of the human species. For instance, we find as a cure for the "kingly disease" or jaundice, "the head of a mad dog pounded and mingled for a drink with wine, healeth." And for cancer, "the head of a mad dog burnt to ashes and spread on, healeth the cancer wounds."

However much we may feel inclined to smile at the absurdities of our forefathers, particularly with regard to this malady, we must not forget that many almost as absurd ideas yet prevail respecting the diseases of the lower animals, and that it is not so very long ago that, according to Lipscomb, charms, consisting of a number of words written with ink on paper or

---

bitten by mad animals, by opening with the point of a knife small abscesses which formed beneath the tongue, and thoroughly removing the matter from them. In 1819, Salvatori, a physician at St. Petersburg, stated that during his residence in Pultawa, he discovered that the people of Galicia knew of the existence, about the frænum of the tongue of a man or animal which had been bitten by a rabid creature, of some pustules which opened spontaneously about the fourteenth day after the accident. So early as 1813, a peasant of the Ukraine had called the attention of Dr. Marochetti to the presence of pustules beneath the tongue of persons who had been bitten by rabid animals, and assured him that if these were not evacuated within twenty-four hours after their appearance the matter would be absorbed, and the disease would soon manifest itself. It was therefore necessary to examine carefully, for at least six weeks, the lower part of the tongue of any one who had been so injured, and if these pustules appeared they were to be at once opened and cauterized. If they did not appear the individual would not suffer from hydrophobia. Marochetti imagined he had verified the correctness of this description five years afterwards in Podolia, and his published account caused a considerable amount of interest and curiosity in the medical and scientific world of that day. The pretended pustules were named the "lysses of Marochetti."—See Marochetti, "Observations sur l'Hydrophobie," St. Petersburg, 1821; *Gazette de St. Petersbourg*, August, 1823; *Journal de Physiologie*, 1825; *Nouveau Journal de Médecine*, 1821; *Journal Universel des Sciences Médicales*, vol. xxiv.; *Recueil de Méd. Vétérinaire*, 6th series, vol. xi. p. 9.

parchment, were thrust down the throats of mad dogs to cure them.

Jahiah-Ebn-Serapion, a native of Syria, who lived at the commencement of the ninth century, believed the disease produced by the bite of a mad dog to be incurable; though he proposed that the patient should be made to swallow water by enclosing it in a globule of concrete honey, which was to be put in the mouth.*

Rhazes, a celebrated Arab physician, mentions hydrophobia, and says that a certain man barked by night like a dog and died; and that there was one who, when he beheld water, was seized with trembling, horripilatio, and rigors, but when the water was removed from him these symptoms ceased.

The Arab physician, Avicenna, at the commencement of the eleventh century, speaks of rabies. He directs the wound to be dilated and kept open for forty days, and recommends, as an infallible remedy, the ordinary blistering fly (*meloe vesicatories*). He states that he saw the body of a mad dog covered with pustules (*guandoque pustulis scatet seu apostematur*), and the skin of which had an ashy tint (*colore cinerito*).† He alludes to the urinary organs being affected, states that hydrophobous persons barked like dogs; that they had a desire of biting people; that there were instances of patients being suffocated in attempting to drink, and that the malady sometimes terminated in apoplexy.‡ Altogether his treatise is very complete, and certainly marks a step in advance of his predecessors.

Six hundred years afterwards, Baptist Codrondius, in an excellent description of the symptoms of rabies, confirms Avicenna's observation with regard to the skin in hydrophobia.§

* Serapion, "Breviarium," tr. v. cap. 17.

† In mankind, this tint of the skin during an attack of hydrophobia is represented by a dull redness or erythema, which has been designated by the term "rabic roseola." There have also been noted other cutaneous symptoms in man, which have received the names of "rabic pleiads," "rabic bubo," &c.

‡ Canon, book v.

§ "De Rabie Hydrophobia Communiter dicta." Franciforti, 1610.

A work entitled the "Kynosophion" (Κυνοσόφιον), supposed by some to have been written by Phæmon, while others imagine it to have been composed by Demetrius Pepagomenos, a Greek writer who lived at Constantinople in the twelfth century, contains the names of some diseases the dog is liable to, and their remedies, but no symptoms are given. It is marked by the grossest superstition and absurdities. For example, to discover the part in which a dog is suffering, the following singular advice is offered: "Adversus solem constitue canem, et in locum læsum muscæ convolabunt, atque sic locum dolentum deprehendes." Allusion is made to the lysses under the tongue, it is to be presumed; for it is stated that there is a little body beneath the tongue of the dog, which is compared to *a white worm*—or rather, when the sentence is literally translated, to *a hole similar to that of a worm*. It is necessary, continues the writer, to destroy it quickly before it increases and invades the whole throat. "Priusquam augeatur totumque occupet guttur," says a translator.*

Fracastor, or Fracastorius, in the sixteenth century, in a poem entitled "Alcon, sive de Cura Canum Venaticorum," appropriated this idea of the "worm" in the tongue, which he had probably obtained from Pliny; or he may even have seen it in the original Greek manuscript of Pepagomena, which by some chance might have found its way into the library of the Medici. The particular words of the poem are—

"Vulnificus *vermis* suffunditque ora veneno."

Albertus Magnus, Bishop of Ratisbon, in the thirteenth century, alludes to the malady and its appearance in horses; and Laurentius Rusius, a century later, takes cognisance of it.

From this period the literature of rabies gradually expands; observers and writers wonderfully increase; and, with the progress of medicine, their remarks become more valuable and

* Brogiani, "De Veneno Animantium Naturali et Acquisito Tractatus," Florence, 1752.

comprehensive, though so far as the successful prevention or attempts at curing the malady are concerned, but little progress appears to have been made; and the disease, terrible and fatal as in the old times, was, to the popular mind, shrouded in mystery, and obscured by the superstitious rites and ideas devised by ignorance, priestcraft, and fear.*

For instance, in Belgium, the custom is still practised of going to the shrine of St. Hubert, in the Ardennes, for the cure of hydrophobia, as in the early ages. The anonymous author of the "Life of St. Lambert," written about the end of the eleventh century, makes mention of several people who were there cured in A.D. 825. The legend relates that the stole of St. Hubert, which works the miracle, was brought from heaven by an angel, who gave it to the saint while he was praying at the tomb of St. Peter in Rome. The last-named saint also brought him a golden key, assuring him that God would grant him a special power over evil spirits.

The following is the rubric of the regulations to be observed by those who are taken to be cured, in order that the miracle may stand some chance of succeeding; it was printed in 1671:—

"The person, who is attired with the stole in honour of St. Hubert, must begin by confessing and communicating for nine successive days; must sleep alone either in white sheets newly-washed, or else entirely dressed; must drink alone, and not bend the head down in drinking at fountains or rivers. Item, may drink red and white wine, and 'clairet,' mixed with water, or water only; may eat white and other bread; pork of a male pig not more than a year old; capon or pullets of the same age; fish having scales, such as smoked herrings and

* I have made but little reference to the literature of rabies and hydrophobia beyond what was absolutely necessary for my purpose. Commencing with Spackmann's "Declaration," published in 1613—the first English work, I think, on the subject—the writers who have written on these maladies in this country are very numerous, while on the Continent they are legion. A tolerably complete bibliography will be found appended to the article "Rabies" in Copeland's "Dictionary of Practical Medicine."

carp, and hard-boiled eggs; all of which must be eaten cold, and in no other manner. Item, the head must not be combed for forty days, and if the person receives a wound, or the bite of any animal drawing blood, he must practise the same abstinence for the space of three days without returning here. Item, on the tenth day he must have his bandage taken off by a priest, and cause it to be burnt, and the ashes cast into the piscina. Item, he must keep the feast of St. Hubert every year, viz., on the third day of November. Item, he may grant reprieve to all persons bitten by any mad animal from forty to fifty days." *

The Sorbonne, it may be remarked, condemned all these practices as superstitious by a declaration of the 10th of June, 1671, and as early as the fifteenth century the celebrated theologian, Gerson, had pronounced against them. The clergy of St. Hubert, in defending the practices against the attacks of the Sorbonne, drew up an explanation of all the means employed in the cure of people who had been bitten, and caused it to be approved by the Bishop of Liège and the faculty of theology of Louvain. This explanation did not, however, prevent a canon of Rheims, in 1709, from undertaking to refute and attack the

* Van Helmont appears to have been a believer in the virtues of this musty saint's vestment, and the silly practices imposed by the priests. "Our good Catholics, despairing of relief from the faculty, repair to St. Hubert, at whose shrine, by virtue of certain ceremonies, they are cured; but it is worthy of remark, if these ceremonies are not strictly observed, the latent rabies immediately breaks out, and they become irrecoverably hydrophobic. There is a vestment of St. Hubert's, which is preserved in a chest secured by six locks, the keys of which are kept by the six different vergers. For these fourscore years past they have been continually cutting off pieces from this holy vestment; nevertheless it remains to this day perfectly entire. Now it is impossible that there should be any imposture in the case; for they have never been able to discover whether this miraculous robe be of linen, woollen, or of silk; consequently it cannot be annually renewed. They cut off a piece of the robe, and incarnate a thread between the skin of the patient's forehead. Hence another miracle—for a person thus cured becomes possessed of a power to postpone the hydrophobia during forty days, in any of his acquaintance, who, after being bitten, may not have leisure immediately to visit St. Hubert; on the condition, however, that if they exceed the forty days ever so little, without applying for a prorogation of the term, they go mad irrecoverably."

miracles of St. Hubert in a letter which he wrote to M. Hennebel, a theological doctor of Louvain. It is reprinted in the "Critical History of Superstitious Customs," by Father Le Brun. In it the author attacks the vulgar opinion of the non-diminution of the saint's stole, and maintains that the greater part of the afflicted who go to the shrine of St. Hubert become mad, and cites several instances derived, for the most part, from the "Treatise on Superstitions," by Thiers. "Those who are cured," he observes, "have either not been bitten by dogs really mad, or have had other ailments distinct from hydrophobia; or it has been the strength of their constitutions, or the physical remedies which have cured them, and not the miracle denied by the most skilful theologians and medical men." He treats the practice of the *neuvaine* as eminently superstitious, and finally refutes the system adopted.

Of course, the clergy of St. Hubert replied to this attack, but by arguments which failed to meet the objections raised; and the question appears since to have rested where all such questions remain—the world of common sense denies the miracle, the superstitious and priest-led affirm it.

What are called "the keys of St. Hubert" consist of an iron, heated red-hot, and applied to the animals bitten by mad dogs. It appears never to have borne the form of a *key*; for in the town of St. Hubert itself the amulet was an iron ring inserted in the wall of one of the houses in the principal street. It no longer exists, though the belief in the potency of St. Hubert is, among the peasantry, as strong as ever. In other places where this saint is especially venerated, the form of the exorcising instrument in no way resembles the key given by St. Peter. At Liège it is also an iron ring, and at Utrecht an iron cross.*

* Dudley Costello, "A Tour through the Valley of the Meuse," p. 297. For very interesting details of this saint and the ordeal for the prevention of hydrophobia, with its supposed marvellous results, see the "Vie de Saint Hubert," by Stanislaus Prioux, Paris, 1853. Also "Pelegrinage de Saint-Hubert-en-Ardennes," by Bertrand. Namur, 1855.

It is scarcely necessary to say that, up to the eighteenth century, little progress was made in ascertaining the nature of the disease, or devising measures for its prevention. Absurd remedies only were prescribed for those who chanced to be threatened with an attack, or were really affected; and though the writers who allude to the malady are numerous, yet they offer nothing of sufficient importance to necessitate our referring to them in this place.

As already mentioned, the notices of general outbreaks of rabies in the early ages of our era are extremely few, though there can scarcely be a doubt as to their occurrence. Occasionally we meet with allusions to people having been bitten by wolves, foxes, badgers, and even bears,* and afterwards dying of madness; indeed, in the middle ages, notices of these occurrences are frequent. For instance, in 1271, it is stated that in Franconia rabid wolves invaded the towns and villages, attacking the herds and flocks, and that no fewer than thirty persons died in consequence of the bites inflicted on them.† In 1500, Spain was reported to have been ravaged by rabies canina.‡

According to Forster,§ there was an epizoöty of rabies among dogs during the epidemic plague in Flanders, Turkey, Hungary, and Austria in 1586. In 1590, this disease also appeared in

* In my work on "Animal Plagues" (London, 1871), I have given detailed notices of these occurrences. A curious case of rabies in a bear is recorded for A.D. 900, as happening at Lyons. "About the year 900, immense forests covered Burgundy, Mâconnais, Brescia, and part of Lyonnais. These forests were tenanted by wolves, wild boars, bears, and other ferocious animals. One day, a rabid bear, following the course of the river Saône, at last reached the quay at Lyons. Everybody fled at its approach except some boatmen, who, armed with heavy sticks, attempted to kill it. The bear, however, little intimidated by their number, rushed among them and bit many—about twenty. Of this party, six were smothered in about twenty-seven days, in consequence of fearful madness. The other fourteen, however, had thrown themselves into the river to escape the animal's attacks, and, having to swim to the opposite bank, were thus preserved from the effects of the poison, as the water of the river, in beating against their wounds, washed away the venom, and thus saved them." (Page 51.)

† "Pistor. Scrip. rerum German.," vol. i. p. 433.

‡ "Animal Plagues," p. 127. § Ibid., p. 137.

an epizoötic form among wolves at Montbeliard.* In 1604, rabies canina was wide-spread in Paris, and caused great alarm.† In 1708, it was also epizoötic among dogs in Suabia.‡ In Hungary, in 1712, wild beasts of all kinds perished in large numbers at Somogy, and in the woods the country people found dogs which had been driven there by madness. Men bitten by them were quickly seized with frenzy and hydrophobia, imitating the barking and the madness of dogs, and attacking those near by biting at them.§ From 1719 until 1721, rabies was uncommonly frequent in different countries, but especially in France and Silesia.‖ In 1722, it prevailed in the last-named country, and had appeared in Hungary.¶ In 1725, it still continued in Silesia, where it was also discovered that wolves were affected. An observer of this fact says: "The principal reason for this appears to be in the atmosphere and the weather, as well as in the constitution of the animal. Such madness seems to be quite common in some other places."** In the following year complaints continued to be made of the madness of dogs in Silesia and Lusatia.†† In England the disease prevailed in 1734, and in 1735 Huxham speaks of "many mad dogs running up and down" in August. In October he writes that "many were bit by mad dogs;" and in November, that "several mad dogs run about."‡‡

Hughes states that in 1741 many dogs went mad in Barbadoes.§§

* "Animal Plagues," p. 138. † Ibid., p. 139. ‡ Ibid., p. 179.
§ Ibid., p. 190. ‖ Ibid., p. 231. ¶ Ibid., p. 236.
** Ibid., p. 238. †† Ibid., p. 239. ‡‡ Ibid., p. 259.

§§ Ibid., p. 266. Mr. Hughes, in his "History of Barbadoes," mentions the cure of a rabid cow during this outbreak: "When found to be mad, she was confined; but as the usual symptoms attending that terrible distemper appeared more and more, and she growing to extreme madness, the owner determined to destroy her; but as she was a favourite beast, her doom was respited until he had tried the following experiment. Having thrown her down upon a dunghill, he directed his slaves to keep her mouth open by force, whilst he gradually poured down her throat a large pailful of cold water. In a short time after she began to feed, and in about twenty-four hours after drank water as usual, fully recovered, and remained so."

The county of Fife, Scotland, suffered much from mad dogs in 1748. Cows and swine were the animals most injured.

A correspondent, writing from Charles Town, South America, under date of November 10th, 1750, says: "Since the commencement of this year, a kind of madness hath appeared among the dogs in the country, so that most of them have been killed; and lately some have been mad in this town. It is not remembered that there ever was a mad dog seen before in this province. I do not hear that they have yet bitten any person; but as soon as their madness appears, they attack every dog they see, which are, within a few hours after being bit, in the same condition. As it began in the country, some suppose this madness to proceed from these creatures feeding on the infected carcases of dead cattle, as no other cause appears. The mad dogs, if not killed, die in two or three days; and some hogs have been seized in like manner."*

In 1752, several mad dogs were reported about St. James's, London, and orders were issued to shoot all which appeared there. In some country towns the justices gave similar orders.†

According to Layard, "in the years 1759 and 1760, madness raged among dogs in London and its neighbourhood, in consequence of the mild winter and early spring."

"It first appeared in the borough of Southwark, and the consternation diffused itself all over the cities of London and Westminster. The magistrates immediately issued a very prudent and judicious order for every person who kept dogs to confine them during a month within doors; and ordered their beadles and other officers to destroy all dogs found at large, with a reward of two shillings for each dog which should be killed." ‡

Great cruelty was the result of this bribe to slay the

* The *Gentleman's Magazine*, January, 1751.

† Ibid., August, 1752.

‡ "Animal Plagues," p. 409.

unfortunate dogs, and the most barbarous scenes were enacted by the brutal rabble, which had a premium put upon their savage propensities. Moorfields was the burial-place of all the animals so murdered. "No less than the bodies of thirty dead dogs were told in one day in Tower Ditch, by a person of undoubted veracity, who was only casually passing by that way. . . . Of the dogs that will be massacred on this occasion, not one in a thousand will be mad; and of those that are mad, not one, perhaps, will be killed. Those who make it a revenue to kill the dogs will carefully avoid meddling with any that have bad symptoms, from the dread of the consequences."* The outbreak appears to have lasted until 1762.

In 1763 a disease appeared among dogs in France, Italy, and Spain, which, it is recorded, terminated sooner or later in madness. In Asti, Alexandria, and other places, all dogs, no matter who their owners might chance to be, were slaughtered by the authorities. In Madrid, nine hundred were killed in one day.†

In 1768 rabies was alarmingly frequent in Boston and other towns in North America;‡ and again in 1770 and 1771 it was extremely prevalent among dogs and foxes in Boston and its neighbourhood; swine were the principal victims of these animals' fury. The malady appears to have been looked upon as novel in that part of the world at this period.

In the early part of 1774, it was causing much alarm in Lancashire, and we find that at a general meeting of the parishioners of Eccles, near Manchester, it was unanimously agreed to strike off from the poor's-rates all paupers who should keep dogs. They also agreed to pay five shillings for every mad dog killed in their parish.§ Lipscomb says the disease was very general in England.‖

* The *Gentleman's Magazine*, August, 1760.

† "Animal Plagues," p. 420. ‡ Ibid., p. 429.

§ The *Gentleman's Magazine*, June, 1774.

‖ "The History of Canine Madness." London, 1809, p. 41.

From 1776 to 1778, the French West Indies was visited for the first time by rabies, and in an epizoötic form. "It was believed for a long time that the Antilles were exempted from rabies, because until now no mad animals had been seen; but from 1776 to 1778 it has reigned almost continually. At Guadaloupe, the dogs were at first attacked with dumb madness, such as we had observed many years before, but without any other consequences. To this dumb madness succeeded that of a furious character; many cattle have been bitten and have died of rabies; we have also seen many human beings perish from this malady, negroes as well as white people. Numbers of dogs which have been bitten, died only with symptoms of dumb madness (*rage muet*); but others have become really mad, and bit whoever and whatever came in their way."*

In 1779, in the district of Belluno, Italy, it was reported that a number of people and domesticated animals had been bitten by a mad wolf in March, and that many of these died of hydrophobia.† At Bourges, France, in the same year and month, a mad wolf bit a child, which afterwards became affected with rabies.‡ In this year, also, rabies canina was very common at Philadelphia and in Maryland, America.§ In 1783, the malady was epizoötic in Hispaniola and Jamaica, and this appears to have been its advent in these regions. "During my residence in the West Indies," says Mosedey, "I never heard anything of this disease; and from the most particular inquiries I have made, I am fully convinced that before 1783 rabies had not appeared upon many, if any, of the islands." It appeared in spring in Hispaniola, and in June in Jamaica, where it continued until March, 1784. It was supposed to have originated spontaneously, and it soon became general. Many negroes were bitten, and died; and swine, goats, and horses were also injured, and perished with symptoms of hydro-

* "De Moyens de Conserver la Santé des Blancs et des Nègres." St. Domingo, 1786. "Animal Plagues," p. 486.

† "Animal Plagues," p. 490.

‡ Ibid., *loc. cit.*

§ Ibid., p. 490.

phobia.* "It was said at first that it was brought to Jamaica from Hispaniola; but experience proved the fact to be otherwise. The common notion that this disease among dogs can only proceed from the poison of an external bite, or that it originates in some particular dog from internal disease, and from thence is disseminated, has excluded the idea of spontaneous madness, arising from some peculiar influence in the air. But this influence of the air generated the canine madness in the year 1783, in the West Indies; for it was general, and many dogs were seized with it that had no communication with others; and some dogs which were brought from Europe and North America, and that were not on shore, went mad on their arrival in the harbours of the islands. . . . In 1783 this disease was general in Jamaica. Many negroes were bitten, and died hydrophobous. A boy belonging to Mrs. Inglis, in Kingston, was bitten by a little dog supposed to be mad. . . . An attorney-at-law in Kingston was bitten by his own dog. . . . One of his negroes was also bitten. Many dogs and goats were bitten, and died mad. A horse belonging to Mr. Edward East, in Liguanea, was bitten, and, being seized with madness, was shot. Another horse, belonging to a merchant in Kingston, was bitten. He broke out of the stable and ran about mad, until by beating his head against a wall he killed himself."

The outbreak of the disease in Hispaniola appears to have been very serious, if we may credit the information conveyed in a letter dated October 29th, 1783, from Kingston, Jamaica. "By the arrival of a brig from Port-au-Prince, we learn that

* "Animal Plagues," p. 520. In the *Gentleman's Magazine* for August, 1760, it is mentioned that Mr. Ingram stated that "in one season of the year the dogs in the West Indies are particularly subject to madness. In this season I have known a great number of negroes bit by them." Speaking of the efficacy of the actual cautery, he adds: "The first ten negroes were all cauterized, and every one was cured. One year, near twenty negroes were bit in one day; nineteen were cured, the other negro would not submit to the cautery, the hydrophobia came on, and he died mad." He knew of more than two hundred who had been so treated successfully, showing how prevalent the disease must have been at that early period.

D

the madness among the dogs was almost universal throughout the island of Hispaniola, and that orders had been issued by the Government to destroy the whole race of them in that country, which had been so effectually carried into execution by the military, that the surface of the water in the harbour of Port-au-Prince was covered with their dead bodies. The said disorder is said to rage among the dogs at Kingston."*

Canine madness was raging all over the Northern States of America in 1785, and the Gazettes of that year abound with accounts of its dreadful effects. It continued during the following year. Many cases of hydrophobia were observed in the Southern States of America;† and in 1789 it was again prevalent in that country. In the State of New York a man died of hydrophobia, induced, it was supposed, from his having skinned a cow that had died of that malady.‡ According to Moseley,§ canine madness raged in England in 1788, and the disease was epizoötic at Münster, in Westphalia, in 1789.‖ In 1797 it was also epizoötic in Rhode Island, North America."¶

In the nineteenth century rabies appears to have become much more frequent than in the previous eras, especially in France, Germany, and England, and also to have extended its geographical limits very considerably. In 1803 it appeared for the first time in Peru. "This disease appears to have been unknown on the shores of Peru, until in the excessively hot summers of 1803 and 1804, when it broke out in the scorched valleys along the northern part of the coasts, from whence it proceeded, with an epidemic course, southward to Ica and Arequipa. It is stated that of forty-two individuals bitten by rabid dogs, and who died in the town of Ica, the greater

* The *Gentleman's Magazine*, February, 1784. The disease does not appear to have been seen in Hispaniola (St. Domingo) until the latter half of the eighteenth century, as Pouppe Desportes, who practised medicine there from 1732 until 1748, says it was unknown in the island. "A Saint Dominique on a l'avantage de ne pas connoitre la rage."—*Histoire des Maladies de S. Dominique*, vol. ii. p. 157.

† "Animal Plagues," p. 524.

‡ Ibid., p. 528.

§ "On Hydrophobia" (London, 1808), p. 32.

‖ "Animal Plagues," p. 528.

¶ Ibid., p. 540.

number died in from twelve to ninety days after being bitten. It appears that the foresight of the Viceroy, Abascal, had saved Lima from the ravages of this furious epidemic, for he ordered a general slaughter of the dogs in the city. During my long residence in Peru, I never witnessed a single case of declared hydrophobia." * Another more detailed and interesting account is as follows: "Neither in Peru, nor in the neighbouring sections of South America, were dogs ever known to be attacked by hydrophobia prior to 1803; but about this time the malady broke out, during the heat of summer, in the valleys of the northern coast, from whence it extended southward along the maritime plains, having arrived at the city of Arequipa in the spring of 1807, while in Lima it was observed between the summer and autumn of the same year. . . . This disease arose spontaneously from the increased atmospherical temperature of the years 1803 and 1804. It commenced on the northern coast, commonly called Costa Abajo, where the air was so heated that Reaumur's thermometer indicated the temperature of 30 degrees in some of the valleys. The calms were extreme, without the lightest breeze that could ripple the surface of the ocean. Animals rushed into lakes and pools of still water to

* A. Smith. "Diseases in Peru," *Edinburgh Med. and Surgical Journal*, 1841. See also Unanue, "Observaciones sobre el Clima de Lima," p. 76. The slaughter thus commenced has passed into a custom of annually destroying these confiding companions of man, when the howl or piteous death-cry of the poor animal rings upon the ear, on fine summer mornings, as the watermen are employed in knocking them down with their iron-pointed sticks in all the streets, and even at the very doors or gates where the persecuted creatures seek protection in vain. To see them dragged along the streets, bound together by the waterman's lasso, leaving a bloody track behind them, and then heaped up in the public squares, where they are often allowed to lie for days, is truly one of the most painful and disgusting sights which Lima presents, and to which the bloody scenes of the bull-ring are comparatively nothing.—*Translator.*

The same dismal proceedings used to be enacted at Kertch, according to Prince Demidoff ("Travels in the Crimea"). Tennent, in his work on Ceylon, describes a similar disgusting performance, dogs being pursued and destroyed by clubs in the streets, and a premium given for each unfortunate animal so butchered. Since his book was published, however, I am glad to be assured that the hideous practice has been discontinued, owing to the remonstrances of the Royal Society for the Prevention of Cruelty to Animals.

relieve themselves from the sensation of excessive heat. This disorder affected every sort of quadruped without distinction, and such was the degree of frenzy excited by it, that some animals, in their fury, bit and tore themselves to pieces; and in situations where the heat was extreme, several men fell ill with all the symptoms of hydrophobia without having been bit. . . . . The malady attached itself more especially to dogs, and some of them suffered so mild an attack that their bite was not mortal; but the greater number were severely affected, and propagated the infection to their kind, to other quadrupeds, and to man. . . . The mean and niggardly overseer of a sugar estate had distributed among his negroes, though advised not to do so, some head of cattle that died rabid; which he did under the impression that they were only *tocado*, or touched with that disease which in hot weather usually affects cattle from the mountains; and the result was, that of the poor negroes who had partaken of this meat, many died with symptoms of hydrophobia. . . . . In the towns of Ica and Arequipa the number of individuals who died, after having been bit by mad dogs, was greater, and their cases less equivocal than the preceding. In Ica a single rabid bitch bit fourteen persons in one night, and all died with the exception of two men, who agreed to be placed under medical treatment. . . . In the city of Arequipa it was much disputed whether or not the malady was a legitimate hydrophobia, and learned papers *pro* and *con* were written by the Drs. Rosas and Salvani. In this paper-war much time was lost. . . . Immediately upon being made acquainted that the epidemic hydrophobia approached the capital, the Viceroy of Peru, Abascal, ordered all the dogs in the place to be killed, by means of which he liberated Lima from the impending scourge; for though a few hydrophobia patients entered at this period into the hospitals, they were not inhabitants of the city, but some individuals who had come in from the neighbouring farms and valleys. When this calamitous epidemic commenced in the valleys of Costa Abajo, Done Jose Figueroa wrote me to say, that the dogs went about with their tails between their feet; they slavered much, hid themselves from human sight, howled lustily, and presently they fell down and moved no more. The cats, with their hair on end, ran about the house-tops. Horses and asses got enraged the one against the other; they threw themselves on the ground, rolled about, and instantly, on being dead, they swelled and putrefied. Black cattle, roaring and lowing, bounded about, fought with each other, in the contest even broke their horns, and they died quickly. . . . Professor Estrada confidently stated, that of forty-two individuals who died in the city of Ica, after having been bit by mad dogs, the greater number were cut off in from twelve to ninety days after the accident. The symptoms which followed the ingraftment of the poison disclosed themselves in the form of convulsions, oppression at the breast, sighs, sadness, laborious breathing, horror at liquids and shining objects, fury, vomiting of dark bilious matter, and an incessant, urgent call on the part of the patients that the assistants should depart from them, because they felt themselves impelled to attack, bite, and tear them to pieces. None in this state survived beyond the term of five days. . . . Since the year 1808 this terrible epidemic has been disappearing. From time to time, however, a dog may be seen running violently hither and thither, and biting all whom he may happen to meet, in the same way as is done by the really mad dog."*

According to the statements of competent authorities, rabies was imported into La Plata in 1806, by sporting dogs belonging to English officers, and since that time it has continued there.

In 1803 also commenced one of the most remarkable epizoöties of vulpine rabies on record. It began in December, in the districts of Aubonne, Cossonay, Orbe, and Yverdon, at the foot of the Jura Alps, where dead foxes were observed, and people, dogs, pigs, and other animals were bitten. The epizoöty

* Smith, "Peru as it is," vol. ii. p. 248.

continued with more or less intensity until 1835, and in the interval spread over nearly the whole of Switzerland. In 1804 it appeared in the Kingdom of Wurtemburg and the Grand Duchy of Baden. In 1819 it had considerably increased in intensity and extent, having extended into the circle of the Upper Danube and Bavaria, and up to 1825 it raged with much fierceness in the Black Forest. In 1821 and 1822, it reigned in the forest of Thuringia, and at Jena a young captive fox became rabid on the chain and bit its owner. In the Voralberg, between May and September, 1821, seventeen goats and cows had perished from the effects of bites inflicted by rabid foxes. In 1824 it was very common among the foxes in Upper Hesse, and it was observed that it spread like any other contagious malady, generally from district to district, and from south to north. It reached Lower Hesse and the frontiers of Hanover at a later period. In Southern Germany the malady continued for several years. In 1834 it was very frequent in the Principality of Hohenzollern; and in August, 1836, a man and a girl were bitten by a fox in the district of Rottenburg. The girl died of hydrophobia. In the winter and spring of 1837 mad foxes were killed at Ulm. It appears that this vulpine epizoöty did not reach so far as North Germany. The symptoms observed in these animals were undoubtedly those of rabies. They attacked people in the woods or on the public highways, even entering villages; and during the continuance of the outbreak every kind of domestic animal suffered from the transmission of the virus by wounds occasioned by these creatures; even fowls were not exempt. Badgers were observed to be infected. In some places all the foxes died, and so many people suffered that there was a regular panic among the villagers.*

* I regret I cannot in this place afford further details of this most remarkable and interesting epizoöty. In another volume, on "Animal Plagues," which I trust will be published before long, I have given full particulars of the progress, symptoms, and other noteworthy features of the outbreak.

At Crema, in Italy, in 1804, a mad wolf descended from the mountains in November and bit thirteen persons, of whom nine died of hydrophobia.* In 1806 rabies was very common in England, according to Blaine, and abounded in the vicinity of London. In the two succeeding years it continued to rage, after which, for several subsequent years, it was less prevalent, "but it never became apparently extinct or rare as before."† In the winter of 1807 it raged as an epizoöty at Dover, and in some of the neighbouring towns. Many cases of hydrophobia occurred in the human species.‡ Until 1823 it was more or less prevalent in the City of London and suburbs every year. It was frequent in North America in 1810,§ but in Ohio it appears to have assumed an epizoötic character, affecting dogs, wolves, and foxes.‖

Rabies was very common in the Ukraine in 1813. Marochetti witnessed it in fourteen persons.¶ A rabid wolf appeared at Bar-sur-Ornain, France, and wounded many persons, some of whom afterwards died.**

According to Unienville, it appeared for the first time in the island of Mauritius in 1813, and was supposed to have been introduced by an English ship from the Bay of Bengal, which had English-bred dogs on board.†† In 1815 the malady was much more frequent than usual in Austria, and particularly in Vienna. According to the most reliable accounts, there did not occur, annually, more than four or five cases of sporadic madness among dogs in Vienna and its neighbourhood between

* Brera, "Prospetto della Clinica Med. di Padova." 1819-20.

† "Canine Pathology," p. 97.

‡ Lipscomb, "The History of Canine Madness," p. 30. Moseley, "On Hydrophobia," p. 1.

§ Thacker, *American Med. and Philosophical Register*, vol. i. p. 457.

‖ Hildreth, *American Journal of Medical Science*, 1830.

¶ "Observations sur l'Hydrophobie."

** Champion, "Relation Historique des Accidens causé par un Loup Enragé." Paris, 1813.

†† "Statist. de l'Ile Maurice," vol. ii. p. 322. Pridham ("The Mauritius and its Dependencies," London, 1846, vol. i. p. 237) asserts that dogs "have never been known to go mad in this island."

1808 and 1814. The disease broke out as an epizoöty in the latter year, when it commenced in the month of October with five, and terminated in December with fifteen cases. In 1815 the disease increased in virulence, seven cases occurring in January; the number increased during the year to forty-six cases. There could be no doubt as to the epizoötic character of the malady, according to the veterinary professor, Waldinger, who watched its progress and described its characteristics, as in by far the larger proportion of cases—viz., forty-three—the dogs attacked by it had not been bitten. Peculiar atmospheric conditions preceded and accompanied the epizoöty, and at last diseases dependent upon the weather, with disturbance of the functions of the skin, as, for example, rheumatism, arthritis, and mange (*schäbe*) appeared.* In 1815 it prevailed in an epizoötic form at Copenhagen, according to Viborg.†

In May, 1817, a rabid wolf attacked and wounded several people in the department of Isère, France. Hydrophobia affected several of the injured.‡ In Podolia, in 1818, Marochetti had no fewer than twenty-six persons in his care affected with hydrophobia.

In 1819 the Duke of Richmond, then Governor-General of Canada, was bitten by a captive fox, and afterwards perished of hydrophobia. In 1822 Forster states that rabies was common in Holland; § and in 1824 it was epizoötic in Sweden, extending also to the foxes, wolves, cats, and even to the reindeer.‖ It was likewise general in England, Norway, and Russia.¶ From 1823 to 1828, Hertwig reports that it was more than usually common at Berlin.**

* Waldinger, "Œsterriche Jahrbuch," 1816. Also "Abhandlung über die gewöhnlichen Krankheiten der Hunde." Vienna and Trieste, 1818.

† "Conspect. Præcip. mom. quæ Comm. de Enzootia Canina atque Hydrophobia." Hafniensa, 1817.

‡ Troillet, "Nouveau Traité de la Rage." Lyons, 1820.

§ "The Disorders of Health," p. 179. ‖ "Suenska Läk. Sellsk. Arb.," 1824.

¶ Gerson und Julius, "Magazin," vol. viii. p. 273.

** "Magazin für Thierheilkunde," "Beiträge zur nahern Kenntniss der Wuthkrankheit." Berlin, 1829.

In 1825 two children, a horse, and an ox were bitten by a mad badger at Langenaufnach, Bavaria. It may have been infected by a rabid fox, as the malady was then raging among these creatures in Germany. Indeed, Count Sponek appears to have been of this opinion when he wrote: "Had it not been madness (*toll*), the great dread of mankind, which Urian Bergmann mentions as peculiar to these animals, would have deterred it from attacking human beings in broad daylight; this is sufficient to stamp the disease as rabies, which was probably due to the badger having had a combat with a mad fox." * In 1828, according to the Registrar-General's Report, no fewer than twenty-eight persons died of hydrophobia in England and Wales. The veterinary professor, Prinz, reports its destructiveness in Dresden in 1829.†

In 1828 to 1830 Böhme asserts that rabies was frequent in Saxony; and in the latter year it was also prevalent in England and Vienna. In the latter city thirty-nine cases were reported. In 1831 and 1832 it was wide-spread in the Grand Duchy of Posen; and in 1833 it prevailed to an alarming extent at Barbadoes.‡ In 1834 it was general in Saxony, and in 1835 it was unusually frequent in Pomerania. On the 15th of February of this year, the government of the canton of Thurgau ordered the destruction of all the foxes, as rabies yet reigned among these creatures. In the canton of Zurich, in this year, a cat and a horse were affected with rabies, and in Lausanne sheep were attacked with it.§ Fitzroy says that, in 1835, hydrophobia was very prevalent in Chile; and men were bitten and succumbed to the malady. The valley of Copiapó, it is incidentally mentioned, is more particularly visited by the scourge.‖

In 1836 the disease was still more common in Pomerania

* "Sammlung Naturhist. Jägerbeobachten." Heidelberg, 1826.
† "De Wuth der Hunde als Seuche." Leipsic, 1832.
‡ Schomburgh, "History of Barbadoes."
§ "Archiv für Thierheilkunde, Schweiz. Thierärzte," vol. vii. pp. 268, 325, 329.
‖ "Narrative of the Beagle."

than in the previous year, and it was also present in Brandenburg and Saxony. In Brandenburg, horses, cattle, and sheep, as well as people, were bitten, and suffered from the effects of the malady.* At Paris it was also seriously prevalent.† In the following year its presence in Austria is reported by Knolz; and in 1838 commenced an epizoöty at Vienna, which continued until 1841. Between the years 1830 and 1840, only a very few cases were observed in that city. During the very hot summer of 1834, it was particularly noted that only one case of rabies occurred in Vienna and its immediate neighbourhood. In 1838 it appeared in an epizoötic form, and 17 cases were recorded; in 1839 there were 63; in 1840 only 42; but in 1841 no fewer than 141 cases were reported ‡—an unprecedented number, and which caused the greatest alarm to prevail. The following year there were 42 cases, and in 1843 only 2. It is also frequently mentioned in the annual report of the Dresden Veterinary School, by Professor Prinz, for 1838.§ In Wurtemburg the malady was epizoötic from September, 1839, to the end of 1842; and the veterinary professor, Hering, believed it to have been transmitted from the foxes.‖ From the 1st of January, 1840, until the end of February, 1842, rabies was observed to affect 230 dogs and 21 bitches.¶

For 1839-40, the *compte-rendu* of the Veterinary School of Lyons reports but few cases of rabies; but in the next report—that for 1840-41—Professor Rey states that "during the year cases of rabies occurred in great numbers in the dog species; out of sixty-four cases under observation as suspected, thirty-three showed symptoms of the disease and died. It is to the sudden diminution of temperature after great warmth,

* "Sanitatsbericht der Provinz. Brandenburg," 1836.

† "Recueil de Méd. Vét.," vol. xiv. p. 473.

‡ "Mittheilungen Osterr. Veter.," vol. i. p. 55.

§ "Magazin für die Gesammte Thierheilkunde," 1838.

‖ "Repertorium für Thierheilkunde," vol. ii. "Wurtemberger Correspondenzblat," vols. x., xii., xiii.

¶ "Repertorium," vol. iii. Faber, "Wuthkrankheit," vol. i. p. 218.

and to the consequent chilling of the skin, that the so frequent and spontaneous outbreaks of this redoubtable malady should be attributed. The autopsies did not furnish anything remarkable. We had occasion to observe four new cases of rabies transmitted accidentally by dogs to solipeds—two horses, an ass, and a mule. Two dogs were inoculated with the saliva of the mule, but without any result. . . . . We are already in possession of some facts which only too clearly prove that the virus preserves its virulency in passing through several animals. In two instances dogs attacked with communicated rabies have produced the malady in others animal of the same species. A ram, fifteen months old, bitten in the lip by a dog suffering from spontaneous rabies, was affected eleven days after. By inoculation with the lancet, the virus of this ruminant induced the disease in about thirty-five days in another ram of the same age. Here is an example of the transmission from one herbivore to another of rabies communicated by a carnivore. In three experiments, we have noted that of two dogs bitten at the same time, the first alone has contracted rabies. Might we from this infer, as Dr. Marochetti has done, that after the first bites the virus is expended?" *

The same talented veterinarian, in the *compte-rendu* of this school for the succeeding twelve months, 1841-1842, again alludes to the uncommon prevalence of the plague:—

"During this year the city of Lyons has been alarmed by the frequent occurrence of rabies (*rage*); eight people have perished in consequence of bites from dogs affected with this disease. Energetic measures have been adopted by the authorities, and three thousand wandering dogs have been sacrificed. Never at any period has the school received so large a number of hydrophobic animals: out of one hundred and four dogs which have died in the hospital from various diseases, sixty-two perished from rabies. It is not easy to assign any cause for the frequency of so redoubtable a malady; and it is in

* "Recueil de Méd. Vétérinaire," vol. xviii. p. 760.

this respect that we are forced to confess how difficult it often is to fix upon the etiology of a disease. In 1842 rabies showed itself in an enzoötic manner, not only in this city, but also at Aix, Nismes, and at Rouen—in different climates, under opposite atmospherical conditions, and at various epochs. Nevertheless, it was during the month of June last, in the hot weather, that the cases were most numerous.

"Up to the present time we have found that it is necessary to seek for one of the most active causes in the production of rabies in the vicissitudes of the weather, and especially in the sudden transition from an elevated temperature to the cold rains which are so frequent in the vicinity of the mountains. But, above all, it is necessary, with regard to sanitary policy, to point out the facility with which the malady may be transmitted by stray dogs, which, subjected to no surveillance, and exposed in large numbers to the attacks of the hydrophobic, in their turn may contract rabies, and thus spread it in a frightfully progressive manner. In support of this assertion, we may state that the instances of communicated rabies have been much more frequent than the spontaneous cases, and that the scourge has soon disappeared after the destructive measures instituted by the authorities have been carried into effect. In comparing our registers of mortality for the canine species, we find that since 1811, a period of thirty years, 779 dogs affected with rabies have died in the hospital. They have been admitted at all seasons of the year, but in different proportions; June has most, April comes next; then in decreasing proportions come May, July, August, March, and September, February and October, January and November, until in December the number is reduced to one-half." *

In the following year, 1843, only fourteen cases were admitted to the hospital of the school.†

Sir W. Maxwell, Bart., of Monreith, Wigtonshire, Scotland, informs me that in January, 1841, the disease was introduced

* "Recueil de Méd. Vét.," vol. xx. p. 121. † Ibid., p. 756.

into his kennels by a strange, mud-covered dog, and caused the destruction of the foxhounds and other dogs. Rabies was not known in the county at that time.

Dr. Adolphi, Imperial Veterinary Superintendent of Mitau, reports, in 1844, an epizoöty among cattle so closely resembling rabies that he believed it to be this disease, though no mad dog had been seen in the district of Heyden, Reinland—the place where the outbreak first occurred. It commenced in June, 1843, and prevailed until the end of July, 1844. The affected animals ran with tossed-up heads and wild looks madly round the pastures, goring and striking at all other animals with their horns. Every now and again the upper lip was drawn upwards in that peculiar manner in which vicious animals are apt to twitch it, and they kept up a continuous bellowing, which struck all hearers with terror, and which was not excited by the sight of a dog or any other creature, though it increased it. They foamed at the mouth; the hind parts were weak, and the weakness increased so rapidly that on the third day the animals were usually stretched on the ground, and could not be raised but with great difficulty. The muscles of the thighs, shoulders, and face were contracted at intervals as by spasms; and if the cattle chanced to be tied up they were restless, gazed wildly about, and bellowed frequently; if free, they rushed straight onwards over everything until some obstacle impeded their progress, and then they fell heels-over-head and lay still, apparently exhausted. There was no unusual thirst, and the power to swallow remained unimpaired. Any fluids poured in the mouth, as water, bran gruel, &c., were sucked down, and the only peculiarity observable was a motion as of choking, and a twitching of the muscles of the face. The disease was very fatal, most of the affected dying about the end of the fourth day. Adolphi believed it to be spontaneous rabies, as he could not discover that the animals had been wounded by any mad dog.*

* "Magazin für die Gesammte Thierheilkunde," 1844.

In 1847 great numbers of mad dogs were seen, in May, in Roscommon, Ireland.* My friend, Deputy-Controller Rogers, informs me that rabies also appeared at Malta this year, and, it was supposed, for the first time. It was very serious in its consequences, as several people bitten by dogs and cats perished. From 1843 to this date, only a few cases occurred annually in Vienna and neighbourhood, but in this year the number commenced to increase, there being 14 mad dogs; next year, 19; 1849, 17; 1850, 20.

Rabies canina raged epizoötically in 1851 in Northern Germany. At Hamburg alone no fewer than 267 cases were observed among dogs.† At this place, according to Schrader, it appeared after an interval of twenty-three years, in October, 1851. In September of the following year the number of ascertained cases had already reached 203: in August alone there were 44 cases. Active measures were then taken—all stray dogs killed, and orders given to keep others tied up. The total number killed at this time was 1,400, in addition to some 300 or 400 killed by their owners. In October the number of cases had diminished to 17; November, 11; December, 9; and January, 4. But on the restrictions being relaxed, the cases again increased, until in June, 1853, they were 14, and July, 17. Vigorous action was again resorted to, and a reduction once more took place. This was succeeded by another increase, until at last it was subdued, or wore itself out, in 1856. The total number of cases reported during this epizoöty, by the veterinary authorities at Hamburg, was nearly 600. Schrader states, that though the epizoöty prevailed on both banks of the Elbe, yet it was not observed on any of the islands in that river, probably because it was not carried to them by contagion.‡ A rabid wolf also caused much damage in France in 1851. "A mad wolf in the vicinity of Hue-au-Gal, in France, has, during a single day, bitten no less than forty-six persons and eighty-two head

* *Freeman's Journal.* † The *Lancet* and *Medical Times*, March, 1862.

‡ Hertwig, "Jahresbericht für 1853," p. 50.

of cattle. The accounts are very afflicting. The consequences have begun to show themselves. One person is dying after another in the most frightful agonies. All the cattle were purposely destroyed. The treatment recommended in similar cases—namely, that the wound should be kept in a state of suppuration for fifty days—has not been adopted, so that probably none of those bitten can be saved."*

In the Turkish territories, in 1852, a similar occurrence was noted. "The small town of Adalia, in the Turkish territories, has just been the scene of a sad catastrophe. On the 7th July a mad wolf rushed into the place, attacked and severely bit several individuals in the street; but becoming at length alarmed at the cries of the people, he made for the gardens at the skirts of the town. In consequence of this being the time of the silkworm harvest, several hundred individuals slept in one and the same garden, and 128 of them were severely wounded. Owing to the governor having recently taken from the inhabitants every kind of weapon, the unhappy people found themselves without any means of defence. The wolf was at length driven thence also; but the same night he attacked a flock of sheep, and killed eighty-five of them. It was not until the following day that the people, to whom the governor had returned their arms, succeeded in destroying the beast. The report of a medical man resident in the town, in regard to the wounded, is frightful. The most shocking part of the affair is, that several of those bitten have already died raving mad, and the population of the place are in a state of the most terrible consternation."†

* L. Lloyd, "Scandinavian Adventures," vol. i. p. 451. This author, when describing the Northern wolf, says: "The Scandinavian wolf, though subject to several diseases, is happily, I believe, exempt from rabies. This is well; for were they liable to that horrid infliction, the consequences would be dreadful from their numbers, and their being so generally distributed throughout the peninsula. In warmer climates, as is known, the destruction caused by this animal when the fatal malady is at work within him, is awful to contemplate." —*Ibid.*, p. 451.

† Ibid., p. 452.

M. Stanislaus Prioux, in his "Vie de Saint Hubert," refers to the dread rabies was causing on the Continent in 1851: "At the time when rabies had spread the utmost terror over the greater portion of the northern countries (about two years ago, in 1851), I knew an old man at Brussels who, in his youth, had undergone the ordeal prescribed by St. Hubert, and who yet carried on his forehead the precious cicatrix; he assured me he had saved the lives of several people by granting them delays, while others bitten at the same time by the mad animals died."

In England, in 1856, rabies showed itself among dogs and in a herd of deer to a serious extent. "Rabies, or hydrophobia, has shown itself to such an extent at Stainbrough, near Barnsley, as to excite the alarm of the inhabitants of that locality, and to attract the attention of medical men. The disease began to exhibit itself on a small scale in a herd of deer in the latter part of last or early in the present year, immediately after one or more mad dogs had been seen roaming about the locality, one of which is supposed to have communicated the contagion. Nearly one hundred deer have already fallen victims to its effects. While in a state of disease, these otherwise innocent and playful animals foam at the mouth, worry each other like dogs, and tear off each other's hair and flesh, and, when placed in a state of confinement, bite at whatever comes within their reach. With these symptoms the above number have already died, and others are continually being affected by the disease. Five or six dogs have also died at the same place, exhibiting the same symptoms. Until recently the disease was not suspected to be rabies; but attention has been drawn particularly to the matter, through a child belonging to one of the workmen having been bitten by one of the dogs. This caused an alarm, which led to a medical gentleman being called in; and, on investigating the circumstances, he has pronounced the disease to be rabies. In his official capacity of medical officer of the Barnsley Local Board of Health, he has issued a timely notice or caution to the inhabitants, in which he states that there cannot be any reasonable doubt that hydrophobia has manifested itself to a serious extent in the neighbourhood, and he calls upon all persons to be on their guard to protect themselves and their families from the infliction of this terrible malady."*

In Berkshire, likewise, in this year, rabies was reported in a flock of sheep belonging to a farmer at Nuffield. On the morning of February 17th, in a fold containing seventy-two very fine ewes heavy in lamb, a strange dog was found by the farmer's son, and beside it two of the ewes dead, and two others so seriously injured that they were afterwards killed. The dog growled at the boy, but, being pelted with stones, it ran away towards the village. It was then discovered that about twenty more sheep were wounded, more or less, about the nose and ears. The wounds were dressed, and these sheep were put in a fold by themselves; but two or three weeks afterwards several of them began to exhibit symptoms of madness, and fifteen of them lambed, the lambs being brought up by hand. The ewes that became rabid trotted backwards and forwards by the sides of the fold, and repeatedly bit at the hurdles, tearing mouthfuls of wool out of each other, foamed at the mouth, &c. "Twenty-two are since dead, and there are five more that were slightly bitten, which no doubt will also die before many days. The mad lurcher afterwards attacked two dogs, which were soon shot. It next ran to Mr. Corderer's farm at Lashbrook, and fell on his dogs; but that gentleman, suspecting the dog to be mad, shot him, and then his own dogs, and consigned their bodies to the Thames."†

My friend, Mr. Michie of Shanghai, China, informs me that while he was in Hong Kong, in 1857, an English bloodhound suddenly became rabid and bit several people; one man died of hydrophobia. It was remarked that this was the first case which had occurred on the island, and none have been reported since that time.

* The *Veterinarian*, vol. xxix. p. 341. † The *Reading Mercury*, May, 1856.

From 1855 to 1860 rabies was extensively prevalent over a large portion of Northern Germany, France, and Spain; but, strangely enough, the cases in Vienna were very few, except in 1855, when there were sixteen. In 1858, the disease was so serious in Algeria that the Governor-General issued a circular relative to preventive measures.*

In 1860 rabies was prevalent in America, especially in the west, "attributable to the large number of idle dogs everywhere kept, or, rather, allowed to prowl about without much keeping." † In this year there were several cases of canine madness in various towns of France.‡ Captain Malcom, Royal Engineers, informs me that while stationed at Canton, South China, a man died near that town, in 1860 or 1861, of hydrophobia. In 1861, while I was quartered with the British army of occupation at Tientsin, near Peking, North China, cases of hydrophobia, caused by bites from rabid dogs, occurred among the native Chinese.§

About this time, and for a few years subsequently, the presence of rabies was more than usually noted in Rhenish Prussia, and it appeared in an epizoötic form at Vienna. In reality it began in 1860 with 12 cases, in 1861 there were 10, and in 1862, 32. In 1863 there were 29 cases, and in 1864, 24. As in 1841, when this dreaded malady was epizoötic in the same city, the dogs which were generally affected belonged to people who were in tolerable circumstances; the animals had been well fed and carefully preserved from the vicissitudes of the weather; but did not get sufficient exercise, and were seldom, if ever, allowed to gratify their animal passions. As in 1841 also, the majority of the dogs affected were mongrels, or belonged to irritable and nervous breeds; or they

* "Annales d'Hygiène Publique," 1866, p. 97.

† The *Veterinarian*, vol. xxxiii. p. 393.

‡ Ibid., *loc. cit.*

§ The grotesqueness of the Chinese mind in general matters is perhaps most conspicuous in those relating to medicine, and more particularly to diseases. I am assured on the best authority that, in some parts of the Flowery Land, it is the universal belief that a man affected with hydrophobia is *enceinte*, and that he is so distressed and ultimately perishes because he cannot be delivered.

were dogs which, having been kept all their lives chained up, had become very vicious. The males appeared to be more frequently attacked than the females; but this might have been accounted for by the fact, that in Vienna dogs are more numerous than bitches. The adult age, as in 1841, seemed to be the most favourable for the development of the malady. Thirty-two animals were admitted to the Imperial Veterinary Institute; eight of these were dead on their arrival, and of the others only seven showed symptoms of furious rabies, the other seventeen being affected with that form which is known as "dumb madness."

Professor Pillwax, of the Veterinary Institute, has given an excellent description of the outbreak, to which we shall have occasion to refer again. In the meantime it may be mentioned that in one of the thirty-two dogs which, during life, presented all the symptoms of rabies, the most characteristic lesions of typhus were found; also, that nine of the mad dogs sent to the Institute had bitten twelve people, and only one of these, a young lad, contracted the malady. He had been bitten by the dog which, on a necroscopic examination, had offered such evident lesions of typhus. Four weeks after being wounded the first symptoms of hydrophobia appeared, and he soon succumbed. Three other persons bitten by this dog had their wounds immediately cauterised (the boy's wounds had not been so treated, because of their number and extent), and they escaped.*

In Saxony the disease appears to have been prevalent at this time. Haubner says that, previous to 1860, only a small number of mad dogs had been observed in that kingdom; but in that year a few isolated outbreaks were reported. In Dresden, however, for more than ten years, not a mad dog had been seen. In 1863 it began to spread gradually, and at length it prevailed over the whole kingdom. In this year 10 cases were

* "Œsterreichische Vierteljahresschrift für Wissenschaftliche Thierheilkunde," 1863.

reported; in the following year, 33; in 1865, 227; in 1866, 287; and in 1867, 250.*

About 1862 Sir Samuel Baker, exploring the Nile tributaries of Abyssinia, informs us not only of the existence of hydrophobia—or, rather, rabies—in that part of Africa, but also of its appearance in an epizoötic form. "One night we were sitting at dinner, when we suddenly heard a great noise, and the air was illumined by the blaze of a hut on fire. In the midst of the tumult I heard the unmistakable cries of dogs, and thinking that they were unable to escape from the fire, I ran towards the spot. As I approached, first one and then another dog ran screaming from the flames, until a regular pack of about twenty scorched animals appeared in quick succession, all half mad with fright and fire. I was informed that hydrophobia was very prevalent in the country, and that the certain preventive from that frightful malady was to make all the dogs of the village pass through the fire. Accordingly an old hut had been filled with straw and fired, after which each dog was brought by its owner and thrown into the flames." †

In 1864 great apprehensions were entertained in Lancashire as to a severe outbreak of the disease; and to such an extreme degree had the alarm attained, that in June of this year it was calculated that upwards of one thousand dogs had been destroyed in Liverpool alone—seven hundred by the police, and three hundred by private individuals. The number of deaths from hydrophobia registered in England was twelve. In Ireland seven persons died of hydrophobia (six males, one female). No deaths are reported from Scotland.

For two or three months in the middle of 1865, rabies prevailed to a very unusual extent among dogs in and around London. In the neighbourhood of Enfield, several sheep were bitten, some of which fell victims to the dreadful malady, and

* "Handbuch der Veterinär-Polizei." Dresden, 1870, p. 308.

† "The Nile Tributaries of Abyssinia," p. 164.

others were killed. Many persons were bitten, and two or three deaths occurred from hydrophobia.* The total number of deaths registered in the human species in England was nineteen.

At Lyons, France, in 1865, the malady also appears to have been largely on the increase, as Professor Saint-Cyr, of the Veterinary School in that town, reports the admission of no fewer than 159 dogs into its canine infirmary, being an excess of 62 over the number admitted in the previous year. Some of these (78) were actually rabid, and others (81) only suspected. Altogether 87 were affected, and all these perished.†

But in 1866 the disease appears to have assumed a formidable extension and virulency in England, and especially in Lancashire, as no fewer than thirty-six deaths from hydrophobia are reported by the Registrar-General. Eleven of these were of persons residing in London, thirteen in Lancashire, three in Northumberland, two in Buckinghamshire, two in Durham, one each in Kent, Hampshire, Staffordshire, Leicestershire, and Cheshire. In 1867 a "Metropolitan Streets Act" was passed which enabled the police to seize all vagrant dogs. In June, 1868, it was put in force, and the number of cases of hydrophobia immediately became greatly diminished in and around London.

At Shanghai, North China, according to the testimony of my friend Mr. Michie, merchant of that town, rabies showed itself among English dogs during the summer of 1867, and several persons were wounded. Two Europeans, bitten by their own dogs, perished soon after from hydrophobia. At this time a cat had also evinced symptoms of the disease and was destroyed. Dr. Michie informs me that in the two fatal cases, the disease followed within a few weeks of the injury, and that within the two months succeeding the death of these persons, rabies became extraordinarily common amongst the dogs of the

* The *Veterinarian*, July, 1865, p. 439.
† *Journal de Méd. Vétérinaire de Lyon*, 1866.

European residents of the settlement, and several persons were bitten. Owing to the alarm occasioned by these events, immediately the injuries were inflicted surgical aid was sought, and it was remarked in none of the cases in which precautions were taken did the disease occur. Excision beyond the marks of the teeth on every side, and cauterisation, in all probability were the means of saving several lives. Dr. Michie saw several of the dogs that were suffering from the disease, and by his advice not only were these shot, but also other apparently healthy dogs belonging to the same kennels which had been bitten by the original rabid dogs.

In 1868 so many cases of rabies were reported in Belgium, where the disease is usually very rare, that the authorities had to issue stringent regulations for its prevention and suppression. It appears to have commenced about January, and was reported from several provinces. Up to May no fewer than thirty-two dogs, a horse, and a cat, had been admitted to the infirmary of the veterinary school at Cureghem, near Brussels, according to the report on the disease drawn up by order of the government, by Professors Defays and Thiernesse. In two cases the malady had been transmitted to the human species.* Mr. Michie informs me that in the winter of 1869-70, a Scotch terrier became rabid at Chinkiang, China, and bit a buffalo, which subsequently died of the disease, the symptoms being well marked.†

In 1869 rabies was noted in Paris, and the transmission of the disease from the cat to the human species was reported.‡

* *Journal de Méd. Vétérinaire de Bruxelles*, 1868, p. 349.

† Hydrophobia appears to be well known to the Chinese physicians, and for a long time it has been the subject of their ingenuity in the matter of remedies. Among these is a preparation which is lauded as an infallible cure. This is composed of musk, half an ounce; native and artificial cinnabar, of each five drachms. These substances are rubbed down together to an impalpable powder, and then given suspended in a spoonful of rice-spirit. Calm sleep and copious perspiration comes on after two or three hours; otherwise, a second dose of the powder is given, and a cure, they say, is sure to follow.

‡ "Recueil de Méd. Vétérinaire," 1869, p. 836.

Early in this year cases of rabies began to be observed in Lancashire, and up to the present time (January, 1872) the epizoöty—for the malady really assumed an epizoötic form—has continued and extended, reaching as far as Yorkshire, where it caused much damage and destruction of human life, and the borders of Scotland. So early as November, 1868, a young woman was wounded by a mad dog at Preston, and in March, 1869, six rabid animals were destroyed there, two deaths among people having occurred.* In this month all the dogs captured at large in that town were destroyed. In the neighbourhood of Wigan, and at Chorley, rabid dogs were seen, and cows and dogs were wounded by them and died of rabies. Other animals bitten—dogs, pigs, &c.—were destroyed as a preventive measure.† The cases occurring in Preston and its environs were followed by others some miles further south, and almost simultaneously outbreaks were reported in the counties lying east and north of that town, the disease gradually extending further from this supposed centre.‡

In September several cases were reported as occurring at Huddersfield, Yorkshire, and a boy aged three years died of hydrophobia.§ At Newburgh, in the same month, a mad dog bit a man and several other animals; the man died. A rabid retriever dog attacked and wounded several persons and dogs in and about Derby, Nottingham, and Loughborough, in November. It was supposed this animal had been bitten in the commencement of the month near Wigan. In January, 1870, in the neighbourhood of Hebden Bridge, near Halifax, a strange dog prowling about a farmstead bit a cow and a dog. The cow died of rabies. "During the past few months many cases of this kind have occurred in the same neighbourhood. Dogs, pigs, cats, cows, and horses, have been attacked, destroyed,

* The *Standard*, March, 1869.
† The *Veterinarian*, vol. xlii. p. 283.
‡ Ibid., vol. xlii. p. 199.
§ *British Medical Journal*, Sept. 25, 1869.

or died from the effects of hydrophobia. Several human beings have been bitten, and last week a man died from the effects." *

In February (20th) a man died in the Nottingham general hospital from hydrophobia, having been bitten on the 25th December, 1869. The dog which bit him was traced from a neighbouring village through twenty miles of country and many villages, having in its course wounded many dogs and men.† In March also two men perished from hydrophobia in this town, another in the hospital in May, and a child in September. In February a boy seven years old died of the disease at Carlisle, and in the next month a man succumbed to it.‡ In March a fatal case in mankind occurred at Stalybridge, and another at Dundee, Scotland.§ In the district of Windermere, Cumberland, towards the middle of 1870, the authorities were compelled to order all dogs to be confined. In the North Riding of Yorkshire much alarm likewise prevailed in consequence of the frequency and extension of the malady. In Huddersfield Mr. Kirk reports the district around as a centre of infection, and as having had several indisputable cases of rabies in dogs, and one in the horse, in this year.‖

In Bolton, Lancashire, in December, my friend Mr. Lawson reports rabies in the human species, cows, and sheep;¶ and Mr. Worthington of Wigan, in the same county, states that since

* The *Standard*, January, 1870.

† *British Medical Journal*, February 26, 1870; December 2, 1871.

‡ Ibid., April 30, 1870.

§ Ibid.

‖ The *Veterinarian*, December, 1870. For Huddersfield there is the following proclamation, dated May 30th, 1870: "This is to certify that we, the undersigned, being two of Her Majesty's Justices of the Peace, do hereby direct that from the date hereof, until the 31st day of August next, all Dogs, within the borough of Huddersfield, shall be confined on suspicion of canine madness. And notice is hereby given, that every person who, during the period set forth in the foregoing Notice, suffers any dog to be at large, incurs a penalty of any sum not exceeding forty shillings, or, in the discretion of the justices before whom he may be convicted, may be imprisoned for a period not exceeding fourteen days. All dogs found in the streets or highways will be considered to be at large, unless held in check by a string, chain, strap, or other fastening.

"(Signed) C. H. Jones, Mayor, J.P.
Wright Mellor, Deputy Mayor, J.P."

¶ The *Veterinarian*, May, 1871.

August the disease had assumed most alarming proportions, scarcely a week having passed without three or four animals falling victims to it. He was able to enumerate no fewer than forty-two cases which had occurred within a radius of nine miles during the previous eighteen or twenty months, many of which had come under his own notice. The list comprised four human beings, one horse, eleven cattle, twelve sheep, and fourteen dogs.* Referring to the extension of the disease and the facility with which it could be propagated over a wide expanse of country, he gives the following striking illustrations: A terrier belonging to a gentleman in his neighbourhood was severely bitten in November, 1869, by a dog that had wounded four cows, which subsequently perished of rabies. Soon afterwards the owner of the terrier, who was ignorant of the serious nature of the injury inflicted on the animal, and the danger he was incurring, sold the dog to a dealer in that town, who again sold it shortly after it came into his possession. Immediately this became known inquiries were made by the police for the purpose of having the dog either kept under surveillance or destroyed. The dealer was applied to, but either could not or would not furnish the slightest information as to its whereabouts. As these men are in the habit of trading with dealers in other towns, it is not improbable that this dog may have been sent many miles away, and had become the source of incalculable mischief in its new locality.†

On the 9th February the inhabitants of Shevington and Mawdesley were thrown into a state of great alarm by a rabid dog which made its appearance in these townships (near Wigan), and after committing an immense amount of mischief, was destroyed the following morning, at the farm of Mr. Henry Alty, Black Moor Hall, Mawdesley. The animal was a small-sized sheep-dog of a light-brown colour, with a broad band of white hair round the neck, white stripe down the face, white fore-legs, and about three inches of white at the extremity of

* The *Veterinarian*, May, 1871. † Ibid., August, 1870.

the tail. This description was given in order to warn people who might have seen the animal in other places than those mentioned, without suspecting it to be mad. From inquiries made at the time, the dog was first seen on the preceding Sunday at Rufford, from whence it passed through Mawdesley, over Hunter's Hill, through Wrightington, to Welsh Whittle, in which neighbourhood it seems to have remained during the night. Early next morning it was again seen at Mossy Lee, in Wrightington, and after severely injuring a sheep near Wrightington Hall, passed into the lower part of Shevington, traversing nearly the whole of the township during the day, and attacking indiscriminately every animal with which it came in contact. About four o'clock in the afternoon it again passed through Wrightington, by way of Anderton's Mill, in Mawdesley, and here for the remainder of its brief existence its depredations were indeed fearful, scarcely a farm having escaped its visitation during the night and following morning. In this township alone nearly a score of dogs which had been bitten by it were shot and buried in one week, and many others were probably afterwards destroyed. Among the victims at Shevington were several dogs, a sheep, calf, and a cow. A horse was also ferociously attacked by it whilst at work near Appley Bridge, but being seized by the hairy part of the tail, fortunately sustained no injury. No people were injured, though several had narrow escapes. The whole of the dogs known to have been bitten in Shevington were destroyed, and the other animals, being under the immediate notice of Mr. Worthington, were to be destroyed directly the disease manifested itself. That the strange dog was rabid there was not the shadow of a doubt; the characteristic symptoms of the disease being well developed during life, and, besides, an examination made after death revealed unmistakable evidence of rabies. "As a rabid dog in the latter stages of the malady," adds Mr. Worthington, "is invariably irresistibly impelled to ramble and do mischief, and is almost incessantly on the move, it is probable that many dogs in the above townships have received slight and unsuspected bites." As a means, therefore, of preventing the extension of the disease, it was earnestly suggested that every dog to which even a shadow of suspicion might be attached, should be immediately destroyed, or kept in the most rigorous confinement for a period of at least ten months. "Those who have once seen this truly horrible disease," he says, "or who entertain the slightest regard for public safety, will not, I am sure, for a moment hesitate to adopt such an easy and effectual precaution."*

It is afterwards intimated that several dogs and cattle which had been wounded by this errant dog had become rabid.

During the summer months, rabies in its two forms appeared among the Lyme (Cheshire) harriers, and led to their extermination.

On the 14th March, 1871, the disease was observed in the vicinity of Disley and Marple, in Cheshire. A bull-terrier dog suddenly appeared in a farmyard at Stanley Hall, Disley, and bit a sheep-dog. It then went through the village of Disley, and bit two other dogs. These were subsequently destroyed, exhibiting all the symptoms of rabies. It then appears to have left this neighbourhood, and gone through Lyne to Wimblehurst, in Marple, where a flock of twenty sheep were attacked by it, and nearly all were wounded, thirteen showing bites about the head and neck. Two were severely torn, one had a large piece bitten from its cheek, and the other had its lips lacerated to a great extent. The dog was killed soon after in Wimblehurst.

About the 15th April several of the sheep were observed to be strange in their habits, and especially to exhibit pugnacious symptoms, by butting at each other. Four died on the 18th; on the 19th eight were destroyed; and in June only five of the flock remained.

The sheep-dog at Stanley Hall appeared "strange in his

* The *Veterinarian*, March, 1871.

habits," according to the farmer, about a fortnight after being bitten, and, breaking away from its kennel, it bit another dog in the village. Running afterwards to Cheadle Hulme, it was killed.

On April 9th a rabid harrier made its appearance at Disley, and, after an exciting chase, it was shot at Strines, but not before biting four other dogs, which were at once destroyed. It also came in contact with two or three dogs which, from their not showing any wounds, were not destroyed. One of these was a large mastiff, which seized the harrier, and shook it. In about three weeks afterwards the mastiff appeared to be quite altered in its usual habits, which caused his owner to give it some laxative medicine. The animal, to all appearance, recovered; but while it was indisposed another dog, a retriever, began to play with it. This retriever was subsequently destroyed for rabies, though there existed a doubt as to whether it was infected by the mastiff or from a black-and-tan dog which bit it a few weeks previously. The black-and-tan was a stranger in the locality, and was seen to chase some hens after biting the retriever. This led to its being shot.*

Mad dogs were seen in Glossop and Werneth, in Derbyshire.

Up to the present time the disease has been noted as more or less prevalent among dogs in the North of England, and other animals have become infected with rabies. Many people have also died from hydrophobia, induced by the bites inflicted by rabid dogs and cats, notably in Liverpool and other parts of Lancashire, and in Leeds. For instance, in the *Leeds Mercury* for June 7th alone we find the following records of bites:—A dog wearing a wire muzzle too large for its head, bit a man in the leg. A female servant playing with a poodle dog, was bitten by it through the lip; and a valuable dog of the "snap" breed, lying asleep on the sofa in a room where a child belonging to its master was at play on the carpet, suddenly jumped up, and attacked the infant, lacerating its cheek in a

* The *Veterinarian*, vol. xliv. p. 478.

shocking manner. The animal had never exhibited a savage disposition before this occurrence. It was at once destroyed.

Elsewhere the disease was appearing in a really epizoötic and alarming manner.

In Cleveland the disease showed itself in the commencement of June. "At Skelton, in Cleveland, on Friday, a stray dog visited the village, and bit several others, and also a man and two boys at Hobhill, where it was afterwards shot. Another dog visited Saltburn-by-the-Sea, and bit eight dogs, which were subsequently shot. A third visited Markse-by-the-Sea, where several were bitten; and a fourth, about a fortnight ago, was shot between Lazenby and Redcar, after having bit a man, a cow, a pig, and several dogs." *

In Nottinghamshire it was also causing alarm in this month. On June 19th a dog belonging to a person at Gedling went mad, bit one of his children, broke loose, ran away, and was not afterwards heard of in the locality. The following morning it was seen at the Lenton Ford, on the Trent, where it turned into a field in which was a large flock of sheep, one of which was bitten by it, it not having run away with the others. Then the dog ran across the canal to another field, and attacked a youth who was digging up thistles. The boy fought him manfully with his implement, which the animal seized with great ferocity, indenting the handle with its teeth, and covering it with foam and blood. Beaten off, it turned into the public street of Beeston, where it met a flock of sheep, bit many of them, and then wounded the young man who was driving them severely in the nose.† It then tried to attack a dog that was being led by a man, but being outmanœuvred, it ran miles without any one being able to trace the damage it committed, until at length, biting the policeman on duty at Lockington, it was lost sight of.‡

* *Leeds Mercury*, June 7, 1871.

† This man's wounds were promptly attended to, and up to the present time (January, 1872) he continues in good health at Atherstone.

‡ The *Nottingham Journal*, June 20, 22, 1871. The following is a copy of

In the *Sporting Gazette* for July 1, 1871, we read: "Very alarming intelligence has reached us of the outbreak of hydrophobia in several hunting kennels. The Quorn have lost all their entry, and many of the Albrighton have died; whilst, still more serious, fears are entertained for the fate of the huntsman and one of his assistants in the latter pack, both of whom were bitten.* We also hear that the disease has

---

the magisterial notice placarded in Nottingham in 1871:—"Borough of Nottingham.—Dogs.—I, John Manning, Esquire, Mayor of the Town and County of the Town of Nottingham, in pursuance of 'The Town Police Clauses Act, 1847,' do hereby direct that on account of Canine Madness existing in this Town, all dogs shall be confined for Four Calendar Months from the day of the date hereof.—JOHN MANNING, Mayor, 6th June, 1871. Every person who suffers any Dog to be at large during the time above specified, will be liable to a penalty not exceeding 40s., and any Constable may take the Offender into custody without warrant. Every Dog at any time straying at large in the Borough will be taken charge of by the Police, and if not claimed after the expiration of Six Days will be destroyed."

* My friend, Mr. Cartright, M.R.C.V.S., of Wolverhampton, has kindly sent me the following interesting description of the outbreak among the Albrighton and Quorn hounds. He writes on August 28th: "I was requested by the Master of the Albrighton Hunt to go on May 19th to the kennels, and make a *post-mortem* examination of a young hound (of this year's entry), which the huntsman had shot and buried the day before, as he suspected it was affected with 'dumb madness.' The body, after it was exhumed, appeared fresh and in good condition. The abdominal cavity presented nothing remarkable; the stomach contained only a little slimy mucus, and there were a few patches of inflammation on the peritoneal coat of the large intestines. The liver and kidneys were quite healthy, as also were the heart and lungs. There was no enlargement or other abnormal appearance of any of the glands of the throat, and the mucous membrane of the mouth and pharynx appeared quite natural. On removing the bones of the cranium, the dura mater presented a highly injected appearance; there was an increase of the arachnoideal fluid, and there was a larger quantity of fluid than natural in the lateral ventricles. The substance of the brain was also affected, and the blood vessels at its base were very much congested. From the attendants, I learned that this hound had been reared by a butcher at Newport, and had been at the kennels about two months before it began to show symptoms of illness. These symptoms were an altered manner, loss of appetite, and a disposition to snap at men or dogs—more especially dogs—and as it had bitten the huntsman and his dogman, it was at once destroyed.

"On the 3rd of June, I was again requested to attend at the kennels. The day previous, the huntsman observed something the matter with the mouth of another of the young hounds. On examination, he saw several small wart-like excrescences on the base of the tongue; these he at once removed with nippers, and bled and physicked the animal. When I saw it, the glands of the throat were enlarged, the lower jaw dropped, but there was no discharge of saliva, and

spread amongst some of the Scotch packs." Cases continued to occur in the Albrighton pack, of both furious and mad

---

the mouth felt slightly warm. It appeared weak, with a peculiar husk, was off its feed, lapped water freely, but was unable to swallow; it was retired in manner, and had to be dragged out of the kennel into the open: it was quiet with its attendants, but very savage with other dogs; indeed, it worried a terrier, which was immediately destroyed. On the night of the 4th the symptoms became more violent; the animal continued gnawing at the doors and brickwork of the yard, and when I saw it on the morning of the 5th it had become quite exhausted; the lower jaw and lips were more pendulous—in fact, it appeared sinking, and died during the night. *Post-mortem* examination on the 6th: the stomach was found to contain a small quantity of straw, hair, grass, and some partly digested food; its coats were not inflamed, and the intestines and other abdominal viscera were healthy; the lungs and heart were normal; the parotid and other salivary glands were larger than natural, and had a pallid appearance. The mucous membrane of the mouth and throat was much inflamed, and peeled off very easily. An abscess had formed on each side of the fauces, from which between two and three teaspoonfuls of thin, greyish matter issued. The brain was not examined.

"On the 15th, a third hound (same entry) was brought to my establishment to be examined. It had presented symptoms similar to the former cases, but had been lying in an unconscious state for nearly twelve hours before death. The *post-mortem* appearances were also similar: the abdominal viscera were healthy; stomach contained some straw, hair, and earth; a little straw, half-masticated, was in the pharynx, and its lining membrane was inflamed. There was an increased quantity of fluid on the brain and in the lateral ventricles, and the brain itself, as well as its membranes, had a pallid appearance.

"On the same day, two hounds were sent for *post-mortem* examination from the Quorn kennels. No satisfactory account of the symptoms was forwarded, except that one of them had appeared strange in manner, and showed a disposition to bite other dogs. The body of one was much swollen, and a large quantity of fœtid gas escaped when the abdominal cavity was opened; the stomach and intestines were also distended with gas, and very much inflamed. A small quantity of food, partly digested, was in the stomach; the lungs were black, and filled with blood; and the membranes of the brain, as well as the blood vessels at its base, were very much congested. The *post-mortem* appearances of the other hound were similar to those presented by the cases from Albrighton, but the brain could not be examined, as the animal had been shot through the head. I went to Quorn next day and examined the bodies of three other hounds; they had evidently been suffering from the same disease as those at the Albrighton kennels, and had shown similar symptoms during life—altogether, they had lost seven hounds by the disease.

"Another hound was taken ill on the 17th June at the Albrighton kennels, with symptoms similar to the former cases. It was shot, and buried without any *post-mortem* examination being made; and as the disease had confined itself to the young hounds, and appeared likely to attack them all in turn, it was deemed advisable to destroy the others. The remaining six couple were accordingly shot. About a month ago an old hound showed symptoms of the first stage of the disease, and it was immediately destroyed. No other cases have occurred

rabies, until at last in November, 1871, those remaining were destroyed.

On August 15th, according to the *Daily News* for the 18th of that month, Mr. Berry, a minister in Mossley, died from hydrophobia, arising from the bite of a cat three months previously.

Towards the end of 1871, cattle were dying from rabies in Cheshire. Sheep were also bitten by a rabid dog at West Hartlepool, and died of rabies.*

In Cumberland and Durham the disease was also committing great havoc. Mr. Wilkinson, M.R.C.V.S., of Newcastle-on-Tyne, informs me, under date of November 30th, that he had seen and heard of more cases of both forms of rabies for the last three years than he could have believed possible, and had pointed out its apparent increase to veterinary surgeons and others. In Durham the most notable occurrence was the outbreak of the malady among the county foxhounds, which necessitated the entire destruction of those still unaffected. A correspondent in the *Field* for December 2, gives the following interesting relation of the event:—

"Perhaps no more striking instance of the uncertainty attendant on the most promising and best-laid plans in hunting affairs has ever been demonstrated than the destruction of the Durham county hounds, which, from the rapid spread of hydrophobia and dumb madness in the kennels, had become an absolute necessity, in order to obviate the danger of spreading a disease the most dreadful and fatal in its consequences of any to which human or animal life is subject. A short history of the case may be useful as well as interesting, not only to masters of hounds and hunting-men, but, from its peculiar physiological characteristics, to all who take an interest in and

since, and when I saw the pack a few days ago all were in good health and condition." As stated above, the whole pack (a dog one), consisting of twenty-nine couples, was finally destroyed in November, fresh cases having occurred.

* The *Veterinarian*, December, 1871.

watch those visitations which appear at different times among human beings and animals.

"For the last seven or eight years the Durham county hounds, under the management of a committee, have had Thomas Dowdswell, from Lord Macclesfield's, as their huntsman; and it is not too much to say that by careful breeding, with the advantage of some of the best blood, the pack had been brought to a state of perfection never surpassed since the time of Mr. Ralph Lambton, who for so many years hunted the country at present occupied by these unfortunate hounds. The pack of forty-one couples commenced the season under the most promising auspices, with a country well stocked with foxes and every prospect of success; but, alas for men's calculations! a check has come, and every hope apparently so well founded has been destroyed by a visitation as sudden as it was unexpected.

"About five weeks ago, after a very good and severe run, in breaking up their fox, Dowdswell observed a fine young hound, called Carver, by Lord Macclesfield's Foiler, going from hound to hound in a very unusual manner. Taking alarm, he had the hound led home, and by direction kept confined in a place by himself for a few days in order to prove the nature of the disease, which increased in intensity, and on the third day the dog was perfectly mad, biting and gnawing everything he could reach. Four hounds he had bitten previously were at once put down. On a post-mortem examination the stomach was found in a state of extreme irritation, and full of extraneous matter, such as straw, chips of wood, &c. This, of course, was sufficiently alarming, and those in charge of the pack watched anxiously for any unpleasant symptoms among the other hounds. All went well for a fortnight, then two bitches were seized on successive days with a disease in the throat, which prevented them swallowing, and was accompanied by a loss of the use of the lower jaw. These were treated by blistering the throat with doses of calomel, and feeding them as well as could be accomplished with strong broth and stimulants, by means of the horn. Both died. On a post-mortem examination, all the parts appeared in a natural condition except a mucous covering in the throat, the general appearance of the internal organs being similar to that when death is caused by suffocation. A few days elapsed, and other hounds were seized in precisely the same manner, all dying in about three or four days. As a rule the hounds so attacked were quite harmless, following the huntsman, and apparently grateful for anything done for them. The attacks continued, and some few began to show signs of rabies. The general features of the disease were, however, what is usually called dumb madness, which, beyond doubt, is contagious in its character; and seeing that no hound once attacked ever recovered, the decision come to was to put them down immediately on the first appearance of the symptoms, in order to avoid infection. Up to last week about nine couples had been attacked and died, the disease still running on. Of course hunting was dropped, and the committee, feeling deeply their responsibility, called a meeting of the subscribers in Durham on Monday last, to take into consideration the proper course to be adopted under these painful circumstances. The question to be decided was, whether, looking at the danger to life and the uncertainty as to any known mode of cure, the pack should be destroyed, or an attempt be made to stamp out the disease by isolating every hound. Up to Saturday it was thought the latter plan might be adopted and tried with safety; but the Monday morning's report showed the attack on several more hounds had assumed unmistakable symptoms of rabies. This fact induced the meeting to come to an unanimous resolution: 'That it was a duty they owed to the country to sacrifice the whole of their gallant pack, and to appeal to masters of hounds for a few hounds to enable them to finish the season so disastrously cut short.'

"The most singular feature of the matter has been that it

commenced with a case of decided hydrophobia—successive attacks being clearly the disease called dumb madness—then, again, a case or two of rabies followed by more dumb madness, and lastly, before the fatal order was given, several cases of hydrophobia. Now it is not probable that two diseases would be concomitant in the kennels at the same time; and, as the premonitory symptoms were to a great extent the same in all the cases, it is but fair to assume that the whole of the attacks were different phases of the same disorder, and that, whatever had been its origin, it eventually took the shape of a contagious epidemic of the most violent character."

To the kindness of Mr. C. Stephenson, veterinary surgeon of Newcastle-on-Tyne, I am indebted for an important fact, communicated to him by Mr. Harvey of that town. It would appear that Carver, the hound first affected, was bitten before it was sent to the kennels, and that none of the diseased hounds were attacked by dumb madness in the earlier stages of the malady. The remarkable feature in the history of the outbreak, however, consisted in the fact that some drafts of the pack were sent to India towards the end of July, and it was reported in Durham at the commencement of December that many of these had been attacked by a "disease of the throat," as the reporters termed it, and "hanging of the lower jaw," and that "all died." The hound Carver did not exhibit any marked symptoms until long after these drafts were despatched, and it was therefore concluded that there was no probability of its having bitten any of them, and that the rabific poison must have been introduced into the kennels before they were sent away.

In consequence of the great prevalence of rabies at the commencement of 1872, the Duke of Rutland would not allow any bitches to be sent to the stud hounds at Belvoir, and the Hon. G. Fitzwilliam issued similar orders with regard to Milton; neither would he allow hounds to be sent to other kennels.

The wide and serious extension of this epizoöty over the

country appears to have been largely, if not altogether, due to the insufficiency of the police measures adopted in the different towns and districts, the late period at which they were introduced, the want of a proper and uniform sanitary organisation to combat the spread of this and other contagious diseases of animals, and the general ignorance prevailing with regard to its symptoms and nature.

A writer in *Land and Water* for September 23rd, 1871, says that "hydrophobia has been very fatal in Barbadoes during the summer." The custos of the public library at Bridgetown, in separating two dogs which were fighting, was severely bitten, and afterwards died of hydrophobia. "In one coloured family three children died of hydrophobia; in another two."

GEOGRAPHICAL EXTENT OF RABIES.

Though rabies is undoubtedly most prevalent in the temperate regions of the world, and incomparably less frequent in the torrid and frigid zones, and though it is altogether unknown in some parts, yet it would appear that the facilities for increased communication with different and hitherto very remote quarters of the globe have, of late years, tended much to diffuse and generalise the malady, and to introduce it to countries where, until recently, its terrible presence had not been felt. In this respect it does not differ from a multitude of diseases which, like it, are transmissible, and whose geographical limits, apparently well defined and fixed less than a century ago, are now indefinitely extended, and will be further increased just in proportion as the animals liable to them are carried further beyond their present location. The most striking example of this is, perhaps, to be found in the case of bovine pleuro-pneumonia, a contagious disease which was confined to a comparably small area in Central Europe towards the end of last century, and is now as destructive among the herds in North America, Australia, New Zealand, and even in the interior of South Africa, as it is in the cattle-sheds and pasture lands of our own country.

Only in this way can we explain why rabies was reported by travellers and others, only a short time ago, as unknown in certain countries where its effects are now most painfully experienced; unless we admit that their inquiries were not sufficiently close or skilful, or that their knowledge of the people, their customs and traditions, was too superficial.

Nevertheless, it is very remarkable that certain regions with which Western communication has been uninterruptedly and increasingly maintained for a somewhat considerable period, and into which European-bred dogs have been largely introduced, should have remained free from the canine scourge up to the present day. I have carefully inquired, and have also examined the writings of every available authority, yet cannot find that the disease has ever been witnessed in either Australia or New Zealand, though the number of dogs imported into these two countries must have been very great. The malady has never been observed in Van Diemen's Land, according to Darwin;* nor yet in the Azores or St. Helena. In North America, as we have noticed in the history of the disease, it is well known, and sometimes assumes an epizoötic form; but in South America, if we are to form an opinion from various trustworthy sources, it would appear to be only partially distributed. As we have seen, it was present as a wide-spread epizoöty in Chile in 1835, and it haunts the valley of Copiapó. The memorable outbreak of 1803 proves that it has been in Peru; according to Sigaud† it is observed in the Brazils from time to time, and, indeed, on occasions it is somewhat prevalent. This is confirmed by Spix and Martius.‡

In the time of Azara, it must have either been extremely rare or altogether unknown on the eastern side of the Andes; for that traveller thought the American continent was exempt from rabies.§ Ulloa never heard of the disease in Quito.‖

In Mexico, according to M. Liguistin, chief veterinary surgeon in the French expedition to that country, rabies, though not often seen, is yet known. "It is observed from time to time in the dog and cat particularly, and it is notorious that it especially attacks European dogs imported into the country. In our own experience, since our arrival in Mexico, we have had

* "The Journal of a Naturalist."

† "Travels in the Brazils," p. 424.

‡ "Reisen in Brasilien."

§ "Voyages dans l'Amérique Méridionale, depuis 1781—1801."

‖ "A Voyage to South America," vol. i, p. 281.

occasion to destroy two European dogs affected with confirmed rabies, within three months of each other. The first belonged to Marshal Bazaine, and presented all the characteristics of primary or spontaneous madness; the other also belonged to an officer on the staff, and became rabid in consequence of a bite it had received some days before it was destroyed." M. Pernaud, veterinary surgeon in the artillery, has also described a well-marked case of rabies in an imported dog in Mexico.* M. Liguistin gives the particulars of three cases of hydrophobia in the human species—one from the bite of a cat, and two by dogs. In Mexico the extract of the plant "huaco" is believed to be a specific against the effects of bites from rabid or venomous animals.†

Rabies is also well known in the West Indies. Hillary says that canine madness "is so frequently seen in most hot countries, and especially in the West Indies, that it may be said to be endemial."‡ We have seen that it was prevalent at Barbadoes so early as 1741, in Hispaniola and Jamaica in 1783, in St. Domingo in 1776, and in Guadaloupe. It is a frequent disease in Hayti, and appears in all seasons. Ceylon has suffered severely from it, and hyænas frequently become mad.§ Forbes writes of Ceylon as follows: "The native doctors acknowledge their inability to cure hydrophobia, saying they can heal the bites, but the gods must do the rest. Three months is the time after which they consider any one safe who has been bitten by a mad dog. . . . . At one time, when mad dogs were very numerous in the Mitalé district, mad jackals were also to be met with; and two men, who had lain down to rest in an open shed, were severely bitten by a jackal, which, from their description, was evidently in a rabid state. As these men were travellers I did not learn their fate; but I have known an instance of a horse dying from the bite of a mad jackal. One

* "Journal de Méd. Vétérinaire Militaire," vol. iv. p. 535.

† Ibid., 1867, p. 456.

‡ "On the Diseases of Barbadoes," p. 245.

§ Tennent, "Ceylon."

day, in that same season, I discovered that three terriers, which I had inherited from the commandant who preceded me, were wandering about the house, all of them suffering from hydrophobia, and one of them so far gone as to be unable to close his mouth. . . . . They were destroyed without having done any mischief. A few days after this a servant, standing near the door of a room in which my family were sitting, seeing a strange dog rushing in, snatched up a rice-pounder, which fortunately lay within his reach, and killed the animal at a blow; soon after a half-armed crowd appeared, and recognised this as the mad dog of which they were in pursuit. It was about the same time that, when riding out one evening, I met a moorman who had been severely lacerated by a mad dog, but the wounds healed up in about three weeks." This man died of hydrophobia six weeks afterwards.* The disease has also visited the Mauritius, as noticed in our history, but Marsden never heard of a case at Sumatra.† We have described its appearance in North and South China. The Abbé Vinzot has heard the virtues of a particular species of *Polygala* much vaunted as a remedy for hydrophobia in China. Père Legrand states that it is prevalent in the empire of Annam, and says it is cured by the thorn-apple (*Stramonium*) in such strong doses as to produce phenomena of intoxication simulating the symptoms of furious madness. The once famous Tonquin remedy, consisting of native and artificial cinnabar, was derived from that country more than half a century ago.

The malady is perfectly known in India, and the Hon. Mountstuart Elphinstone says that in Afghanistan it affects wolves, jackals, and dogs, and is attributed to the simoon or pestilential

* "Eleven Years in Ceylon," vol. i. p. 363.

† "History of Sumatra," p. 115. "Those dogs brought from Europe lose in a few years their distinctive qualities, and degenerate at length into the cur with erect ears, *Kuyu*, vulgarly called the pariah dog. An instance did not occur of any one going mad during the period of my residence. Many of them are affected with a kind of gonorrhœa."

wind.* Choisel, a Jesuit residing at Pondicherry, so early as 1756, published a pamphlet in which he relates many examples of rabies being transmitted to the human species at that place. The disease appears to be pretty generally diffused over the Asiatic continent, though in some regions it is much less frequent than in others. In Syria and the Holy Land I found upon inquiry when there in 1867, that it is by no means a rare malady, though in scriptural times we can find no mention of its having been noticed. In Syria I was informed that when a person was affected with hydrophobia he was shut in a dark room, the greatest care being taken to keep him tranquil and prevent his seeing any red-coloured object, and that if he lived for a certain period he was thrown from an eminence into the sea, evidently after the manner, and with the same intention as is indicated by Celsus. In Syria and the Levant, according to Dr. Nicora, the malady has been so well known for a long time that certain so-called "specific remedies" are the property of some families, who keep their composition a secret, as they look upon them as heir-looms. And Dr. Camescasse has collected the reports of twenty-five cases observed in the Smyrna hospital and neighbouring localities.† Dr. Suquet, in 1857, communicates three cases of hydrophobia reported to him by Dr. Rerles of Latakia. He also mentions that there are families in Syria who possess secret specifics against the disease. And Dr. Guillar, at Damascus, after alluding to a very conclusive and well-observed case of hydrophobia that occurred there, terminates a report he drew up on the 26th September, 1856, by saying that it is impossible to deny the existence of rabies in the East. "Every one knows and dreads it, and in various localities there are empirics who sell preservative remedies, for the Arabs also look upon it as incurable." In Turkey its presence has been noted even in wolves, as in 1852. Dr. Michel, of Salie, Turkey, informed M. Camescasse that a rabid wolf

* "Account of the Kingdom of Caubul."

‡ Tardieu, "Dictionnaire d'Hygiène," art. "Rage."

had bitten forty-seven persons, forty-five of whom had died of hydrophobia, the remaining two being preserved by the chloride of antimony having been immediately applied to their wounds. Trustworthy witnesses also certify to the fact that cats have become rabid in Egypt and Turkey, and have produced hydrophobia in human beings.

Ahmed Effendi, veterinary professor in the Military Academy at Constantinople, stated at the International Veterinary Congress held at Vienna in 1865, that "in the East—that is to say, in Turkey—the disease known as canine madness exists, and it appears, though very seldom, not only in dogs in villages and in the country, but likewise in those in large towns." In Roumania, situated in the same zone as Turkey, rabies and hydrophobia are frequent, especially in the vicinity of the mountains, where the disease is generally communicated by wolves to the shepherds' dogs, and from these to mankind. Among the peasantry in that country it is commonly believed that birds of prey, such as eagles, hawks, vultures, &c., fall dead from an elevation in the air which is never reached by any other creatures, and are eaten by wolves; these latter communicate the madness due to this food to the dogs, in their frequent battles with these around the herds or the sheep-folds, and the dogs in their turn transmit it to the cattle and people by the simple fact of inhalation, as when the wind blows towards man or beast from the quarter in which the diseased dog is situated.* In El Hejaz, that part of Arabia bordering on the Red Sea, hydrophobia is known, though it is rare, according to Burton. The people have many superstitions about it, and imagine that a bit of meat falls from the sky, and that the man who eats it becomes mad. "I was assured by respectable persons that when a man is bitten they shut him up with food in a solitary chamber for four days, and if at the end of that time he still howls like a dog they expel the *ghul* (devil) from him by

* Constantinescu, "De la Rage."

pouring over him boiling water mixed with ashes—a certain cure, I can readily believe," adds Burton.*

Until a recent period it seems to have been extremely unfrequent in, or altogether absent from Africa. Even in South Africa, up to the present time, it is generally believed that no well-marked case of rabies has occurred. Livingstone certainly heard of a chief who died from the bite of a mad dog; but he appears to have been doubtful. He says: "In conversation with some of my friends (at Litubaruba) I learned that Maleke, a chief of the Bakwains, who formerly lived on the hill Litubaruba, had been killed by the bite of a mad dog. My curiosity was strongly excited by this statement, as rabies is so rare in this country. I never heard of another case, and could not satisfy myself that even this was real hydrophobia. While I was at Mabotsa, some dogs became affected by a disease which led them to run about in an incoherent state; but I doubt whether it was anything but an affection of the brain.† No individual or animal got the complaint by inoculation from the animals' teeth" (Did the animals attempt to bite?); "and, from all I could hear, the prevailing idea of hydrophobia not existing within the tropics seems to be quite correct." ‡ Numerous travellers and residents have asserted that the disease has not been witnessed at the Cape of Good Hope.

It is not known on the Gold Coast, according to Clarke;§ and Du Chaillu, from inquiries among the natives of West Africa, during his brief residence there, could learn nothing of its existence in that part of the continent.‖ Neither have we any proof of its appearing in East Africa, though Burton

* "Pilgrimage to El Medinah and Meccah," vol. i. p. 372.

† Rabies is more or less an affection of the brain and its continuation—the upper part of the spinal cord.

‡ "Missionary Travels and Researches in South Africa," p. 127. As will be seen from our history and this geographical notice, the prevailing idea that hydrophobia does not exist within the tropics is an erroneous one.

§ "Remarks on the Topography and Diseases of the Gold Coast."

‖ "A Journey to Ashango Land, and further penetration into Equatorial Africa."

informs us that the settled Somal "have a holy horror of dogs, and, Wahabi-like, treat man's faithful slave most cruelly." * Whether this dread is inspired by the liability of the animal to rabies we are left to conjecture.

But if in South, East, and West Africa the canine pest is either so rare as not to attract attention, or does not visit these regions at all, it is not so in North Africa. Sir W. Baker, as we have observed, speaks of it when he was surveying the Nile tributaries of Abyssinia. Indeed, in Northern Abyssinia rabies would appear to be by no means unfrequent, according to M. Rochette d'Héricourt, who says that the Abyssinians employ the root of a plant of the *Cucurbitaceæ* as a preventive of hydrophobia, which acts as an emetico-cathartic, and also as a curative agent. "As soon as the dose has produced its effect, the patient suffers from nothing but the results of the medicament. On my arrival at Devra Tabor, a mad dog having attacked and wounded three other dogs and a soldier of Bas-Ali, the king called me, and said, 'You will see the efficacy of the remedy of which I have spoken.' All the dogs were then ordered to be shut up in separate compartments; and next day, while the rabid animal was calm, he caused to be given in our presence a quantity of this root in powder. It produced all the effects indicated, and the dog was saved. Of the three dogs wounded two were also preserved by the same procedure, but the third died, the remedy not having been administered to it, in order to prove its death from rabies. The soldier, who manifested all the symptoms of hydrophobia towards the ninth day, was subjected on the tenth day to this treatment, and he was also cured." M. Bouchardat, who alludes to this relation by Héricourt, appears to think some success might be derived from the exhibition of the active drastic principle found in this family of plants, especially the *Cucumis elatherium.*† Larrey, Volney,

* "First Footsteps in East Africa," p. 143.

† "Annuaire de Thérapeutie de 1850."

Brown, and Prosper Alpinus denied the existence of canine rabies in Egypt; and Professor Prince, late of the Veterinary School at Aboozabel, states he had not witnessed a case in ten years; but in more recent times its occurrence has been repeatedly observed by Pruner.* Dr. Punel reports four undoubted cases of hydrophobia in Alexandria in 1850, 1855, 1856, and 1857; and Dr. Amstein, cited by Tardieu, reports having witnessed no fewer than thirty-nine well-defined cases of rabies in that country, Syria, and Turkey. In 1857 Burguières-Bey, sanitary physician at Cairo, mentions three cases of hydrophobia as having occurred there; the disease had been communicated by imported dogs living in a state of domesticity. During the first ten years of the French occupation of Algeria, the malady appeared to be so extremely unfrequent as to lead some writers to suppose that the canine race did not suffer from it in that country; but for many years it has been prevalent, and its transmission to mankind, even among the Arab tribes, is not at all an unusual circumstance. The malady, however, according to some writers, is confined principally to the centres of civilisation, such as Bône, Philippeville, Oran, Tlemcen, Ténès, Orléansville, Monstaganem, and Novi; it is in these places, which are chiefly peopled by Europeans, that rabies has been more particularly noted. Yet it is by no means unfrequent in the country. On the 25th December, 1845, at the Hanif bivouac of the French troops under General Bedeau, a fine charger belonging to Commandant Paër, of the 33rd Regiment, died of rabies. It had been bitten by a dog that showed all the symptoms of this disease, and was killed fifteen days before. In 1846, Dr. Lelouis saw an Arab chief die from hydrophobia; he had been bitten by a dog some time previously; and in the "Recueil de Memoires de Médecine et de Pharmacie Militaires" for 1856, is to be found a collection of twelve observations extending from 1844 to 1855, recording the, at times simultaneous, appearance

* "Die Krankheiten des Orientes" (Erlangen, 1847), p. 431.

of rabies in the most distant parts of the three provinces of Algeria.

"Contrary to what the majority of writers have advanced," says M. Dussourt in 1851, "we may remark that rabaïc hydrophobia is far from being rare in Africa—in our Algerian colony at least. The Arabs know it perfectly well, and even agree in regarding it as very common, especially among animals, which they kill, and, if herbivores, eat their flesh. The name they give to rabies and to the rabid individual (*mkloub*, or changed into a dog) is proof of this, for it is derived from *kelb*, dog, and *mkelb*, mad dog. . . . . . Rabies is very common among the Arabs in Africa, who apply the term 'dogified' (*mkloub*) to those who are affected, and they have also their jugglers who pretend to cure it. At a few leagues from Orléansville there is an Arab who is well known in the country as the owner of a secret remedy (for which any one pays very dear), by the aid of which he pretends not only to cure but to prevent the disease. Besides, all the Arabs we have questioned on the subject have uniformly stated that every year they have cases of hydrophobia in their tribes, though they do not appear to be so afraid of it as we are."* These remarks were occasioned by the occurrence of two cases of hydrophobia, and alluding to the frequent appearance of the malady in the lower animals, this writer continues: "Since the death of these two women, in the space of eight days M. Breton, veterinary surgeon to the squadron of Spahis at Orléansville, has seen two horses and a mule die from rabies. The three had been bitten by dogs. M. Rossignol, assistant-surgeon, has just informed me that the disease has been seen in several dogs and horses at Ténès, from which place he has just arrived."† This testimony as to the existence of rabies in Africa comes from Orléansville, but similar evidence, and particularly with regard to the antiquity of the disease, is supplied by various medical men

* "Recueil des Mem. de Méd. Chirur. et Pharm. Militaire," 1856, p. 139.
† Ibid., p. 161.

from Douéra.* "We know at present," writes M. Costa in 1862, "that rabies is by no means rare in Algeria. In a period of five years, at Muscara only, M. Durand, chief of the hospital, has witnessed among the Europeans four cases of confirmed rabies terminating in death, in a population of less than 4,000." In two years, Veterinary-Surgeon Decroix had knowledge of twenty-four cases in Algiers and its suburbs: four men and a young girl, two cats and seventeen dogs.†

Dr. Bergot, from inquiries instituted among the Arabs in the neighbourhood of the village of Gastu, learned that they were quite cognizant of the disease; they had their opinions as to its duration, causes, and treatment. The old men whom he consulted remembered perfectly well that, before the arrival of the French, cases were at least as frequent as subsequently, and they gave the names of seven individuals who had died from hydrophobia in the space of fifteen years.‡

The Medical Society of Algiers, after investigating the subject very carefully, came to the conclusion (1) that rabies existed in Algeria before the French conquest, the terms relating to it being found in the oral language, and are in use among the natives; (2) and that the knowledge of the Arabs with regard to hydrophobia is sufficiently complete to confirm this proposition—their ideas and practices concerning it date from a remote period.§ And Dr. Roucher,‖ an excellent authority on the disease in that country, is decidedly of opinion that rabies was not imported, but is indigenous, and was known at a period long anterior to 1830. He accounts for its not being better known during the first ten years of the French occupation by the fact "that the European population was very small;

* "Bulletin de la Société de Méd. d'Alger," 1861, p. 43. "Bulletin de la Société de Médecine," 1861, p. 50.

† "Reflexions sur la Rage." Abeille Médicale, 1863.

‡ "Cas d'Hydrophobie rencontré dans les Zerdezas" ("Bulletin de la Soc. de Méd. d'Alger.," 1864, p. 93).

§ "Bulletin des Travaux de la Soc. de Méd. d'Alger.," 1860, p. 78.

‖ "Annales d'Hygiène Publique," &c., 1866, p. 106.

that the army was accompanied by only a few animals susceptible of contracting or transmitting the disease; that observations among the natives were impossible, and the intercourse between them or their domestic animals, and the soldiers or the animals following them, was extremely rare; that the state of concentration and continual surveillance of the troops prevented the attacks of wild animals; and, finally, that the extent of territory already conquered and occupied was extremely limited." The Doctor concludes this statement by expressing his belief that "Algeria is the country for which rabies—perhaps even spontaneous rabies—has a special predilection." In Algeria the jackal suffers from rabies, and takes the place of the wolf in France.

As we have before observed, it appeared in the island of Malta in an alarming manner in 1847; Gibraltar is sometimes severely visited, and I am informed that about two years ago, thirteen persons were bitten by a rabid dog, and of these eleven perished.

The colder regions of the globe are not exempt from the ravages of rabies, though in the very coldest it may be so seldom witnessed as to lead to the belief that it is not known. In Sweden, Denmark, Norway, Russia, and Lapland it has been frequently seen in an epizoötic form, as in 1815 and 1824. The Old Bushman says of Sweden: "Madness is, I fancy, rare; but the regulations respecting loose dogs in the towns are very stringent during the summer season." * In Russia and Denmark it is always more or less prevalent. But in Greenland and Kamschatka it is said to be quite unknown. Erman, when describing the Ostyaks of Siberia and their dog-sledges, notices this circumstance. "Madness among the dogs would be, in this country, a most formidable scourge, and would infallibly cause the destruction of whole races of men; but every one here (at Obdorsk) assured us that the disease is wholly unknown to them. Steller has stated the same thing

* "Ten Years in Sweden," p. 169.

respecting the dogs of Kamschatka; so that hydrophobia would seem to be one of the European results of living in towns. One essential and unfailing distinction between the dogs of Siberia and those of Europe lies in the very moderate food of the former; whence it might be inferred that it is excess, and not want, which generates the morbid habit."*

Dr. Kane, when frozen-up in the Arctic regions (latitude 70° 41′) in 1854, alludes to a disease appearing among his dogs, which so closely resembled rabies as to occasion alarm. On October 5th he writes: "Yesterday the mother of one batch (of puppies), a pair of fine white pups, showed peculiar symtoms. We recalled the fact that for some days past she had avoided water, or had drunk with spasm and evident aversion; but hydrophobia, which is unknown north of 70°, never occurred to us. The animal was noticed this morning walking up and down the deck with a staggering gait, her head depressed, and her mouth foaming and tumid. Finally, she snapped at Petersen, and fell foaming and biting at his feet. He reluctantly pronounced it hydrophobia, and advised me to shoot her. The advice was well-timed; I had hardly cleared the deck before she snapped at Hans, the Esquimaux, and recommenced her walking trot. It was quite an anxious moment to me; for my Newfoundlanders (dogs) were around the housing, and the hatches were open. We shot her, of course." Speaking of the sunless Arctic winter, it is further remarked: "The influence of this long, intense darkness was most depressing. Even our dogs, although the greater part of them were natives of the Arctic circle, were unable to withstand it. Most of them died from an anomalous form of disease, to which, I am satisfied, the absence of light contributed as much as the extreme cold. January 25th.—The mouse-coloured dogs, the leaders of my Newfoundland team, have for the past fortnight been nursed like babies. No one can tell how anxiously I watch them. They are kept below, tended, fed, cleaned, caressed,

* "Travels in Siberia," vol. ii. p. 34.

and *doctored*, to the infinite discomfort of all hands. To-day I give up the last hope of saving them. Their disease is as clearly mental as in the case of any human being. The material functions of the poor brutes go on without interruption; they eat voraciously, retain their strength, and sleep well. But all the indications beyond this go to prove that the original epilepsy, which was the first manifestation of brain disease among them, has been followed by a true lunacy. They barked frenzically at nothing, and walked in straight and curved lines with anxious and unwearying perseverance. They fawn on you, but without seeming to appreciate the notice you give them in return, pushing their heads against your person, or oscillating with a strange pantomime of fear. Their most intelligent actions seem automatic; sometimes they remain for hours in moody silence, and then start off howling as if pursued, and run up and down for hours. So it was with poor Flora, our 'wise dog.' She was seized with the endemic spasms, and after a few wild paroxysms lapsed into a lethargic condition, eating voraciously, but gaining no strength. This passing off, the same crazy wildness took possession of her, and she died of brain disease (*arachnoidal effusion*) in about six weeks. Generally, they perish with symptoms resembling locked-jaw in less than thirty-six hours after the first attack. . . . . My dogs that I had counted on so largely, the nine splendid Newfoundlanders and thirty-five Esquimaux of six months before, had perished; there were only six survivors of the whole pack, and one of these was unfit for draught." "Tiger, our last remaining dog, was seized with a fit ominously resembling the last winter's curse. In the delirium which followed his seizure, he ran into the water and drowned himself." In a note, it is added: "Hydrophobia. The caption at the head of the page is not intended to affirm the existence of this disease in this high North. Some of the tetanoid symptoms attendant upon tonic spasms closely simulated it; but the disease, strictly speaking, is unknown there." And in the Appendix to Vol. II. (p. 305), this able explorer again observes: "A strong tendency to tonic spasm, probably induced by the lengthened cold and darkness, was the chief trial of our party. General disease was readily controlled by a careful hygiene . . . . . but this anomalous form of spasmodic disease was encountered with difficulty. It extended to our dogs, assuming the aspect of tetanus; in spite of every effort, no less than fifty-seven perished, many of them with symptoms not unlike those of hydrophobia. The loss of these animals interfered seriously with my original scheme of search." *

Mr. McDougall also speaks of the dogs belonging to the *Resolute*, in the Arctic regions in 1853, having serious fits, none of which, however, terminated fatally; though evidence of their injurious effects could be traced in the very expression of these animals. During one of these fits a bitch ran away, and was no more heard of.†

It must be admitted that the symptoms described by Kane, especially in the first case he alludes to, bear a most striking resemblance to those noted in rabies, as we shall see hereafter; the duration of the disease and its fatality were also characteristic of rabies; while the pathological alterations in the brain, particularly the effusion, are, as will be pointed out in the proper place, very frequently found in this disease.

But however rare and sometimes disputable the malady may be in tropical or frigid regions, there can be no doubt whatever as to its being always present, to a greater or less extent, in temperate countries, and in an unmistakable form. Europe appears to be particularly afflicted with the scourge, which we have reason to believe is increasing in virulency and in frequency. But even in Europe it would appear that certain regions are more tormented with it than others. France and Germany, and Upper Italy and Holland, seem to suffer more than other Continental nations. Spain is also sometimes severely visited; but

* "Arctic Explorations," vol. i. pp. 106, 123, 156, 163, 459.
† "Voyage of H.M.S. *Resolute* to the Arctic Regions," pp. 369, 376.

in Portugal, according to De Souza, although there are many stray dogs, cases of canine madness occur very seldom. Though in this country, owing to our very culpable neglect of comparative pathology, we have nothing to guide us in forming an estimate of the extent of the disease among the lower animals; yet from the casual notices that appear at intervals, and the number of people who perish from hydrophobia, we are almost justified in asserting that Great Britain is frequently seriously visited by rabies, and while it has always been present, our history shows that since the commencement of this century, and particularly in later years, it has been largely on the increase; so that we may soon expect, if no energetic and general measures are adopted, to be as severely punished as France or Germany. Of the three kingdoms, England appears to furnish the majority of cases, Scotland being, apparently, remarkably exempt. For instance, in 1866, while thirty-six cases of death from hydrophobia were reported by the Registrar-General as occurring in England, no person was affected with the disease in Scotland. For the twelve years commencing with 1855 and terminating with 1866, the number of persons who succumbed to the malady in England was ninety-five, and in Scotland only twelve. From this we might hazard the opinion that rabies was not nearly so frequent in the northern parts of our island. But it must be confessed that this is a mere inference, as the veterinary schools do not publish any statistics of cases admitted to their hospitals, nor make any report as to the extent of the malady in the respective countries; and the Government, we believe, does not take any steps to register the prevailing diseases among the domestic animals in the various counties—a grave and inexplicable omission, which has been the cause of immense loss, and has greatly retarded the progress of veterinary medicine and sanitary police, two subjects which have been considered as well deserving the attention of other enlightened governments.

ETIOLOGY OF RABIES.

THE investigation of the cause or causes of rabies—of the conditions which predispose the organism to the development of the disease, or which act directly in producing it—is, in this instance, as it is generally in other maladies, a study of the greatest importance; as on it depends, in a large degree, the prevention of the scourge—terrible alike to man, to the dog, and to all animals. And perhaps with no other disorder to which the inferior creatures are liable has the study of causation been more closely pursued, or been more prolific in suggesting hypotheses and furnishing suggestions than the one now under consideration. In the canine and feline species, the origin of the malady is frequently obscure and involved in doubt, and the consideration of this at once opens up the, for a long time warmly contested, question as to the spontaneous origin of contagious diseases.

SPONTANEOUS ORIGIN.

For many years, and even now, the spontaneous origin of rabies in the species of animals in which it is most frequently witnessed has been denied by authorities who have ranged themselves on the side of the contagionists, whose belief it is that contagious diseases are propagated and maintained solely by the transmission of a specific virus from the diseased to the healthy, and that no transmissible disease ever arises spontaneously, but that its infecting element is always in existence.

Whatever weight this line of argument may have in human medicine, there can be no doubt whatever that in comparative pathology it cannot be entertained as absolutely unassailable.

In certain maladies which develop a contagium capable of producing the same morbid disturbance that characterises them when transferred to healthy animals, we are almost, if not altogether, compelled by the force of reasoning and the power of indisputable facts to admit their spontaneous origin from a concurrence of circumstances—many of them perhaps obscure—whose operation we are not always able to trace, save in the effects produced in the creatures subjected to their operation. Several virulent and well-known diseases in the lower animals must be placed in this category, and among them we need only now mention those vulgarly designated "glanders," "farcy," and "strangles" in the horse, anthrax in cattle, the so-called "typhus" in pigs, and "distemper" in the dog. Numberless facts, indeed almost every day's veterinary experience, appear to demonstrate in the most unmistakable manner that these affections may be developed directly, without the intervention of any infecting medium. And rabies, we feel we are justified in asserting, must also be included in the list of diseases which, generated under certain favourable conditions, during their course develop a virus that, like a ferment, acts as a leaven in producing morbid and characteristic changes when it obtains admission to a previously healthy body.

Notwithstanding the arguments of the distinguished veterinarians and amateurs (among whom, in this country, Blaine, Youatt, and Meynell were prominent) who have affirmed that rabies only owes its origin to a traumatic action—*i.e.*, to a wound inflicted by the teeth of a rabid creature on the body of one hitherto free from every trace of the disease—there are few nowadays who are not convinced that it will occasionally appear in a spontaneous manner, and without any certain assignable cause. No doubt the transmission of the disease by inoculation furnishes by far the largest number of cases, and many of these, from the obscure manner in which the inoculation has been effected, appear to be due to other causes than those of a traumatic character; but, notwithstanding, the disease must have had a commencement. Several of the ancient Greek and Roman writers, while admitting that the disease was contagious, nevertheless acknowledge that, in the dog at least, it could appear without the influence of the contagious element being invoked.* Our history shows that, while rabies has frequently followed the introduction of European dogs into new regions, it has also appeared in an epizoötic form in countries where it had been previously unknown—as in Peru in 1803—and its appearance could not be traced to any foreign source.

There are localities where rabies does not appear except at rare intervals; years may elapse without a single case being observed, and all at once many cases occur; indeed, it is a matter of common observation that at various epochs the malady breaks out with exceptional violence and frequency, and may even assume an epizoötic form, while at other times it is entirely absent for many years, or isolated cases may only be noted now and again in districts widely apart.

Dr. Roucher adduces the appearance of the malady in Algeria as confirmatory, to some extent, of its spontaneous origin. The marked intermittence in its manifestations at different geographical centres; its regular propagation from each centre; the multiplicity of cases at certain epochs of very short duration, contrasting strikingly with their rarity at other times; the intervals between the outbreaks, which are longer than the period of incubation of the virus; the small number of cases compared with the crowds of wandering dogs; the difficulty of explaining by contagion alone the maintenance of the disease in every region after long interruptions—all this would lead to the supposition that inoculation is not the sole cause in Algeria, and, we might add, in other countries. A reference to the history of the malady, as it has been noted by French

* Galen is, I think, the first who positively asserts that dogs are the only animals which become mad without being bitten, or having had the least communication with infected creatures ("De Loc. Affect.," book vi.).

surgeons and veterinary surgeons since the occupation of that country, will show, in tracing it by zones at its different irruptions, that it proceeds from more or less extensive centres.

In 1834, for instance, there was only one case in Algiers. In 1844 it broke out at Bône in the month of March, and radiated in July and October as far as Philippeville, Constantine, Batna, and that part of the mountain chain of Bou-Taleb adjoining Sétif. In 1845 it was seen in December on the Oued-Isser, and in the following month at Dellys. In 1847 an isolated case occurred at Blidah. In the period extending from December, 1850, to August, 1851, rabies only occupied two distinct centres—Bône, in the east, where three cases appeared in the first quarter; and in the west, where it arose at Orléansville, and from January to March, 1851, travelled to Tenès and Cherchell, to appear in August of the same year at Tlemcen, on the extreme western limit of the French possessions.

In November and December, 1854, it was again witnessed at Tenès and Orléansville; then in January, 1855, at Mostaganem; in February, at the village of Damesme, near Arzew. In 1856 there was an isolated case at Mostaganem; in 1857 one at Tlemcen; and in 1858 two at the first-named place.

For the first time, in 1860, rabies appeared simultaneously at Oran, Arzew, and Mascara, in February and March, and again in October and December. It afterwards reappeared at Hamma, near Constantine; and in June of that year, after an absence of sixteen years, it broke out in Algiers, killing five persons in four months. From that time it seemed to cling, with a kind of predilection, to that capital, as it exclusively persisted there in 1861, and in April, June, and November, 1862, whence it was propagated to Blidah in December. In May of that year it prevailed at Bône, and in May and June, 1863, it extended to Philippeville, and to the village of Gastu, between Guelma and Jemmapes; subsequently, deaths from hydrophobia were reported from Hennaya, near Tlemcen, Constantine, Médéah, and Algiers.

Besides the bearing this historical *résumé* has on the question with which we are now occupied, there are some other points of interest and importance to be noted, which have not failed to attract the attention of Dr. Roucher.

The last period, he observes—that from 1860 to 1863 included—does not offer the same order of progression as the first, and there is nothing to show that in the future the periods of invasion of rabies are likely to be separated by long intervals of immunity; indeed, the contrary seems probable, if the increasing frequency of the disease in later years is taken into consideration—this frequency, by multiplying the cases, having a tendency to efface the intervals of exemption. And in this period, also, it is easy to distinguish the outbreaks at definite geographical centres. There is likewise to be observed a certain regularity in the progress of the disease, which might lead to the suspicion that there was a mode of propagation dependent at once upon time and distance.

A review of the periods in which the disease was manifested would also go some way to prove the occurrence of rabies from some other cause than contagion alone. Thus, in 1834, there was one case (Roucher does not state whether the cases noted in this *résumé* were those of man or the lower animals; he only observes that in the total of 65, 47 were of men and animals, and 18 of animals exclusively). In 1844, ten years afterwards, there were seven cases in eight months; and in December, 1845, fourteen months later, there was another case, followed by one in January. In 1847 there was an isolated case, the last for four years; then, from the month of December, 1850, to August, 1851, there were eleven cases in nine months; after which three years passed without any being recorded, until, from November, 1854, to February, 1855, there were five cases in four months. From this period to June, 1856, there was another blank of sixteen months, when two isolated outbreaks were reported—one at this date, and another in August, 1857. In May and June, 1858, there occurred two cases very close in point of time, and another in an unknown month; the same may be said for three other cases, which are only reported to have occurred in the interval between 1856 and 1858. During a year and eight months the scourge slept, but only to appear more destructive than ever in 1860, when eleven cases were noted in as many months. It again disappeared until May, 1861, when, up to September, two cases were observed. In 1862, from January to December, there were six cases: and in 1863 there were three outbreaks in May and three in December, in addition to two cases at undetermined periods of the year, making a total of twenty-seven cases.

Knowing the extreme limit of the incubatory period in the canine species, it is surely unreasonable to pretend that the malady can lurk unobserved in a dog for ten years, or even for one year. The disease is frequently observed attacking dogs which have been isolated for months together on farms, chained up in courtyards, or kept in rooms as lap-dogs, and having no communication with other creatures of the same species. And, besides, experiments undertaken to discover the length of time required for the incubation of rabies have strikingly demonstrated the fact, that this period goes on increasing in proportion as the virus is further removed from its origin—*i.e.*, the rabid animal from which it was first derived—until at last its virulency becomes extinct.

Many years ago, M. Rey, the talented professor of the Lyons Veterinary School, anxious to set at rest the question then agitating veterinary surgeons as to whether communicated rabies in the canine species was transmissible to ruminant animals, instituted a long series of very remarkable experiments, which proved not only that this contagion exists, but that it can be transmitted to the fifth degree in sheep, and finally disappears, the effects of the virus being more and more slowly developed as the re-inoculations are multiplied;* showing that in passing through different bodies it gradually loses its activity and

* "Recueil de Méd. Vétérinaire," 1844.

potency. And there are the strange outbreaks of rabies among feral creatures—such as the fox and wolf, jackal and hyæna—in which we have sometimes only one animal appearing in districts where the disease does not then exist, and wounding other beings who afterwards become hydrophobic; and at other times many instances of the malady are noted among these creatures over a wide region for a number of years, without any assignable cause. The disease must be spontaneous, one would be inclined to assert, in the wolf at least; for how can this creature, which is not unfrequently affected with rabies, become inoculated with the virus of the malady? The conditions in which it lives differ too widely from those of the dog to enable us to apply the same arguments to both.

Another point in favour of the view that rabies is due to some other influence than propagation by rabid animals, is to be found in the circumstance, that at intervals it appears in a general or epizoötic form, spreading far and wide in countries in which mad dogs are seen every year only here and there. If the malady owed its diffusion solely to rabid animals, surely it must always, in these regions, be more or less general. Making every allowance for the fact that during these epizoöties the virus is elaborated on an extensive scale, and the affected animals transmit it freely to all other creatures with which they come into contact, yet, taking into consideration the history of the disease, and the circumstances so frequently attending its advent and progress, we are constrained to agree with those veterinarians who maintain that it is spontaneously developed; that during its development a contagion or infecting element is generated, which is capable of giving origin to the disease in other animals, when introduced into their bodies; and that though the spread of the malady among a large number of animals, over a wide extent of country, may be largely or even entirely due to inoculation, yet that in these circumstances some mysterious influence is at work, which we might designate the epizoötic constitution of the disease. Certainly, we cannot directly prove that the disease arises spontaneously, the proofs necessary to establish this with all the necessary rigour and precision fail us. We can only found our belief on collateral circumstances, which in themselves, nevertheless, strongly favour our view.

Vernois* and Tardieu,† among modern observers, believe in its spontaneity in the dog and cat. The former knew of several unmistakable instances, and was of opinion that its occurring in this manner is the principal cause of its appearance in many regions where it could not be ascribed to contagion. Tardieu cites two cases of spontaneous rabies in the cat; one in which the malady was induced by depriving a cat of its kittens, and another in which it was caused by a severe burn. Blatin‡ also affirms that it originates spontaneously in the wolf and fox, as well as in the dog and cat. And Bouley, one of the highest living authorities on the subject, does not deny this, but, on the contrary, favours the supposition.

An instance which has been quoted as tending to prove the spontaneous generation of rabies in the dog, is alluded to by Roucher as having occurred in Algeria, and reported by Moreau of Bône. A little pug dog was kept tied up in a cellar for fifteen or twenty days without being let loose during that period, at the end of which it bit its mistress, who died of hydrophobia. Nothing is said as to what eventually became of the animal, but it was generally believed that the disease was developed spontaneously in it. It must be remarked, however, that this is not a satisfactory instance to quote, as fifteen or twenty days is not a long period of incubation, and the dog might have been inoculated before it was confined to the cellar.

Supposed Causes.

But though we hold the above opinion, we are nevertheless far from having arrived at a knowledge of what occasions the

* "Etude sur la Prophylaxie Administrative de la Rage." Paris, 1863.

† "Dictionnaire d'Hygiène Publique," art. "Rage."

‡ "De la Rage chez le Chien et des Mesures Preservative." Paris, 1863.

direct or spontaneous development of rabies—knowledge which is of the greatest moment with regard to the prevention of this, the most calamitous of all diseases; for of the many causes which have been adduced by different authorities, none can be received without hesitation, and some must be rejected as altogether unsatisfactory. Indeed, the etiology of rabies has yet to be elucidated; as it may be said that we are in complete ignorance of the circumstances on which its spontaneous production depends. Nevertheless, it is necessary, in a dissertation on the disease, to notice the principal constant or occasional causes which have, in later years, been from time to time fixed upon to account for its appearance, more particularly in an epizoötic form.

Influence of Climate.

Though the species in which spontaneous rabies becomes developed are to be found in a wild or domestic condition in every inhabited region of the globe, yet, as we have seen, it is the temperate regions which suffer most frequently and extensively from its ravages, while in some of those of extreme temperature it is rare or altogether absent. Indeed, in different climates of the same country a notable diversity has been observed. For instance, in Italy, Dr. Gramegna, after an examination of the statistics of rabies occurring there during 1868 and 1869, shows that the disease is much more rare in the warm parts of that kingdom, such as Sardinia and Sicily.* The reason for its appearing in temperate climates has been said to be owing to the disturbance of the cutaneous transpiration from the vicissitudes of the weather. But it must be remembered that in none of the domestic animals is this process less active than in the dog, whose skin is so very rarely seen bedewed with perspiration; indeed, the malady is generated in those creatures whose skins are least active in function, and, besides, other creatures are quite as much, if not more exposed to the weather

* "Sull' Origine e Cura della Rabbia Canina." Florence, 1871.

June	1 case.
July	1 ,,
August	1 ,,
September	2 ,,
October	2 ,,
November	2 ,,
December	2 ,, *

Sometimes the annual statistics show a predominance of cases in the summer months, as for instance in Professor Rey's *compte rendu* for 1841-42, alluded to in our history. More recently, the talented veterinarian, Professor Bouley, in a most interesting communication made to the French Academy of Sciences on the 4th April, 1870, gives the results of an analysis of departmental reports for the six years from 1863 to 1868. The reports, though it would appear they were far from complete, give for the spring months, March, April, and May, 89 cases; for the summer, June, July, and August, 74 cases; for autumn, September, October, and November, 64 cases; and for the three winter months, December, January, and February, 75 cases. From these figures it might be inferred, as was suggested by M. Bouley, that there is not a very great difference in the seasons with regard to the prevalence of rabies; that the winter season is, in this respect, about the same as the summer; that the cases are most numerous in the spring, and least so in the autumn; therefore, that the opinion which exempts the winter months from outbreaks of the disease, and attributes them to the summer season, is not in harmony with the facts displayed by these returns.

According to M. Boudin, in 97 cases of hydrophobia in the human subject, and which, of course, terminated in death, 25 occurred in March, April, and May; 42 in June, July, and August; 13 in September, October, and November; and 17 in December, January, and February.† But as these were cases in which the malady had been produced by inoculation, and as

* *Journal de Méd. Vét. de Lyon*, 1869.

† "Traité de Géographie et de Statistique Médicales," vol. ii. p. 683.

the incubation of the disease would, in all probability, be different in each case, we cannot place any great reliance on these figures. It may be observed, however, that, allowing for the incubatory period, this would carry back the infliction of the injuries sustained by the forty-two summer cases to an earlier period, possibly the spring, and thus support M. Bouley's conclusion with regard to the preponderance of cases occurring in that season. But knowing that cases of communicated rabies are more common than those which may be regarded as arising spontaneously, it is evident that the former cannot be looked upon as influenced by the seasons; or, at any rate, it might be asked if the cases occurring in extreme seasons have not really received the infection in the temperate ones, or *vice versâ*.

However the question might be answered, it is a fact beyond all dispute that hot weather does not exert any marked influence in the genesis or prevalence of rabies; for, apart from the striking evidence afforded by European statistics, if the disease was due to a high temperature, then we should expect to find the malady much more prevalent in warm than in temperate regions—to find it in South Africa and Australia, for instance, countries in which its presence has not yet been positively attested.

In Algeria, the disease, although occurring in every season, yet appears to be most prevalent in the months when the temperature is not high, as in the autumn; and it is in the winter season that man has most to fear from suspected animals, a greater number of persons being bitten by rabid dogs at that season than any other.

So far, then, as observation has extended, we are led to the conclusion that meteorological conditions and the different seasons have but little effect in exciting or determining the evolution of spontaneous rabies; and that it is a disease which may appear in any season or in any kind of weather. As remarked by Professor Röll, the meteorological characters of the years 1814, 1815, 1830, 1838 to 1842, and 1862 were very different at Vienna, and yet canine rabies prevailed at these periods in an epizoötic form. And Professor Saint-Cyr, who has devoted many years to an attentive study of the malady, does not hesitate to assert that cold, heat, drought, or humidity—in a word, all the meteorological influences, whatever they may be, are absolutely without action, or at least without any known and perceptible influence, on the development of rabies. What confirms this opinion, he adds, is the very irregular manner in which the cases observed during several consecutive years are distributed. The two months of 1865, April and September, which are usually wet months at Lyons, were in 1865 remarkably dry and warm; so that if the hygrometrical state of the atmosphere had any influence in the production of the disease, these two months ought to resemble each other in the number of cases they afforded. But in *April there were fifteen mad dogs*, and in *September only one*.

The majority of veterinary observers appear to be of opinion that damp, relatively warm weather seems to be the most favourable to the evolution of rabies.

Influence of Hunger, Thirst, and Food.

Hunger and thirst,* and putrified food and bad water, have at times been assigned as the cause of madness in dogs, but with no more show of probability than attends the belief in the influence of seasons and weather. In countries where the disease is unfrequently seen, or quite unknown, dogs suffer more from abstinence from food and water, and are therefore much more likely to greedily ingest both, no matter how putrified or unhealthy, than the canine race of milder climates. We might cite Turkey, Syria, Egypt, and Africa generally,

* "In Venice, I found the common opinion to be, that the disease is often occasioned by thirst; for which reason all barbers, shoemakers, and coffee-house keepers, are obliged to have a small tub or pan of water before their doors, particularly in hot weather, that the dogs running about the streets may drink when they want, as there are no places in that city where they can otherwise supply themselves with fresh water."—*Moseley*, "On Hydrophobia," p. 26.

and India and Australia, as countries in which these animals are much exposed to the torments of thirst and hunger, and frequently compelled, in their capacity of scavengers, to eat garbage in a state of putrefaction, and imbibe water at rare intervals the very opposite of pure; yet we have seen that these regions do not suffer from this canine pest like those in which the dog is better cared for.

Besides, unfortunate dogs have been subjected to these influences experimentally, with a view to the production of the disease, but without any other result than death from inanition and exhaustion. Bourgelat, the celebrated founder of the French Veterinary Schools, confined six dogs together, and kept them without food and water until they began to devour each other, and finally perished, but none of them presented symptoms of rabies. This cruel experiment has since been performed on an extensive scale by Dupuytren, Magendie, Breschet, and others, but with negative results, so far as the production of the disease was concerned. For instance, at the Alfort Veterinary School, three dogs were chained apart, but fully exposed to the heat and glare of the sun. Salted flesh alone was given to one, only water to another, and neither food nor water to the third. As might have been foretold, these poor creatures died, but did not exhibit any symptoms of rabies.

It should be mentioned, however, that Rossi, of Turin, according to Constantinescu, caused cats to become mad by shutting them up in a room without food or water; though whether virulent rabies was produced is a matter for doubt.

Influence of Sex and Generative Functions.

The sex of the animals in which the disease has been supposed to appear spontaneously has, according to the celebrated veterinarian and inspector of the French Veterinary Schools, the late M. Renault, and others of perhaps less authority, a powerful influence in the production of rabies; and it has been asserted that it is only spontaneous in the males. Nothing is more unlikely, nor yet more difficult to prove. In the first place, the proportion of male to female dogs is, at least in this country, very great, and for the simple reason that dogs are generally considered more valuable than bitches, and the latter are more frequently destroyed in litters of puppies. And in the next place, because it is by no means an easy matter to determine between a case of spontaneous and a case of communicated rabies.

Professor Lafosse gives two instances of female dogs in which rabies appeared spontaneously, to all appearance at least, for they were always kept indoors, and never went out except under the surveillance of their owners; and another of a female cat which never left the house of its mistress. And M. Tardieu cites the case of a female cat which became mad in consequence of its kittens being taken away from it; and another that was rabid from the pain caused by a large wound. Besides, bitches do become rabid, though whether spontaneously or from contagion is, as we have said, difficult indeed to prove; but their number is much less than that of dogs; and if we could only arrive at the relative proportions usually existing between the two sexes, we could then determine how far the supposition that the disease is only generated in the male is likely to be correct.

Professor Eckel, of Vienna, whose report we have already alluded to, noted, in 1841, that in 141 cases of canine rabies, 126 were males and only 15 females, or about 8 to 1. According to the registers of the Toulouse Veterinary School from 1843 to 1858, 13 dogs and 2 bitches affected with rabies were admitted, or 6 to 1; while from 1852 to 1862, the total number of dogs brought to the school for examination was 7,806, of which 5,855 were dogs, and 1,951 bitches, or a proportion of about 3 to 1.

In 1863, during the epizoöty at Vienna, Professor Pillwax remarked that the males were more frequently affected than the females; but he observes that this might be accounted for by the fact that in Vienna dogs are more numerous, proportionately, than bitches.

In 1865, Professor Saint-Cyr reported, out of the 87 cases admitted to the Lyons School that year, 15 bitches against 72 dogs, or 24 per cent. But, he asks, Does not this number nearly represent the normal proportion of bitches, compared with the total number of the canine population? He refers to a case of rabies occurring in an emasculated dog at the school in May of the same year, as a proof that the absence of virility does not afford exemption.

In 1868, Professor Peuch, of the same school, carefully noted the sex of all dogs admitted to the hospital. From his report it appears that 251 dogs and 88 bitches were treated for various diseases; while for rabies there were 20 males and 7 females. From this comparison, he says, it must be concluded that the sex of the animal does not exercise any action on the development of rabies

Of 8,649 dogs treated for different maladies at M. Bourrel's hospital in eight years, there were 6,597 males and 2,052 females, or a proportion of 3 to 1 in males. The 6,597 males furnished 344 cases of rabies, or a trifle more than 4 per cent., while of the 2,052 females, there were only 49 cases, or slightly over 2 per cent.

From this it would be inferred that bitches are less liable to become affected than dogs. In Algiers, in 47 cases of rabies in the dog, 37 were males and 10 females.

Professor Bouley, in the report already referred to, mentions that in 320 cases of wounds inflicted on people, 284 were by dogs and 26 by bitches; and at an earlier period he found that the registers of the Alfort school gave a list of 175 dogs and only 15 bitches affected with rabies.

There can scarcely be a doubt that bitches are as susceptible to the contagion by inoculation as dogs. This is well exemplified in what occurred a few years ago to a bitch pack of fox-hounds belonging to Mr. Standish, South Shoreham, Southampton. This pack was nearly exterminated by rabies, through the disease having been introduced to the kennels by a hound which had strayed away for several days, and on its return was discovered to have been bitten.*

It would appear, then, that the influence exercised by the sex of the animal is at least doubtful, though it must be admitted that more males than females suffer from the disease, a fact which might be taken to support the opinion that it is only spontaneous in the former. But, as we have said, this disproportion may coincide with that existing between the sexes; and in any case it is most difficult to arrive at any other solution of the question from the statistics already furnished. To ascertain with certainty the influence of sex, it would be necessary to discover the proportion existing between the number of cases occurring spontaneously and those due to contagion in the male and female; as observation has demonstrated that dogs in health very rarely bite the opposite sex, while they are frequently wounded by the latter. Perhaps, as Lafosse remarks, the physiological instincts are preserved in the diseased state; and if this be so, and if the proportion of infected or transmitted cases continues to remain greater with the males than the females, then we have an explanation of the difference in frequency between the two sexes.

In connection with this question of sex comes another which has been in existence and warmly discussed for some years; this is the influence of the generative acts in producing or preventing the disease. Several veterinarians and medical men have held to the opinion that a predisposing cause of rabies was to be found in the torments dogs experienced through the abeyance in which the gratification of their sexual desires was usually maintained, or the excitement and irritability so frequently attendant upon attempts to satisfy these desires.

* The *Veterinarian*, vol. xliv. p. 549.

Those who hold this opinion invoke in its favour the greater frequency of rabies in the civilised countries of the West than in the regions where dogs have their liberty and lead a vagabond life, and where the sexes are allowed to remain in their natural proportion, as among the Bedouins in the desert, and with the pariah dogs of the East generally. M. Desjardins, for instance, has recently announced that heat and the deprivation of food and water are not likely causes in the production of rabies in the dog, for in hot countries, as in Algeria and the East generally, the disease is unknown among the dogs living in a state of liberty without any restraint. The cause he believes to be the restriction as to intercourse between the sexes, and also the barbarous and ridiculous use of the muzzle. "Leave the dog at liberty," he says, "to lead a wandering or vagabond life, no matter which." During his travels in the East, he questioned the old mountaineers, the inhabitants of Constantinople and of Smyrna, as well as they of Upper and Lower Egypt, and, notwithstanding the high temperature of these regions, he learned that everywhere, with full liberty and no restriction as to coupling, the malady tends to disappear. He therefore recommends that dogs should be allowed to go about at large, and be submitted only to the great influence of nature, feeling satisfied that rabies would soon disappear from the list of maladies.* M. Sacc, another of the advocates for this hypothesis, after enumerating the principal causes to which the disease is generally attributed, concludes that it is produced in dogs by prolonged and enforced continence. In support of this, he gives the following as the most convincing proof. Travelling in Hungary in 1852, he learned that on both banks of the Danube there was only one breed of dogs—the wolf or pariah dog (*chien-loup*)—and that on the left, or Christian bank, there were every year some cases of rabies; while on the other, or Turkish bank, the malady was unknown. He attributed this difference to the circumstance

* *L'Indépendance Scientifique et Littéraire*, 1869.

that the Christians only preserved the male dogs, while the Turks allowed nearly as many females as males to live.

If this report was founded on irrefragable proofs, as Lafosse observes, it ought to be seriously reflected upon before being rejected. But is it very likely that it is based upon facts? If so, how comes it to pass that the dogs belonging to the Christians are not driven by their desires to visit the canine females on the Turkish bank? Is there no communication between the two shores of the Danube? and are the dogs less capable of swimming across a river than Leander was across the Hellespont? And what is to prevent the civilised dogs of the French towns in Algeria from visiting those of the Arabs? Is it not possible that when the dogs of the Europeans or Christians become rabid, they might not sometimes vent their fury on those of the nomad tribes and Turks, and thus inoculate them with the death-producing virus?

But no reliance can be placed upon the evidence hitherto produced to substantiate the above opinion. In opposition to it, indeed, we have the evidence of Roucher, who states that, in Algeria, the dogs wandering at large are not exempted from rabies, and a large proportion of those in villages, or which lead a nomadic existence, suffer from it. Thus, of 65 cases of hydrophobia (in man, of course) occurring within a certain period, 25 were reported from the country districts as having taken place either in Arab tribes, in sparsely-populated villages, or in the suburbs of important towns. And the same authority, after investigating the facts collected as to the frequency of rabies among various breeds of dogs in that country, remarks that nearly all those living in a domestic state, and which have become rabid, have generally been bitten by stray dogs, and that therefore the rabific virus should have another origin more general, perhaps, than domesticity. "We are more disposed to place above it, and in the first line, the effects of vagabondage, with the *cortège* of miseries accompanying it. . . . They are the stray dogs, those which are unknown and without an owner, which predominate among the rabid." When we reflect that rabies is developed in wolves and foxes, animals which live in a wild state, and are not thwarted in their generative desires, we may suspect that prolonged continence has but little, if anything, to do with the development of madness. Other domestic animals, as the ass and horse, are in some countries, particularly the East, frequently kept in an entire state during their lives, without being permitted to exercise their procreative faculties, and yet no disease simulating rabies appears in them in consequence of this compulsory abstention. But, it has been contended by others, if the actual enforced abstinence from sexual intercourse does not develop rabies, the jealousy, excitement, irritation, and anger among dogs, consequent on several competing for the same female, is sufficient to, and even does, occasion the appearance of rabies in them; and the exemption of the bitch from these influences is, in all probability, the reason why she is so seldom affected with the disease. The incessant competition, the extreme excitement, and the savage fights among amorous dogs in pursuit of a female in rut, have been decided upon as sufficient to predispose them to madness; and it has even been believed that their bites, when disputing for the possession of a bitch during the rutting season, will engender rabies. Several occurrences have also been brought forward to support the opinion, the most striking of which are to be found in a memoir on canine madness which L. Toffoli, of Bassano, published in 1840. It was these occurrences which led this author to believe that *l'amour contrarié* might give rise to spontaneous rabies. At Compèse, a little village some miles from Bassano, there was a mongrel bitch which showed signs of rut, and a multitude of admirers attended upon her, as is usually the case. Among them was one, a surly mongrel, which, extremely enamoured and jealous, always hung about her, and closely followed upon her steps. But as this dog was driven away and maltreated by his more vigorous rivals, he always failed in his attempts to gain her affections; nevertheless, he continued day and night to brave all danger and withstand all worrying, until at last, discouraged and peevish, he withdrew from the contest. Then he exhibited a new phase in his character, by biting a cat which previously had been his playfellow; afterwards he attacked every dog he met, particularly those who had been his rivals, and wounded them all more or less, no matter how strong and ferocious they might be. Finally, he cruelly injured a child, and would no doubt have resorted to other dangerous performances had he not been promptly killed. On hearing of this circumstance, Toffoli carefully investigated the matter, and gathered all the information he could, the result being that he was convinced the dog had become affected with primary or spontaneous rabies through the influence of the above-cited causes, without any other dog having communicated the malady by wounding him. But he was not quite satisfied with this solitary instance, as to others it might appear to offer insufficient evidence. So he associated himself with an old sportsman who had passed fifty years of his life among numerous packs of hounds, and with this man he retired to a country house, away from all traffic and people, in order to conduct his experiments and carry out his investigations, so as to put the subject beyond the reach of a doubt.

For example, he got a bitch in rut and put beside her a dog which she did not know and did not care for. He excited the dog to the utmost degree, but would not allow him to go near the bitch, and yet there was no sign of rabies. It was not the same, however, when several dogs were admitted to the place where the female was kept. The same exciting competition commenced as in ordinary cases, accompanied by the same maddening jealousy and fierce combats, and eventually the dog first introduced became rabid.

The results obtained in this way by Toffoli were so constant and decisive, that he was perfectly convinced as to the effect of jealousy and rage, conjoined with a powerful sexual desire, in producing a rabid condition.*

These experiments do not appear to have been repeated by any other observer, and it must be confessed that they require repetition before being received as worthy of dependence, for the reason that daily observation invalidates the results which might be derived from them to uphold such an hypothesis as that now under examination. True, one or two casual observations have certainly been recorded in favour of it, and these are worth noticing here.

A cross-bred spaniel, aged five and a-half months, was brought to the infirmary of M. Leblanc, the eminent veterinary surgeon in Paris, on the 18th October, 1863. This animal offered all the symptoms of rabies; the eyes were sparkling and fixed, bark hoarse and broken, and it had a tendency to fly at everything put before it, as well as gnawing the wood of its kennel, &c. The owner, a watchmaker, declared that he had bred the dog, and that since its birth it had not left its mother. It never went out, and it was naturally very quiet. Towards the commencement of the month, the mother showed signs of rutting, and the young dog, excited by the odour, made unsuccessful attempts to approach her. Its ardour was extreme, its agitation incessant, and its appetite became almost null. On the 14th, the owner's daughter, wishing to play with it, was slightly bitten. On the 16th, the bitch, fatigued no doubt by the caresses and tentatives of the dog, drove it off by biting it, and it then escaped from the house in the evening, and did not make its appearance until the middle of the next day. Then it was offered some milk, which it lapped up with avidity, and went to sleep until the evening. When one of the workmen went to light the gas in the shop, the dog wakened up from its torpor and flew at the man, trying to bite his heel, which it did not succeed in doing, leaving only a red mark on the skin. Next day it

* *Journal Vétérinaire de Belgique*, 1843.

was taken to M. Leblanc's establishment, when his son at once recognised the presence of a rabid animal among his patients by the characteristic howling only. During the three succeeding days it refused all kinds of food; on the 21st it was paralysed, and died on the morning of the 22nd. Immediately afterwards, an examination was made of the body. The blood was black in all the vessels, and the liver, kidneys, and heart were gorged, but there were no lesions in the larynx or trachea. Straw and the *débris* of wood were found in the stomach; the lining membrane of the intestines had red patches here and there, and the bladder was empty.*

M. Weber, another Parisian veterinary surgeon, relates a similar case in favour of the spontaneous origin of the disease from this undue excitement of the venereal organism. The dog which subsequently became rabid was so valuable that it was not allowed to stray, but was kept in a loose box in a stable. In the adjoining box was a bitch in rut, and the effluvia from her caused the most ardent generic excitation in the neighbouring animal. For nearly fifteen days this unfortunate creature, condemned to such tantalising proximity, manifested the utmost agitation, and continued making as high jumps as it could to get over the partition that separated it from the object of its desires; but its aspirations, like its efforts, were not successful. Fifteen days afterwards this dog became furiously rabid, and its owner affirmed that it had never been bitten.†

But it must be evident that more facts of this kind are required before any satisfactory conclusion can be arrived at. In the meantime, it would be well to decide that it is not improbable that there may be some foundation for the supposition that intense sexual excitement may produce rabies, though at present there are only probabilities in favour of it.

* It must be mentioned that M. Decroix made inquiries into the history of this case of so-called "spontaneous rabies," and afterwards announced that M. Leblanc had not been told the correct version. (See the *Abeille Médicale*, 1863, p. 358.)

† Bouley, "Bulletin de l'Academie Impériale de Médecine," 1863-64, p. 92.

There is another point of view which must be taken into consideration in discussing the question as to the origin of rabies from this cause. This is the relation the periods of rutting bear to the periods when the disease is most prevalent.

The dog-bitch is usually in rut in February and August, and if procreation does not take place it is sometimes renewed three months later—in May and November. Of course in domesticity there are exceptions to this rule.

The cat usually ruts in spring and autumn, but in this animal also a domestic condition sometimes produces deviations from the general law.

The female fox commences to be in rut about January and February; and the she wolf, when aged, towards the end of December and in January; younger animals are so in February and the beginning of March.

If the production of rabies was at all connected with this condition of the generative system, then we might expect the malady would be only prevalent at the periods when rutting is general; whereas, we find that it is observed at all seasons. If the foregoing causes are capable of engendering rabies, we should observe most cases of that disease in February and August, allowing for the period of incubation; but, according to the statistics, these months do not furnish the most numerous cases. Indeed, if the causes enumerated were at all influential in producing the disease, we should not only have it much more frequently than it now is, but it would be common in countries where it is at present rare, or never witnessed.

Influence of Anger.

The same may be said with regard to the effect of bites inflicted by angry dogs during the rutting or any other season, or caused by other creatures. The Abbé Rozier, in his Dictionary, mentions a man who became mad through having bitten himself in a fit of rage; a case is also recorded in which a soldier became rabid in consequence of bites inflicted by a comrade; and Pelletier, of Mans, reports the case of a woman who contracted the disease through having been bitten in the breast by the child she was nursing. Dr. Camille Gros has recorded a case that occurred in the *clinique* of M. Tardieu at the Lariboisière Hospital, which would tend to prove, if accurately recorded, that the bite of an angry dog is dangerous. "An individual was bitten by an angry—but not rabid—dog. The wound was washed with clean water and spirits of camphor, and it healed in ten days. Afterwards he became ill, symptoms of hydrophobia manifested themselves, he was brought to the hospital, and died in four days; at the autopsy the lesions observed in hydrophobic patients were found. The premonitory symptoms and the progress and duration of the malady, were the same as with them." From this fact, this author imagined that the bite of an irritated dog, or one in rut, might become momentarily virulent and cause rabies.*

But surely if the bite given in anger by man or animals not rabid had such an influence, cases of hydrophobia and rabies would be quite every-day events. Cur and other dogs are continually biting each other all over the world; and whoever has struggled, as I have, to sleep through the night in a Turkish locality—Scutari, for instance—in Damascus, in Cairo, or in one of the main thoroughfares of a North China town, such as Tientsin, will be ready to testify that sanguinary battles among the half-starved and mangy canine scavengers are matters of at least hourly occurrence. Besides, in this country, so far as our observation has extended, dogs kept purposely for fighting—the notorious bulldogs—are those least frequently affected with rabies.

Certain it is, that nothing can be more erroneous or terrifying than the assertion that rabies may be induced by the bite of a healthy animal; and it must be strenuously denied that such a result is possible. No wound, injury, or bite from a healthy dog will produce the specific disease we term rabies.

* Camille Gros, "Thèse sur la Rage." Paris, 1860.

Of the abundant proofs we might bring forward to support this assertion, we need only quote what Professor Pillwax of Vienna has adduced against the alarming statement. In 1862, when rabies appeared as an epizoöty at Vienna, 552 dogs were brought for examination to the Veterinary Institute, and all these, with the exception of 32, were found to be free from this disease; among the remaining 490 were only a few cases of mange and epilepsy. Yet the official report stated that the majority of these dogs had bitten people, and, notwithstanding, not one of those who had been wounded by the 490 non-rabid dogs died of hydrophobia. Only one individual—a boy—who had been bitten in the face by a dog suffering from paroxysms of rabies, was attacked by the disease on the twenty-fourth day, and died in three days. "Since the year 1848," says the Professor, "during which period I have had the examination of suspected and really rabid animals, 300 and 400 dogs have been annually brought to the Veterinary Institute because they had bitten people. Until the state of their health had been ascertained, they were looked upon as suspicious by the authorities. Although the number of these non-rabid animals amounts to more than 5,000, yet not one of the persons so injured by them has had hydrophobia. If the bite of a non-rabid dog is capable of inducing hydrophobia, surely a large number of these people must have been affected and have perished."

Influence of Pain.

By some writers, extreme pain has been mentioned as likely to produce madness, and instances are given in which dogs have become rabid, apparently through intense suffering. One of the most striking of these is given by Eck, a veterinary surgeon at Berent. A dog had been castrated by some cruel boys, who used a bad knife and caused the animal great torture. Soon after the mutilation, the poor dog found its way home, and retired to a corner of the house, refusing all kinds of food. Some time afterwards, it came out of its retreat, obedient to the voice of its master, though it would not permit him to seize it; on the contrary, it was irritable and morose, threatening to bite the farm people it had previously been very fond of. It took refuge in a corner of the stable, from whence it issued the following day to bite some cattle, and could not be driven off by its master's voice nor threatenings with a stick. It escaped through a hedge, again bit some cattle it met in the village, and disappeared. Some time afterwards, the owner of the dog, returning from the market with two horses, was astonished to observe that in a very short time one of them had become very emaciated, and that it indulged in all kinds of disorderly movements, jumping about and kicking as it had never done before. The same evening, this horse was being led about, when it escaped and seized a goose, which it crushed with its teeth. Eventually this horse died mad. Some days subsequently, the other animals bitten by the dog became ill, and died exhibiting symptoms which left no doubt as to the nature of their disease; and the neighbouring cattle also suffered. M. Eck saw the horse and five cattle succumb to rabies, communicated to them by the maltreated dog, which he had every reason to believe became affected with spontaneous rabies in consequence of the pain it experienced.*

But may not this tortured dog have been bitten by a rabid animal previous to the mutilation? Tardieu alludes, in one of the reports of the Comité Consultatif d'Hygiène, to the case of a cat that became rabid in consequence, it appeared, of a large wound. If pain could produce rabies, surely the disease would be much more prevalent. Serious operations are sometimes performed on dogs, and it is the animal, perhaps, of all others, which is preferred for experiments—often of a terribly cruel character—by the vivisector and experimentalist. Cropping the ears is also atrociously painful, and yet from these causes we have never heard of a case of madness—real rabies—produced.

* Magazin für Thierheilkunde, 1865.

Influence of Breed.

Rabies may be said to attack all breeds of dogs indiscriminately, though but little attention has yet been paid to the class of animal in which it appears most frequently. Some writers have averred that small English dogs, spaniels, poodles, terriers, Pomeranian, and other dogs—in fact, all those of an irritable temperament, and which usually appear surly or vicious—are more particularly predisposed to contract the malady spontaneously.*

In the epizoöty in Vienna, during 1841, Professor Eckel, in 141 cases of canine rabies, established the following per centage:—

Mongrels of all kinds	53¼
Small English breed	12¼
Foxhounds	6⅓
Poodles	5
Pomeranian dogs	2 6/7
Danish dogs and Pointers	2 5/7
Pugs and Bassets, or Turnspits	2 1/7
Mastiffs	1 3/7
Hounds, Sheep-dogs	0 5/7

This veterinarian remarked, in reference to the above proportions, that the total number of each breed could not be ascertained; so that no definite conclusion can be arrived from his statistics. Nevertheless he was of opinion, that whatever the breed might be, the dogs *de luxe* kept in apartments, petted and abundantly fed, and whose venereal appetites were incompletely or never gratified, were the dogs most liable to rabies.

Professor Pillwax, in the epizoöty in the same city in 1862, corroborates Eckel to some extent by stating that the majority of the rabid dogs in that year were mongrels, or belonged to irritable and nervous breeds, or else were dogs which, having

* "Among dogs, such as are noted to be most apt to become mad are swiftest of foot, fullest of agility in body, leanest of constitution, and in colour red or blacke."—*Spackman*, "A Declaration of such grievous Accidents as commonly follow the bitting of Mad Dogges" (London, 1613), p. 32.

been kept all their lives chained up, had become very vicious. He also observes that, as in 1841, the largest number so affected belonged to people who were in tolerable circumstances, and the animals themselves had been well fed and carefully preserved from the weather, but insufficiently exercised, and seldom allowed to gratify their sexual propensities.

Hertwig is also of opinion that dogs kept only for luxury are the most dangerous.

Professor Saint-Cyr's observations do not substantiate those of Eckel and Pillwax. In 54 cases of rabies in 1864 he found the following proportions:—

1. Sporting Dogs.	
Hounds	3
Pointers and Spaniels	16
	19 or 35 per cent.
2. Watch Dogs.	
Pomeranian dogs	12
Mastiffs	6
Bulldogs and House-dogs	4
Newfoundland dogs	3
	25 or 46·20 per cent.
Mongrels	4
"Moutons"	2
Terrier	1
King Charles Spaniel	1
Greyhound	1
Pug	1
	10 or 18·80 per cent.

According to this table, says the author, it is the dogs which lead the least sedentary lives that are most frequently diseased. And the report he furnishes for the next year again bears out his opinion. In 87 cases of rabies, the breeds are enumerated as follows:—

Pugs	7
Pomeranians	22
Hounds	4
Pointers	20
Mastiffs and Newfoundland dogs	9
House-dogs and Bulldogs	6
King Charles dogs	8

Poodles	7
Greyhounds	2
"Moutons"	2
	87

And in 1868, in the same city (Lyons), Professor Peuch's observations still further confirm those of Saint-Cyr. In 27 cases there were :—

Bulldogs, Newfoundland dogs, and Mastiffs	8
Pugs	7
Pointers	7
Pomeranian dogs	4
Poodle	1
	27

In the 393 cases quoted by M. Bourrel, of Paris, we find the different breeds of dogs yield the following proportions :—

Breed.	Males.	Females.	Totals.
Mongrels	102	8	110
Pomeranians	76	8	84
Terriers	61	16	77
Sporting-dogs	47	8	55
Griffons, or Poodles	19	6	25
Spaniels (small breed)	22	2	24
Water-Spaniels	5	0	5
Newfoundlands	5	0	5
Greyhounds	3	0	3
Half-bred Pugs	1	1	2
Lap-dogs	2	0	2
Danish dogs	1	0	1
	344	49	393

Roucher has collected a list of the animals reported in Algeria whose bites were followed by death from rabies, which died of the disease, or were bitten by rabid creatures. He classifies them as follows :—

Dogs	70
Horses	7
Cats	4
Mules	2
Calves	2
Goat	1
Jackal	1
Small wild animal	1
Species unknown	3
	91

The number of dogs he afterwards estimated to be about 100; but the 70 he allotted in the following proportions, according to breed and *régime* :—

Dogs belonging to European owners		20
" " Arab tribes		3
Stray European dogs	3	
Arab dogs	8	15
Unknown breeds	4	
Dogs not known, or whose *régime* was not reported		32

There was reason to believe that the majority of those which were not seen, or whose manner of living was not known, belonged to the category of stray dogs, among which there was certain to be a good proportion of the Arab breed. A small wild animal, supposed to be a ratel or ferret, was the cause of rabies in one case.

In this country we have no statistics to refer to, but from casual reports and notices it might be concluded that dogs at large and dogs in confinement are alike susceptible to the malady, and that no particular breed suffers more than another.

Influence of Age.

Age has been considered by several authorities as influencing to some extent the production of rabies; and, as usual, the majority of the Continental observers have not failed to note this particular also. We will only refer to a few of these.

Eckel, in 1841, found that the adult age appeared to be the most favourable for the development of rabies; and Pillwax, in 1862, made a similar observation. Saint-Cyr, in 52 cases, reported the ages to be as follows:—

Less than 6 months	1
From 6 months to a year	5
" 1 to 2 years	12
" 2 to 3 "	8
" 3 to 4 "	5
" 4 to 5 "	5
" 5 to 6 "	5
" 6 to 7 "	1
" 7 to 8 "	1

From 8 to 9 „	2
„ 9 to 10 „	3
„ 10 to 11 „	2
Age unknown	2
	52

In 1865 the ages of the rabid dogs admitted to his *clinique* were in 87 cases—

Less than 6 months	6
From 6 months to a year	7
„ 1 to 2 years	12
„ 2 to 3 „	11
„ 3 to 4 „	8
„ 4 to 5 „	9
„ 5 to 6 „	4
„ 6 to 7 „	10
„ 7 to 8 „	1
„ 8 to 9 „	3
„ 9 to 10 „	3
„ 10 to 11 „	0
„ 11 to 12 „	0
„ 12 to 13 „	1
Unknown age	12
	87

From these tables we might conclude that young and adult dogs—that is, animals aged from one to seven years—are most frequently attacked by rabies.

Peuch, in the 27 cases already alluded to, found the following to be the ages:—

1 dog	aged 7 months.
5 dogs	„ 15 to 20 months.
6 „	„ 2 to 3 years.
9 „	„ 4 to 5 „
3 „	„ 6 to 7 „
1 dog	„ 8 to 9 „
2 dogs	age unknown.

Out of 8,639 dogs admitted to the Canine Hospital of Paris, which is under the direction of M. Bourrel, in the period from 1859 to 1866, no fewer than 393 were rabid, or rather more than 4 per cent. This high rate M. Bourrel attributed chiefly to the influence of agglomeration. At any rate, it will be seen that his large field for observation gave him an excellent opportunity of noting several features in the disease which does not fall to the lot of many.

With regard to age and sex in the early months of the dog's life, he gives the following proportion as suffering from rabies:—

	Months.										
	1	2	3	4	5	6	7	8	9	10	Total.
Males......	0	0	2	1	2	4	3	8	1	5	26
Females..	0	0	0	0	0	1	1	1	2	0	5
Totals ...	0	0	2	1	2	5	4	9	3	5	31

One year and upwards.

	Years.															
	1	2	3	4	5	6	7	8	9	10	11	12	13	14	15	Totals.
Males......	42	64	53	36	40	32	16	12	6	9	1	4	0	2	1	318
Females...	3	11	7	8	4	4	3	1	1	0	1	1	0	0	0	44
Totals ...	45	75	60	44	44	36	19	13	7	9	2	5	0	2	1	362

From these figures it will be seen that from the earliest up to the latest period of its life the dog is liable to rabies; but that from one to seven years it would appear to be most susceptible to the invasion or generation of the malady.

Thus far, then, we have examined some of the causes which have been supposed by various writers, and often accepted by the public, to be concerned in predisposing to, or exciting the direct development of, canine rabies, and in none of them have we found a satisfactory solution of the problem. Few veterinarians now deny, in an absolute manner, the spontaneous generation of the malady; yet none can assign its genesis to any specific cause. It is a malady *sui generis*, but how it is primarily induced we must confess we know not. It certainly appears to be on the increase in the great centres of civilisation in Europe, and its development would seem to coincide, as has justly been remarked by Professor Röll, with the degree of domestication and over-refinement, or "softness," of the dog; the *régime* to which it is usually submitted being directly opposed to the conditions which nature provides for the existence of carnivorous animals.

But it must not be forgotten that the disease has existed from the earliest times, and that creatures not subjected to the refining, enervating, and, in many respects, unnatural process of domestication—the fox and wolf, for example—are capable, we have every reason to believe, of developing the pest, and oftentimes in a particularly severe form.

In view of the obscurity which prevails with regard to the genesis of rabies, and the inefficiency of the various causes which have, from time to time, been brought forward to account for its appearance otherwise than through the medium of a contagious element, we are almost forced to accept the conclusion that there exists a special miasm capable of provoking the disease when acting on animals naturally irritable or vicious, or in a morbid condition. Or we might conclude that the spontaneous disease depends upon several causes in combination, which, in the dog at least, act upon the stomach, air-passages, and nervous system; though what they are, or how they operate, we must confess we know not, and in this respect we find ourselves in the same difficulty with regard to rabies as we are with so many other equally serious diseases of man and beast.

CONTAGION.

If there have been grave doubts among some comparative pathologists as to the spontaneous development of rabies, there have never been any entertained by the most competent authorities as to the *contagiousness* of the disease when once it is present in an animal. Since the days of Aristotle and Celsus, this important fact has been recognised; and it is now fully established that it is the only evident, efficient, and incontestable cause in effecting the production of the disease in other creatures of the same or different species than those immediately affected. Indeed, as has been already mentioned, several veterinarians of the highest reputation have given it as their settled conviction that the disease is maintained and spread solely by its contagious element, and that there is no other cause in operation. And certainly, when we begin to inquire into the subtle nature of the infecting element, the character of the animals in which it is elaborated, and the peculiar tendency they have to wander away when affected by rabies—a rabid dog sometimes travelling many miles from its home, and wounding nearly every creature it meets, without its course being always clearly tracked, or the number of its victims accurately noted, or even discovered—we must admit that what would in many instances be designated spontaneous rabies in the inferior creatures might only turn out, on rigid inquiry, to be cases of inoculation by the bites of dogs strangers to the district. In this respect we are quite willing to coincide with those veterinary authorities who assert that, in the immense majority of cases, the malady is the result of inoculation by animals affected with the disease. Bouley was so convinced of this fact, that he believed that nine hundred and ninety-nine cases in every thousand were due to contagion.

Vitality of the Virus.

This "contagium" or deleterious principle is present at the commencement of the malady, and continues to be formed until the termination of life; but it has been determined that it does not preserve its potency long after that event—observations and experiments having proved that the disease is not transmissible to man, mammifers, or birds by the usual media at a later period than twenty-four hours after the death of the rabid animal, or after the cadaveric rigidity (*rigor mortis*) has completely invaded the dead body. According to Hertwig, the infecting principle loses its potency within from twenty-four to forty-eight hours—when the body is quite cold and rigid—in the flesh and blood of dogs that have died rabid; but the period is longer in large animals. Eckel inoculated the blood of a man who had died from hydrophobia, two days after decease, but with a negative result. He experimented on a large scale with the saliva and blood of rabid dogs which had been dead for more than twenty-four hours, but could not produce the disease. And we must not forget to notice the remarkable case of a pupil at the Veterinary School of Copenhagen, who, in examining the body of a dog that had died mad the previous evening, cut his finger slightly. This inoculated him with the virus, and he died of hydrophobia in six weeks.*

Little reliance can be placed upon the statements concerning the fatal inoculations occurring a long time after the death of the diseased creature, and Haubner says that there is no proof with regard to the virulency of dried saliva.†

NATURE OF THE VIRUS.

We know nothing as to the intimate nature or composition of this animal poison, except that it is organic matter in a peculiar condition, capable of reproduction when transferred to other creatures, and producing specific effects in them resembling those developed in the animal from which it was originally derived; and we can only judge as to its presence and virulency by the results it produces when introduced into the blood of previously healthy animals.

This specific principle is what is technically designated a "fixed virus," in contradistinction to some other animal contagions which are termed "volatile," from their capability of being transmitted through the medium of the air, breath, &c., surrounding infected creatures. The infecting element in rabies may, nevertheless, be volatile, though nearly all obser-

* Hertwig, "Jahresbuch," 1859, p. 60.

† Some experiments performed by Count Salm would seem to negative this statement. He inoculated animals with the dried saliva of a rabid dog, and in this way produced rabies in them. Whether the saliva was more than twenty-four hours old is not stated; and I am not aware that the experiments have been repeated.

vation, and certainly all experiment, go to prove it "fixed." Further observation, however, is required before this important question in the etiology of the disease can be determined, as it has been quite recently stated that the hunting dogs of the Albrighton pack received the infection by smelling through the yard railings at the young hounds which were suffering from rabies. And other instances of presumed volatile infection might be adduced, but some of these will be referred to hereafter.

The Saliva.

The vehicles in which the poison is conveyed are various. From the earliest times the saliva, or mucus from the mouth, has justly been considered as the medium *par excellence*, and there can be no doubt whatever as to its being the agent of transmission in nearly every case of communicated rabies. But nothing has been discovered in the morbid saliva or foam from the mouth of the mad dog to account for its poisonous properties; it is the same clear ropy fluid in the rabid as in the healthy animal, and the microscopist seeks in vain for the secret of its death-bringing power;* neither can the chemist trace any alteration in the quantity or quality of its constituents, or distinguish the presence of any new or unusual element. Perhaps the disease germs are transferred from the blood to this fluid. The hypothesis that certain ferments—an improper term—may be developed in great abundance in the saliva under the influence of psychical disturbance, would account for those instances in which rabies shows itself in dogs bitten by others which are excited or furious by sexual desire, though themselves healthy.

* M. Boucher, of Ville-Jossy, believing with Trolliet, Féréal, and Villermé, that the bronchial mucus contains the virulent element, says: "Nevertheless, at the autopsy of a person who had died of rabies, the salivary glands were examined by Ordonez, and in the saliva found in them were observed crystalline elements (*éléments cristallins*) which this able micrographist had never before met with in these glands."—*L'Union Médicale*, 1869.

Until within a comparatively recent period it does not appear to have been suggested whether other products of secretion or excretion might not also contain it, and up to the present time some important points connected with this question have not yet been solved.

The Blood.

With regard to the blood as an infecting agent, we have the interesting experiments of Professor Eckel, of Vienna, undertaken in 1841. With the yet warm blood obtained from a he-goat affected with rabies, he inoculated a sheep at the nose, lip, and tail. Twenty-five days afterwards this sheep became unwell, and it died on the twenty-eighth day, having exhibited symptoms which were certainly not exactly those of rabies, and yet had no analogy to those of any other known malady. Nothing was found after death to account for this result.

Eckel also inoculated the head and ears of a dog with the saliva of a hog which had become mad from the bite of a rabid dog. Four months afterwards the subject of the experiment was still healthy; it was then re-inoculated with the blood of a locksmith who was affected with hydrophobia. On the sixty-second day subsequent to the second inoculation, the dog was seized with unmistakable rabies and died.

The circumstance must not be overlooked, in appreciating these results, that at the time the experiments were performed, rabies was prevalent as an epizoöty in Vienna.

Lafosse inoculated three dogs with blood from as many animals of the same species affected with confirmed rabies. Only one of these inoculated dogs died, after presenting symptoms which this able veterinarian could not ascribe to any known disease, but which he thought belonged to that form of rabies which the French have named *rage tranquille*. No lesion was observed on a *post mortem* examination which would account for death taking place.*

* "Traité de Pathologie Vétérinaire," vol. iii. p. 841.

The experiments of Breschet, Magendie, and Dupuytren are opposed in their results to those of Eckel and Lafosse, they having transferred the blood of rabid animals into healthy ones without producing the malady. And Hertwig gave the blood and saliva of rabid animals to healthy dogs with no definite result. Nevertheless, as Lafosse has well observed, there exists strong presumptive evidence that the blood in rabies, as in several other contagious diseases, is impregnated with the virus. And Eckel, Röll, Haubner, and other distinguished veterinarians, are decidedly of opinion that the virus of the disease is present in the blood, flesh, and other blood-containing tissues and organs, and appears in them with the outbreak of the malady. Consequently, it is as presumable that fresh flesh, soaked in blood, might also produce rabies if brought into contact with other absorbing surfaces than those of the digestive organs; and perhaps even the latter may be unable always to destroy the virus supposed to be contained in this medium. The recent experiments of the distinguished veterinarian of Lyons, Professor Chauveau, have incontestably proved that the virus of a contagious malady may be absorbed by the digestive organs. Conducted with all the care and sagacity that marks the researches of this able physiologist, there is every reason to place entire confidence in these experiments, opposed though they are in their results to those of Renault and Roche Lubin. The subject is one of much moment as affecting health, animals used for food being liable to the disease, and are therefore not unlikely to find their way into the butcher's stall.

The Flesh.

This, of course, leads to the question, Whether the *flesh* of creatures which have died of rabies or been killed while affected with it, can communicate the malady? It is to be regretted that the facts upon which the solution of this serious problem in veterinary sanitary police depend should be more or less contradictory; but it nevertheless appears that a large preponderance of evidence of a very trustworthy kind affirms the question.

With regard to the use of the flesh as food, the question would of course apply to its being ingested in a raw as well as a cooked state, and also the condition of the absorbing surfaces with which it comes into contact.

Cooked Flesh.

In the matter of *cooked flesh* from rabid animals, we find that Dr. Lecamus, of the Faculty of Paris, has eaten it with impunity. Jean Baptiste Castelli reported in 1777 to the Medical Society of Paris, that in the previous year a butcher had sold at Medola, near Mantua, the flesh of a cow which had been killed while exhibiting all the symptoms of rabies, after being bitten by a mad dog. None of the people who consumed its flesh were inconvenienced.

Schœnkius, on the contrary, stated that an innkeeper in the duchy of Wurtemberg gave several persons the flesh of a pig that had been affected with rabies, and these suffered from hydrophobia.

Lanzoni of Ferrara saw a whole family affected with hydrophobia after eating the flesh of a cow that had been attacked with the disease, but only three died, the others having recovered "through the help of Providence and the administration of remedies"—a circumstance which diminishes our confidence as to the nature of the malady.

Our "History" affords some instances of the pernicious effects of the flesh of rabid animals when eaten, and particularly that of the epizoöty in Peru in 1803 (p. 36), when negroes perished through having to consume the cattle that died mad.

Fernelius states that a mad wolf was hunted and killed, and that several persons ate of the flesh; all died of the disease soon afterwards.*

* "De Morbo Contag.," book ii. chap. 14.

condition, which, in its symptoms, bears some resemblance to a certain variety of that disease.

The number of authors who have stated that accidents have arisen from the consumption of the flesh of rabid animals as food is not meagre, nor are they of slender repute. The question as to the innocuousness of this flesh would appear, for these reasons, to be based upon negative and affirmative facts, and though no rigid conclusion can be arrived at when it is so divided by contrary opinions, yet it must be remembered that the negative facts only demonstrate the inconstancy of the communication of the disease in this manner; while the affirmative facts, if properly observed by reliable authorities, should solve the problem.

But if the disease has been sometimes induced by means of the flesh of rabid animals, is it certain that the virus has been absorbed in the digestive organs? Might there not be abrasions about the lips and mouth through which it would obtain direct access to the blood, and thus develop the malady? At any rate, knowing the powerful neutralising action generally ascribed to the digestive apparatus on several active animal poisons, when these are introduced by the mouth, it is very probable that in those instances in which rabies has been produced by the administration of uncooked flesh, the membrane covering the lips and gums, or lining the cheeks, may have been abraded, or in a condition to permit the ready absorption of the contagious matter contained in this food. Experiments have demonstrated that rabies will follow the application of the flesh and blood of a mad animal to a wound on the body of a healthy one.*

Milk.

The influence of the *milk* obtained from animals supposed to be infected with rabies, has received much attention;

* Lafosse, Op. cit., p. 839. Galen, in his book on Temperaments, says that the saliva of the mad dog is not equally dangerous when admitted into the stomach as when introduced by a wound.

and, as in the case of the flesh, the facts relating to its virulence are negative and positive. Among the negative facts, however, those must be distinguished which have reference to the milk derived from animals only bitten by mad dogs, and those really affected with the disease.

Andray reports that peasants have used, for more than a month, the milk of a cow which was wounded by a mad dog, without experiencing any inconvenience.*

An infant fed on the milk of a goat until the day the animal became mad, remained in perfect health. And, what is more striking, another child drank the warm milk drawn from a rabid cow, and no ill effects followed. The veterinarian, Gellé, has stated that he was commissioned by the Préfet of the Haute-Garonne, to inquire into an occurrence reported from the commune of Gagnac, near Toulouse, in which several persons had drunk the milk of a rabid cow every day from the commencement until the fatal termination of the disease. Though some of them were plunged into the greatest terror, yet none were affected with the disease.

The experiments made by Baumgarten and Valentin concord with the observations made by Gellé; they are also confirmed by the researches instituted by Baudot, who, a great number of times, noted that neither the milk nor butter obtained from rabid cows produced unpleasant effects on whole families who had consumed these articles of food.†

At the Alfort Veterinary School, a ewe which had been wounded by a rabid dog was soon after delivered of twin lambs, which it of course suckled. Twenty-one days after the infliction of the bite the ewe became rabid, and died, but the lambs did not manifest any signs of the disease.

The only positive statements I can meet with as to the milk of a mad cow producing rabies are the following. Soranus of Ephesus, the most distinguished disciple of the Methodic School

* "Recherches sur la Rage." Paris, 1781.

† "Mémoires de la Soc. Royale de Médecine," vol. ii. p. 911.

of Medicine, averred that infants at the breast are sometimes attacked with hydrophobia.* Balthazar Timæus speaks of a peasant, with his wife and children, as well as several other persons, becoming rabid through drinking the milk of an affected cow. Eleven of these died; but the peasant and his eldest child were restored by medical treatment—a circumstance which might tend to throw some doubt on the occurrence. Faber mentions instances in which the milk has proved injurious. An observation made by M. Dussourt, and quoted by Roucher, offers a very probable instance of transmission by the milk of a hydrophobic patient. This was the case of a negress in Algeria, whose child died presenting symptoms similar to those of the mother before she perished. In the same country, however, M. Hugo relates the case of a rabid bitch whose puppies were suckled by her, and remained in good health. But, again, an instance is given in *Cassell's Magazine* for July, 1871, in which the puppies suckled by a mad bitch also became rabid.†

It will be seen, then, that a large share of proof is in favour of the innocuousness of the milk derived from cows or other creatures while affected with rabies; though the question as to whether this liquid would also prove inoffensive when drawn immediately from the mammary gland and brought into contact with any other absorbing surface than that of the digestive organs, has not yet been responded to. Neither has

* Cæl. Aurelianus, Op. cit., lib. iii. cap. 2.

† "A friend of mine once owned a favourite terrier which had recently littered five puppies, and as she was kept constantly in his garden, she could not possibly have been bitten for some considerable time. But she suddenly displayed unmistakable symptoms of madness, and ran up and down the garden, with the saliva flying from her jaws, and her head twitching from side to side, as the heads of all mad dogs do. . . . But even in her frenzy her maternal instinct was too strong, and she ran back to her kennel, and began suckling her puppies. . . . But here is the strangest part of the story, and to me it seems very pathetic:—all her little puppies were raving mad too, and the foam hung in flakes about their mouths, and their poor little heads twitched, just as the mother's had done. They had sucked in madness with the milk, for she had not bitten any of them. This was, in my experience at least, a new feature in the history of hydrophobia."

a distinction been drawn, with regard to the ingestion of milk from rabid creatures, between the secretion as it is obtained fresh from this gland, and after it has been altered by the action of heat or commixture with other articles of food, as coffee, tea, &c., which might more or less destroy the virus, supposing it to exist in this fluid.

In the uncertainty in which the question remains, it would be well to proscribe the use of milk obtained from animals supposed to be, or actually rabid: for it must be always remembered that one positive fact is worth a thousand negative ones.

Does the Virus exist in the Nerves?

The malady being one which appears to be more or less of a nervous character, several authorities have imagined that the contagious material might be lodged in the nerves; and Rossi made some experiments with the view of proving that it was so. He was led, from these experiments, to affirm that rabies could be induced by transferring a portion of nerve from a diseased to a healthy animal; and, indeed, he describes how he produced madness in a dog by inoculating it with a morsel of nerve, yet warm, from the thigh of a rabid cat. And Hertwig, the talented professor of the Berlin Veterinary School, has several times carefully repeated this experiment with pieces of nerve and muscle, and has produced the disease, though less frequently than if he had inoculated with the saliva.

Is the Virus contained in the Breath?

Since the days of Aretius,* the learned physician of Cappadocia, the idea has more or less prevailed that the breath of rabid animals or hydrophobic persons could transmit the disease; and at intervals we find names of some importance endeavouring to support the idea by citing cases of rabies which they had observed, and the origin of which they thought

* "De Signis et Causis Acutor. Morb.," book ii. chap. 7.

could be ascribed to no other cause than the inhalation of the pulmonary transpiration.

"But," says Lafosse, and his remarks will be endorsed by those who have had most experience among rabies in the lower animals, "how often have we ourselves been compelled to inhale the breath of mad dogs? At the Veterinary School the dog-kennels are only separated from each other by boards, and these partitions are perforated with holes in their upper part in such a fashion that the air, charged with the transpiration from the lungs, circulates from the one kennel to the other. Though the thickness of the boards is the only separation between dogs that are rabid and those which are not, and though we can reckon no less than fifty-six cases in which mad dogs have had this indirect relation with others which were not affected with the disease, yet no transmission of the malady has been known."

Yet in this country at least there have been instances recorded which would seem to prove that the disease may be transmitted by the pulmonary and other exhalations; though it must be confessed that we require more carefully-observed experiments and facts of this kind before assenting affirmatively to the question.

Does it exist in the Perspiration?

It enters into the category of popular ideas with regard to this disease, that the contagion lurks in the perspiration; but up to the present time there is no proof whatever that the nurses, physicians, and others who attend to the hydrophobic patients, and frequently touch them when perspiring, have ever had the malady transmitted to them by this medium. Neither has any observation been made with regard to this question by those who have had experience among rabid animals.

Does it exist in other Secretions or Excretions?

There do not appear to be any observations which might lead to the inference that the special virus of rabies exists in other secretions or excretions, and no experiments have been instituted, so far as we are aware, to ascertain whether the mucus from other parts than the mouth, or the tears and the urine, could become the vehicles of contagion. Röll, however, in stating that the saliva, the foam from the mouth, and the blood are the agents in which the virus is most potent, states that "the other products of secretion and excretion are equally charged with it." *

Certainly, Eckel's experiments appear to demonstrate that the contagium is present in the blood, and it would therefore be rash, without negative proof, to conclude that it did not exist in all the secreted or excreted fluids.

Is the Virus present in the Secretions of the Generative Organs?

This question has been submitted by Lafosse; and yet he has been obliged to reply, that no observation made on animals has definitively settled it. It is usually so difficult to follow out the course of the malady in those creatures which are most liable to it, and to ascertain their various acts from the moment when the disease begins to affect them in its latent state until it reaches its apogee.

Does the Virus exist during the Incubation of the Disease?

The facts relating to this question have only had reference, for the most part, to the human species.

Chabert, a former director of the Alfort Veterinary School, relates that a female, the wife of the executioner (*guillotière*), contracted the disease; she had cohabited with her husband up to the evening previous to his being attacked with hydrophobia, due to his having been bitten by a rabid dog. Hoffman relates a similar case.

But Baudot mentions the case of a young woman who had

* Op. cit. p. 464.

cohabited with a soldier for a month, from the day when he had been bitten by a mad dog until hydrophobia manifested itself in him, without becoming affected.

The Memoirs of the Royal Society of Medicine of Paris also contain an account of several peasants of Trigance who were bitten by a wolf, and who lived with their wives until the day before the disease appeared, without the latter participating in the malady.

Bouteille, Boissière, and Rivollier mention cases in which sexual intercourse took place within only six hours of the appearance of hydrophobia, and yet there was nothing to prove that the malady could be transmitted during the period of incubation.

M. Canillac, a veterinary surgeon of Allier, France, reports that a cow became rabid forty days after having been bitten by a mad dog. During the attack she calved, and though every care was taken to prevent her licking the calf, which she only suckled for one day, the progeny also exhibited symptoms of rabies on the third day after birth.*

Veterinary-Surgeon Hickman, describing an outbreak of rabies among some ewes, states that the lambs of all the ewes which had yeaned before the symptoms appeared did well; but when the symptoms became manifest before yeaning, the lambs were born dead, or very soon died.†

The evidence, it will be seen, is contradictory as to whether the deleterious principle is present as an infecting agent before the disease has become developed. But pending the settlement of the question by observation or experiment, it will be well to remember that a contagious malady of the horse species—glanders—may be transmitted by means of the blood abstracted from an inoculated animal which has not yet become affected with the disorder in an apparent manner.

* Lafosse, Op. cit., p. 841.

† The *Veterinarian*, vol. xi. p. 356.

Between what Species is the Disease communicable?

Though it has long been decided that animals of the canine and feline species could transmit the disease to various species and to each other, yet that the malady could be conveyed from others than the cat and dog tribes does not appear in recent times to have been clearly understood, and the experiments undertaken with the object of proving whether it could or could not be communicated in this way have been somewhat conflicting in their results.

For instance, it was doubted whether, in the case of herbivorous animals affected with rabies, their bite could convey the malady in the same manner that it had been conveyed to them. Notwithstanding that common observation, in accidental cases, had long ago decided the matter, experiments made by Betti, surgeon of the Florence Hospital, and afterwards repeated by the veterinarians Girard, Vatel, Huzard, sen., and Dupuy, as well as at the Lyons Veterinary School, were unsuccessful in transmitting rabies from herbivorous animals. Lafosse inoculated a cow, two horses, and two dogs with the saliva from a rabid sheep, but without any result; he also inoculated a horse and three dogs with the saliva from a rabid ox, but had no better success. For several years the highest authority, perhaps, on this malady in Europe—the late veterinary professor Renault—believed, from numerous experiments, that the rabies of the herbivora could not be communicated to the dog; and it indeed appeared to be the impression that the rabäic virus of the carnivora, though potent in producing the disease in herbivorous creatures, lost this potency in them, and hence the non-virulence of their saliva.

Vaughan and Babington in this country were unsuccessful in their attempts to convey the malady from herbivores, and it was thought by some eminent men—among them Sir Astley Cooper and the veterinary professor Coleman—that the power to propagate the disease was confined to such animals as naturally employed their teeth as weapons of offence.

But experiments of a later date have proved this assumption to be erroneous. Eckel, as we have seen, succeeded in conveying the disease from a he-goat to a sheep; he also successfully inoculated the dog with the saliva of rabid herbivores. Berndt inoculated four sheep with the saliva of a mad ox, and they became mad. Breschet asserted that he had conveyed the disease by inoculation with the foam from the mouths of rabid horses and asses. Professor Rey, of the Lyons Veterinary School, having produced rabies in sheep by causing them to be bitten by mad dogs, succeeded in developing this disease in other sheep by inoculating them with the saliva or by bites from the mad creatures; and Renault finally succeeded in obtaining the transmission of rabies from herbivores to the dog.

Youatt gives an instance in which rabies was conveyed from a horse to a man; this excellent veterinarian also communicated the disease on two occasions from the horse to the dog, and once from the ox to the dog.*

Professor Tombari, of Turin, reports the admission of a rabid heifer into the Veterinary School of that city, on the 14th July, 1863. It died at the end of the second day after its arrival; but an hour and a half before death, a quantity of the saliva which flowed abundantly from its mouth was collected in a sponge, and with it a horse was inoculated (at the neck), a sheep (at the flanks), and two bitches. The sheep was the first to die, in about two days, after refusing water and all kinds of nourishment, and showing great prostration. On the fourteenth day, the horse began to show symptoms of dulness; it trembled, became covered with perspiration, and refused to eat and drink; the breathing was accelerated, and the animal lost condition, but remained tranquil; it did not attempt to kick, but tried to bite when any one approached it. It succumbed on the nineteenth day. On the 28th July, one of the bitches

* The *Veterinarian*, vol. iv. p. 223.

showed all the characteristic symptoms of rabies, and the other died of the disease in the beginning of September.*

The saliva of rabid sheep has produced rabies in rabbits. Tardieu mentions that in 1855, in the department of Creuse, France, a sheep that had been bitten by a mad dog, bit in its turn the shepherd, who was seized with hydrophobia fifteen days afterwards, and died.†

The result of the experiments carried out by various authorities led Röll to assert that the bite of herbivorous animals suffering from rabies, as well as inoculation with their saliva or blood, will communicate the affection, though the contagious principle is not so active or intense as that derived from the carnivora.

The disease has been communicated from the ox to fowls, as demonstrated by Dr. Ashburner, in 1828, and later by Mr. King, of Clifton, who produced rabies in a fowl by inoculating it with the saliva of a cow that had just succumbed to the disease.

Zincke, of Jena, produced rabies in fowls by inoculating them with the canine virus; and Van Swieten reports that an old woman died with all the symptoms of rabies, after a wound inflicted on her by an irate cock; but, as he could not admit that a virus not present in an animal could be communicated by that animal, he conjectured that the cock was suffering from rabies which had been imparted to it by a fox.

It must not be forgotten that the facility with which the disease can be transmitted by different species depends, besides the activity or degree of viruleney of the infecting principle, upon the organisation and habits, or rather nature, of the diseased. Flesh-eating or carnivorous animals, as is well known, generally attack other creatures with their teeth, which are well adapted for wounding and tearing; consequently, they are the most successful in inoculating with the poison. Cases

* "Il Medico Veterinario," 1865.

† "Dictionnaire d'Hygiène Public et de Salubrité."

are reported in which the malady has appeared in mankind without any other injury having been inflicted than scratches by cats' claws. For instance, Lipscomb mentions the history of Daniel Perrin, aged twenty, who, in the autumn, was only scratched by a mad cat, so that the cuticle of his right thumb was wounded. In the following March he was seized with hydrophobia, and died mad;* but in all probability these weapons had been previously contaminated by the saliva, as rabid animals frequently use their paws to remove the viscid secretion that obstructs their mouths.

Herbivorous animals differ in their habits and instincts, as well as in their aggressive weapons, from the carnivora, which render them less dangerous enemies when affected with rabies. The horse's natural weapons are its hoofs, and it comparatively rarely employs the teeth; while the cow, sheep, and goat use their horns. The transmission of the disease from these animals is, therefore, less likely to occur, though not from any other cause than their instinctive reluctance to use their teeth in inflicting injury. And even when, at a late stage of the disease, these instruments are resorted to, particularly by the horse, the bite is not so liable to produce inoculation, simply from the fact that, owing to the shape of the teeth, and the disposition of their tables or biting surfaces, they cannot readily penetrate the skin.

With regard to the communicability of rabies from the human species to the lower animals, the evidence is not less conclusive, notwithstanding the fact that negative experiments have been recorded. On the 19th of June, 1823, Magendie and Breschet, in the Hôtel Dieu, and in the presence of many witnesses, gathered some saliva from the mouth of a man who was dying of hydrophobia, and with it inoculated two healthy dogs, near the patient's bed. One of these animals was seized with rabies on the 27th of July, and bit two others, one of which was mad on the 26th of August. Eckel, as we have seen,

* "The History of Canine Madness," p. 64.

mentions a similar instance. Mr. Earle, of St. George's Hospital, London, inoculated several rabbits with the saliva of a woman affected with hydrophobia; some of these became rabid. Hertwig successfully transplanted the virus from a dying man to a dog; and Renault, of Alfort, also proved experimentally that the disease could be transmitted from mankind to the canine species. And Aurelianus, Enaux, Chaussier, and others mention instances in which hydrophobia has been induced in persons who have accidentally had the saliva of hydrophobic patients applied to their lips.

In the past year (1871) a girl named Bence died in Liverpool from hydrophobia. It was believed she had not been bitten; but the death of her little brother from the disease occurred about three weeks previously, and the supposition was that the virus had been communicated in some way to the girl through a wound in her foot.

From the above and other facts, which it is not deemed necessary to allude to in this place, it may be safely affirmed that the virus of every rabid animal will communicate the disease, and that there is every reason to believe that all warm-blooded creatures are susceptible to its influence.

Frequency of Transmission.

Another important and interesting question connected with the foregoing subjects, is that which has reference to the frequency with which rabies follows the bite or inoculation with the infecting material of a mad animal. For the lower animals, there are a sufficient number of observations recorded to enable us to form an approximative idea on this subject, though it must be borne in mind that some unavoidable contingencies rather tend to depreciate the value of the figures given in cases of wounds; for instance, it is not always possible to assure one's self that bites have really been inflicted by mad animals, or, if so inflicted, that they have been sufficient to insure inoculation.

Lafosse, of Toulouse, states that out of 60 animals suspected of having been bitten by rabid creatures, 21 died from the disease. According to Renault, out of 244 dogs brought to the Alfort School between the years 1827 and 1837, having been bitten in the streets by mad or suspected dogs, and which remained for two months under observation without receiving any treatment, 74, or about one-third, became rabid. This veterinarian states that some uncertainty always prevailed with regard to the existence of the malady in the dogs which inflicted the injuries; that the traces of bites had not always been sought for and noted in all the dogs left at the school, and that therefore there was no proof that they had been bitten; and, besides, they might have been wounded in parts of the body where the thickness of the hair would prevent the saliva reaching the wound. It was in consequence of this uncertainty that, at different periods between 1830 and 1851, he caused dogs and herbivores—horses and sheep—to be bitten several times by really rabid dogs, in his presence, and on those parts of their bodies where the skin is thinnest and has least hair; on other occasions he obtained saliva from the mouths of the mad dogs when they were most furious, and with it inoculated healthy animals by punctures in the skin. The number thus experimented upon was 99, of which 67 contracted the malady; the other 32 were kept under observation for more than a hundred days without manifesting any symptoms of the disease.*

Though everything in these experiments appears to have been favourable to the production of the malady, yet it will be observed that only three-fourths became affected—the other fourth, without any preventive treatment, entirely escaping.

According to the registers of the Lyons Veterinary School, the proportion of animals bitten accidentally in the streets, and which afterwards became mad, was, for the dogs one-fifth, and

* Renault, "Rapport sur la Rage" (Bulletin de l'Académie de Médecine. Paris, 1852).

horses one-fourth. This proportion is not much less than that reported by Renault as the result of his experiments.

For Berlin, Hertwig reports that from 1823 to 1837, out of 137 dogs bitten in the streets of that city, and brought to the hospital of the Veterinary School to be kept under observation, only 16 became rabid—a proportion of one to eight. The same talented veterinarian inoculated 59 dogs, of which number 14, or 23.7 per cent., contracted the disease; but of 25 others which he either inoculated with the saliva of mad dogs, or caused to be bitten by them experimentally, 10 became rabid, and the other 15 remained healthy. In some cases he found that several inoculations—from two to four—were necessary. It is worthy of remark that a young mastiff resisted for three years all Hertwig's attempts at inoculation, although seven others inoculated at the same time, and with the same saliva, succumbed to the malady.*

Faber has stated that of 114 dogs bitten by others which were rabid, 77, or 68 per cent., were afterwards affected; of 68 to 78 cattle bitten by rabid dogs, 45, or 64 per cent., died of rabies; and of 127 sheep, 51, or 40 per cent., became rabid.

From these statistics, collected in different places and at different times, it might be inferred that at least two-thirds of the animals bitten accidentally by dogs supposed to be, or which are really mad, escape, without being submitted to any treatment; while of those experimentally exposed to receive the contagion under the most favourable conditions for its transmission, about one-third do not contract the malady, even when abandoned to their fate. Lafosse is of opinion that the degree of contagion appears to vary from one-third to one-eighth. Nevertheless, as Renault has justly observed, it must not be accepted as correct that these results, obtained in a large number of observations, represent the consequences which might follow the bite of each rabid dog; for it often happens that a dog undoubtedly mad bites a certain number of animals,

* Beiträge zur näheren Kenntniss der Wuthkrankheit.

or furnishes saliva with which to inoculate them, and out of this number the sixth or seventh portion only will contract the disease, while, in consequence of the bites or inoculations with the saliva of another dog, which appears to be in the same condition as to rabies, nearly all the individuals wounded or inoculated—the five-sixths or six-sevenths, for example—will become mad. It may be as well to mention here that a mad dog, when at liberty and on its tour of destruction, will frequently bite as many as sixty or seventy other dogs, in addition to the people and cattle it may encounter; and that these wandering rabid dogs are the chief agents in diffusing the malady.

The virus of the rabid wolf would appear to be more violent and prompt in its action than that of the dog, as a greater percentage of those bitten by this animal will perish than in the same number wounded by the latter.*

As with the lower animals, so with mankind—for, providentially, many of those injured by dogs, cats, wolves, foxes, or other creatures affected with rabies remain unaffected; but, as has been just stated, particularly in our history, the injuries caused by wolves have been most frequently followed by rabies. Renault gathered from different sources that out of 254 persons bitten by these animals, 164, or nearly two-thirds, became hydrophobic. Of 114 cases collated by Dr. Watson of persons bitten by mad wolves, 67 died. In the "Memoirs of the Paris Royal Society of Medicine," an instance is recorded for 1772, in which a rabid wolf bit two persons, and many cows and horses; all perished.† Troilliet relates that of 23 persons wounded by a rabid wolf, 13 died. Baudot also gives an account of no less than 40 oxen, cows, horses, dogs, and other creatures bitten by a mad wolf in June, 1765, the majority of

* "Die Wuthkrankheit."

† Wolves are still very numerous in some of the departments of France. Geoffrey Saint-Hilaire, for instance, states that in only one department—the Nièvre—a wolf-killer, aided by his helpers, destroyed no fewer than 1,134 wolves.

which succumbed. Dr. Camescasse, sanitary officer in Turkey, gives the history of 47 persons bitten by a rabid wolf, 45 of whom perished of hydrophobia. Palmarius has seen twenty wolves, driven either through hunger or madness, sally out of a forest, and seize every living creature that came in their way; all bitten by them perished afterwards. Renault estimated the mortality arising from the bites of rabid wolves at 66 per cent.

Tardieu mentions that in 99 individuals bitten by animals manifestly rabid, 41 only became ultimately affected with hydrophobia; and from the inquiry instituted in France by the Comité Consultatif d'Hygiène Publique, we learn that from 1855 to 1858 included, out of 198 individuals injured by virulent bites, 112 afterwards died from hydrophobia, or 6 in every ten. This, of course, does not include those cases in which preservative remedies were adopted, but is merely the number of those left to chance.

Aitken states that out of 153 persons bitten by dogs, only 94 are known to have perished—making the chances of escape as nearly three to two. Watson says that of 15 persons bitten by a mad dog, only 3 succumbed; and John Hunter states that he knew an instance in which 21 were bitten and only one died; though he estimated the mortality at 5 per cent. Vaughan relates an instance in which between twenty and thirty persons were wounded by a mad dog, and only one perished; and Sully speaks of 4 persons and 12 dogs having been bitten by the same rabid dog; all the dogs perished, but the people escaped.* Tardieu gives an instance, however, in which one dog in a department of France gave the disease to ten persons.

In the communication already alluded to as furnished by Professor Bouley in 1870, it would appear that in the forty-nine departments of France in which the existence of rabies was announced by 108 reports, 320 persons were bitten by mad

* "Observations on the Bites of Animals," p. 23.

animals. Of these, 129 perished from hydrophobia—a mortality of 40.31 per cent.; and in 123 cases known and specified by these documents, no harm followed—making 38 per cent. in which the bites have proved innocuous. But it will be noticed that 68 cases remain to be accounted for; of these there is no further reference in the reports—a circumstance which would lead to the supposition that they had not a fatal issue, since a death due to the bite of a mad animal always causes more alarm and commotion than if the accident was followed by complete immunity.

According to Renault, the percentage of deaths from hydrophobia in persons bitten by rabid dogs is 33.

In Algeria, of 63 persons wounded by animals, 47 died from hydrophobia, the remaining 16 escaping the malady, although they had been, like the others, bitten by animals which afterwards died rabid, or had transmitted the disease to other persons.

Of the 63 bites, 39 were single—that is to say, inflicted by one animal on one person only. One of these bites did not produce any after consequences. In 8 multiple bites 4 were double—or inflicted by one animal on two persons—1 triple, 2 quadruple, 1 quintuple. One of these double bites caused two deaths; the other three one death each.

Three persons attacked at the same time by the same animal did not become hydrophobic. Two quadruple bites caused, on two occasions, two deaths; on another occasion one death. And the quintuple bite only produced one victim. The details point to the curious result of 8 rabid animals having wounded 24 persons, and yet only 9 of these dying of the malady. The proportionately small number of fatal cases was ascribed to the precautions taken after the wounds had been inflicted, and it is curious to note that those who thus escaped evil consequences were almost exclusively French people.

Some interesting instances of immunity are recorded in Algeria by Roucher. One reported by M. Miguérès was as follows: a strange dog bit a cat, which died immediately, and a dog, which was killed on the following day; likewise a child, that did not suffer any bad results from the wound, and the father of this child, who in attempting to capture the animal, was bitten, and afterwards perished of hydrophobia. Dr. Moreau, of Bône, alludes to an instance in which a dog bit two persons, one of whom succumbed to hydrophobia in two days, after forty-eight days' incubation; the other in seven days, after one hundred and sixteen days' incubation. This animal also wounded a tailor, twenty-three years of age, in the hip, and although he took no precautions he escaped hydrophobia. The brute also attacked a child seven years old, and wounded it extensively in the chest, yet it exhibited no symptom of hydrophobia—though it must not be overlooked that a surgeon who was called in immediately cauterised the injuries by the deflagration of cones of moist gunpowder.

With regard to the animals which inflicted the wounds in the 320 cases that Bouley reports, 284 were male dogs and 26 females, 5 he or she cats, and 5 male or female wolves. Out of 48 persons who perished of hydrophobia in France in 1852, only one had been bitten by a cat.* In 85 cases of death from hydrophobia, Boudin announces that 58 were due to dogs, 20 to wolves, and 7 to cats.

In 228 cases of hydrophobia occurring in France from 1850 to 1859, in which the animals inflicting the injuries had been noted, Tardieu found the following:—

Produced by bite of dog	188
" " wolf	26
" " cat	13
" " fox	1

Of the varieties of dogs whose bites caused the death of people in 14 cases, the following were noted:—

Sheep-dog	5 cases.
Setter	2 "

* Tardieu, "Dictionnaire d'Hygiène et de Salubrité." Paris, 1854. Art. "Rage."

Terrier or "Griffon"	2 cases.
Poodle	1 "
Spaniel bitch (suckling)	1 "
Lap-dog (small)	2 "
Mastiff (large)	1 "

There are several other points connected with the transmission of the disease to mankind which deserve notice, though they are, perhaps, not of so much moment with regard to the existence or extension of the malady among the lower animals.

The transmission of rabies to the human subject is not so frequent as is generally believed, though from the foregoing figures it will be seen that the number who suffer from the disease is painfully large. No doubt, insusceptibility to the influence of the virus may have much to do in exempting those who are bitten by rabid animals from the serious consequences which ensue in the majority of cases. That such susceptibility exists in rabies, as in other diseases, there can be no doubt whatever, after what has been noted in the lower animals as well as in mankind. Renault's careful experiments proved that one-fourth of the inoculated creatures escaped the effects of the inoculations which were mortal in the other three-fourths; and what better instance can we have than that of the mastiff which Hering unsuccessfully inoculated many times during three years, while other dogs experimented upon at the same periods, and with the same virus, contracted rabies? This predisposition or susceptibility is more conspicuous, generally speaking, in the canine and feline species than in the herbivora or the human species. Dogs and cats hold the first place in the scale of susceptibility; then man and the pig; next ruminants—the sheep and goat being more susceptible than the ox; and, lastly, the horse.

It is in admitting the existence of this aptitude or predisposition—so strangely overlooked or ignored by the non-contagionists—that we can explain the fact that, in many instances, the saliva of a mad dog introduced into a wound has not induced the disease, while in other cases the slightest abrasion of the skin has permitted the absorption of the poison and the production of the malady. This aptitude and immunity is observed in other contagious diseases besides rabies. In addition to this, repeated observations have demonstrated that certain mad dogs have infected the greater part of the animals they have wounded, while others, labouring under the same disease and equally guilty of biting, have only exceptionally transmitted it to those they attacked. This peculiarity would go far to prove that there is a difference in the virulency or intensity of action of the contagium, not only in certain animals, but in certain outbreaks. It is necessary to remember these facts when considering the probabilities of the occurrence or extension of rabies, and also when endeavouring to draw inferences from statistics. And there also arises the question as to the virus becoming less active after passing through several organisms. The experiments of Professor Rey, of Lyons, show that there is some foundation for the belief that repeated transmissions attenuate the power of the infecting element. This veterinarian, by successive inoculations in several different animals with the rabific virus obtained from a single primitive source, found that it appeared to act with much less promptitude on the last than the first inoculated, and that with sheep it had no effect after the fifth removal or generation. There also remains the presumption that the first bites of a mad animal are more dangerous than those afterwards made, especially if they are numerous and inflicted at short intervals, as there is less likelihood of the teeth being so thickly covered with saliva after they have been several times used—or, in other words, after they have been wiped by penetrating the fur, clothing, skin, or flesh of another creature.* And it may even be surmised that only a certain quantity of the virus is secreted in a given

* In June, 1871, a rabid dog in the suburbs of Nottingham attacked a flock of sheep on the highway, and bit about twenty; it then immediately sprang at the face of the young man who was driving them, and wounded him severely; the wounds were subsequently dressed, though they were so serious that the gravest

time, and that this may be soon expended when the bites are repeated in quick succession. One more consideration must be noticed in connection with the apparent innocuousness of the bites received from rabid animals. Wool and thick hair may be, and no doubt is, in many cases, a safeguard against the introduction of the virus into wounds inflicted on the lower creatures, owing to these materials cleaning the fangs while they are passing through them. The clothes worn by people will serve a like purpose; free hæmorrhage from the wounds will also aid in carrying away the saliva from contact with the living tissues.

These considerations, which cannot be lost sight of, will serve to explain much that is supposed to be obscure in the transmission of rabies in the lower animals, as well as to man.

Sex in Mankind.

In the human species, the male sex (as with the canine species) appears to be the most exposed to this transmission. In England, from 1847 to 1858, 133 deaths took place from hydrophobia; of these 103 were males and only 30 females. In 1866, when the deaths from this disease were no less than 36, the males were 27 and the females 9; in 1867, 9 males perished and only 1 female; in 1868, there were 7 males, no females; and in 1869, 16 males and 2 females.

In Ireland, in 1864, 6 men and 1 woman died of the malady.

In Scotland, however, for the ten years from 1855 to 1864, 12 deaths are reported, and the proportion of males and females is equal.

From 1844 to 1850, 39 deaths from hydrophobia were reported in Bavaria; of these 21 belonged to the male sex and 18 were females.

---

apprehensions were entertained as to his being inoculated. Up to the present time, however (January, 1872), he remains in health; and we might ask if his immunity from the mortal disease was not mainly owing to the dog having previously bitten so many woolly animals.

In France, in 1852, in 48 cases of hydrophobia, 36 were men and 12 women. The same proportion had been observed in preceding years; and in summing up all the results of different inquiries in that country, it was found that in a total of 136 deaths from this disease there were 104 men and 32 women.

In 239 cases of hydrophobia, the statistics of which were collected by M. Tardieu from departmental reports compiled in France from 1850 to 1859, the sexes were enumerated in the following proportions:—

Males	175
Females	64

In Bouley's analysis, out of the 320 persons bitten, 206 belonged to the masculine sex, and 81 to the feminine; the sex is not indicated for the remaining 33.

This statement is in harmony with the preceding, and indeed with general observation; the number of women injured by mad dogs is always much inferior to that of men, and may be explained by the less risk they incur by reason of their dress and their mode of life.

With regard to the mortality following these bites, the more ample dress may also have had some share in diminishing the number of deaths among the females; for while of the 206 persons of the male sex who were bitten, the mortality was 100—a little less than one-half, or 48 per cent.—among 81 of the opposite sex the deaths were only 29—slightly more than a third, or 36 per cent. M. Bouley, who does not allude to the influence of dress in the respective rates of mortality, thinks the privilege of relative immunity only a statistical accident due to the small number of cases registered.

Age in Mankind.

The age of the persons bitten is not without interest.

In England, in 1866, the number of deaths being 36, the ages were as follows:—

Under 5 years	6
From 5 to 10 years	9
„ 10 to 15 „	2
„ 15 to 20 „	4
„ 20 to 25 „	4
„ 25 to 30 „	5
„ 30 to 40 „	2
„ 50 to 60 „	2
„ 60 to 80 „	2

In 1867, in 10 deaths the ages were :—

Under 5 years	2
From 5 to 10 years	2
„ 10 to 15 „	2
„ 15 to 35 „	1
„ 35 to 45 „	2
„ 45 to 55 „	1

In Scotland, for the ten years from 1855 to 1864, in 12 deaths the ages are :—

Under 1 year (male)	1
„ 5 years (females)	3
„ 10 years	3
„ 15 „	1
„ 30 „	2
„ 45 „	1
„ 65 „	1

The 39 deaths from hydrophobia reported in Bavaria as occurring between the years 1844 and 1850, were of persons whose ages were found to be :—

Under 1 year	3
From 1 to 5 years	17
„ 5 to 10 „	1
„ 10 to 20 „	3
„ 20 to 30 „	4
„ 30 to 40 „	1
„ 40 to 50 „	3
„ 50 to 60 „	1
„ 60 to 70 „	1
„ 70 to 80 „	5

Boudin gives the following ages of 136 persons in France, who died from hydrophobia :—

Under 5 years	7
From 5 to 15 years	30
„ 15 to 20 „	15

From 20 to 30 „	12
„ 30 to 60 „	54
„ 60 to 70 „	8
Above 70 years	6
Not indicated	4

Of 47 cases in Algeria, the ages were thus distributed :—

Under 5 years	1
From 5 to 10 years	2
„ 11 to 20 „	9
„ 21 to 30 „	6
„ 31 to 40 „	5
„ 41 to 50 „	5
Above 50 years	2
Age unknown (adults)	16
„ „ (children)	1

In Bouley's statistics the ages of individuals bitten are given in 274 cases, the distribution of which into decimal series further substantiates the interesting fact revealed by the above tables, that the largest number of accidents from this cause—97 out of 274—corresponds to the series from 5 to 15 years; this is the age of childhood, marked by thoughtlessness, imprudence, and helplessness, as well as a tendency to tease and play with animals. Numbers of dogs, during the fit of madness, observes M. Bouley, would spare the children with which they are so familiar, if the latter did not tease them more than usual, from finding they were not in their ordinary humour, owing to the disease. On the other side, he adds, this large proportion of bitten children is to be explained by the greater risks they run of being attacked by stray dogs in the streets of towns or in villages, where they are so frequently seen playing in groups.

Another interesting fact M. Bouley points out has reference to the series in which the number of persons bitten is highest, for in it the mortality is lowest. In the 97 cases reported as occurring at from 5 to 15 years of age, there were only 26 deaths; while in the succeeding series, the mortality is 12 in 25, 21 in 34, and 17 in 28—better shown in decimals as 26·77 for childhood, and 48, 61, and 60 per cent., for the subsequent series. From whence the conclusion to be derived is, says this authority, that if children are more exposed to the bites of rabid animals, it must also follow that they are less predisposed to contract the disease, perhaps owing to their natural heedlessness and their perfect moral quietude.

Seat of Injury.

The influence the situation of the injury has in the transmission of rabies to the human species is not only of great interest, but is a subject of the highest importance.

In 1852, in the 48 cases of hydrophobia cited by Boudin, the bites were localised as follows:—

On the face	13 cases.
„ lower limbs	15 „
„ upper limbs	12 „
Not indicated	8 „

In 178 cases collected between 1855 and 1858, they were:—

On the hands	86 cases.
„ face	47 „
„ limbs	40 „

Tardieu states that in 145 cases of hydrophobia in which the situation of the wounds was noted, he found the following:—

On the upper limbs, and chiefly on the hands	79 cases.
On the face	37 „
On the lower limbs	29 „

In the *résumé* of Bouley's statement it is remarked: "If we compare with each other the bites occupying the same situation, some of which were mortal in their results, while others were not followed by rabies, it is found that, in the 32 cases in which the wounds were made on the face, death has occurred in 29, and only 3 escaped; or a mortality of 90 per cent., and innocuity of about 9 per cent. In the 73 cases in which the virulent wounds were inflicted on the hands, the statistics demonstrate that they were fatal in 46, and inoffensive, so far as rabies is concerned, in 27; or a mortality of 63 per cent., and innocuity of 36 per cent. With regard to the wounds of the upper and lower limbs, when compared with those of the face and hands, the relations are inverse: the 28 cases in which the wounds were inflicted on the upper extremities were only fatal in 8 instances, and remained inoffensive in 20; and the 24 cases of wounds on the lower limbs were followed by hydrophobia in 7 patients, while 17 escaped the disease. This gives a mortality of 28 and 29 per cent., and of innocuity of 70 and 71 per cent."

Lastly, for the wounds on the body, which were generally multiple, the mortality is again in the ascendant; out of 19 cases of this description, 12 perished from hydrophobia, and 7 did not contract the malady.

These facts confirm the results of previous inquiries in France, and once more demonstrate that the bites inflicted by rabid animals upon uncovered parts of the body, such as the face and hands, more certainly afford access to the contagium than those which are made on the arms or legs when the teeth of the mad creature has, before reaching the skin, to traverse the clothing, and thus be deprived of their virulent humidity.*

* One day in the summer of 1865, a mad dog appeared in a commune in Roumania. In its course, it crossed the garden of a peasant and showed itself at the door of his house, pursued by several people intent on killing it. The peasant, hearing the alarm, hurried to the door, accompanied by his daughter, and attacked the dog with a stick. The animal turned upon its aggressor, bit him in the left arm through the clothes, inflicting several wonnds. The daughter, on her part, also attacked the dog, which left the father, flew at her, and wounded her in the face. Some days afterwards, both went to the hospital. The father, sixty years of age, of a strong constitution, had on the fore-arm four wounds that had all the appearance of having been inflicted by bites; they were not inflamed. During his stay at the hospital he did not manifest any anxiety on account of these bites, and went away in eight days, cured. The daughter had on her left cheek a large complicated wound, which was swollen and painful on pressure. The swelling disappeared in a few days. What was most remarkable in her case was, that to every one who would listen to her she expressed her fear of becoming mad, after the examples she had seen. In forty days, the wound being almost cicatrised, this woman suddenly lost her appetite, and manifested symptoms of anorexia; she had bilious vomitings, became dull and very restless, and the wound swelled and broke out anew. After four days' duration of these precursory signs, nervous symptoms became apparent, such as great perversion of the intellectual faculties, spasms in the chest and throat,

It is true that the consequences of bites inflicted on the body appear to contradict this proposition; but it must be observed, in explanation, that the wounds in this part are generally multiple, a circumstance which increases the chances of successful inoculation; that among these wounds there are some on naked parts, as the neck and chest; and also that, when a man is attacked by a mad animal, if he is bitten on the body he is also certain to be so on the hands, which are his natural instruments of defence.

The great mortality attending the wounds inflicted by rabid wolves is probably due to the fact that these animals generally fly at the faces of those persons whom they attack.

Rate of Mortality from Hydrophobia.

As before mentioned, no estimate can be formed of the deaths among animals from rabies in this country; but with regard to those occurring in the human species in England, we are indebted to the returns of the Registrar-General for the following information:—

In 1838 there died of hydrophobia		.	24 persons.
1839	" "	. .	15 "
1840	" "	. .	12 "
1841	" "	. .	7 "
1842	" "	. .	15 "
1847 *	" "	. .	5 "
1848	" "	. .	7 "
1849	" "	. .	17 "
1850	" "	. .	13 "
1851	" "	. .	25 "
1852	" "	. .	15 "
1853	" "	. .	11 "
1854	" "	. .	16 "

alternating with cramp in the legs; there was also well-marked hydrophobia, sputation, altered voice, dilated pupils—in fine, all the classical symptoms which characterise virulent rabies.—*Constantinescu*, "De la Rage," p. 44.

The same author states that in the mountains of Roumania, persons bitten by mad dogs or wolves have no fear for the consequences if the wounds have been made through their clothes, while they pretend to be much alarmed if they are bitten through the uncovered skin.

* From 1842 until this year, I cannot obtain the exact number of deaths.

In 1855 there died of hydrophobia	.	14 persons.
1856 ,, ,,	. .	5 ,,
1857 ,, ,,	. .	3 ,,
1858 ,, ,,	. .	2 ,,
1859 ,, ,,	. .	4 ,,
1860 ,, ,,	. .	3 ,,
1861 ,, ,,	. .	4 ,,
1862 ,, ,,	. .	1 ,,
1863 ,, ,,	. .	4 ,,
1864 ,, ,,	. .	12 ,,
1865 ,, ,,	. .	19 ,,
1866 ,, ,,	. .	36 ,,
1867 ,, ,,	. .	10 ,,
1868 ,, ,,	. .	7 ,,
1869 ,, ,,	. .	8 ,,

To every 1,000,000 persons the number of deaths from 1851 to 1867 has been :—

1851	1852	1853	1854	1855	1856	1857	1858	1859
1	·8	·6	·9	·1	·3	·2	·1	·2

1860	1861	1862	1863	1864	1865	1866	1867
·2	·2	·05	·2	·6	1	2	·5

The mean annual rate of mortality from hydrophobia in England for fifteen years, to every 1,000,000 inhabitants, was ·5.

In Scotland, the deaths from this disease were :—

In 1855	1
1856	1
1857	1
1858	1
1859	1
1860	4
1861	1
1862	1
1863	1
1864	0
1865	0
1866	0

From 1855 to 1864, a period of ten years, the proportion of victims to hydrophobia in every 100,000 deaths from every disease in that country was 6.

The statistics of deaths from hydrophobia in France do not appear to have been very generally or regularly obtained;

according to Boudin, they have been received only from the chief places in that country. The list prepared by the Minister of Public Works, from documents furnished by the large towns, gives the following numbers :—

	Died from hydrophobia.	Died from other causes.
In 1854	47	194,222
1855	34	196,088
1856	12	111,906
1857	18	132,192
1858	39	121,799
1860	17	145,354

This minimum of deaths from hydrophobia, however, only comprises those occurring in a fraction of the French population, and the same authority argues that there is no reason to believe that they are less numerous in the country and in small localities, than in the chief towns of the arrondissements and other towns having at least 10,000 inhabitants ; indeed, the contrary is more probable, for preventive measures should be generally better enforced, and bitten persons more speedily attended to, in large towns than in the country ; besides, in the latter, people are also liable to come in contact with wolves and foxes, animals which furnish their contingent to the disease. Taking, therefore, the localities for which the cause of death is not specified, and assigning to them the same proportions as for the towns, the probable number of persons who perished in France would be in—

1854	249
1855	162
1856	70
1857	117
1858	288
1860	91

This estmate gives a mean annual rate of deaths from hydrophobia for the whole of France of 162, a very high rate indeed.

In Prussia, according to Dieterich, the number of deaths from the malady were :—

In 1844	20
1845	15
1846	28

From 1820 to 1834 inclusive, a period of fifteen years, 1,073 persons succumbed to hydrophobia in that kingdom, or about 71 every year.

In Bavaria the deaths from 1844 to 1850 inclusive, were 39.

Austria appears to have suffered severely during the period from 1830 to 1838, and again from 1839 to 1847. The following statement is interesting, as showing the divisions of the empire in which hydrophobia was most prevalent:—

	1830 to 1838.	1839 to 1847.
Lower Austria	22	29
Upper Austria	7	6
Salzbourg	0	2
Styria	7	4
Carinthia	0	1
Carniola	0	5
Goertz, Gradis, Istria	33	20
Trieste	0	1
Tyrol and Vorarlberg	8	9
Bohemia	48	34
Moravia	18	8
Silesia	5	3
Galicia	63	81
Bukowina	12	24
Dalmatia	122	14
Lombardy	107	85
Venice	54	66
Military Frontier	83	57
	589	449

These figures will afford some idea of the danger the human species incurs from the prevalence of rabies.

In Sweden, according to Boudin, the mean annual death-rate from hydrophobia at four different periods was:—

From 1776 to 1785	58
„ 1786 to 1790	138
„ 1831 to 1835	6
„ 1856 to 1860	42

In Belgium, from 1856 to 1860, there were only 26 deaths.

The number of persons who have perished annually from hydrophobia in Algeria since the French occupation cannot, for obvious reasons, be satisfactorily determined. Roucher has collected the records of 47 cases from 1844 to 1863, which give a mean annual mortality of 2·35. From 1860 to 1863 no fewer than 19 cases were recorded, a proportion exceeding that noted in France. The 47 cases were thus apportioned among the population—

Europeans	34
Natives	7
Nationality unknown	6

Proportions between Rabies and Hydrophobia.

In connection with the mortality from hydrophobia in the human species, to whom the disease is communicated by rabid animals, it would be very interesting and valuable if we could arrive at an idea as to the proportions existing between the people who perish from this disease, and the number of creatures affected with rabies in any country like our own, and especially of those animals which generate and propagate the malady. No government has yet attempted to collect statistics with this object, and, indeed, in England rabies has received so little notice that it is not deemed worthy of being included among the contagious animal diseases which merit the attention of the legislature; so that we are quite at a loss with regard to data which might enable us to arrive at a satisfactory conclusion as to the extent of the danger incurred to the human population through the frequency of this scourge in the canine and feline species. Our history and the foregoing statistics may, however, aid us to some extent, and this aid may be supplemented by a reference to some other available facts and figures supplied by continental authorities.

The foreign veterinary schools keep and publish an annual register of the diseased animals admitted to their infirmaries, and it is not unusual for the veterinary surgeons in large cities to do the same; so that if we compare the number of cases of rabies recorded in these registers with the deaths from hydrophobia which are accurately noted in nearly every country, we shall be able to form some estimate, perhaps, of the relative proportions between rabies and hydrophobia. But it will be seen that this estimate will be far from correct, inasmuch as every rabid dog does not come under the cognizance of these public-spirited men; many die or are killed without being reported; so that the valuation, so far as the dogs are concerned, will be under rather than over the truth.

We will take Paris as a city in which the canine race is tolerably numerous, and where the number of rabid dogs has been pretty accurately registered, either on their admission to the excellent Veterinary School at Alfort, or to the private infirmaries kept by skilful veterinary surgeons. The Alfort register gives, for ten years, the list of mad dogs admitted annually, as follows:—

1853	11
1854	3
1855	16
1856	20
1857	17
1858	19
1859	17
1860	20
1861	37
1862	32
Total	192

For the four last years of the above decade, M. Bourrel admitted into the canine infirmary in Paris 85 rabid dogs, and if we add these figures to those of Alfort for these years, we shall find an annual mean of nearly 48 mad dogs in these two establishments alone; while in the entire department in which Paris is situated, the average number of deaths from hydrophobia is only 2·35 a year. These figures certainly prove that the number of victims to this disease in mankind is far below that of the canine race, and this disproportion is no doubt largely due to the intense desire the mad dog manifests to wound its own species and to avoid injuring its human codenizens—tendencies which will be alluded to hereafter when describing the symptoms of rabies.

The history of the outbreak of rabies in Hamburg in 1851, also testifies that the danger incurred by man, through cohabitation with the dog, sometimes bears no relation to the multiplicity of cases of rabies; for though no fewer than 267 mad dogs were destroyed during the intensity of the epizoöty, according to Boudin there was no case of hydrophobia recorded. Other eruptions might be quoted with the same object; though some, again, show a large implication of the human species and a grave mortality from hydrophobia, which only peculiar circumstances—such as the greater virulency of the contagium and exaggerated violence of the malady in the dog—can account for.

No estimate can be made of the relative mortality in other species of animals besides the canine and human species.

Mode of Access of the Virus.

There can be no doubt whatever as to the fact that a recent wound, or, as it is technically termed, a "traumatic surface," is capable of absorbing the contagium of rabies; and also that the most dangerous injuries are those which bleed least, or an abrasion on any part of the body. But there is not the same certainty with regard to the absorption of the contagium by other channels, though some facts would go far to prove the possibility of such an occurrence, as we have already noticed. The mucous membranes would appear to be most exposed to absorb the poison, particularly those of the mouth, though unperceived abrasions of their surface may in reality be present.

Enaux and Chaussier speak of persons who were affected with hydrophobia through wiping their mouths and noses with clothes soiled with the saliva of rabid creatures; and Cælius Aurelianus says that a woman suffered the same fate in consequence of wetting with her tongue the folds of a cloak which had been torn by a mad animal.* And a still more marvellous instance is given by Schenkius, in which the malady was produced by a scratch from a hunting knife that had been used to kill a mad dog some years before.† It is also stated by Palmarius that horses, goats, and sheep have become affected through eating the straw on which rabid swine had lain.‡

These instances, if they appear somewhat incredible, yet ought to render us circumspect as to allowing the saliva of rabid animals to come into contact with the membrane lining the mouth, nose, or eyelids, or even on the hands. Indeed, it would seem doubtful whether even the gastric fluid has much influence in depriving the virus of its activity, since Zincke inoculated a fowl with virulent saliva mixed with some of the gastric fluid of a cat, and it died in fourteen days afterwards.

The ancients appear to have been fully alive to the danger of allowing the contagious principle to come into contact with the lining membrane of the mouth, as Celsus states that on a sound condition of it depended the safety of the Psylli who sucked the wounds of bitten people; and at a later period Dioscorides is particularly urgent in recommending those who perform this judicious and humane operation to rinse out the mouth with astringent wine, and afterwards lubricate it with oil before commencing.

Van Swieten, quoting Palmarius, says that a countryman was dying of hydrophobia, and being informed of this, in an intermission of the fits he desired that be might take a farewell of his children, which the people who kept him tied down consented to; he kissed them, and then was suffocated. On the seventh day the children were seized with the same illness, and died in great agony.§

* "Acutor Morb.," book iii. chap. 9.
† "Observ. Medicin.," book vii. p. 848.
‡ "Lib. de Morb. Contag."
§ "De Morbis Contagiosis."

Bardsley mentions the case of a man who, while sleeping on the ground, was licked about the mouth by a rabid dog, and afterwards had hydrophobia and died. Another man was attacked with the malady, and no proof could be adduced that he had been bitten; it was subsequently remembered that he had used his teeth to untie the rope with which a rabid dog had been hanged.

Two of the cases of death from hydrophobia included in the table furnished by Boudin, were due to small dogs accustomed to lick the faces of their owners, to whom the disease was in this way communicated. And Mr. Lawrence mentions the case of a lady who had a French poodle, of which she was very fond, and which she was in the habit of allowing to lick her face. She had a small pimple on her chin, the top of which she had rubbed off; and, allowing the dog to indulge in his usual caresses, it licked this pimple, of which the surface was excoriated. Thus she acquired hydrophobia, of which she died. In the *Gentleman's Magazine* (vol. xx., p. 429), an instance is given in which a woolcomber in Derby died of hydrophobia, having become fatally infected by taking off the skin of a mad dog, and casually putting the knife to his mouth. Lipscomb mentions the case of a poor man in Kent who was seized with the malady through allowing a dog, apparently in health, to lick an ulcer on his leg, having been persuaded of the sanative influence of that practice.

Youatt asserts that in more than a score of cases of rabies in the horse, the disease was induced by their stable companions, Dalmatian dogs, licking them about the nose; but we are inclined to believe that bites were more probably the means of inoculation.

The unbroken skin of the hands would appear to be perfectly impervious to the poison, as there is no mention of any evil consequences having ever befallen the many veterinary surgeons who, in studying the malady, ministering to diseased animals when alive, or examining their bodies after death, must oftentimes have had saliva and blood smeared upon these parts. But the danger must be great when there are recent excoriations or abrasions on the skin.

Incubation.

The poison of rabies having obtained access to the living tissues by a wound, an abrasion of surface, or perhaps through a very thin but intact membrane—though this is doubtful—gives rise to pathological manifestations after a variable period of time, according to the predisposition of the creature inoculated; in other words, according as the organic soil in which the mortiferous seed is sown is more or less prepared for its evolution. And the early appearance of the morbid symptoms may, perhaps, depend upon the activity of the virus, as we have evidence to show that it is more prompt in producing its effects in some species of animals than others, and is even more virulent in the same species the nearer it is to its primary source.

What takes place during this incubatory or latent period we know not; but it may be confidently asserted that in no other malady is this interregnum more variable and uncertain; indeed, if we are to credit some reports, the duration of the latent stage is indefinite. The capriciousness of the virus of rabies in this respect is certainly very remarkable and unaccountable. The wounds produced by rabid animals generally heal up readily, and leave but slight traces, and to all appearance those who have been injured appear to be as well as usual. True, in some rare instances in the human subject, pain has been experienced in the region of the wound for a considerable time after the receipt of the injury, and still more rarely a quickened pulse and slight fever have been present from this time until the disease became manifest. In other exceptional cases, silent changes seemed to be taking place in the constitution, evidenced by general debility, a quick, weak, and easily excited pulse, sallow looks, and sunken eyes. But, as a rule, the health remains to all appearance the same as before the inoculation; and so subtle is the poison that, according to Van Swieten, persons who afterwards die of hydrophobia may, in the incubatory stage, contract diseases of various kinds, even virulent diseases, such as variola, without the course of the rabies being thereby modified in the least, or its evolution retarded. What occult influence is at work, what changes may be taking place previous to the manifestation of the first symptoms, is a matter of pure hypothesis. The venom of the cobra, hydrocyanic acid, strychnine, and other poisons, produce effects more or less prompt and decided, according to the amount introduced into the body of any animal, and we can exactly prognosticate not only the result, but the time about which it should occur. The virus of contagious diseases, and more particularly hydrophobia, differs from these, inasmuch as a minute quantity is as potent in inducing its particular malady, in a certain time, as a large quantity; and in the special disease now under consideration it may lie in a latent condition for a long period without affording the slightest indication of its presence.

Faber imagined that the contagious principle became encysted after its introduction into the body, and that it was only under the influence of certain favourable conditions — such as the inflammation of the cyst—that it entered the blood.

Dr. Brown Séquard is of opinion that an alteration takes place in the part of the body that has been bitten by a rabid dog, before the convulsive and other phenomena of hydrophobia appear; and also that the convulsions of hydrophobia occur by fits following a kind of *aura* (pain or other sensations) starting from the wound of the bite or its cicatrix, which then very often gives way, and is replaced by a bleeding or suppurating sore. He admits that there is a poisonous principle in the saliva of rabid individuals; but he thinks that it is in consequence of changes produced locally in the nerves wounded by the bite that the phenomena of hydrophobia occur. In support of this view he mentions a most interesting case communicated to him by Dr. Stokes, of Dublin, and which occurred in the practice of Dr. Stokes's father. A tourniquet was applied to the bitten limb of a patient attacked with hydrophobia, and the symptoms quickly improved, and even seemed to cease altogether. The surgeon then proposed to his colleagues to amputate the limb; but they declined to assent to the operation. It was ascertained several times that so long as the tourniquet was applied to the limb no convulsions occurred, while they came on as soon as the tourniquet was removed. As from a fear of inducing gangrene the tourniquet was not constantly applied, the spasms returned, and the patient ultimately died.* As in man so in the animal; for Röll states that in many cases there appears to be a greater amount of sensibility in the cicatrix, which is manifested by the creature licking, rubbing, or scratching it.

Virchow was of opinion that the contagium of rabies has an action similar to that of ferments, and that the new elements introduced at the point of inoculation are being continually introduced into the blood, by means of which they act on the nervous system. He also says that in the latent period the contagium should be eliminated from the blood during the course of the regulating metamorphic movements, and that rabies only appears when these elements have accumulated in an excessive quantity—as may perhaps occur in consequence of the multiplication of the ferment at the time of a new inflammation of the wound.

Röll thought that, after inoculation, there might be produced insensible alterations in the nervous apparatus, as is the case in alcoholic intoxication—these alterations becoming manifest by the symptomatic *ensemble* when the animal is submitted to certain unfavourable conditions.

However this may be, it would appear that a certain stage must be attained in the development or increase of the poison before the disease manifests itself; and, as has been suggested, a double zymosis or fermentation (if the term may be allowed)

* "Lectures on the Central Nervous System," p. 261.

may also take place, first in the part, and afterwards in the system, the result of which is either to multiply the poison or to increase its virulency. Many instances are on record which appear to support this surmise, particularly those in which local disturbance in the seat of the injury has preceded the more urgent symptoms of the disease. For example, Pouteau gives the history of a case of hydrophobia in which, about thirty-two days after the man was bitten, and the day previous to the first symptoms showing themselves, two red pimples, white at the top, appeared precisely at the spot on the back of the hand, where the dog had made the wound, and which was then only a scar. They soon disappeared.*

Boerhaave states that when hydrophobia is in its latent condition the wound becomes painful again, and vague pains are subsequently perceived in neighbouring parts. And Salius Diversus, who imagined he had discovered an infallible sign of threatening rabies, asserted that a peculiar pain was set up at the seat of the bite, and from thence it ascended by insensible degrees to the brain in the space of three or four days, and gave rise to vertigo.†

This local *aura*, however, is not always present, and many cases are observed in the human species in which it is entirely absent.

* "Essai sur le Rage." Lyons, 1763, p. 31.

† "When the bitten body beginneth to grow into madness, he sensibly feeleth a paine, though not very great, in the place that he was bitten in, which, creeping from place to place, about three or fower days after it beginneth, or a little more, ascendeth to the brain, where it causeth a kind of giddynesse and a certaine manner of confusion withall, whereby the sicke bodie beginneth to stagger and reele this way and that way, and shortly after falleth starke mad." —*Spackman*, "A Declaration of such Grievous Accidents as commonly follow the Bitting of Mad Dogges." London, 1613, p. 23.

"The first effects of a poisonous saliva appear rarely before the third day, sometimes not till the thirtieth or fortieth, and some instances are related of the poison laying dormant two or three years—nay longer—and then breaking out. It generally shows itself at the full or new moon, when a sharp pricking pain is felt in the part where the bite was given, although the wound shall have been healed some time."—*Layard*, "An Essay on the Bite of a Mad Dog." London, 1762, p. 27.

The supposed localisation of the infecting principle in or around the wound in the form of pustules or vesicles, after the injury has been almost or quite healed up, and to which the designation of "primary lysses" has been given, has been frequently alluded to.

And again, there are the "secondary lyssi," so long traditionally believed in by the inhabitants of Greece and Russia before made known to the world by Xanthos and Marochetti. This sign, as before noticed, consisted of a pustular or vesicular eruption beneath the tongue, which appeared soon after the commencement of the incubation stage—within a few days, according to these authors. Magistel, who paid particular attention to this subject, says that he saw the "lyssi" in different individuals on the sixth, eleventh, and twentieth day after the bite of a rabid dog, and that after the twenty-second day he never succeeded in finding them, although he looked for them, until the thirty-fourth day after the inoculation of the virus.*

The existence of these secondary lyssi has given rise to much dispute, the majority of the most competent authorities being incredulous as to their ever appearing in this situation, and though for a time the subject was allowed to subside, it has recently been brought forward again by Auzias-Turenne.†

* "Mémoire sur l'Hydrophobie" ("Journal de l'Hôpital de Burley." Paris, 1824.)

† "Aperçu Historique et Philosophique sur les Lysses ou Vesicles de la Rage" ("Recueil de Méd. Vétérinaire," vol. v. 5th series, p. 658.)

Marochetti asserted that in a person bitten by a mad animal, the virus accumulates and is temporarily retained about the orifices of the sublingual ducts, on the sides of the frænum of the tongue, and on the lower aspect of that organ. In these places several ephemeral pustules show themselves, whose fluctuation can be perceived by means of a probe. The time at which they appear is not certain, but they usually correspond to the interval between the third and ninth day after the bite, though they have been seen so late as the thirty-fourth day. If the virus in these pustules is not destroyed within twenty-four hours after they appear, it is resorbed and the disease soon manifests itself. It is therefore necessary, during six weeks at least, to examine carefully, several times each day, the lower part of the tongue of a person who has been bitten. If the pustules appear, open and cauterise them promptly; but if they do not form, it is certain that the individual will not suffer from hydrophobia.

The celebrated Trousseau is not a disbeliever in their presence; for he admits that this peculiar sublingual eruption may be met with in a certain number of cases of rabies (in man), but that one must know how, and particularly when, to look for it, namely, at the commencement of the incubation stage, and not in the period of invasion or of confirmed rabies, since the eruption has disappeared by that time, without leaving any trace behind. "In the present state of science we may not, perhaps, have the right to deny, as has been done, the presence of lyssi in rabies. This eruption should, therefore, be searched for in persons who have been recently bitten by a rabid animal, and whose wounds have not been cauterised. The accuracy of the statements made by Marochetti and Xanthos may easily be tested, because the wounds inflicted by rabid animals are rarely cauterised sufficiently early, and to a sufficient depth, to prevent absorption of the virus; so that in a certain proportion of cases, the presence of lyssi ought to be made out from the third to the twentieth day after the inoculation. I need not dwell on the advantages that would be obtained if the statements made by Marochetti, Xanthos, and Magistel were confirmed. Rabies could then be diagnosed during its incubation stage, and if by laying open and cauterising these vesicles the ulterior manifestations of the disease can be prevented, the complaint could be cured as soon as the sub-lingual eruption was detected. I cannot, therefore, too strongly recommend practitioners to look out for the presence of lyssi in individuals who have been exposed to the risk of being inoculated with rabies. The examination should be made regularly twice a day, according to Marochetti, because the eruption does not show itself on a fixed day, and the vesicles break easily. The same authority adds, that the eruption comes on at an earlier period in proportion to the amount of poison deposited in the wound, and that the invasion of the confirmed disease comes on also earlier, according to the early date of the appearance of the eruption."

Trousseau likewise adds: "There seems to have been of late

a disinclination to attach any importance to the presence of this eruption, and it has been said that it was a very extraordinary circumstance, without its analogue in pathology, that the virus of rabies should be localised—stored-up in a particular region I cannot entirely concur in this opinion ; and, without desiring to prove that this localisation of the virus is a perfectly natural phenomenon, which might have been foreseen, I will merely call attention to the fact that in most virulent diseases, a primary localisation of the virus may be detected in a particular tissue organ, and that the disease gives rise to general manifestations only secondarily. Thus, in eruptive fevers, we see the morbid principle affect the skin primarily, and the lumbar portion of the spinal cord in small-pox, the bronchial and laryngeal mucous membrane in measles, and the kidneys in scarlatina. We see syphilis limit itself, in the first instance, to the lymphatic ganglia in the groin and in the occipital region, and station itself for a time in the lymphatic system before giving rise to secondary manifestations in mucous membranes and in the skin. Again, we see the poison of glanders affect the mucous membrane of the nose in the beginning, and it is only after a time that other mucous membranes are involved, together with the skin, the cellular tissue, the joints, and viscera.

"If in virulent diseases in general, therefore, the virulent principle has a primary elective seat, why should one refuse to admit, on *à priori* grounds, that the virus of rabies, when inoculated into any part of the body, can act primarily on a determinate and localised region? Why should any surprise be felt at its selecting the free extremities of the excretory ducts of the salivary glands, when no doubt is nowadays entertained as to the saliva itself being the vehicle of the poison? Again, why wonder that a special eruption should be confined to the region where the excretory ducts of the sublingual and submaxillary glands terminate, when experiments by Claude Bernard have proved that all the salivary glands do not possess similar properties? Lastly, when it has been experimentally shown that certain substances, such as iodine and the iodides of potassium and of iron, are more rapidly eliminated by the salivary glands than by any other organs, why should it not be admitted that these glands may eliminate a virulent principle which, after a definite time and by virtue of special circumstances, lodges and is stored up in the extremities of the excretory ducts of these glands, or in the salivary follicles in their vicinity? Marochetti thought that the virus which had been thus deposited was, after a certain time, absorbed, and then gave rise to all the symptoms of confirmed rabies. He therefore followed the traditional practice of the inhabitants of Thessaly and Ukraine, and made an early incision through the vesicles, so as to give issue to the virulent matter, and then cauterised them with a red-hod iron. He affirms that this plan always succeeded in the numerous cases which came under his observation in Ukraine. One cannot take too much pains to look for this peculiar eruption, since it would be the only sign by which the incubation stage of rabies can be diagnosed, and since by cauterising it one may arrest the fatal progress of the disease."*

Whatever the results of more extended and careful observation may develope in the future, with regard to the localisation of the rabid virus, either at the point of inoculation, the region of the tongue, or elsewhere, during the latent period of the disease, it may be accepted at present that, of several individuals inoculated, all do not become affected with the malady; and yet during this interval there is nothing to indicate which will be attacked and which escape, neither is there anything by which to foretell when it may appear. In the words of Dr. Beale, we might say, "Just as a seed may remain perfectly quiescent, but nevertheless in a living state, for a long period of time, without growing or giving any evidence of vitality, so there is reason to think that many kinds of bioplasm (of which

* "Lectures on Clinical Medicine." By A. Trousseau. London, 1867.

the virulent principle of rabies is no doubt one) may remain in a living, but almost dormant, state in the system, ready to spring into active existence should the conditions favourable to their existence be brought about, and the pabulum for their nutrition be at hand . . . . . the development of the forms of disease characteristic of their presence being determined by the state of the system and the conditions to which it is exposed."*

We know not whether the contagium is present in the saliva,† the blood, or other fluids, while the disease is yet in its occult state, and are only made aware of its existence when it begins to produce its painfully characteristic effects.

In many instances rabies appears without any apparently exciting cause, the poison having germinated sufficiently to induce those morbid changes or physiological derangements which mark the presence of this malady. At other times some internal or external influence promptly puts an end to its latency, and developes the disorder in all its malignancy. Excitement, anger, sexual irritability, terror, injury to the cicatrix, sudden changes of temperature, and morbid disturbance, &c., appear sometimes to exercise a powerful influence in hastening its advent in the lower animals. A remarkable instance of the effect of terror in inducing what appeared to be rabies, occurred in my own experience in 1865, while stationed with my regiment at Manchester. A very small toy terrier, the gift of a friend, had been in my possession about three weeks, and had not been wounded by any dog to my knowledge. It appeared perfectly healthy, and was as playful as usual, when, in August of that year, going on leave to Warwickshire, I took this little creature with me, and had it in the railway carriage during the journey. Playful at starting, it soon lay down on a cushion

* "Disease Germs: their Real Nature," p. 164.

† It is much to be regretted that Marochetti and others who have seen the secondary lyssi did not resort to inoculation with the contents of the vesicles to prove whether they really contained the morbific element. This, I imagine, would have established the correctness of their hypothesis, or altogether disproved it, and could have been easily carried out.

and slept, as there were no other passengers in the compartment, and continued in this state until, on entering Crewe station, the engine of a passing train suddenly blew the whistle close to our carriage. The shrill sound and the noise caused the dog to spring up apparently in a frantic state of alarm. It gave vent to strange yelps, something between a howl, a scream, and a bark, and commenced to run round the compartment, jumping up on the seats, climbing the walls as if trying to escape, and behaving like an animal perfectly furious. Though before extremely obedient and affectionate, now it would not listen to me; indeed, it seemed to be deaf, and I had much difficulty in securing it. Buttoning it up firmly in the breast of my light overcoat, it continued to scream in the same manner, and was perfectly indifferent to all kind words. Soon after, quantities of ropy saliva began to flow from the mouth, and this, through the incessant struggles of the poor beast to get away, was not long in saturating the clothes it was in contact with. It also showed an urgent disposition to bite when taken hold of, snapping at the hand which seized its neck, an action it had never previously exhibited. The occurrence was so unusual and so startling, that though I half suspected rabies, I could not bring myself to believe that the disease would appear in this very sudden manner, and be excited by such a cause; for the creature was more or less accustomed to noises from the time it had been given to me. Nevertheless, I was careful to keep my hands covered by strong gloves, and to prevent the saliva reaching my face.

On reaching my destination some time after the manifestation of these symptoms, the dog, still in the same condition, was let loose on the platform of the railway station, and it ran into the station-master's house and under the bed of a back room. Here it was seized with difficulty, and taken home, where it was turned out in the garden, and all the characteristic symptoms of rabies in a violent form were soon noted: the peculiar expression of the physiognomy, the curled-up lip, exposing the canine teeth, the foamy saliva hanging from the mouth in long strings, the arched back, head held low on the ground, and—most curious symptom of all—a perpetual gulping, as if the creature was trying to swallow something. It started away among the trees, beneath shrubs, and crept into all the remote corners, as if to hide itself. It appeared to be almost blind, as it ran against objects in its way, and its hearing at intervals being also evidently affected, it would allow me to approach to within a short distance, when it immediately rushed off again like a hunted hare, until it reached another out-of-the-way spot, where it once more assumed the striking attitude just mentioned. The chirp of a bird, or the rustling of the leaves of a shrub, appeared to throw it into a convulsive fit, and gave it a most alarming and distressing appearance. There could be no doubt now, it was thought, as to the nature of the disorder, and as the dog was a household pet, and much valued, it was determined to try the effect of treatment, which the very small size of the animal and a pair of gardener's gloves on the hands permitted to be carried out without injury to the attendant, though without success, as it died on the second day. An examination of the body revealed the existence of the most common pathological lesions of the disease: congestion of the brain and the mucous membrane at the base of the tongue; the lining membrane of the stomach and intestines was also deeply injected.

Was this a case of spontaneous rabies, produced by terror, or had the dog been bitten by a rabid animal before it came into my possession? If the latter, the usual premonitory symptoms, or "first stage," had passed unnoticed.

It has been suggested that it may have been a case of epilepsy, but the symptoms were certainly very different to those I have witnessed in that diseased condition.

In the human being, the influence of a moral cause in the development of the hydrophobic symptoms has been noted at various times; but the most interesting, perhaps, are the following:—

A man, aged thirty-seven years, was admitted to the Saint Louis Hospital, Paris. His case is reported by M. Malherbe. Six weeks before admission he had been bitten by a cat, but this circumstance he did not allude to when first seen. He then complained of a pain in his left arm. Being afterwards interrogated, it was discovered that the cat had been ill for some days, and had been killed soon after it bit him. The bite, which was in the left arm, had been cauterised by a druggist. Cicatrisation had been complete for some time, when one of his neighbours said to him, "I have hanged my cat. Yours bit it, and it went mad." The unfortunate man was greatly moved by this statement, and immediately afterwards experienced the first symptoms of the disease, which were not severe until the 12th August, 1869, the date on which he was admitted to the hospital, where he soon after died, of course.

Sauvages alludes to an instance of hydrophobia occurring in a man who had been bitten by a mad wolf. This individual continued in good health until the thirty-third day after the bite, when, as he was dressing his vines, a person who was passing by, entering into conversation on the subject of his accident, inadvertently told him of several people who had died of hydrophobia six months after they were bitten. This made such an impression upon the man, that, on his return home, he became low-spirited and pensive, and had no appetite for food; the injured parts, which had healed up, inflamed in a very violent manner; a fever ensued, for which he was bled four times in twelve hours—together with a dread of water, and other symptoms of the disease. On the fifth day he put an end to his sufferings by hanging himself.*

The *Tribune* (vol. i., p. 245) alludes to the case of a woman who had been bitten in the face, and who was admitted to the Hôtel Dieu, Paris. After a few days she was cured of

* "Dissertation sur la Rage. Chefs d'Œuvre de M. Sauvages."

her wounds and discharged. Going about her usual avocations one day, she heard a man exclaim, "She has not yet gone mad, then?" From that time she could not swallow liquids, and on the same day re-entered the Hôtel Dieu, but this time to die of hydrophobia.*

One of the most recent examples of this dangerous impressionability of the imagination I can find, is that related by M. Bucquoy. A woman in the clinic of Dr. Maisonneuve had been bitten by a dog, which was supposed not to be rabid, and the injury had healed; when, two months after the accident, she was met by two students who had been with the doctor at the time, and who asked her if she was not yet mad. Immediately she was seized with nervous symptoms, became intensely anxious and uneasy, and went into the hospital in the belief that she was hydrophobic. She was put under the care of M. Langier, and the following day was evidently affected with the disease; hemiplegia appeared, with a violent delirium, accompanied by an irrepressible amount of fear, and she died asphyxiated in forty-eight hours.†

As has been said, the period of incubation of rabies is very uncertain, and in many cases it cannot be ascertained with any degree of probability; as animals are frequently wounded by others without any particular notice being taken of the circumstance, and also as frequently without any one observing the injuries at the time of, or even after, their infliction. Indeed, it is common to hear the owners of rabid dogs assert that their dogs had never been from home; or, if abroad, had never left

* These instances would appear to have nothing very surprising in them, when we know what a powerful influence the mind, or rather moral causes, exercise on the composition and secretion of the humours; when we see, for example, the urine, usually neutral or even alkaline in character, become suddenly acid as a result of bad news. The secretion of this fluid in a hysterical paroxysm, the flow of bile and subsequent diarrhœa by terror, the gush of tears which grief excites, and the production of milk by a mother while in a fit of anger so hurtful as to poison her offspring—are all so many proofs of the influence referred to. The green frog, irritated by pain, secretes a venom which, for deadliness, has been compared to that of the rattlesnake.

† *Cosmos*, June, 1860.

them for a second; that they could not, therefore, be bitten without their knowledge, and they were not cognizant of such an occurrence; while others do not deny that their animals were bitten, but they do not know when, where, or how.* Yet it is most essential, with a view to preventive measures, that we should know everything about the duration of the incubatory period.

In the Dog, Lafosse states that the shortest authenticated

* In illustration of this fact, I may adduce the following incidents related by Blaine. He says: "I was requested by a gentleman residing in Wimpole Street, to examine a dog, which I at once pronounced rabid; on which he promptly informed me that if the dog was so, he certainly must have become so without infection (which he knew was in direct opposition to my opinion): for that this dog, which was a very great favourite, had never, for many months, been out of doors alone, nor, indeed, at any time out of the sight of either himself or his valet, who was also attached to the dog, and had the express care of him when his master was absent. As, therefore, neither of them had ever seen him bitten, they were positive on the subject. Anxious to arrive at the truth where so important a matter was concerned, I commenced a close examination of the other servants; and it was at length remembered by the footman that one morning, when the master's bell rang for the valet to take this dog from the bedroom, as he was accustomed to do, his absence occasioned the footman to answer it; and this man distinctly recollected the dog accompanying him to the street door, and also that, while engaged in receiving a message brought, he as distinctly remembered that the dog went a little way into the street, and was suddenly attacked by another that passed, seemingly without an owner. Here was an explanation of the apparent difficulty: this passing dog, there is little reason to doubt, was rabid, and, pursuing the usual march of mischief, he bit the favourite. Another case, even more confirmatory of the possibility of becoming mistaken on this subject, is that of a Newfoundland dog, which was constantly chained to his kennel during the day, and suffered to be at large during the night within an enclosed yard. This dog became rabid, and as no dog was known to have had access to the yard, it seemed to be an established certainty in the mind of his owner that he *generated* the disease *spontaneously*. This case I also sifted with great perseverance, to elicit the truth, which was this,—that the gardener to the family remembered, one night in bed, hearing an unusual noise, as though the Newfoundland dog was quarrelling with another, but which from the dog's confined situation, made him believe was impossible, and he therefore took no notice of the subject. He also recollected that about this time marks of a dog appeared in his garden, which, on account of the height of the wall, surprised him; and he further remembered that remains of hair were discovered on the wall which separated the garden from the yard where the dog was confined, but which circumstances, until strict inquiry was made, had excited no attention. About the same time the neighbourhood, it appeared, had been alarmed by the absence of a large dog belonging to one of the inhabitants, which had escaped from confinement during the night, evidently under symptoms of disease. Here also a ready solution of the difficulty occurred."

period that occurred in his experience was 7 days, and the longest 155 days. Röll gives, for the same animal, from 3 to 6, and rarely from 7 to 10 weeks. Blaine asserts that the majority of cases occur between the third and seventh week, though some are protracted to three, four, or even a greater number of months. A week was the shortest period he had noted. Youatt has known instances in which the first symptoms have only become manifest after from 5 to 7 months, and he never knew of a case occurring before 17 days intervening. Other authorities have related cases in which the disease was developed within from 3 to 10 days after contamination. Of 9 cases which Peuch could rely upon, the symptoms appeared after the bite, in each, at an interval of 95, 88, 35, 26, 24, 22, 18, 15, and 10 days respectively.

In 1863, Renault reported that of 68 dogs inoculcated experimentally or bitten, the malady was developed in :—

1	from the	5th	to the	10th	day.	7	from the	45th	to the	50th	day.
4	„	10th	„	15th	„	2	„	50th	„	55th	„
6	„	15th	„	20th	„	2	„	55th	„	60th	„
5	„	20th	„	25th	„	4	„	60th	„	65th	„
9	„	25th	„	30th	„	1	„	65th	„	70th	„
10	„	30th	„	35th	„	4	„	70th	„	75th	„
2	„	35th	„	40th	„	2	„	80th	„	90th	„
8	„	40th	„	45th	„	1	„	100th	„	118th	„

In Saint-Cyr's 87 cases of confirmed rabies in 1865, there were only 26 the date of whose inoculation could be positively ascertained. In these the latent period was :—

Cases.	Days.	Cases.	Days.
1	16	1	36
1	18	1	38
3	21	1	41
2	24	2	50
1	30	2	60
1	31	1	62
2	32	1	86
1	33	2	90 to 100
1	35	2	105 to 115

Bouley has known instances in which the latent period was

twelve days and seven months, though they were rare; it was usually from six to twelve weeks.

According to Haubner, in 200 cases the appearance of the disease within 2 months was 83 per cent.; 3 months, 16 per cent.; 4 months, 1 per cent. He mentions an instance in which the incubatory period was from 7 to 8 months, and another in which it was 14 months. He gives an average of 3 months.

On the 8th of June, 1791, the man who slept in the kennel, and who had the charge of Earl Fitzwilliam's foxhounds, was unusually disturbed during the night by the hounds fighting. He got up several times to quiet them, but always found the same hound quarrelling. He was induced, in consequence, to notice this animal, and finding it stupid and pugnacious, he confined it by itself. The other hounds were quiet the remainder of the night. At the end of the third day after this occurrence the dog became quite rabid, and on the fifth day it died. Preparations were made for confining forty-two couple of hounds separately. Six of these became rabid in the following order: the first on July 1st; the second on August 3rd; the third on September 3rd; the fourth on September 4th; the fifth on November 10th; and the sixth on December 8th. In the Albrighton kennels, the latent term was from two to five weeks.

From these statistics and facts, it will be seen that nothing can be said with certainty, or in a positive manner, as to the length of the interval which elapses between the receipt of the injury and the appearance of rabies; and that it is therefore hazardous to say, when a dog has been wounded by one that is rabid, at what period it may be considered safe from an attack of the disease, as there are no reliable limits to this latent period.* Young dogs are sooner affected than old ones.

* Sir William Maxwell, of Monreith, in giving me the history of the outbreak of rabies among his hounds already alluded to (p. 45), refers to an instance in which the malady appeared in a dog, "Frank," much beyond the ordinary

With the CAT the incubation is said to be from 2 to 4 weeks.

In the HORSE it varies from 15 days to more than 2 months, according to Röll; other authorities state that rabies does not appear in this animal before 9 weeks. Blaine was of opinion that the average time is the same as in the dog. Youatt speaks of a case occurring 4 months after inoculation. Haubner, in 40 cases, gives the latent period after 3 months as 15 per cent.; of these 15 extended to 9 months, and 1 even to 15 months. Peyronie gives a minimum of 15, and a maximum of 74 days; and Lafosse speaks of 72, and even 92 days' incubation in this animal. There is a very interesting case recorded in the *Lyons Veterinary Journal* for 1869 (p. 541), of a horse that was bitten in the nose by a bull-dog. In an hour and a

---

period of latency. I make no apology for giving the interesting account of this case in his own words. Speaking of the entire disappearance of the contagion from the county with the destruction of the infected animals in his kennels, he writes: "Among the survivors was one—a magnificent dog of the St. John's breed, with a close, thick coat, strong and active as a panther, as intelligent as he was handsome, and the terror of all poachers and trespassers. He never was in the kennel, and one of his characteristics was, that though treating us all with dignified urbanity, he never condescended to any familiarity with any one but his own master, the head gamekeeper. To me a slight quiver of the tip of his tail and a look of kindly recognition in the eye, was all the notice he ever gave. *Fully eleven months* after the last case of rabies I have mentioned, I walked with a friend past the gamekeeper's house, and stopped to speak to him as he stood at the door, with his dog "Frank" in close attendance at his heel. Suddenly Frank left him and came over to me, and began licking my hand with a hot, dry tongue—laying on with all his force, as if he would take the skin off. The keeper called him away, but he always returned, and as we moved on seemed inclined to follow us. I ordered them to look to him; this departure from his usual habits striking me forcibly. Next morning I had a message from the keeper asking for authority to destroy Frank, as he was unmistakably mad "just like the others." However, though it would have been merciful to the poor dog, yet it seemed desirable from the circumstances to allow the disease to run its course, and so ascertain its identity. A frightful business it was, *but no hydrophobia* as long as the poor beast could lap; on the contrary, everything of liquid about the place he laid his tongue in. He died on the fifth day. . . . . It seems a subject of grave inquiry whether Frank had carried the virus for eleven months before it incubated into the fearful vigour of the disease, or whether such virus could have existed in any form about fragments gnawed by the previous victims and raked up by him afterwards; or what theory to adopt to account for his taking the disease so long after it had totally ceased in the district: which, by-the-bye, being a peninsula leading to nowhere but the sea, no passing mad dog could have escaped notice."

half after the injury, which was inflicted on the 25th March, the wounds were cauterized by the red-hot iron at the Veterinary School in that city; and the animal continued apparently quite well, and performed its usual work until the 30th May, when the first symptoms showed themselves.

M. Bouley refers to four horses admitted to the Alfort School in 1862, in which the disease appeared from 8 to 12 weeks after the bites were inflicted. Boudin mentions an instance in which a mad dog, on the 8th July, 1849, bit a man, three horses, a cow, and three pigs: all of which were successively affected with the disease during that year, with the exception of one of the horses, in which it did not appear until 26th September, 1850—an incubation of 14 months. This period is so extraordinarily protracted, that it might be questioned whether the horse had not been bitten again in the interval.

In the Ox, Röll gives the latent stage at from nine days to several months, and even more than a year, according to his authorities. Young animals are usually affected about the third or fourth week after inoculation. Blaine and Youatt think it is much the same as in horses and dogs. In England several cases are recorded in which this period averaged about two months. In one case death occurred in twenty-one days.

Haubner, from the statistics of 234 cases, states that 10 per cent. occurred after 3 months; 8 per cent. after 4 months; the last extending to 9 months. He, however, speaks of instances in which the incubation was prolonged up to the end of the year, 2 months beyond this, and even to 2½ years.

For the Sheep and Goat, Vatel has stated the time of incubation for the first-named animal to be 74 days; and Röll gives from several days to several months, but ordinarily from 2 to 4 weeks. During the present epizoöty in Lancashire, a sheep died from the disease within 14 days after the injury. In 180 rabid sheep, Haubner found the latent stage to have been over one month in 8 per cent.; two months, 18 per cent.; up to 68 days, 2 per cent. Pigs, according to the last-named authority, have a period of from 9 days to several weeks or months. Thorel speaks of 49 days; and Gervi affirms that he has known it extend in this creature to two years, but this is very doubtful. Haubner gives this period as less than two months; but Bénion says it never exceeds eight days.* The malady usually shows itself in the pig, I believe, about the fourth week.

Spinola mentions a noteworthy circumstance in connection with rabies in animals. He states that gestation appears to prolong the duration of incubation, and that all the long-deferred cases which he knew of occurred in cows with calf; in these circumstances the disease did not usually appear until calving time was over. This would be a curious feature in the malady if it should be further confirmed by other observers. But doubts may be entertained as to the circumstance being general. During the present epizoöty in Lancashire, we find in the *Veterinarian* for March, 1869, two cases of rabies in pregnant heifers reported by Mr. Worthington, of Wigan. Both of these animals died—one in 21 days after being bitten—without aborting or calving.

In MAN, the time that elapses between the deposition of the virus in the wound and the announcement of the earliest signs of its constitutional effects, has been fixed at wide intervals, and there does not appear to be the same amount of certainty as to the limit which is observed in the lower animals.

Romberg made an analysis of sixty authentic observations, and found that the shortest period of incubation was fifteen days, and the most extended from seven to nine months: the average period being from four to seven weeks.

In this country, the majority of cases have shown this interval to be from thirty to fifty-nine days. John Hunter says the longest period is seventeen months.

According to Tardieu, in 26 cases it was less than a month; in 93 cases, from one to three months; in 19 cases, from three

* "Traité de l'Elevage et des Maladies du Porc," Paris, 1872, p. 270.

to six months; and in 9 cases from six to twelve months. In 87 undoubted cases, the period was a month for 17; one to three months for 57; three to six months for 6; and six to twelve months for the other 6. This observer also states that it is shorter in young people than in adults or the aged. In the majority of cases occurring in children aged from two to ten years, the period was reduced to a month, and even to from twenty-five to twenty-eight days in those aged two and a-half, seven, and ten or eleven years. This was a constant feature.

In the above 147 cases of hydrophobia, this authority found the incubatory period then to be—

1 month in	26 cases.
1 to 3 months in	93 „
3 to 6 „	19 „
6 to 12 „	9 „

The period also appears to have been brief as the patients were young, being as low as twenty-four days in a child two and a-half years old.

Trousseau says that the incubation may vary from a few days to a year.

Boudin states that, in 69 cases, there was an incubation of less than a month in 14; from one to three months in 41; from three to six months in 8; and six to twelve months in 6.

In 224 cases also noted in France, it was less than a month in 40; from one to three months in 143; from three to six months in 30; and from six to twelve months in 11 cases.

In Algiers, hydrophobia has been found to vary in its incubatory stage from twenty to two hundred days; an exceptional case is mentioned as occurring in nine hundred days after the infliction of the injury; but the mean duration of the latent period, according to the result of Roucher's analysis, has been fifty-one days; its ordinary minimum, thirty days; and maximum, three months. Other Algerian authorities assert that it is not so long, the mean period being thirty or forty days.

Bouley mentions that out of the 129 fatal cases already referred to, the period of incubation is given in 106; and it results from the information furnished, that it is during the sixty days following the bite of the dog that the manifestations of hydrophobia have been most numerous—73 in the 106 occurring during this period. The remaining 33 cases are dispersed in the following days up to the 240th day—or a period of exactly eight months; but they gradually become less numerous, so that beyond the hundredth day the cases are only represented by the figures 1 and 2. At the eighth month there was only one case.

From these statistics Bouley concludes, that after a bite from a rabid dog, the chances of escape from hydrophobia augment considerably when two months have passed without any symptom of the malady appearing, and that beyond the ninetieth day, the probability is in favour of complete immunity. But he adds that beyond this period the danger has not entirely passed away, and those who have submitted to virulent bites cannot be altogether re-assured; though their future prospects become less and less sombre, and the victims to these injuries, as well as their friends, may reasonably entertain sanguine hopes of safety. In previous inquiries it had been established that the duration of the incubatory period was brief in proportion as the patient was young. The results furnished by his investigation are confirmative of those derived from the preceding statistics. In comparing the series of periods of incubation with each other—from three to twenty years on the one side, and from twenty to seventy-two on the opposite—for the first there was a mean period of forty-four days, and for the other of seventy-five days—a sensible difference, and one which has a great interest with regard to prognosticating the possible consequences of bites from mad animals in the first period of life.

The limits at which hydrophobia has appeared in man after the bite of a mad animal are very wide, and in some instances almost, if not quite, incredible. For instance, Haguenot, citing Sauvages as the authority, gives the history of a peasant who was suffering from the most urgent symptoms of hydrophobia on the third day after he had been bitten by a mad wolf. Troilliet even quotes instances in which the characteristic symptoms appeared as early as the day following the injury, and others on the eighth day. Sidey mentions their appearance on the twelfth day.

The other extreme has furnished still more startling cases. Chirac describes the case of a merchant who was bitten by a rabid dog at Montpellier, afterwards resided ten years in Holland, and was only attacked by hydrophobia on his return to France, when he learnt that a brother cadet, who was bitten at the same time by the same animal, had died of the disease.

Finco, of Padua, gives an instance, in an Italian medical journal, of a young woman who became affected with hydrophobia fourteen years after receiving a wound from a rabid dog. In the "Transactions of the Vienna Medical Association," Hassinger records a case in which the incubatory stage extended over two years. And Mr. Thomson mentions the case of a lad eighteen years of age, who had been twenty-five months in close confinement in prison, and of course during that time had not been exposed to the bite of any animal. Seven years before his admission, he had been severely bitten in the right hip by a dog, and the scar was still apparent. During the whole period he was under observation he was sullen, gloomy, and reserved, and was never known to look any person in the face to whom he spoke. Death occurred after a three days' illness, during which "the most decided symptoms of hydrophobia were manifested."* On the 15th May, 1854, a case was admitted into Guy's Hospital, in which

* Aitken, *Op. cit.*, p. 719. *Lancet*, vol. i.

hydrophobia appeared to have been developed five years after the bite was inflicted.*

In the daily papers for January 6, 1872, there appeared a notice of a boy, fourteen years of age, who died at Nottingham from hydrophobia, induced by a bite on the eyebrow from a dog which had bitten his father at the same time; the latter had perished of the disease seven months before.

In 1831, Trousseau saw a young man suffering from hydrophobia, who had been bitten by a cat seven or eight months previously; the animal, immediately after inflicting the injury, disappeared from the house and had not afterwards returned.

The cases in which the incubatory stage has been so greatly prolonged, while they have been discredited by some of the best authorities, yet are in some instances vouched for by men who would not allow themselves to be deceived, if possible; and it would be injudicious to ignore the lesson they inculcate, with respect to adopting every precaution likely to avert the appearance of the disease. At the same time, we are ready to agree with Trousseau, that "the disease generally shows itself (in man) in from one to three months after the infliction of the bite. The cases are rare in which it has developed itself after three months, and still more rare in which it came on from the sixth to the twelfth month; and one is almost authorised, from the statistical observations that have been made, to question the authenticity of the cases in which the disease set in a year after the person had been bitten. *A fortiori*, must one regard with suspicion those instances of the disease in which the incubation is stated to have been more prolonged. These latter may not have been cases of true rabies, but of nervous hydrophobia, in which the mere recollection of this awful complaint sufficed to bring on a more or less prolonged dysphagia (choking, difficulty of swallowing)."

* Aitken, *Op. cit.*, p. 720. *Medical Times*, 1854.

SYMPTOMS.

The virulent germs having fructified under the influence of favourable circumstances, and being now ready to commence the series of pathological changes which mark the course of the disease, the latent period comes to an end, and the operation of the virus on the organism is betrayed by certain signs or indications to which have been given the name of "symptoms."

The symptoms of rabies in the different creatures attacked by it are marked by some striking peculiarities, which give a particularly distinctive character to the malady; while the symptoms themselves, in whatever species of animal they may be manifested, have the greatest analogy, and in each are characteristic of the affection to an eminent degree: the only differences presented in the various classes being chiefly due to their dissimilarity in organisation, nature, and habits—dissimilarities which more or less influence the development and course of the symptom in every malady.

A knowledge of the symptoms of rabies in all the domesticated animals is of the highest importance; but for the dog it is more essential than for any other creature, as it is most susceptible to attacks of the disease, is far more frequently affected than any other animal, and is always with us—the pet and playmate of our families, the constant companion of ourselves, and the associate of other creatures. As the prompt recognition of the presence of the malady in its earliest phase may be the means of preventing alarm, or obviating an outbreak of the pest over a wide district, and may be useful in averting the harassing anxiety and dread which follows the infliction of a bite from a suspected animal, or may even be serviceable in saving the lives of our fellow-creatures, too much stress cannot be laid upon the urgent necessity there exists for every one who keeps a dog, or has anything to do with animals, becoming acquainted with those signs which indicate the presence of madness; for on the measures devised by this acquaintance really depends the prevention of the disease. If, in ordinary maladies, prevention is better than cure, then in this perhaps most terrible of all afflictions, for which there is no relief, and to be affected with which is to be doomed to a certain and horrible death, any known means by which it may be hindered from reaching ourselves or other creatures, must surely command the most earnest attention and solicitude.

For this reason, we will commence our description of the symptoms of the disease as they are manifested in those animals which transmit the contagion to our own species; and if our enumeration of these appears to be too detailed and minute, it must be ascribed to our extreme anxiety that nothing should be omitted likely to lead to the early detection of the malady, with the view to prevent alarm and loss of life.

After these, the symptoms of hydrophobia in man will merit description, if only for the purpose of comparison; lastly, those offered by other creatures when affected with rabies will be alluded to.

Symptoms in the Dog.

Before commencing a description of the symptoms of rabies in the dog, it may be as well to state that there is in reality no appreciable difference between those presented in cases in which the disease has been communicated, and those in which it is spontaneous. The only distinction worthy of notice is one which is sometimes dependent upon the condition of the wound in communicated rabies, and has reference to what has already been mentioned with regard to the localisation of the virus at the seat of its introduction. It has been frequently stated that the wounds inflicted by a rabid animal were difficult to heal, and that they always ulcerated when the disease was about to appear; but there seems to be some exaggeration in these statements. It is only when the wounds are deep and lacerated that they are slow to cicatrise, but in this respect they do not differ from similar injuries inflicted by non-rabid animals; when they are simple and superficial, they are as readily repaired as on ordinary occasions.

But, as in mankind, it has been frequently observed that in animals which were about to exhibit the symptoms of rabies, due to a wound, there has appeared to be an irresistible tendency to scratch, rub, lick, or even gnaw the spot where inoculation took place, as if it were the seat of annoying pruritis or hyperæsthesia; and in consequence of this disturbance, the part becomes swollen, the cicatrix is not unusually torn open, and there results a violet-coloured wound which increases in size until the animal dies. This is most frequently observed in swine.

These phenomena pertaining to communicated rabies are all the more surprising when we see them produced in animals two or three months after the infliction of the virulent wound, and after a solid cicatrix has been formed; though it is less astonishing and more frequent to find them appear within from fifteen days to a month after the receipt of the injury.

Lafosse asserts that these phenomena are more frequently absent than present; he having observed them in only one-third of the cases of communicated rabies that came under his observation.

Otherwise, in transmitted and spontaneous rabies the symptoms may be said to be identical.

The disease has been divided into three stages, or periods, and has also sometimes been described as presenting itself in two or three forms, according to the peculiarities in the symptoms. But, as a rule, one period of the malady does not pass suddenly into another, but by an almost imperceptible transition; and the forms do not differ essentially from each other, but appear merely to constitute varieties of the same disease, due to the natural disposition of the animal, or other modifying circumstances. These forms have been designated "true rabies" (*rage vrai, rasendi wuth*), "dumb rabies" (*rage mue, stille wuth*), and "tranquil rabies" (*rage tranquille*), the latter designation given by Berndt to a peculiar, but, it would appear, a well-marked variety.

It is a great and dangerous error to suppose that the disease commences with signs of raging madness, and that the earliest phase of the malady is ushered in with fury and destruction. The first perceptible or initial symptoms of rabies in the dog are related to its habits. A change is observed in the animal's aspect, behaviour, and external characteristics. The habits of the creature are anomalous and strange. It becomes dull, gloomy, and taciturn; seeks to isolate itself, and chooses solitude and obscurity—hiding in out-of-the-way places, or retiring below chairs and other pieces of furniture; whereas in health it may have been lively, good-natured, and sociable. But in its retirement it cannot rest; it is uneasy and fidgety, and betrays an unmistakable state of *malaise;* no sooner has it lain down and gathered itself together in the usual fashion of a dog reposing, than all at once it jumps up in an agitated manner, walks hither and thither several times, again lies down and assumes a sleeping attitude, but has only maintained it for a few minutes when it is once more moving about, "seeking rest but finding none." Then it retires to its obscure corner—to the deepest recess it can find—and huddles itself up in a heap, with its head concealed beneath its chest and its fore paws. This state of continual agitation and inquietude is in striking contrast with its ordinary habits, and should therefore attract the attention of mindful people. Not unfrequently there are a few moments when the creature appears more lively than usual, and displays an extraordinary amount of affection. Sometimes in pet dogs there is evinced a disposition to gather up small objects, such as straws, thread, bits of wood, &c., which are industriously picked up and carried away. A tendency to lick anything cold, as iron, stones, &c., is also observed in many instances; even the cold nose of another dog will be favoured with this mark of attention; and it is not uncommon to observe an inclination to lick other animals. Sexual excitement is also frequently an early symptom, and is likewise present, at times, in other creatures when rabid.

At this period no propensity to bite is observed; the animal is docile with its master, and obeys his voice, though not so readily as before, nor with the same pleased countenance. If it shakes its tail, the act is more slowly performed than usual, and there is something strange in the expression of its face; the voice of its master can scarcely change it for a few seconds from a sullen gloominess to its ordinary animated aspect; and when no longer influenced by the familiar talk or presence, it returns to its sad thoughts, for—as has been well and truthfully said by Bouley—"the dog thinks and has its own ideas, which, for dogs' ideas, are, nevertheless, from its point of view, very good ideas when it is well."

These initial symptoms gradually become more marked; the restlessness and agitation increase; if on straw, the dog scatters and pulls it about with its paws, and if in a room, it scratches and tumbles the cushions or rugs on which it ordinarily lies; and nowhere can it find a suitable place for repose, but is incessantly on the move, rambling about, scratching the ground, snuffing in corners and at the doors, as if on the scent, or seeking for something.

With this restlessness there is manifested a curious group of symptoms due to some defect or aberration in mind, vision, hearing, or feeling, which causes the animal to indulge in strange movements, as if it were affected by some imaginary influences, or subject to hallucinations. Its brain is in a morbid condition, and its mind evidently haunted by phantoms and horrid fancies. When not excited by any external cause, and its movements are observed in silence, the poor creature will remain for a brief period perfectly still and attentive, as if watching something, or following the movements of some creature on the wall; then suddenly it will dart forward and bite at the vacant air, as if it were pursuing some annoying object, or as if it tried to seize a fly.* At another time it throws itself yelling and furious against the wall, as if it heard threatening noises on the other side, or as if enemies were before it, and it must chase and injure them.

But though apparently so ready and so determined to employ its teeth against imaginary foes, and to resort to aggressive movements which appear to be quite under the influence of the will, the unfortunate beast is still docile and submissive. To rouse it out of its pitiful frenzy, it is only necessary that it should hear its master's voice calling it by name; then the hideous phantom vanishes at once, and the dog runs to receive the caress it loves so well, with all its old expression of attachment and regard.

It cannot be too much or too strongly insisted upon, that, at the initial period of the disease, the dog is not really furious

* "In 1845," says M. Dulac, of Bordeaux, "I was asked to see a small English-bred dog, which was tied by a slender cord in a room where two children were at play. It was feared the animal was mad, as it had bitten an old woman two days before, and that morning it had attacked several dogs. Naturally it was excessively quiet and affectionate. When I entered the room, it was lying on a chair, and *it stared at me with a strange, indefinable look, expressive at once of sadness and fury*, and this gaze it maintained for nearly ten minutes; then it turned away its head, closed its eyes, and appeared sleepy. Soon after the head drooped over the chair and dragged the body to the ground, where it lay huddled up, as if it tried to reduce itself to the smallest possible volume. It only remained an instant in this situation when it seemed to rouse up, opened its eyes, and made several dashes towards the wall. Its owner said to me that it was chasing flies. Being again placed on the chair, it went through the same performance of slipping off it on to the floor. Within half-an-hour, this was repeated eight times: the animal roused out of its lethargy, and sprang at the wall as if it tried to seize some object within its reach." The sight of another dog which was brought before it brought on a paroxysm of rage, and it gave out a rabid howl, which left no doubt as to its condition; it was then killed.

by his presence or voice. This influence, by maintaining a kind of fascination over the animal, keeps the more ferocious symptoms of the disease in abeyance, and thus averts dangerous consequences. The sentiment of submission and attachment remains superior to the rabid instinct, and the animal continues quiet, even when strangers are present. Instances have been known in which dogs in the first stage of the disease have lived in their master's house, moved about without restriction, slept in the room and even on the bed, without doing any injury to the members of the family, or even to the children, who may have frolicked with it, and perhaps annoyed it. This good behaviour has continued for one, two, or three days, and even for a period sufficiently long for the disease to have reached its climax. Bouley has seen rabid dogs in the hospital court at Alfort which were not muzzled, but merely held by a leash; and yet, owing to their master's presence, they remained completely inoffensive in the midst of the crowd surrounding them: only manifesting their rabidity after being separated from the person who brought them.

It seems strange that even during the paroxysms of rabies, when the dog is a prey to the agony of furious madness, the voice of its master has a magical influence in mitigating the delirium: it is sometimes sufficient that a few words should be spoken to bring about a brief interval of calmness in the middle of a fit, and the tail will then be freely moved from side to side in token of recognition; while a gleam of the affectionate light which used to shine before the advent of the horrid disease will for an instant lighten up the sombre and haggard-looking eye. Even when the dog has escaped from all control, and wanders erratically abroad, ferocious and restless, and haunted by horrid phantoms, the well-known voice has yet power to attract the attention of the poor demented creature, and it will respond to its name and approach its owner as submissively, sometimes, as in health. "Dispersed by the magical influence of the familiar voice, all these dreadful objects vanish, and the

health, is in as great danger as if the injury had been inflicted when the animal was really diseased.* On the other hand, if a sick dog can drink it is pronounced free from madness. So universal is this opinion, even among those who ought to know better, that we frequently meet with instances where foolish credulity has occasioned serious mischief. Blaine tells us of Dr. H., an eminent London physician, who, on being consulted by a person actually bitten by a mad dog, immediately inquired whether the animal could drink; and on being informed that it was able to do so, he peremptorily pronounced that the animal could not be mad, and proceeded to recommend that no precautions whatever should be adopted. Had this advice been followed, three persons might have lost their lives; but, fortunately for them, his opinion was not received as worthy of confidence, and Blaine attended to the wounds. In five weeks an unfortunate spaniel, which had been bitten by this dog, became rabid, and in six weeks a horse, also wounded by it, was affected. Dr. Gillman relates a case of hydrophobia where a fatal security had been indulged in, owing to the fact that the dog which inflicted the wound ate and drank during its illness.† Mr. Youatt had a dog brought to him which was unquestionably rabid. The owner, a poor woman, had her hands excoriated by an eruption, and these hands the dog had

* This notion is so absurd that it scarcely deserves alluding to, were it not attended with inconvenient results and the sacrifice of the life of the poor dog, which may be in perfect health when it chances to inflict the bite. To say that hydrophobia will attack the wounded individual, should the animal at any future time become rabid, is just as reasonable as to say that we are liable to receive the infection of small-pox, typhus, or any other contagious malady from a person we have to-day shaken hands with, should he at any future time become affected with either of these diseases. It would be far more satisfactory, if there was any doubt as to the condition of the animal, to keep it secured and under observation. A few days would decide whether or not it was rabid when it inflicted the injury; and if the result proved the latter, then the mind of the wounded person and his friends would be relieved from the anxiety and dread of perhaps many months' duration, and the animal's life would be spared; even if he dog happened to be mad, no further harm could result, and every precaution would, in the interval, have been adopted to prevent infection.

† "A Dissertation on the Bite of a Rabid Animal."

repeatedly licked during its illness. On Mr. Youatt's intimation that it was necessary she should adopt some precaution, she applied to a medical gentleman, who assured her that if the dog attempted to drink it was not mad, and no precautions were necessary.

Quite recently, a professed sportsman — Grantley F. Berkeley—in several letters to the *Times* newspaper, persistently attempted to perpetuate this most dangerous fallacy, by asserting that hydrophobia was present in the dog, and adding (December 16, 1871): "Let all who read this believe me when I say, no hydrophobic dog will either approach to or lap water; the very sight of it will put him in convulsions." It was only this writer's inexperience of the malady that prompted him to emit such an absurd opinion, for he elsewhere *naïvely* confesses that, "I have in all my experience—over fifty years —known of but one case of hydrophobia." It is surely more than a blunder to give an opinion on such a subject, by which the lives of human beings may be sacrificed, without apparently the slightest proof or knowledge to support it!

It is not true that a rabid dog is hydrophobous; water does not inspire it with fear or horror, and when it is put before the animal it does not produce aversion; from the commencement to the termination of the disease there is no antipathy to water. The many hundreds of rabid dogs seen by Blaine, Youatt, and others, did not evince any marked aversion to that fluid. On the contrary, the animal is generally thirsty; and if water be offered, it will lap it up with avidity, and will always swallow it at the commencement of the disease. When, at a later period, the constriction about the throat—symptomatic of the malady—renders swallowing difficult, it does not the less endeavour to drink, and the lappings are as frequent and prolonged as deglutition is retarded. Even then we see the suffering creature in despair plunge its entire muzzle into the vessel and gulp at the water, as if determined to overcome the convulsive closure of its throat by forcing down the fluid.

Tantalus could not experience a greater torment with regard to water than does the unlucky dog.

So little dread have the canine species of water, that they will ford streams and swim rivers; and when in the ferocious stage of the malady, they will even do this in order to attack other creatures on the opposite bank. The experience of more than twenty-five years did not, according to Mr. Blaine, afford an instance in which anything like a dread of water was manifested, or in which a spasm followed attempts to swallow it.

Every observer and writer on the malady testifies to the correctness of this statement; and innumerable instances might be adduced in which rabid dogs, from whose bites people and animals afterwards perished, had no fear of water, but swallowed it greedily. Gillman gives many examples, and we have already alluded to some. In John Hunter's celebrated case of hydrophobia in the boy Rowley, the dog ate and drank with voracity; and in another case reported in the *Edinburgh Medical and Surgical Journal* for 1808, a man was bitten by a dog which "ate and drank heartily, showed no signs of indisposition, hunted as usual," until it began to snap at dogs and was destroyed. M. Pierquin, in "De la Folie des Animaux," published not long ago, relates the case of a lady who owned a greyhound, which was in the habit of sleeping on her bed. One morning she discovered that it had torn and gnawed the coverlet, and the same day *it was observed to drink a larger quantity of water than usual*, though it ate little. Alarmed by this change in its conduct, the lady consulted a veterinary surgeon, who did not find anything to cause anxiety. The next day, when she offered it some food, it wounded her slightly at the end of the finger, near the nail. This occurred on December 26. On the following day it died, "and it had never ceased," says M. Pierquin, "to drink very copiously of water until the end." On February 4, in the succeeding year, the unfortunate woman was seized with hydrophobia, and on the 7th died.

M. Duluc, veterinary surgeon of Bordeaux, was called in one day to see a bitch that had returned home covered with mud and prostrated with fatigue, after running about for twenty-four hours and attacking every dog it met: though fortunately without doing them harm, as it was muzzled. It obeyed the voice of its master, and as soon as he spoke it looked anxious; its eyes were fixed on his, and it continued quiet, though its tail remained motionless between its legs. This animal had a puppy two months old, which M. Duluc placed before it; it made no opposition to its taking the teat, but a moment afterwards it pushed it away with its paws; though without attempting to bite it, and making only a kind of growl. Several times the puppy tried to retake the teat, but it was always repulsed in the same manner. For several days this bitch had eaten less than usual, *but it drank* as much as before. The next day it came before its master, who took off its muzzle and offered it water. *It lapped for a long time and drank with avidity.* Reassured by this that it was not hydrophobic, he thought he might allow it to run at large in the garden without danger. No sooner was it untied than it ran about in a violent manner, uttering most unusual sounds. Frightened by this extraordinary behaviour, he called it to him, and it obeyed, though with a certain amount of hesitation; he immediately tied it up, and had scarcely done so when a duck passed within reach of its chain; this it seized furiously, and crushed its foot. Afterwards it flew at a mare that a servant had brought too near it, and bit it severely in the upper lip. No doubt now existing as to the nature of the malady, the dog was sacrificed, as well as its progeny; and although the mare's lip was deeply cauterised three hours after the accident, it became rabid in twenty-five days.

A writer in *Land and Water*, for December 23, 1871 ("Salopiensis"), speaks of having had his pack of foxhounds twice decimated by rabies within the last few years, and adds: "I never saw one (hound) so attacked that exhibited any fear of water." Another writer in the same journal (J. W. Hill, M.R.C.V.S., Wolverhampton) says: "In the recent dumb madness (at Albrighton), I have seen the hounds bury their muzzles up to the eyes in water, as if to quench their insatiable thirst, but paralysis prevented their swallowing any of the liquid." Mr. Henderson, in his letter to the *Times* for December 13, mentions that the first hound of the Durham county pack attacked with rabies, crossed a brook without reluctance and lapped water freely. "Two days later I saw him lap broth when in a condition so mad, that he flew at any one coming near the door of the kennel in which he was confined."

The idea that dogs are not rabid when they can drink and do not seem afraid of water is, therefore, utterly erroneous, and would appear to owe its origin to the presence of hydrophobia in man, which, as we shall see hereafter, is a marked symptom in him. Therefore, beware of a sick dog even when it drinks with avidity, for an aversion to water in rabies does not exist at any period of the disease.*

* "Parlons maintenant de l'*hydrophobie*. Nous y sommes aussi bien naturellement conduits par l'une des circonstances de la relation faite plus haut. 'Comment pouvions-nous soupçonner la rage chez notre chien?' nous disaient les personnes qui conduisaient l'animal dont il vient d'être question; 'il buvait sans difficulté, et allait souvent boire!' Le préjugé de l'hydrophobie est l'un des plus dangereux qui règne à l'égard de la rage canine; et l'on peut dire que le mot *hydrophobie*, qui s'est peu à peu substitué, même dans le langage usuel, à celui de *rage*, est une des plus détestables inventions du néologisme, parce que cette invention a été fertile pour l'espèce humaine en une multitude de désastres. C'est que, en effet, ce mot implique une idée aujourd'hui profondément ancrée dans l'opinion du public, bien qu'elle soit radicalement fausse, et démontrée fausse par les faits de tous les jours. De par le nom grec imposé à la rage, un chien enragé doit *avoir horreur de l'eau*. Donc, s'il boit, il n'est pas enragé; et partant de ce raisonnement, on ne peut plus logique, un très-grand nombre de personnes s'endorment dans une sécurité trompeuse, à côté de chiens enragés qui vivent avec elles et couchent même sur leur lit. Et cela, parce qu'il a passé par la cervelle de je ne sais quel savant de faire du mot *hydrophobie* le synonyme de celui de *rage* . . . . Le chien enragé n'est pas hydrophobe; il n'a pas horreur de l'eau. Quand on lui donne à boire, il ne recule pas épouvanté. Loin de là: il s'approche du vase; il lappe le liquide avec sa langue; il le déglutit souvent, surtout dans les premières périodes de sa maladie, et lorsque la constriction de sa gorge rend la déglutition difficile, il n'en essaye pas moins de boire, et alors ses lappements sont d'autant plus répétés et prolongés qu'ils demeurent plus

With regard to food, at the commencement of the attack the dog does not usually refuse to eat, and some animals are even voracious to an unusual degree. But in a brief space the appetite for food is modified, and the creature becomes fastidious, eating only what it usually has a special predilection for, and refusing what it used to take without hesitation;. this soon gives place to a most characteristic symptom. Either the appetite has become extremely depraved, or the creature is compelled to submit to a fatal and imperious desire to bite and ingest everything; for it seizes with its teeth, tears, crushes, and finally swallows, substances which are generally indi-

---

inefficaces. Souvent même, en désespoir de cause, on le voit plonger le museau tout entier dans le vase, et mordre, pour ainsi dire, l'eau qu'il ne peut parvenir à pomper suivant le mode physiologique habituel."—*Discourse on Rabies delivered before the Imperial Academy of Medicine by M. Bouley* in 1863.

"L'hydrophobie proprement dite, telle qu'on l'acceptait autrefois comme symptôme de la rage, n'existe pas: au contraire, on remarque que des chiens enragés lèchent leur propre urine, barbotent dans l'eau qu'on leur présente, et même la boivent avidement .... Les chiens enragés supportent également la vue de l'eau et même les arrosements; seulement ceux-ci les excitent fortement. Les exemples des chiens enragés qui ont traversé des eaux courantes ne font pas défaut."—*Röll, op. cit.*, p. 470.

"S'il importe de détruire le préjugé qui consiste à croire que tout carnivore enragé est sans cesse en proie à des accès de fureur, pendant lesquels il chercherait à faire usage de ses armes offensives, il n'est pas moins nécessaire d'extirper l'idée fausse qui attribue à ces animaux une *horreur des liquides* et un *refus obstiné des aliments:* bien des observateurs signalent des cas où, dans le début de la rage, les chiens étaient tourmentés par une soif ardente et buvaient de l'eau avec une extrême avidité. Maintes fois nous avons vu ce fait se produire. Vers le déclin même, la soif ne se calme pas toujours, et le malheureux enragé s'efforce encore, mais en vain, de la satisfaire, en approchant sa gueule du liquide qu'il ne peut plus déglutir, que souvent même il lui est impossible de laper, soit à cause de la paralysie des mâchoires, soit à cause du spasme du pharynx. Il faudrait donc bien se garder d'induire de ce qu'il conserve le désir et la faculté de boire, de ce qu'il n'entre pas en fureur à la vue de l'eau, qu'un animal n'est pas affecté de la rage. Bien souvent nous avons eu à nous féliciter d'avoir résisté aux sollicitations de personnes voulant rentrer en possession de chiens qu'elles avaient confiés à nos soins, et qu'elles s'obstinaient à ne pas croire enragés, parce qu'elles les voyaient boire avec facilité."—*Lafosse*, "Traité de Pathologie Vétérinaire," vol. iii. p. 851.

"Il est désormais acquis à la science, que c'est précisément un signe de la rage lorsque la soif est trop ardente, et que jamais appellation plus fausse, plus absurde, et en même temps plus dangereuse, ne fût appliquée à aucune maladie que celle d'*hydrophobie* à la rage du chien."—*Sanson*, "Le Meilleur Préservatif de la Rage," p. 26.

gestible, and certainly not alimentary. The litter of its kennel, wool from cushions, the cover of the bed on which it sleeps,—if allowed to spend the night with its master,—carpets, stockings, slippers, wood, grass, earth, stones, coal, glass, horse-dung, human excrement,—even its own fæces and urine,—or whatever else may come in its way, are devoured.

At the examination of the body of a dog that had died of rabies, it is so common to find in the stomach a quantity of dissimilar matters on which the teeth have been exercised, that if there was nothing known of the animal's history these would be strong evidence of the presence of the disease.

Therefore, whenever a dog is observed to persist in tearing the carpets, cushions, or other articles in rooms; when it gnaws boards or the wood of its kennel, devours its straw, soil, &c., without exhibiting any tendency to bite people, it ought to be suspected; for these signs are but a prelude to those of a more serious character, and the poor animal is in reality venting that ferocity on inanimate objects which will soon be directed towards everything animated.

It is generally believed that the mad dog slavers or foams abundantly, and that the mouth is always filled with this secretion; when such is not the case, it is imagined that the animal is not rabid. This is another serious error; for the secretion of saliva is not much increased, if at all, until the disease has reached its furious stage, and before this period a dog may be quite mad without foaming or slavering at the mouth. Youatt says there is at first an increased secretion of saliva; but it soon lessens in quantity, becomes thicker, viscid, adhesive, and glutinous; and it adheres to the corners of the mouth, fauces, and teeth. It is at this period that the thirst is so ardent, owing to the inflammation or congestion at the back part of the throat. The dog sometimes furiously attempts to detach the saliva with its paws; and if, after a while, it loses its balance in these attempts and tumbles over, there can no longer be any mistake as to the nature of the malady.

There is another symptom connected with the mouth in that form of the disease called "dumb madness," which might mislead, and in fact has frequently done so. The lower jaw drops, in consequence of paralysis of its muscles, and the mouth remains open. The membrane which lines its interior is dry from the constant current of air passing over it, and assumes a deep red tint; while its surface is covered with brown patches of dust or dried earth, which more especially adhere to the upper surface of the tongue and to the lips.* The membrane lining the mouth sometimes shows cracks, due to its dryness. The strange alteration produced in the dog's physiognomy by its constantly open mouth and the dark colour of its interior, is rendered still more remarkable and characteristic by the dull, sad, or dead expression of the animal's eyes.

In this condition the creature is not very dangerous, because it usually cannot bite if it tried; but the saliva is none the less virulent, and inoculations with it through imprudent handling will be as fatal as if they had been made with the teeth. It is most dangerous in these circumstances to interfere much with the mouth; and it is not unusual for people who do not understand the disease, to imagine there is something lodged about the dog's jaws or throat that prevents the mouth being closed, and to endeavour to relieve the animal by thrusting their

* Mr. Carlisle, the eminent teacher of surgery, writes to Dr. Gillman: "I saw, on July 26th, 1810, a dog which had been bitten fourteen days since by a reputed mad dog. This was the second day of the attack. He was walking loose in a stable, reeled, and seemed feeble; his eyes were bright but not fierce; *his tongue protruded about an inch and a half beyond his lips, as if occasioned by a swelling of the fauces and root of the tongue. The protruded part was dry, and covered with a blackish crust; his lips were covered with dusty dry horse-dung.* He received from my hand a piece of flesh quietly, and turned it about on the ground with his nose as if pleased with it, but was unable to chew or receive it into his mouth. The dog knew his feeders, and answered to their call, looking at them, but not with expressions of pleasure; he had gnawed the wooden stalls. July 27th. Saw the dog again; he was lying on his side, with little use of his hinder limbs, breathing with difficulty; his tongue less protruded and less swelled. He knew his master and *lapped water;* he made several attempts to rise on his legs, and at length succeeded, and ran forward against the wall." The dog died next day.

fingers into its mouth with the intention of removing the obstacle. Should there be any scratch or sore upon the fingers, or should an abrasion take place from contact with the teeth, or through a convulsive effort of the animal to close its jaws, inoculation may take place, and serious consequences follow.*

There is another indication of rabies which is apt to mislead, and which is not unfrequent. This arises from the sensation of constriction and astriction which the animal experiences at the upper part of the throat, under the influence of the rabic spasm, and also in consequence of the aridity of its mouth. The creature acts as if a bone or some foreign body were lodged between its teeth or in its throat, and uses its front paws as if trying to remove the annoyance. This is a very deceptive symptom, and is apt to induce any one witnessing it, and who did not understand its real purport, to venture on giving the animal assistance. This, without due precautions, is even more hazardous than in the other case, as the dog in this condition can bite; and the opposition it offers to the examination of its mouth may cause injury to the hands, and result in inoculation.

Another symptom in the early period of rabies is the appearance of the so-called "lysses," or eruption at each side of the tongue; but this is, according to the testimony of the best observers, if at all present, too fugitive and concealed a feature in the malady to be of any real importance in recognising the presence of the malady.

In addition to these signs furnished by the digestive apparatus at the initial period of the disease, there is another somewhat exceptional one, and which for this reason is perhaps

* Numerous deaths have occurred from hydrophobia through this mistake. A very melancholy instance was that of M. Nicolin, a veterinary surgeon in Lons-le-Saulnier, France, who, believing the owner of a dog that a bone was lodged in the animal's throat, proceeded to remove it without first inquiring into the beast's condition. Either through the paralysed jaw suddenly closing, from the irritation caused by M. Nicolin's manipulations, or through the virulent saliva obtaining access by a sore on the hand, he afterwards became affected with hydrophobia, and of course perished.

more insidious than the others. This is vomiting; and not unfrequently the ejected matters are tinged with blood, or may even be entirely composed of that fluid: which is derived, according to Bouley, from the wounds caused in the lining membrane of the stomach by the hard, sharp-edged substances the animal has swallowed—a symptom which, rare though it be, it is well to associate with the probable existence of rabies in the animal exhibiting it, and to be guarded accordingly.* Indeed, in all internal diseases of the dog, it is prudent for amateurs or unskilled persons to consider the animal as in principle "suspected," and, to avoid danger, to adopt every precaution until it is positively ascertained that rabies is not present.

The blood vomited at the commencement of rabies is said to be derived from wounds and abrasions in the interior of the stomach, due to the foreign substances ingested by the sick animal. This may be true in some cases, though certainly not in all; as the symptom has been observed in dogs whose stomachs did not contain anything likely to produce such injuries, and were even sometimes empty. Besides, this vomiting of blood or a chocolate-coloured fluid is at times noted in human hydrophobic patients, whose appetite is not depraved like the dog's, and who do not swallow straw, stones, glass, &c. When we come to treat of the pathological alterations found in rabid animals, we shall be able to account more satisfactorily for the appearance of this symptom.

The *barking* of the rabid dog is very peculiar, and so characteristic, that to those acquainted with it nothing more is needed

* The necessity for this caution is exemplified in a case that occurred to M. Bouley at Alfort, in 1862. A dog was brought to the clinic of that school, which had, according to the statement of the owner, vomited blood since the previous evening. On seeing the animal, M. Bouley had no suspicion that it was affected with rabies, and merely prescribing an alum potion, ordered it to be confined in one of the kennels. No sooner was it removed from its master's influence, by being shut up in the cage, than it denounced its real morbid condition by unmistakable signs. The pupil charged with its supervision reported the circumstance to the professor, and, most fortunately, the prescription had not been executed; so that the error in diagnosing the disease had not the terrible consequences it might have had.

to indicate the presence of the disease. It is not even necessary to have heard it frequently; for so strong an impression does it make on the mind, that those who have heard it once or twice never forget it or its signification. In health, as is well known, the bark consists of a series of sonorous sounds or cries, each distinct from that which follows, and equal in duration and intensity. In rabies, the voice is frequently changed at an early period of the malady, owing to the alterations occurring in the larynx; and, instead of the sharp succession of clear tones, we have a noise which is neither a bark, howl, growl, nor snarl, but a seemingly curious jumble of all these—the howl being predominant. The tone is hoarse, altered in *timbre*, indistinct, and lower in pitch; a preliminary bark is made in a somewhat elevated tone, and with open mouth; this is immediately succeeded by five, six, or eight decreasing howls, which appear to come from the depths of the throat, the jaws not coming together and closing the mouth during each emission, as in the healthy bark.

The sound of the bark is altogether so peculiar, that it has been likened to that of a cock-crow, and hence experienced French veterinarians say that the rabid dog has "la voix de coq;" others again, as Blaine, have compared it to the "giving tongue" of the old heavy Southern harrier; while others have imagined it to resemble the cough in croup. It is very difficult to express in words the character of the voice in this howling, which is frequently the first indication of the disease; it is emitted when the animal is sitting or standing, and always with the nose elevated, and is usually most frequent at night. To indicate its compass, M. Sanson has had recourse to musical notation, which may give some idea of the three varieties of sounds usually heard.

In the three bars the *C* crotchet represents the bark, which slides up into the howl indicated by the minims *A*, *B*, and *C*—the last, the octave, being incomparably more common than the other two.

These prolonged howlings have something so sinister and lugubrious about them, that they strike those who understand their import with a kind of terror; and it is not improbable that the presentiments of misfortune which, according to popular tradition, are derived from dogs barking at the moon, have had no other origin than the remembrance of the disasters caused by mad dogs, which, some time before showing the furious symptoms of rabies, were wont to exercise their vocal organs during the night in the emission of the doleful sounds that certainly presaged no good to other creatures.

A sudden and strange alteration in the familiar voice of a dog should at once attract attention and elicit inquiry; the rabic cry or howl is a sure warning, and affords just grounds for alarm, as it is one of the precursory symptoms of the furious stage of the disease.

To show the importance of recognising the modified bark of a mad dog, Bouley gives the following authentic anecdote. Some years ago, two veterinary students, returning to the Alfort School about nine o'clock in the evening, heard the howl of a rabid dog proceeding from a house in Charenton. They felt impelled to knock at the door and warn the proprietor of the danger that menaced him; and he, fortunately taking the warning as seriously as it was given, kept the animal, a watch-dog, on the chain during the night, and the next day took it to Alfort. The students had not been deceived, for M. Bouley certified that the dog was mad; and its master could scarcely recover from his astonishment when told so—he could not believe that the creature he held in his hand, and still as docile, affectionate, and obedient as usual, could be attacked by so redoubtable a disease. It was so, nevertheless; and from the time it occupied the cage destined for sick dogs, the symptoms of rabies manifested themselves in the most evident manner.

This dog was very large and powerful, and if it had been detached from the chain, as it was customary for it to be, and had contrived to escape, it might have caused some terrible accidents. Too much praise cannot, therefore, be awarded the two students for their presence of mind and promptitude, by which they in all probability prevented serious mischief.

These rabic howlings are emitted frequently by the majority of mad dogs; others only make them when excited, and in very rare cases the voice is not modified. In dogs affected with that form of the disease termed "dumb madness"—which will be alluded to hereafter—the voice is completely lost from the commencement of the malady, a circumstance to which this form owes its distinctive appellation.

The symptoms which proceed from the sentient faculties in the dog are noteworthy and remarkable. Contrary to what takes place in man in hydrophobia, the dog's sensibility appears to be considerably blunted; and the animal seems to have lost the faculty of expressing, in its own language, the sensations it experiences. The mad dog is mute under the infliction of pain. No matter what amount of suffering it may be subjected to, it never emits the slightest nasal sound—the first expression of complaint in the dog—nor the acute yell by which it betrays the perception of severe torture. Beaten, pricked, wounded, even burned, the mad dog remains silent, though not insensible. The sentiment of preservation still remains; for when the litter upon which it is lying is set on fire, it flies away from it and gathers itself up in a corner to escape the flames. When a bar of red-hot iron is put before it, and, impelled by fury, it flies to bite it, it nevertheless retires from it immediately. A red-hot iron applied to its paws likewise makes it fly. These observations have been made by M. Bouley, who adds, that it is evident in these diverse circumstances that the animal suffers—the expression of its figure proves this—but, notwithstanding, it never gives a cry or moan. If sensibility is not extinct in the mad dog, as is evidenced by the results of the experiments above cited, it is certainly less acute than in ordinary conditions. When the blazing torch has been thrown beneath it, the animal does not move at once, but takes time; so that when it really has decided to escape it is already seriously burned. Certain dogs, though they are exceptions, will not let go the bar of red-hot iron which they have seized between their teeth.

Thus Ellis, in his "Shepherd's Guide," mentions that the grooms in the Godderden kennels held a red-hot poker before a mad dog, which the animal furiously seized, and held in its mouth until it was seriously burned.

It would then appear from these facts, that dogs attacked with rabies do not perceive painful sensations so readily as in health, and this explains why they may wreak their fury sometimes on themselves; for many facts in the history of the disease testify to their insensibility to their own self-inflicted injuries. One of the most curious and convincing is that recorded by Bouley. He was called in by Count Demidoff, in Paris, to examine a spaniel which had a small bleeding wound at the base of the croup and commencement of the tail; this wound had appeared recently; the animal was quite lively, obeyed the voice that called it, and approached in the usual docile manner, wagging its tail. There was nothing to give rise to the suspicion that it might be affected with rabies; and, indeed, M. Bouley confesses that as this incident happened very many years previously to the time at which he was relating it, he was all the more easily led astray, because at that period he only knew the disease at its stage of exacerbation and fury—the only phase in which it was described in those days. He looked upon the sore as one of the skin diseases so common in the dog, and ordered an appropriate treatment: recommending at the same time, as a matter of cleanliness, that the animal should not be allowed to lie in the room, nor yet on its master's bed, as it was accustomed to do; so it lay on the landing-place of the stairs. The next morning a domestic found, on the first step, the tail of the favourite spaniel completely separated from the body: the dog had inflicted this mutilation upon itself. Astonished and disgusted at the accident, the Count, without inquiring into the motives which prompted the spaniel to perpetrate such an act, put a collar upon it with a chain attached, and sent it off to Alfort. The animal went the whole distance without exhibiting any unusual sign, and without giving the servant cause to suspect in the slightest degree that he was followed so closely by a mad dog. On arrival at the court of the hospital, the creature, with the remains of its tail raw and bleeding, its mouth of a dusky bluish colour, and its eyes wild and wandering, had now too characteristic a physiognomy to admit of any mistake being made. It was prudently led to the kennel, where, under the influence of the excitation produced by the barking of the other dogs, a fit of madness soon declared itself. In two days it was dead.

This animal, therefore, exhibited in a striking manner the principal features which belong to rabies in its initial stage: a pet dog so dominated by the sentiment of affection and the influences of domesticity, that, although the desire to bite was already developed in it, yet it spared its master and the servants of the house, and only attacked itself, without appearing to feel its self-inflicted injuries; during the whole distance from Paris to Alfort it submitted itself to the man who led it, and whom it knew, without evincing any access of the disease; and it, finally, did not exhibit rabies in all its fury until after being separated from the conductor, and when it was left to itself and its delirium.

With regard to sensibility, then, suspicion should always attach strongly to a dog which does not manifest a certain degree of pain, and receives punishment without uttering any cry or complaint. When, for instance, a dog is pursued in a locality because it is without an owner, and is a stranger, if it remains mute notwithstanding the menaces and the blows to which it is subjected, there is every cause for suspicion.

There is also reason for apprehension when a dog bites itself persistently in any part of its body, and does not stop because of the pain it should experience. True, it may act in this manner from the presence of some skin disease accompanied with itching; but, on the other hand, it is possible that the creature is impelled to use its teeth in this manner from the instinct to bite already developed in it, or perhaps owing to the peculiar sensation experienced in the cicatrix of the wound by which it was inoculated. The latter may have been the cause of Count Demidoff's dog biting its tail off. At any rate, when this symptom appears, it is judicious to take precautions.

There is also another peculiar symptom of rabies in the dog and other animals, though in man it is not frequent, which is very important in a diagnostic point of view. This is the impression made on a rabid dog at the sight of an animal of its own species—an impression which is so powerful as to excite at once a fit of fury; so that it may be said that the dog is the certain reagent by whose influence we may reveal the presence of the disease yet latent in the creature we suspect.

In practice, this means is generally resorted to by M. Bouley, in order to dissipate any doubts when the diagnosis is otherwise uncertain; and it is rare that it fails. As soon as the suspected dog finds itself in the presence of another of its species, if it is really mad it at once assumes an aggressive attitude, and if it can reach the latter it will bite it furiously. It is remarkable that this special excitability of the rabid state is not peculiar to the dog alone, but that all mad animals manifest the same sensibility when in the presence of one of the canine species; all become excited, exasperated, and furious at the sight of a dog, and fly at it to attack it with their natural weapons. The horse assaults it with teeth and hoofs; the bull, cow, and ram with their horns; even the timid sheep, when rabid, so far from exhibiting fear at the view of a dog, under the influence of the malady loses its natural pusillanimity, becomes the assailant, and butts furiously at the enemy before which, in health, it would have fled in abject terror.

This strange interversion of sentiment,—when the most timorous of creatures becomes all at once animated with the most bellicose spirit,—is a remarkable symptom of rabies, and its diagnostic value is evidenced in the following anecdotes related by Bouley. Some years ago, a fine sporting dog was brought to Alfort in a cabriolet, in which it had lain beneath the legs of its master and the coachman. During the journey, and notwithstanding the excitement that may have been roused in it by the presence of a stranger beside it, the dog remained perfectly inoffensive. The carriage arrived at the courtyard of the school hospital, and the owner lifted out the animal in his arms and carried it to M. Bouley's consulting room. He then informed the professor that for two days it had been dull and refused to eat. Not being then so well acquainted with the disease and its insidious modes of manifestation, M. Bouley placed it on his knees to examine it more carefully. He was opening its lips to ascertain the colour of the mouth, when a poodle belonging to him entered the room. In a moment the dog he was inspecting escaped from his hands without attempting to bite him, and set upon the new arrival, which endeavoured to evade the attack. This unexpected, and also most unusual behaviour on the part of the sporting dog, according to the testimony of its owner, gave rise to a suspicion of rabies; the animal was immediately confined in an isolated place, and in three days afterwards succumbed to the disease.

In another instance a horse was the subject of this peculiar symptom. This creature had been brought to M. Bouley's notice in consequence of its having been unable to swallow for a day or two. It appeared to be, and in fact was, of an extremely mild temper. The professor was in the act of examining the mouth, and had seized the tongue in his hand, when the same poodle appeared and commenced to ramble about him. As soon as the horse perceived it, it disengaged itself from his hands by a rapid movement, and dashed with open jaws after the dog, which again had to take to flight. What proved to be very remarkable in this case was that the horse was very quiet with people; it obeyed the voice of its conductor, followed him in the most docile manner, and without its being necessary to hold the rope of the halter; even after its aggressive demonstration against the poodle it was perfectly inoffensive to the multitude of persons around it. According to the man in charge of it, it was usually very fond of dogs, but during the journey from Vitry to Alfort that day it had attacked all those it met in the road. This man did not attach any importance to this fact, and he would not have mentioned it had the animal not again shown the same tendency towards the poodle.

There were no other symptoms to guide one in forming an opinion of the case; yet the precaution was taken to thoroughly secure the horse between two large trees in the park by a double head-collar. Several times the experiment was repeated of exciting a fit of madness by the sight of a dog brought before it; and, under the influence of these, it was not long before the rabies from which it was suffering reached its most urgent paroxysms. In a few hours the disease had passed through its stages, the animal became exhausted, and died a short time after entering the hospital.

So common is this peculiarity that it may be said to be present in every case of rabies; and it should put people upon their guard, as it is generally an early and striking indication of a change in the dog's manner—appearing even before any other very prominent symptom. Numerous proofs of this might be given, in addition to those already furnished; but it will suffice to adduce the case of the dog which introduced the disease into the Monreith kennels. My friend, Sir William Maxwell, informs me that towards the end of January, 1841, a large

Newfoundland dog, apparently completely worn out from fatigue, and covered with mud, found its way into the kitchen of the factor's house, near Monreith. The children played with it, and after an hour or two the servants turned it out; during the whole time it never attempted to bite any one. On the same afternoon it showed itself at the home-farm offices, and the overseer, thinking it belonged to the gamekeeper, put a rope round its neck and sent a lad with it to that functionary's kennels, about a mile off. It went with him very quietly, and arrived at the kennels just as the keeper returned from shooting, with a couple of pointers at his heel. The sight of the latter seemed to put new life into the strange dog; breaking away from the lad, it savagely attacked one of the pointers and rolled it over; but receiving a blow or kick from the keeper, without attempting to bite him, it ran away and was seen no more in that neighbourhood—though a dog answering its description was shot as mad next day at a place about twelve miles distant. On examination, no wound was found on the pointer, except a small scratch on the lip. No mischief appeared, or was even suspected, until near the end of March, when the animal showed symptoms of rabies, and in April the disease commenced among the other dogs.

The nervous susceptibility of rabid animals would thus appear to be powerfully excited by the presence of one of the canine species, which rouses them from the calm condition they may yet be in, and produces aggressive manifestations more and more furious in proportion to the intensity and number of excitations produced. According to Bouley, this phenomenon is so constant that it may be considered as the expression of a fatal law whose secret is unknown to us. But as there are few laws without an exception, so it appears this affords one in the remarkable instance related by the veterinary professor, Renault, of Alfort. A horse experimentally inoculated by this talented gentleman with the virus from a rabid sheep, contracted the disease, and in such a severe form that it turned its fury upon itself, and tore the skin off its fore-arms with its teeth. But though so violently rabid, the sight of a dog did not produce any excitation. A dog thrown into its manger during a paroxysm was not harmed, and it pushed it about with its nose, as if to get it out of the way without doing it any injury. But when a sheep was placed before it, all at once it became terribly furious, sprang upon it at once, and the poor inoffensive animal, seized between its powerful jaws, was in an instant crushed by its teeth, and shaken as a terrier shakes a rat.

It would almost seem from this fact, which is unique in the annals of science, as if animals inoculated with the rabid virus, by a bite or in any other manner, were conscious of the cause of their disease, and that this idea determined them to manifest their fury at the sight of a creature belonging to the same species as that which furnished the poison whose inoculation produced the malady.

With this curious exception, it may then be laid down as a rule that the sight of animals of the canine species prompts the excitability of rabid creatures; and the recognition of this fact may prove of the greatest utility, if the owners of dogs only know how to profit by it. Every day, says the same observant author so frequently quoted in these pages, affords us a proof of the truth of this; when we interrogate the owners of dogs which have become rabid, we find that, before directing their assaults against mankind, these animals were very excitable at the sight of another of their species. Unfortunately, however, in the majority of cases, this very significant peculiarity has not attracted the attention of those who have observed it, nor aroused suspicion in their mind, simply because as yet there does not appear to be any other notable change in the character of the irritable beast.

When a dog, therefore, contrary to its habits and natural inclination, becomes suddenly aggressive to other dogs, it is time to take precautions. Such manifestations are very significant, and, if understood, they may be utilised in averting danger to other creatures.

From the enumeration of these characteristic symptoms it will be seen that, in the majority of instances, the familiar house-dogs remain inoffensive in the early period of their rabid state to the persons around them, dominated as they are by their affectionate regard for them. And the poor creatures may only be obeying the dictates of these sentiments when, as very often happens, they leave their owners' domicile and disappear; it might be said that they have a consciousness of the harm they might do, and that to prevent it they fly from those to whom they are so much attached. Whatever foundation there may exist for this interpretation, it is nevertheless the fact that very frequently the rabid dog forsakes its master and its home, and does not return again, either because it soon dies in some retired corner; or, which is ordinarily the case in populous localities, it is recognised as mad by the damage it inflicts on animals or people, and is killed.*

But in other instances, and they are only too numerous, the unfortunate dog, after wandering about for a day or two and escaping pursuit, returns to its home and its human companions, in obedience to some fatal attraction; and it is in these circumstances more especially that misfortunes are to be dreaded. The return of the poor wanderer attracts every one's attention and excites the sympathy of the household, so that the first impulse is to succour it; for oftentimes what was the companion and the pet comes back in a miserable plight, reduced almost to a skeleton, and covered with mud, and even with blood. Woe to any one who approaches the unlucky sufferer

* Hertwig says that during a period of forty years, whenever rabies assumed an epizoötic character, he always observed that dogs belonging to peasants or other persons living in the country, and running unhindered and without supervision into the towns, were the principal agents in extending the contagion. This desire to escape is one of the principal characteristics of rabies, and is so notorious where the disease is frequent, that it is sometimes so designated. In Illyria, for instance, it used to be, and may still be, popularly known as "stecklina," or the escape disease.

now; as at this period of the disease the propensity to bite has become imperious with it, and overrules its affection, however strong this may yet be; and for the caresses and care bestowed on it, it is only too apt to return wounds inflicted by its teeth.*

We should always look with suspicion upon a dog which, after being absent from its home for some days, returns again, and especially if it be in the condition just described.

The above may be said to be the precursory symptoms of the true mad or furious period; and it will be observed that rabies is not what it is usually imagined to be—a disease characterised by a continual state of fury; on the contrary, it has been shown that, before this final stage is reached, there is a somewhat long period during which the animal is inoffensive, although to the experienced and observant eye the malady is present, and is easily recognised. And this is the period when the majority, if not all, of the dogs should be sequestrated, before they have time to do mischief. The erratic dogs in the semi-delirium of rabies, inflicting wounds on every animal and man they meet, have not been suddenly seized with the disease; but the largest portion of them are dogs that have deserted their homes, and which, before their flight, exhibited the unequivocal symptoms above mentioned. Were these precursory indications sufficiently known and appreciated by the owners of dogs, and the proper precautionary steps adopted, much would be done to prevent the spreading of the disease. For there can be no doubt

* The maternal affection for its young remains as strong in the rabid as it is in the healthy dog. M. Defays, a professor at the Brussels Veterinary School, gives an instance of a bitch that had three puppies, and two days afterwards suddenly exhibited all the symptoms of rabies. Notwithstanding the severe attacks of the malady, the poor creature continued to suckle its young, and ran anxiously to them when they emitted the slightest cry; not being able to swallow any fluid, however, the secretion of milk was suspended and the puppies died. But this event did not alter its desire to be near and to fondle them, and to cover them over with straw as if to hide them; it was only when complete paralysis had supervened that the unfortunate animal ceased to occupy itself with its dead offspring. ("Annales de Méd. Vétérinaire." Brussels, October, 1871.)

whatever, that the agents which propagate it are the dogs that have escaped from their owners, after having been unwell for a sufficiently long period to have afforded warning and the adoption of preventive measures—so far as the extension of the disease is concerned—if it were only known that the signs then exhibited were precursory of rabies. It will be seen, then, how necessary it is for the prevention of alarm and the preservation of human and animal life, that an acquaintance with, or a knowledge of, these initial symptoms should be acquired by every one; for who is there who is not more or less among dogs, and who might at any moment have to do with an animal in this condition? The insidiousness of rabies, and its terribly destructive character in man and beast, are surely sufficient to impress upon us the necessity of learning all we can with regard to its suppression; and in no way can we more successfully contend with the scourge than by knowing the earliest symptoms which indicate its existence, for then we can adopt measures which will most assuredly prevent its extending beyond the animal affected.

After two or three days, frequently after only twelve hours, the precursory or early signs of rabies have given place to those which mark the confirmed malady or furious period—that in which ferocious instincts are developed in the poor creature, and the desire to bite is irrepressible; there can scarcely then be a doubt in the mind of the most inexperienced as to what is the matter. In the first place, the physiognomy of the rabid dog at this stage is terribly modified. Its confiding and affectionate nature is no longer manifested in its glances, and we have instead an indefinable expression of sombre melancholy and cruelty. The eyes have their pupils excessively dilated, and momentarily emit lightning-like flashes, produced by the reflection of the light from the *tapetum lucidum* at the back of the organ, which in some aspects causes the eyes to look like globes of fire. But when this scintillation ceases, then the eyes become dull and heavy, and so fierce-looking as to excite a lively sentiment of fear in those who find themselves in the presence of a mad dog: even when the animal is seen from before the bars of a cage, where its symptoms and behaviour can be most safely and attentively observed. As a general rule, the conjunctival membrane of the eyes is red and injected, and the eyes themselves are nearly closed; their sensibility to light is increased, and wrinkles which sometimes appear on the forehead above the eyes, add to the repulsive aspect of the animal. No sooner does the mad dog become aware of your presence than it springs at you, and emitting its characteristic howl or bark, seizes the iron bars that hinder it from attacking any one. If anything is presented to it, such as a walking stick, it flies at it immediately with open mouth, and grasps and gnaws it with its teeth, but without giving out a cry or a growl. Water put before it, it is said, will also not unfrequently excite a paroxysm, as will also light reflected from any polished body; these paroxysms can be produced when we choose, according to Haubner. The water in these rare cases, however, will be readily drank in a dark place; it is only when shone upon that it is likely to be avoided.

But this fury is soon succeeded by profound lassitude; the animal becomes exhausted and retires to the furthest corner of its den, where it remains for some time insensible to everything that may be done to irritate it. Then all at once it wakens up, springs forward again, and performs the same frenzied movements if there is anything to excite it. The first paroxysm of madness is usually the most intense, and the fits altogether vary in duration from some hours to a day, and even longer. They are ordinarily shorter in trained and pet dogs than in those which are less domesticated; and in all the remission is so complete after the first paroxysm that the animals appear to be almost, if not quite, in perfect health at this time.

During the paroxysms, the respiration is hurried and difficult, but it is calm in the remissions. The pulse, when it has been examined—for there is danger in manipulating a rabid dog during one of its mad attacks—has been found quick and hard.

In the early stages, it would appear from the thermometrical observations already made that there is no marked increase of temperature, and that it is only at a later period, when the body begins to waste, that the heat becomes exalted. In all febrile diseases, as a rule, there is an augmentation of temperature from the commencement. In one case of "dumb madness," the temperature rose to 104·8°.

If, however, the dog is not excited, and is kept in a cage away from all noises and objects that might rouse its nervous susceptibility, these fits of fury are not observed. Sometimes the suffering creature is agitated, and wanders here and there in a restless, purposeless manner, turns over its straw, and appears to pursue and bark at phantoms; or it will remain crouching for a short period in a drowsy state, until suddenly it makes a bound as far as the dimensions of its cage or the length of its chain will permit, barking in its peculiar manner at the same time; then it will perhaps remain fixed for a few minutes staring strangely at objects and persons with which it used to be perfectly acquainted; at other times it is calm, sleepy, motionless, only moving now and then in a quick nervous manner, but without getting up, as if it were haunted by a disquieting dream. It never becomes really furious or aggressive unless there appear external causes to excite it, and the most potent of these is the presence of one of its own species. No sooner does it behold another dog, even at a distance, than it displays all the symptoms of advanced rabies in the most painful and alarming manner; it bounds towards the new arrival and violently attacks the bars which hinder it from inflicting serious injury on those around it. But, strange to say, if the dog is introduced into the cage, the first impulse of the mad animal is not always to fly upon and bite it; on the contrary, the presence of the unlucky visitor seems to inspire it with sentiments of affection, and it manifests this by caresses and amatory gestures whose signification is not doubtful. Then, almost in the same instant, moved by an antagonistic impulse, its eyes appear to become inflamed with fury, and it madly throws itself upon its victim and freely uses its teeth. The attacked animal rarely retaliates, but usually responds to the bites by acute yells which contrast strangely with the silent anger of the aggressor, and it struggles to guard its head from the attacks directed against it by burying it deeply in the litter, or covering it with its fore paws. This period of violence is soon over, and the mad dog resumes its caresses, which are as ardent as at first; but there is only a short interval before another fit of rage ensues, and when these have been repeated several times, the patient becomes exhausted and feeble, and falls off into a restless kind of somnolescence. No sooner, however, has it rested sufficiently long to have regained a little strength than it recommences its attacks, and continues them until paralysis ensues—which is not long, for these fits repeated in this way have a singular influence in precipitating the course of the malady.

As before mentioned, at this period the mucous membrane of the mouth is most frequently dry, and sometimes even fissured and cracked. The secretion of a great quantity of saliva, and its flowing from the mouth, is usually only witnessed in cases in which swallowing has become impossible, because of the morbid condition of the pharynx. At times the tongue, nose, and also the whole head, appear swollen.

It has been for a long time known that the mad dog is shunned by other animals of its species, and though there are, of course, exceptional cases now and again, yet it is none the less a remarkable fact that dogs appear to know instinctively the danger they incur at the approach of a rabid congener; and it has been frequently observed that the strongest and most courageous manifests weakness and cowardice in its presence.* Instead of attempting to fight with it, they usually

* The following is an old English translation of Ambrose Paré's description of rabies, written in the sixteenth century: "The mad dog hath sparkling and

endeavour to escape from its attacks by flight. If shut up in a cage with it, even fighting dogs appear to lose their pugnacity, and seem to have a presentiment of the terrible danger to which they are exposed: expressing their fear by tremblings over the whole body, and seeking to crouch away in a corner.*

---

fiery eyes, with a fixed look, cruel, and squinting; he carries his head heavily, hanging down towards the ground, and somewhat on one side; he gapes and lolls out his tongue, which is livid and blackish, and being short-breathed, he casts forth much filth at his nose, and much foaming matter from his mouth. In his gait he appears as if he suspected and feared all things; he keepeth no certain path, but runs one while to this side, and another while to that, and stumbling like unto one that is drunk, he oftentimes falleth down on the ground, and violently assails whatsoever he meets withal, whether it be man, tree, wall, dog, or any other thing. Other dogs shun him; but if another dog unawares chances to foul on him, he yields with abject mission to his mercy, fawns upon him, and privily labours to get from him, though he be the strongest and greatest of the two. He is unmindful of eating and drinking; he barks not, yet bites all he meets without distinction, not even sparing his master, who at this time he knows not from a stranger or enemy; but when he sees water, he trembles and shakes, and his hairs bristle up. In all cases dogs affected with hydrophobia betoken a strange antipathy to other dogs, and particularly to cats; but as the disease makes its progress this antipathy is overcome, and the animal not only bites other dogs and cats, but the surrounding persons, as well as things—wood, stones, earth, glass, &c., have been found in their stomachs on dissection."

Spackman, in 1613, gives the following symptoms: "When a dog is become mad, he is commonly altered in the whole habit and temperature of his body, growing leane, dry, and thirstie, yet refusing to drink, and fearing or flying from water and bright things. He is sad and pensive, hanging down his head, or bearing it more toward one side than another; his eyes be red and fierie, his countenance horrible and very unpleasant; and Paulus saith hee is altogether dumbe and seldom able to barke. Yet some say he will now and then barke at his owne shadow, but with a very hoarse voice. His eares hang down, he dreveleth and fometh at the mouth and nose, his tongue hangeth out, being of a red or blackish colour, hee bloweth short, refuseth both meat and drinke, his tayle hangeth loosely, or is clapt betwixt his legs: he goeth drowsily, and when he runneth, he reeleth to and fro, yet runneth he then faster than he was wont. Hee knoweth neither his master nor any of the household, but will bite them as soone as any other. What creature soever he meeteth, either wilde or tame, he will offer to bite it. In his running or going, he will stop sometime upon the sudden. All other dogs are afraid of him, and runne from him if they may; but if they meet him on the sudden, they will crouch down to him and flatter him for feare. These are noted to bee the signes of an absolute mad dog, but many mad dogs want some of these signes."

* A good instance of the danger of relying too implicitly upon this sign, and also the fallacy of the worming operation, is afforded by a correspondent in the *Bath Herald* for February 6th, 1808. "A hound, supposed to be mad, passed

One of the exceptions to the rule is afforded by a case that occurred at Alfort, and which is alluded to by M. Bouley. One day he introduced a bull terrier, a very good fighter, into the cage of a mad dog. The first impression it experienced when shut in was manifestly that of fear; but this it soon overcame, and instead of waiting to be attacked, it began it; at a bound it dashed upon its adversary, and seizing it behind the neck, threw it upon the floor, and put it out of its power to inflict harm. Twenty times this experiment was repeated with different mad dogs, at various times, in the hospital of the school, and the terrier was always as successful. In all these encounters it contrived to escape bites, and did not contract rabies.

---

through my father's garden, skirmishing, as he passed, with several of my father's dogs, and with my spaniel. The former were all destroyed; but as I was not convinced that the hound was mad, I did not destroy the spaniel, and as he had been *wormed* when a puppy, and had overtaken the hound, and *had a second bite with him, I was confirmed in my opinion that there was no danger, from the general notion that dogs in health will not pursue a mad dog.* I came up during this battle, and separated the dogs, when the hound snapped at me and went off, and I could never get any subsequent intelligence of him. This was in the month of *August*. About three weeks afterwards I went to the river to shoot wild fowl, taking the spaniel with me, but soon observed that he would not go into the water, as usual; and when driven in a little way, he soon returned, shivering, and I could not make him go in again. I had with me a young pointer, which the spaniel made up to on his return from the water, turned him on his back, and bit him several times. The next day, as the groom was trimming my horse, the spaniel came out of the stable, jumped up to the horse's lip, and left slight marks of his teeth, but which appeared like two mere scratches. Both dogs were confined. The spaniel daily got worse. About the fourth or fifth day he got loose, with his chain on, went into the kitchen, and lay under the table while the servants were at dinner. He did not molest any one, nor at all incline, like dogs that are not wormed, to run away, and snap indiscriminately at everything they pass; but on being taken back, and fastened up near the stable, *he lay and bit the straw*, refused food, and sprung from water as if it would scald him. In a few days he died. The young pointer had all the symptoms of the malady usually described. Being convinced that he was perfectly mad, he was shot with a pistol. The horse was sent to an eminent farrier, who burnt the bitten part of the lip, and gave him the Ormskirk medicine. I drove him two or three months in a curricle, but observed that he continually rubbed his lip on the manger. At length I found that he had imbibed the fatal poison. The time that had elapsed from the day he was bitten till that when he was taken mad was exactly six months and a fortnight. As his recovery was evidently impossible, I soon had him killed." In all probability, the spaniel was affected with "dumb madness."

But this and similar instances are quite exceptional; and, as before said, the mad dog is to others a source of dread. This is very evident from what happens in packs of hounds. As is well known, these animals are rather curious in their behaviour sometimes, and should two of their number commence to quarrel, woe to the one which manifests its faint-heartedness by cries, for the others immediately set upon and worry it in a most unmerciful manner. But, what is very remarkable, if one of the two quarrelling dogs is rabid, the whole pack holds aloof in a remote part of the kennel, and should there be an open door or window, they will resort to flight. Notwithstanding their cruel habits and somewhat savage disposition, they become quite cowardly in the presence of the threatened danger, and the mad dog is left to worry its victim; if, impelled by its rabid instincts, it selects another out of the pack, the others also instantly leave this one to its fate. M. Bouley vouches for the correctness of this statement by his experience, and mentions that this remarkable peculiarity was especially noted in the Prince of Wagram's pack at Gros-Bois. This pack became infected by a strange dog one day while hunting, and the disease spread so rapidly among them that it was found necessary to destroy the whole; though not before they had given ample demonstration of the truth of what has just been asserted.

Mr. Henderson, alluding to the outbreak in the Durham County pack, in his letter to the *Times* of December 13, says: "The night before the meeting of the members of the Hunt, held in Durham, Dowdeswell, the huntsman, than whom a more careful man does not exist, was much disturbed by the fighting and noise of six hounds he had separated from the pack, they having shown the usual premonitory symptoms. After trying in vain to quiet them several times during the night, at daybreak he found three fighting and worrying each other, covered with blood and furiously mad, the other three crouched up in a corner, frightened and trembling."

I myself know of an instance in which a large mastiff, a savage, aggressive brute that worried every dog that came within its reach when on the chain, flew to the back of its kennel and trembled at the approach of a mad setter, which had bitten dogs, horses, and cattle.

If the mad dog is not confined in a cage, but kept in a room where there is more liberty, it wanders about in every direction, and with all the greater agitation if not accustomed to be separated from its human companions. It is continually on the move, and rambles, seeks, smells, howls at the walls, flies at the phantoms that seem to pursue it, gnaws at the bottoms of doors, furniture, &c., and may at last make an escape through glass doors or windows. If persons are only separated from it by glass it does not hesitate to smash the fragile barrier: being all the more determined to get through it when excited by seeing them, and moved by the fatal desire to bite, which now entirely dominates it. The larger the obstacles the wilder its fury, and no sacrifice is too great to obtain liberty. House-dogs are trying every moment to escape from their dwelling; and those which are kept tied up or shut in a room are constantly endeavouring to break their attachment, or to destroy the doors or partitions that confine them, in order to satisfy their longing to be at large.

When a rabid dog makes its escape it goes freely forward, as if impelled by some irresistible force—travelling considerable distances in a short time, and attacking every living being it meets on its way; preferring dogs, however, to other animals, and the latter rather than mankind. Cats also appear to be, next to dogs, most liable to be injured. A mad dog that had done a considerable amount of mischief in Lancashire in 1869, was seen, in one part of its career, trotting along the road with a cat in its mouth, which it had picked up from a cottage, and which, some time afterwards, it dropped to attack a cow.* Fowls, likewise, are particularly exposed to the assaults of the

* The *Veterinarian*, March, 1870.

rabid dog. When it attacks, and endeavours to tear its victims, it does so in silence, never uttering a snarl or a cry of anger; and should it chance to be injured in return, it emits no cry or yell of pain. Though it will not so readily assault mankind as it will other creatures; yet it is most prudent, when in the presence of a mad dog, to allow it to pass, instead of attacking it, unless there is a certainty of killing it without the risk of being wounded by its teeth. The degree of ferocity would appear to be influenced very much by the natural disposition of the dog, and the training it has received. Some, for instance, only snap or give a slight bite in passing; while others, on the contrary, bite furiously, and tear the objects presented to them or which they meet in their way, and sometimes with such an extreme degree of violence as to injure their mouths and break their teeth, or even their jaws.* If chained up, they will

* A very remarkable instance of this kind occurred at the Lyons Veterinary School in 1865, and as it affords a good example of the disease, no apology is needed for referring to it here. A large watch-dog, five years old, was observed to have lost its usual appetite for four days. It also tried to get hold of animals passing it, especially those of its own species, springing at them and attempting to bite them in such an unusual manner, that it looked as if it were naturally vicious. At last it bit a milkman, with whom it had previously been on the best of terms, and the owner of the dog then had it sent to the school. On its arrival there, it was not under the influence of a paroxysm, and there was nothing in its appearance to indicate that it was unwell. It was even lively, and was so responsive to the caressings bestowed upon it, that the student *de service* took it to a kennel, tied it up, and took off its muzzle without its showing the least viciousness. The following day, however, the symptoms of rabies became manifest in a most unmistakable manner. Finding itself shut up, it became furious. At first sight, the unusual brilliancy of its gaze was most striking, though it was fixed and haggard; the pupils were more dilated than was natural; the conjunctivæ were deeply injected and had a dark red colour. The tail was carried close between the legs and kept immovable, whereas in health it was carried curled over the back. It frequently barked, and any irritating cause, such as the presence of a man, made it bark still more. The voice was brief, jerking, and hoarse, and it alone would have indicated the existence of the disease. It was very restless in the kennel, incessantly turning round; if not excited it did not attempt to bite, and showed a singular propensity to gather its litter into heaps in different places by means of its fore feet. From time to time, even when apparently calm, it opened its mouth and sharply closed it again with a champing noise, as if it were biting at flies. Bits of flesh were offered to it at the end of a stick; these it at once seized and swallowed without masticating. Deglutition was nevertheless difficult, and it might have been the stick that

gnaw the chain until their teeth are worn away and the jaw-bones laid bare.

The rabid dog does not continue its progress very long. Exhausted by fatigue, by the fits of madness excited in it by the objects it meets in its way, by hunger, thirst, and also, no doubt, as a consequence of the disease itself, its limbs soon become feeble. Then it slackens its rate of travelling, and walks unsteadily; its drooping tail, its head inclined towards

---

excited it to seize the food. The following day the madness was quite extraordinary. Every instant it darted at the door of the kennel, seized the bars between its jaws, and tried to break them. A non-viscid saliva, abundant in quantity, and foamy, flowed from its mouth, which was bleeding through contact with the bars. It flew at a single bound towards everything presented to it without appearing to mind the danger to which it might be exposed; in this way it seized a piece of red-hot iron, and even licked it. Its howlings were more frequent, interrupted, and hoarse. In one of its fits of fury, it got its lower jaw fixed between the bars of the kennel, where it was retained by its fangs; it now began to struggle so much, and made such vigorous efforts to free itself, that the jaw was broken, the fangs were torn out, and nearly all the incisor teeth were smashed. The pain caused by this fracture, though it must have been extreme, did not calm its fury; it was still seen with its mouth full of blood, and the extremity of the jaw dangling about, howling, biting at everything offered to it, and attempting to gnaw the bars, which seemed to be the principal object of its fury. If food was thrown to it, it would still try to take it, though it could not. This horrible scene lasted without interruption for nearly half a day, when it was decided to destroy the poor brute. This was done by putting five grammes of strychnine in a small morsel of meat, and giving it to the dog on the end of a stick. It furiously seized this merciful bait, and soon died.—*Journal de Médecine Vétérinaire de Lyon*, 1865.

This case, it must be remembered, is somewhat exceptional. It is remarkable for the intensity and persistence, even in the absence of all external excitation, of the rabid *furore*, which was carried to the highest degree it could attain—even to the fracture of its jaw. Professor Saint-Cyr adds, that it was truly a horrible and pitiful spectacle to see the poor animal throwing itself with open mouth, the blood streaming from it, and the jaw hanging in pieces, against the bars of the cage, seizing them, and still gnawing at them, despite the pain of its broken jaw, as if the excitement of its internal sufferings had overpowered all other sensations. "Certainly," he continues, "if rabies always showed such a fearful assemblage of symptoms, it would well deserve its name. But in the great majority of cases the mad dog, unless imprudently excited, is far from being furious. Even this poor creature, whose end was so cruelly tragical, remained three days with its master, quite rabid, without manifesting any other signs of the horrible disease than an irresistible desire to bite, without any access of fury. And at the time of its admission to the hospital it was yet calm, and betrayed no disease until it was shut up in the kennel."

the ground, the mouth open, and the protruded tongue of a lead-blue colour, and covered with dust,—all this gives the distressed creature a very striking and characteristic physiognomy. In this condition, however, it is much less to be dreaded than in its early fits of fury. If it is still bent on attacking, it is only when it meets with anything directly in its track that it seeks to satisfy its rage; but it is no longer sufficiently excitable to change its direction, or go out of its course to attack an animal or a man not immediately in its path. It is extremely pro-

Furious Rabies: Late Stage.

bable, also, that its fast failing vision and deadened scent prevent its being so easily impressed by surrounding objects as it previously was.

As has been said, to each paroxysm, which is always of short duration, there succeeds a degree of exhaustion as great as the fits have been violent and often repeated. This compels the animal to stop; then it shelters itself in obscure places, frequently in the ditches by the roadside, and lies there in a somnolescent state for perhaps hours. There is great danger, nevertheless, in disturbing the creature at this period; for, when roused from its torpor, it has sometimes strength enough left to inflict a bite. Many people, and particularly children, have perished from hydrophobia through having committed such an imprudent act as disturbing a rabid dog in this condition; indeed, this danger may have given rise to the old proverb to "leave sleeping dogs alone." This period, which we may term the second stage of the malady, is as variable as the first stage, but it rarely indeed exceeds from three to four days. The phenomena we have described insensibly merge into those of the third or last period, when symptoms of paralysis appear, which are promptly followed by death.

When the disease approaches its termination, and during the remissions in the paroxysms, these symptoms of paralysis become manifest, especially in the hind limbs, which look as if they could not support the animal's weight, and cause it to stagger about; or the lower jaw becomes more or less drooping, leaving the dry mouth partially open. Emaciation proceeds rapidly, and the paroxysms diminish in intensity; while the remissions become less marked. The physiognomy assumes a still more sinister and repulsive aspect; the hair is dull and standing on end; the flanks are drawn up; the eyes lose their lustre and are buried in their orbits, the pupils are dilated, and the cornea of the eye is dull and semi-opaque; very often, even at an early period, the eyes squint, and this strabismus adds still more to the terrifying appearance of the poor creature. The voice is husky, if at all heard; the breathing is laborious, and the pulse hurried and irregular. Gradually the paralysis increases, and the hinder extremities are dragged as if the animal's back were broken, until at length it is general, and is then the prelude of death. Or the unfortunate creature remains lying in a stupor, and can only raise itself with difficulty on the fore limbs when it is greatly excited. In this condition it may yet try to snap or bite at objects within its reach. At times convulsions of a tetanic character appear in certain muscles, at other times throughout the body; a comatose condition ensues, and the rabid dog, if permitted to die in a natural manner, perishes, in the great majority of cases, from paralysis and asphyxia.

Such are the phenomena which usually go to make up the category of symptoms appertaining to "furious rabies," as it has frequently been named. But there are two other types or forms of the disease which must be noticed, as their manifestations are peculiar; and though they are accompanied by less dangerous symptoms than that we have just been describing, they are none the less worthy of attention. These types

"Dumb Madness." Drawn from Life. (Sanson.)

have been designated "dumb madness" and "tranquil madness."

"Dumb madness," as already mentioned, owes its name to the diseased creature being unable, perhaps from the commencement of the disease, to emit the characteristic howl or bark of rabies, because of the paralysis or inflamed condition of the vocal organs; as well as, in all likelihood, the paralysis of those muscles of the lower jaw which close the mouth. This paralysis imparts a curious and a very characteristic physiognomy to the poor dog: which is not only unable to utter any sound, but is also incapable of eating and drinking, and remains with the jaw pendant and the mouth open, showing the flaccid or swollen tongue covered with a brownish matter, and a stringy, glutinous saliva lying between it and the lower lip and coating the fauces, which sometimes appear inflamed. Indeed, it may be said that it is only in this form of rabies in the dog that there is slavering. There is, of course, a total inability to lap or to swallow fluids; though the desire to drink is intense, and the creature will thrust its face into the vessel in futile efforts to obtain relief, even until the approach of death. Water may be poured down its throat without inducing a paroxysm. The general physiognomy and demeanour of the poor creature inspires the beholder with pity rather than fear, and almost impels one to afford it assistance. The symptoms due to cerebral excitement are less marked than in the raging form of rabies; the agitation is not so considerable, and the restlessness, tendency to run away, and desire to bite, are also not nearly so great; generally the animal is quite passive. Not unfrequently one or both eyes squint. It is only when very much excited that the creature may rarely contrive to close its mouth. Sometimes, also, there co-exists a certain amount of tumefaction at the back part of the throat (pharynx), and even at the neck; and when the tongue shares in this complication it hangs out of the mouth. In certain cases, according to Röll, there is also a catarrhal condition of the membrane lining the nasal cavities, the larynx, and the bronchi; sometimes the animal denotes, by its attitudes, the existence of abdominal pain, and in this instance the fæces are soft or quite fluid. The other symptoms, such as the mental disorder, rapid and prompt exhaustion, paralysis of the posterior regions of the body towards the termination of the disease, as well as the rapidity with which it runs its course, are the same as in the other type of rabies.

The simultaneous occurrence of cases of "dumb" and "furious madness" is frequently observed in packs of foxhounds. We have already given instances in our History, especially in the outbreak at Guadaloupe, in 1776, and lately in the Albrighton pack, in 1871. The epizoöty among the Durham County foxhounds, already alluded to, furnishes us with another notable instance, for the details of which I am indebted to Mr. Farrow, M.R.C.V.S., of Durham. He informs me that the first case of rabies occurred on October 20, and the second on November 1, eleven days afterwards; the third was noticed on November 3; and from this time the disease became more general through the pack, three or four rabid hounds being reported every week, until eleven couples had either died or been destroyed. The first animal was attacked with "furious" rabies in the most marked form, and the commencement of the disease was indicated by its flying at, and attempting to bite, several hounds after a severe run. It was led home and carefully isolated from the pack. Mr. Farrow saw the animal on the 22nd, and it did not then exhibit much ferocity, though it was not deemed safe to approach within seizing distance; it evinced a certain amount of irritability by continually shifting its position and seeking a fresh resting-place. Some fluid food was set before it, of which a portion was taken. On the following morning it was again seen by this gentleman, and it was then in a very excited state, incessantly biting and tearing to pieces the furniture of the box, &c. It was immediately shot as rabid. The next two cases assumed the "mild" or "quiet character," as Mr. Farrow designates the "dumb form;" there was not the slightest tendency to do harm to any one who came in contact with them, and they died on the fourth day from "exhaustion and suffocation combined." The symptoms in these and other cases of dumb madness that followed were, he says, a disinclination for food, dulness, and moving from place to place. On the second day these symptoms were more marked, and the peculiar brilliancy of the eye was very conspicuous; deglutition was performed with difficulty, and there was partial paralysis of the lower jaw, accompanied by a hoarse peculiar sound in the windpipe, with a discharge of frothy saliva from the mouth. After several cases of "mild" rabies had occurred, the malady again assumed the violent form in the kennels, the hounds affected becoming so furious that it was extremely dangerous to approach them. And Mr. Henderson of Durham, in the letter which appeared in the *Times* on December 20, amply corroborates this statement, especially with regard to the later cases. "The huntsman, on visiting a few hounds separately confined, opened the door of the kennel, when a bitch he had brought up from a puppy flew at him most savagely, and had he not fortunately held the door in his hand and caught her between that and the post, he would most certainly have been bitten. It is needless to say, the bitch was perfectly mad . . . . Again, a day or two after, before leaving home for a rest, Dowdeswell went to take a last leave of such of his pack as remained, when Playmate, a favourite hound, who was accustomed to show his affection by standing up and placing his paws on his master's neck, sometimes being even permitted to lick his face, made his usual demonstration of licking; he was gently put aside and seemed disappointed. The day following Playmate, with three others, went perfectly mad; and would not permit those who were accustomed to feed and attend them to come near."

The "dumb madness" differs, therefore, in its more prominent features, from the form just described by reason of the paralysis of the lower jaw, which hinders it from biting, except in very exceptional circumstances; and also because the ferocious instincts are in abeyance, and there is no tendency to aggression. Nevertheless, there is every cause for circumspection in approaching a dog suffering from this type of rabies, and especially if it has to be handled; for, as has been pointed out, though it may be said to be quite inoffensive, yet its saliva is none the less virulent; and as the peculiar symptom which gives the disease its prenomen, is liable to lead those unaccustomed to rabies to imagine some foreign body is fixed in the creature's throat, and induce them to use their fingers for its removal, great danger is incurred. Therefore it is well to remember that if dumb madness is benignant, so far as its symptoms are concerned, it is not so with regard to its virulence.

It has been calculated that from 15 to 20 per cent. of rabid dogs have this peculiar form. It is uncommonly rare in other animals, and has really never been seen in swine or in mankind.

"Tranquil rabies" was, I believe, first described by Berndt,* and has been certified as not unfrequently present in dogs by Professor Lafosse. In this form of the disease the dog lies rolled up, and does not pay the slightest attention to any noises or movements around it; remaining indifferent even to the food and drink offered to it. Plunged in a kind of coma, it gradually wastes away, and dies quietly about fifteen days after the first symptoms have shown themselves.

This form of rabies has not, to my knowledge, been alluded to by any other comparative pathologists; which would lead us to suppose that it is rare. The disease most commonly assumes the furious type, and it is somewhat remarkable that puppies and young dogs nearly always have it in this form.

Thus far, then, we have endeavoured to depict the symptoms of rabies in the dog, from the initial manifestations to the termination of the disease in death. It only now remains to add, before alluding to the duration of the disease, that it is not necessary, nor is it likely, that all the signs above enumerated should be present in every case. One or more of the most characteristic may be absent now and again, and others may be more or less modified; yet there will always be sufficient evidence of the kind we have adduced present in every instance to indicate the existence of the malady to the careful, or even the casual, observer.†

* "Nouvelle Expériences sur l'Hydrophobie."

† Professor Saint-Cyr makes some very excellent remarks on this subject; and they are so apposite and useful that I make no apology for translating them.

Diagnosis.

The diseases or conditions with which rabies may be, and has been, confounded, are, nevertheless, somewhat numerous. The following are the chief:—

"Epilepsy," in which there are sudden convulsive fits, with loss of consciousness, and accompanied by a flow of foamy saliva from the mouth; at the same time the animal emits cries of distress, lies on the ground, and struggles. There is very

---

Speaking of the rabid or suspected dogs brought to the Lyons Veterinary School, he says: "These dogs are not always sent at the commencement of the malady. Often, very often, they remain with their owners, every moment in contact with the people of the houses in which they reside, and especially the children, for one, two, three, and even four days, and generally without the slightest suspicion of the terrible danger to which they are exposed. Every day there come to our *clinique* persons, and particularly females, carrying in their arms, without even the precaution of a muzzle, dogs said to be affected with something or another, but whose real disease is nothing but rabies. One dog had a *weakness of the hind quarters*, believed to have been caused by a blow with a stick over the back; it still eats a little, does not show any disposition to bite, and is even more affectionate than usual. Received into the infirmary on the 24th March (1864), it dies of unmistakable rabies on the 26th. Another had employed itself pulling shavings about a joiner's shop for two days, and no attention had been paid to this singular, but significant occupation, until, on its owner scolding it, it flew at and bit him; it also attacked a boy, but did not wound him. It was only then that some anxiety was raised as to its condition, and it was brought to the school. It was mad. Another is dull for three days, *but it should not be rabid*, as it still ate and drank, though less than usual. In three days it was dead from rabies. And another, for three days, constantly kept its mouth half open; *it must have a bone in its throat*. This bone was—rabies! These examples might be multiplied, but I will only add one more. In the autumn of 1858, a person of a certain age brought to the school, in his arms, and without being muzzled, a small American poodle. This dog had a paraphymosis, and I was requested to give an opinion. Not suspecting anything, I was about to put my hand on the diseased part, when it darted at me, and bit me severely in the index finger of the right hand. Still dreading nothing, and attributing this movement as merely a defensive one, I went into an adjoining apartment to wash the two or three bleeding and somewhat deep wounds. When I returned to the place where I left the proprietor and the dog, the noise I made in opening the door caused it to bark in the hoarse and broken voice peculiar to the rabid dog. Enlightened by this sinister and pathognomonic sound, I hastened to cauterise deeply each wound, and the accident had no further result. The dog was immediately put in a safe place, and it perished, mad, in two days. Its owner had known it to be ill for three days previous to bringing it to me. . . . . Truly the fear of the mad dog is the beginning of wisdom."—*Journal de Méd. Vét. de Lyon*, vol. xxi. p. 74.

rarely any attempt to bite, though the dog frequently champs with its jaws; and immediately the fit is over there is a return to consciousness, and the creature is the same as before. There is nothing like this in rabies—no loss of consciousness, no convulsive struggles on the ground, and meaningless champings with the jaws.

"Angina," or sore throat, in which all the symptoms of rabies are absent, except the difficulty in swallowing. Besides, there is much sensibility on pressure about the upper region of the throat or pharynx.

"Gastritis" and "Enteritis" (inflammation of the stomach and bowels) may easily be distinguished from madness by the presence of fever, vomiting, abdominal pain, and the absence of nervous symptoms, as well as in the different attitude assumed.

"Spasmodic Colic" does not at all present the same symptoms as rabies. The dog cries from pain while the spasms last, and very rarely at this period it is so irritable as to be disposed to bite, though not purposely. The animal retires, and never barks or howls as in rabies; the moans or yells it makes are those of pain, and are only emitted at uncertain intervals; there is pain on pressing the abdomen.

"Plica Polonica." In certain countries—from the source of the Vistula to the Carpathian Mountains—Lithuania, Red and White Russia, Tartary, Silesia, Bohemia, Suabia, Prussia, Saxony, and other parts of Germany—there is a disease named the "Plica Polonica," which attacks mankind, horses, cows, sheep, wolves, and foxes; and when it affects dogs these exhibit nearly all the symptoms of rabies, so that a large number, according to Lafontaine, are put to death by people who believe them to be mad. They carry the tail between their legs, foam at the mouth, scarcely ever bark, bite every one,—even their owners, whom they do not recognise; they lose their appetite, appear to be blind, and run against the walls; but at this period they drink more than usual, and their bite is not followed by hydrophobia. Foxes, wolves, and sheep offer analogous symptoms. The hair over the body becomes matted, and a vegetable parasite developed in it. Horses have only the mane and tail affected.*

"Distemper" is a disease that might sometimes, by the uninitiated, be confounded with rabies. There is frequently a discharge from the nose and eyes in the latter disease as in the former, and this is particularly apt to mislead. Paralysis, also, of the hinder extremities occurs as a sequel of both. But otherwise there is a wide difference. The commencement of distemper by sneezing and coughing, then a thin and watery discharge from the nose and eyes, becoming eventually purulent; the fever, disinclination to rove—so marked in rabies—absence of irritability and desire to bite; the lassitude, debility, and emaciation attending this malady—are the chief distinguishing features to be noted, in addition to the infrequency of a depraved appetite.

Some nervous symptoms which frequently supervene upon the more acute ones of this catarrhal fever, have at times been mistaken by the inexperienced for those of rabies; but to any one who has paid attention to the maladies of dogs, and who has seen one or two cases of the latter malady, such a mistake could not occur. Besides, the history of the case would at once, in nearly every instance, decide the question as to which disease it was.

The presence of "foreign bodies" in the mouth and throat has often given rise to symptoms which, in some few respects, simulate those of rabies. The animal refuses food and water, has a great difficulty in swallowing, the voice is altered, and there is anxiety and restlessness. But the foreign body can generally be felt or seen, and there is always abundant salivation. The creature is usually making constant attempts to remove the obstacle with its paws; there is cough and expulsive efforts which are almost continuous, and the dog is quite conscious. The extreme agitation and furious delirium are absent, as well

* Lafontaine, "Traité de la Plique Polonaise," Paris, 1808.

as the other notable signs of rabies; and the few symptoms present disappear as soon as the body is removed.

Not long ago a small pet dog was brought to me, said to be mad, and which had caused a great amount of excitement and alarm in the household to which it belonged. For some days it had been very uneasy, wandering about from room to room, attempting to vomit, and incessantly gulping, as if trying to swallow; holding up its head and smacking its lips, as if licking something; retiring to obscure corners, where it lay rubbing its mouth with its paws, and performing other singular manœuvres. There was not much salivation, and the absence of the peculiar physiognomy led me to infer that rabies was not present. No foreign body could be felt in the throat, and a somewhat superficial examination of the interior of the mouth did not lead to the detection of anything that could give rise to the symptoms this dog offered. The fidgetiness, salivation, anxious look, and gulping efforts, however, gave the animal a somewhat suspicious appearance; so much so, that a professional friend who chanced to be with me at the examination, and who had made rabies his study for several years, warned me to be careful in handling it, as its condition was very doubtful. Feeling satisfied, however, that there must be something lodged about the throat, and that it was not a case of rabies, I made a closer inspection of the mouth and fauces, and was not long in discovering a fine thread twisted around one of the upper canine teeth; seizing this with a pair of forceps, it was disengaged from around the tooth, and on pulling it away, it was found to be attached to a piece of rag some inches from the end that had been wrapped round the fang; this rag had been lodged about the pharynx, or upper end of the œsophagus, and had been the cause of the strange symptoms the animal manifested. Being a fixture to the tooth, the piece of cloth, which no doubt had been in its food, could not be swallowed, though it was in the situation in which it could excite the act; while the thread passing along the roof of the mouth, occasioned that kind of convulsive champing which might have been mistaken for the snapping in the air observed in mad dogs. In a second the annoying substance was removed, all the symptoms at once disappeared, and the delighted animal testified its gratitude and its joy by capering about and barking in a very lively manner.

"Tetanus" is a rare malady in the dog, and can scarcely be mistaken for rabies. There are rigid and painful muscular spasms, and the dog does not manifest any inclination to do mischief; the body is contorted, and the jaws usually firmly fixed against each other.

The presence of "worms" (*pentastomata tænioïdes*) in the frontal sinuses, or of a very large number of worms (*tænia echinococcus*) adhering by their hooks to the lining membrane of the small intestine, may also occasion the manifestation of symptoms analogous to those of rabies; but there are other characteristic symptoms of that disease which are absent, and an examination of the body after death demonstrates the nature of the malady. Worms in the nostrils or sinuses of the head will frequently cause the dog to rub his nose incessantly with his paws, against the ground, wall, posts, &c.

The pain and itching consequent on inflammation and ulceration of the inner part of the ear (vulgarly known as "canker") may occasion symptoms which some people might mistake for those of rabies. The ear of the dog is very frequently bitten by mad dogs, and when the disease is about to become developed, it sometimes happens that intense itching is set up in the wound or cicatrix, the animal rubs it against everything, and tries to scratch it with its paws; but in rabies it usually tumbles over while attempting this, and there are the other symptoms to assist in forming an opinion. In disease of the ear we have the symptom continuing for weeks or months, and no material change in the habit of the animal; and from the way in which it constantly carries its head towards the affected side, and the information a cursory inspection of the ear affords, there can scarcely be any mistake made.

To distinguish rabies from the other maladies and accidental conditions we have just enumerated, the peculiarities exhibited in the course of the disease, and which have been alluded to in detail, ought to be kept in memory: more especially the nervous and mental phenomena—the great anxiety, restlessness, irritability, and hallucinations, even while the animal's mind is as yet but little affected; also the peculiar bark or howl, tendency to rove, depraved appetite, desire to bite,—and with a purpose,—the subsequent paralytic symptoms, and the difficulty in swallowing.

Duration of Rabies in the Dog.

The progress of rabies in the dog is always very rapid, and the termination, it may well be said, invariably fatal.

Its duration, in no case, appears to have exceeded ten days; and in the majority of instances death takes places about the fourth, fifth, or sixth day after the appearance of the first morbid symptoms. Of course, it also occurs much earlier. Out of several tables we will only refer to those of Professor Saint-Cyr and Peuch, of the Lyons School, as they afford a fair idea of the duration of the disease in a number of cases. In 1864, fifty-four rabid dogs were reported. Death took place at the following periods:—

Two days	4 instances.
Three ,,	5 ,,
Four ,,	10 ,,
Five ,,	8 ,,
Six ,,	7 ,,
Seven ,,	8 ,,
Eight ,,	2 ,,
Twelve ,,	1 instance.
Thirteen ,,	1 ,,

The last case recovered spontaneously. The duration of the remaining eight cases could not be satisfactorily determined.

In the sixty-eight dogs that were rabid at the school in 1865, the duration of the disease was:—

Two days	. . . . . .	1 instance.
Three "	. . . . . .	6 instances.
Four "	. . . . . .	15 "
Five "	. . . . . .	20 "
Six "	. . . . . .	12 "
Seven "	. . . . . .	8 "
Eight "	. . . . . .	4 "
Nine "	. . . . . .	2 "

In 1868, in seventeen cases at the same school, it was:—

Two days	. . . . . .	2 instances.
Four "	. . . . . .	8 "
Five "	. . . . . .	4 "
Six "	. . . . . .	1 instance.
Seven "	. . . . . .	2 instances.

Resume of the Symptoms in the Dog.

As it is most important that the symptoms of rabies in the dog should be remembered, the following *résumé* of the most notable are given for the guidance of those who keep dogs, or who may have more or less to do with them.

1. The disease is not characterised by fits of fury at its commencement; but is, on the contrary, to all appearance a benignant malady, though even then the saliva or foam is virulent or poisonous. The dog is at this period very dangerous by its licking rather than biting; for as yet it has no tendency to use its teeth.

2. At the commencement of the disease the animal's temper becomes changed; it is dull, gloomy, and silent, seeks solitude, and withdraws into the most obscure corners. But it cannot rest long in one place; it is fidgety and agitated, goes here and there, lies down, and gets up, prowls about, smells, and scratches with its fore paws. Its movements, attitudes, and gestures at times would indicate that it is haunted by, and sees, phantoms; it snaps at nothing, and barks as if attacked by real enemies.

3. Its appearance is altered; it has a gloomy and somewhat ferocious aspect.

4. In this condition, however, it is not aggressive so far as mankind is concerned, but is as docile and obedient to its master as before. It may even appear to be more affectionate towards those it knows, and this it manifests by a greater desire to lick their hands and faces.

5. This affection, which is always so marked and so enduring in the dog, dominates it so strongly in rabies that it will not injure those it loves, not even in a paroxysm of madness; and even when its ferocious instincts are beginning to be manifested, and to gain the supremacy over it, it will yet yield obedience to those to whom it has been accustomed.

6. The mad dog has not a dread of water; but, on the contrary, will greedily swallow it. As long as it can drink it will satisfy its ever-ardent thirst; even when the spasms in its throat prevent its swallowing, it will nevertheless plunge its face deeply into the water, and appear to gulp at it. The dog is therefore not *hydrophobic*, and *hydrophobia* is not a sign of madness in this animal.

7. It does not generally refuse food in the early period of the disease, but sometimes eats with more voracity than usual.

8. When the desire to bite, which is one of the essential characters of rabies at a certain stage, begins to manifest itself, the animal at first attacks inert bodies, gnawing wood, leather, its chain, carpets, straw, hair, coals, earth, the excrement of other animals, or even its own, &c.; and accumulates in its stomach the remains of all the substances it has been tearing with its teeth.

9. An abundance of saliva is not a constant symptom in rabies in the dog. Sometimes its mouth is humid, and sometimes it is dry. Before a fit of madness the secretion of saliva is normal; during this period it may be increased, but towards the end of the malady it is usually decreased.

10. The animal often expresses a sensation of inconvenience

or pain during the spasm in its throat, by using its paws on the side of its mouth, like a dog which has a bone lodged there.

11. In "dumb madness" the lower jaw is paralysed and drops, leaving the mouth open and dry, and its lining membrane exhibiting a reddish-brown hue; the tongue is frequently brown or blue-coloured, one or both eyes squint, and the creature is ordinarily helpless and not aggressive.

12. In some instances the rabid dog vomits a chocolate or blood-coloured fluid.

13. The voice is always changed in tone, and the animal howls or barks in quite a different fashion to what it did in health. The sound is husky and jerking. In "dumb madness," however, this very important symptom is absent.

14. The sensibility of the rabid dog is greatly blunted when it is struck, burned, or wounded, it emits no cry of pain or sign as when it suffers or is afraid in health. It will even sometimes wound itself severely with its teeth, and without attempting to hurt any person it knows.

15. The mad dog is always very much enraged at the sight of an animal of its own species. Even when the malady might be considered as yet in a latent condition, as soon as it sees another dog it shows this strange antipathy, and appears desirous of attacking it. This is a most important indication.

16. It often flees from home when the ferocious instincts commence to gain an ascendancy; and, after one, two, or three days' wanderings, during which it has tried to gratify its mad fancies on all the living creatures it encountered, it often returns to its master to die. At other times it escapes in the night, and after doing as much damage as its violence prompts it to, it will return again towards morning. The distances a mad dog will travel, even in a short period, are sometimes very great.

17. The furious period of rabies is characterised by an expression of ferocity in the animal's physiognomy, and by the desire to bite whenever an opportunity offers. It always

prefers to attack another dog, though other animals are also victims.

18. The paroxysms of fury are succeeded by periods of comparative calm, during which the appearance of the creature is liable to mislead the uninitiated as to the nature of the malady.

19. The mad dog usually attacks other creatures rather than man, when at liberty. When exhausted by the paroxysms and contentions it has experienced, it runs in an unsteady manner, its tail pendant and head inclined towards the ground, its eyes wandering and frequently squinting, and its mouth open, with the bluish-coloured tongue, soiled with dust, protruding. In this condition it has no longer the violent aggressive tendencies of the previous stage, though it will yet bite every one—man or beast—that it can reach with its teeth, especially if irritated.

20. The mad dog that is not killed perishes from paralysis and asphyxia. To the last moment the terrible desire to bite is predominant, even when the poor creature is so prostrated as to appear to be transformed into an inert mass.*

Symptoms in the Cat.

The cat, like the dog, is our life-long companion, and lives on terms of the closest intimacy with us in our dwellings. It is also liable to contract rabies either spontaneously or by inoculation; though, happily, it is rarely affected, for a rabid cat is even more terrible and dangerous than the dog. In fact, when the cat becomes mad, its tiger-like nature is thoroughly awakened, and its bites are more death-dealing than those of the dog.†

* Bouley, "La Rage," p. 80.

† In Algeria, Dr. David, of Lestrade, saw a dog dying of rabies transmit the disease to a cat by biting it. This cat, in its turn, bit two persons, who succumbed a short time afterwards to hydrophobia. Cats are not unfrequently affected with rabies in that country. Roucher mentions four instances, three of which had been caused by bites. One died; another was killed after attacking a

The furious symptoms are preceded by precursory signs which are not to be overlooked, if we wish to guard against serious accidents; though they are not so easily and exactly observed as in the dog, because of the different habits and disposition of the animal.

At the commencement it evinces alteration of the appetite, a gloomy dulness, objectless agitation and restlessness, which is all the more striking as this creature is in its nature somewhat inclined to sleep, and passes the greater part of its life in repose. Frequently the appetite is depraved, and there is thirst, with a strong tendency to bite—which is somewhat unusual, as the cat in a domesticated condition is much more disposed to use its claws than its teeth. There is, then, reason to be suspicious when an animal of this species, contrary to its ordinary habits, becomes all at once restless, offers to attack people without being provoked, moves about evidently without cause, has a tendency to keep aloof, refuses to eat or drink for several days, or has a depraved taste and great thirst, and expresses by its attitudes and its physiognomy that there is something unusual affecting it. In such circumstances it is not too soon to take precautions, and to become master of the creature by a close and sure sequestration.

When the furious symptoms of rabies appear in the cat, its great eyes sparkle with an unnatural light, and express a startling degree of ferocity. There is nothing more terrible than to see a mad cat in a cage, says Bouley; the mouth is partly open and foamy, the back arched, and the tail beating its flanks; its claws are so rigidly protruded as to cause it to walk

---

man who subsequently perished from hydrophobia; the fate of the third was not known. The fourth instance was that of a cat at Orléansville, which communicated the disease, apparently without having been bitten itself. After an absence of several days, it returned home, and wounded the woman who owned it; the latter was soon affected with hydrophobia and died. The animal then disappeared, and in a few days after two dead cats were found in a street of the town in the colony where it had taken refuge. No case of hydrophobia was reported from this town.—*Dussart.*

with difficulty, and they penetrate the floor, leaving their imprint there. When any one presents himself before it, it flies towards him at a single bound, as high as the cage will permit, as if to attack the person's face; for this always appears to be the part of the body for which the mad creature has a special predilection when it is at liberty.

The rabid cat no longer knows its owner. Tamed rather than thoroughly domesticated, it in this condition reassumes all its ferocious instincts, and freely abandons itself to them. In this, as in so many other respects, the cat differs widely from the dog. The latter is intensely devoted to its master, and finds in its affection for him a power sufficiently strong to dominate, for a comparatively long time, the fierce desires that rabies fatally develops in it; rather than obey them, it will fly from its home when it can, and vent its involuntary rage on any one rather than those it loves. The cat will also leave the domestic roof when rabid, though rather through the influence of its savage nature than its devotion to its human companions; and will retire to some obscure loft, cave, or out-of-the-way place to die. It often wanders far from home. The claws are, at times, more frequently brought into use than the teeth, though both are unsparingly employed when the animal is in one of its paroxysms. As with the dog, the cat soon becomes haggard-looking and emaciated; the voice becomes changed, and assumes a special character—hoarse, sinister, and so disagreeable, that it is not unlike the sounds emitted in the midnight serenades of this creature, though the muscles concerned in swallowing are not so much involved as in the dog; paralysis is not long in appearing, and death puts an end to this miserable condition in from two to four days.

Symptoms in the Fox and Wolf.

The fox and wolf, and indeed all the wild carnivores, when rabid, quit their usual habitations, and have no hesitation or dread in entering towns and villages, or encountering men, dogs, and other creatures; on the contrary, when these attempt to obstruct them, they attack in a furious fashion, biting and tearing them, and then pursue their course in an unsteady manner, appearing as if unconscious of their acts. They attack horses, herds, and flocks, on the roads or in meadows and parks, biting them usually about the head and lips; they also ordinarily fly at the face of the human species. We have already observed that among these creatures rabies sometimes prevails on an extensive scale, without its being satisfactorily determined whether this extension is due to some particular atmospheric condition or "epizoötic constitution," or to successive transmissions by bites.

If a wolf bites people or animals without attempting to kill and devour them, it is usually admitted that it may be suspected of rabies.

Symptoms in Man.

We will now consider the symptoms in man and those domesticated animals which receive the infecting element from the creatures we have just referred to.

In many respects there is a striking similarity in the symptoms manifested in the hydrophobic patient and the rabid dog, while in others there is a wide dissimilarity. These resemblances and differences we will note, as we proceed to briefly sketch the phenomena of the disease in our own species.

The period of incubation or latency has been already alluded to, and it has also been mentioned that not unfrequently in man and the dog the earliest indication of approaching indisposition is a sense of pain in, or near, the seat of the wound, extending towards the body should the injury have been inflicted on the limbs. If not acute pain, there is some unusual sensation, such as aching, tingling, burning, coldness, numbness, or stiffness in the cicatrix; which usually in these circumstances swells, becomes of a red or lurid colour, sometimes opens up, and, if yet unhealed, assumes an unhealthy appearance, discharging a thin ichorous fluid instead of pus. In the dog, as we have observed, the peculiar sensation in the seat of the inoculation has at times caused the animal to gnaw the part most severely.

With these local symptoms, some general nervous disturbance is generally experienced. The patient becomes dejected, morose, irritable, and restless; he either does not suspect his complaint, or, if he remembers having been bitten, carefully avoids mentioning the circumstance, and searches for amusement away from home, or prefers solitude; bright and sudden light is disagreeable to him;* his sleep is troubled, and he often starts up; pains are experienced in various parts of the body; and signs of digestive disorder are not unfrequent.

After the continuance of one or more of these preliminary, or rather premonitory, symptoms for a period varying from a

* We have seen that light is unpleasant to the rabid dog, and causes it to seek dark corners and obscure places. The intolerance of the hydrophobic patient to the excitement produced by any shining body, or the sudden effects of a bright light, is well known, and may be one reason why, in Syria and El Héjaz, the popular idea is to keep the person affected with hydrophobia in a darkened apartment. Dr. Marchal, of Calvi, France, relates an instance in which this intolerance to light revealed the nature of the disease. A friend of his, Dr. Lelouis, a surgeon in the Algerian ambulances, was requested to proceed into the enemy's country by an Arab chief, who sent an escort to accompany him. On his arrival, he was ushered into the chief's tent, which was darkened, and found himself in the presence of a tall, noble-looking man, who appeared to be greatly agitated, but yet endeavoured to give himself an air of calmness. After reciprocal salutes, the chief motioned that the doctor should have coffee, after which he showed him his swollen hand as the seat of the disease which had caused him to be sent for. Lelouis made him open his mouth, and was depressing the tongue in order to examine that cavity, when at that moment an Arab entered the tent, and a streak of bright light fell upon the patient, who instantly made a bound backwards, exhibiting the greatest agony and trembling all over. This was a veritable gleam of light on the nature of the case. The chief recovered himself again, passed his hand over his face, and smiled softly, as if to excuse himself. The doctor, in a minute or two after, and in the course of conversation, inquired if the dogs belonging to his tribe were vicious? if they ever bit any one? and if he had ever been bitten? With the greatest indifference, and apparently without attaching the slightest importance to it, the chief showed him his hand, where there was to be seen the cicatrix of a bite, a little more than a month old. This man had no knowledge of hydrophobia. Lelouis left him some opium pills, and departed. In a few days afterwards he learned that the chief was dead.

few hours to five or six days, and, though very rarely, without all, or even many, of them being observed, the patient becomes sensible of a stiffness or tightness about the throat, rigors supervene, and, in attempting to swallow, he experiences some difficulty, especially with liquids. This may be considered as really the commencement of the attack in man.

The difficulty in swallowing rapidly increases, and it is not long before the act becomes impossible, unless it is attempted with determination; though even then it excites the most painful spasms in the back of the throat, with other indescribable sensations, all of which appal the patient, and cause him to dread the very thought of liquids. Singular nervous paroxysms or tremblings become manifest, and sensations of stricture or oppression are felt about the throat and chest. The breathing is painful and embarrassed, and interrupted with frequent sighs or a peculiar kind of sobbing movement; there is a sense of impending suffocation, and of necessity for fresh air. Indeed, the most marked symptoms consist in a horribly violent convulsion or spasm of the muscles of the larynx and pharynx (gullet), by which swallowing is prevented, and at the same time the entrance of air to the windpipe is greatly retarded.*

* Dr. Deroy, of Beton-Bazoches, furnishes a good illustrative case: "On 20th March, 1862, Ch. . . . aged thirty-eight years, in robust health, was slightly bitten in the hands by his dog, which disappeared from the house the same day, and was killed the next day in an adjoining village, after having set upon several dogs. Ch. . . . took no precautions with regard to his wounds, which appeared to him to be insignificant. Nevertheless, six days afterwards, tormented with the idea that his dog had been mad, he came to me. The few excoriations on his hands were completely cicatrised. I reassured him as well as I could, and, to calm his mind, cauterised the scars and gave him a simple prescription, being well persuaded that I had then, unfortunately, no means of averting the danger which he dreaded no less than myself. After this I lost sight of him until the 1st of May, forty-two days subsequent to the injury. He was then seized with well-marked symptoms of hydrophobia, and died at two o'clock in the morning of the 13th, in the midst of crises so terrible, that, during the last evening, notwithstanding the strait-jacket I was compelled to put on him, all the articles composing his bed, to which he was firmly fixed, from the coverlet to the paillasse, were torn into fragments. The following are the most salient features I noted in the case: Intelligence definite; consciousness of his condition; speech jerking; extreme agitation; horrible difficulty in respiration, especially during the access; almost continual spitting; the sight of shining objects did not

Shuddering tremors, sometimes almost amounting to general convulsions, run through the whole frame; and a fearful expression of anxiety, terror, or despair is depicted on the countenance.

The paroxysms are brought on by the slightest causes, and are frequently associated with an attempt to swallow liquids, or with the recollection of the sufferings experienced in former attempts. Hence, anything which suggests the idea of drinking to the patient will throw him into the most painful agitation and convulsive spasms. The morbid sensibility of the auditory nerves has long been known, for Cœlius Aurelianus cautioned practitioners, when bleeding hydrophobous persons, to prevent the noise or sound of the blood flowing into the basin being heard by them lest they should be affected by it (*ne sonitu perculsi commoveantur*).* The sound of water poured from one vessel into another, the sight of liquids or of objects which chance to come before them, the shining surface of a mirror, a current of cold air, or any cold substance applied to the skin, may have this effect.

This is particularly observed when the patient carries water to his lips; then he is seized with the terrors characteristic of the disease, and with those convulsions of the face and the whole of the body, which make so deep an impression on the bystanders. He is perfectly rational, feels thirsty, tries to

---

appear to irritate him, but the difficulty in respiration was such that he could not tolerate any one near him. Every moment he was saying, 'Go away; do not come near me; it is not because I am afraid of biting you; I have no desire to do so, but you stifle me, and prevent my breathing. Open the windows, or allow me to go out that I may respire easily.' . . . The sight of water, wine, or any other liquids did not produce any disagreeable effect on him, and he told us that what tormented him was swallowing. I poured slowly, and at a good height, water from a jug into a plate within two paces of him without his objecting. I said to him, 'If you cannot drink out of a glass or a cup, perhaps you can easily do so out of a saucer.' But he answered sharply and angrily, 'I am not afraid of the liquid you offer me, but how can you expect me to swallow water or anything else, when I cannot even swallow air!' Does not this reply, at once so simple, energetic, and sensible, indicate that, in this disease, the larynx and pharynx are equally affected with the same spasmodic contractions?"—*Gazette des Hôpitaux*, June, 1868.

* "Acut. Morbi.," book iii. chap. 16.

drink, but the liquid has no sooner touched his lips, than he draws back in terror, and sometimes exclaims that he cannot drink; his face expresses pain, his eyes are fixed, and his features contracted; his limbs shake and body trembles. The paroxysm lasts a few seconds, and then he gradually becomes tranquil; but the least touch, nay, mere vibration of the air, is enough to bring on a fresh attack,—so acute is the sensibility of the skin in some instances. A case is mentioned by Trousseau, in which the senses were so exquisitely exalted that the scent of some lilac flowers, distant about thirty metres, greatly distressed a soldier who was hydrophobic; and the least movement of the air, as by the opening of a door, made him complain of a disagreeable sensation, as if his face were slapped, and caused him to jump up in bed. Majendie describes the case of a deaf-and-dumb child who heard distinctly in this stage of the disease. The patient, in some instances, cannot wash his hands or comb his hair without being at once threatened with convulsions.

During the intervals of calm, he sometimes complains of pain in the stomach and of nausea; when he is actually sick, he vomits greenish-coloured matters. In some cases he is seized with sudden terror, and turns abruptly round, fancying that somebody calls to him; and there are hallucinations of sight and of hearing. One patient alluded to by Trousseau, heard the ringing of bells and saw mice run about on his bed. In the dog, we have noted that it is also the victim of hallucinations; but a special difference between rabies and hydrophobia is in the frequent dread of water in the latter, as well as the hyperæsthesia of the skin and exaltation of the other senses. But in another particular there is a similarity.

We have alluded to the presence, at times, of sexual desire on the part of the rabid dog. Since the days of Boerhaave, satyriasis has been noted as occasionally present in men affected with hydrophobia, especially during the period of excitation; indeed, Van Swieten stated that Galen mentions this symptom, and cases are by no means rare nowadays. Nymphomania has also been sometimes witnessed in women suffering from th disease, according to Trousseau.

Another characteristic feature of the disease in man, is a copious secretion of a viscid tenacious mucus in the fauces—the "hydrophobic slaver;" this the patient spits out with a sort of vehemence and rapidity upon everything around him, as if the idea of swallowing occasioned by the liquid induced this eager expulsion of it, lest a drop might pass down the throat. This, to a bystander, is sometimes one of the most striking phenomena of the case. In the last hours preceding dissolution, the patient's mouth is often full of this mucus or froth, which is, in some cases, tinged with blood. The lower jaw would appear to be sometimes partially paralyzed, and then the saliva flows from the corners of the mouth.

Acute and, as it were, electric shocks of pain are now and then felt in the region of the stomach, the back of the neck, and other parts of the spine.

The mind is sometimes calm and collected in the intervals between the paroxysms, and consciousness is generally retained; but, in most cases, there is more or less irregularity, incessant talking, excitement, and occasionally fits approaching to insanity come on. Not unfrequently the victim is aware of the approach of these attacks, and, fearful of doing injury to those around him, begs that he may be restrained. The mental aberration is often exhibited in groundless suspicion or apprehension of something extraneous, which is expressed on the face and in the manner of the patient. Sometimes, on the contrary, he takes a curious fancy to individuals, and lavishes on them marks of fondness and confidence.

In comparatively rare instances he gives way to a wild fury, like that of the dog in one of its fits of rabies; he roars, howls, curses, strikes at persons near him, rends or breaks everything within his reach, bites others or himself, till, at length exhausted, he sinks into a gloomy, listless dejection, from which another paroxysm rouses him.

Eight days	. . . .	3 cases.
Ten "	. . . .	1 case.
Fifteen to twenty days	. . . . .	5 cases.

Tardieu found the duration of hydrophobia not to exceed, in 161 cases, the following periods:—

34 cases	. . . .	2 days.
98 "	. . . .	4 "
24 "	. . . .	6 "
2 "	. . . .	7 "
2 "	. . . .	8 "
1 case	. . . .	9 "

In Algeria the mean duration of the confirmed disease is from three to four days; but it may in rare cases extend to ten.

In ninety instances reported by Professor Bouley, death occurred in seventy-four during the first four days, the largest portion of these being in the second and third day. In only sixteen cases was life prolonged beyond the fourth day. This inquiry, adds the Professor, establishes the fact that now, as always, death has been the inevitable termination of rabid accidents; and that the unfortunate individuals who have been its victims have passed through those dreadful moral and physical tortures which fully explain and justify the terror that the bare idea of hydrophobia inspires among persons in all grades of life.

Diagnosis in Man.

When hydrophobia is fully developed, its peculiar symptoms are so striking and characteristic that it cannot be confounded with any other disease. Those maladies which it most closely resembles are hysteria, and tetanus or "locked-jaw." In hysteria the difficulty of swallowing is present, but none of the other symptoms of hydrophobia. Though tetanus is the disease which, in some of its features, approaches nearest to that under consideration, yet the distinction between them is very marked. The spasm of the muscles is more continued in tetanus, less remitting, and never intermitting. The jaw is usually much in motion in hydrophobia, in the frequent attempts to clear the mouth and throat from the peculiar tenacious mucus; in tetanus it is fixed. Tetanus is rarely attended with aversion to liquids; on the contrary, the bath is grateful; nor are the tetanic paroxysms increased by the sight, hearing, or touch of fluids. Also, tetanus makes its appearance usually at a much earlier period after the infliction of the injury. Physiologically, while tetanus is a disease of the true spinal system of nerves, hydrophobia involves the brain also, as evinced by the disorder of intellectual function and special sense, even early in the disease. Further, the two diseases differ greatly in their mode of induction. Tetanus in the traumatic cases (arising from an injury) is caused by irritation of a nerve, and by disease of the spinal marrow in those which are idiopathic (without any injury). Hydrophobia is the result of a specific poison introduced into the circulation, and thence affecting the nervous system as a poison would. While in tetanus the stimulus which excites the paroxysms operates through the true spinal cord, in hydrophobia it is often conducted from the ganglia of special sense, or even from the brain; so that the sight or sound of fluids, or even the idea of them, occasions, equally with their contact, or with that of a current of air, the most distressing convulsions.*

Though tetanus may be attended with a profuse secretion of mucus or saliva, there is not present the characteristic hydrophobic manner of excreting these fluids.

There is a peculiar hysterical affection, or mental hydrophia, as Dr. Trousseau named it, which simulates the malady, and is brought on by emotion on seeing hydrophobic individuals, through fear of the disease, or, in nervous people, on hearing a description of real cases of it. Dr. Michie, of Shanghai, informs me that when rabies was prevalent there in 1867, he was called up one night to attend a young man, who assured him that he had been unable to drink fluids since the previous afternoon, and who looked excited and haggard. By impressing upon him that the difficulty was imaginary, the

* Aitken, "Science and Practice of Medicine," vol. i. p. 727.

doctor succeeded in getting him to drink some soda-water, and his hydrophobia soon disappeared.*

In this imaginary malady there is only dysphagia, or difficulty in swallowing, and no general convulsions,—the spasm affecting the pharynx alone, while the breathing goes on with regularity. The sudden invasion of the complaint, generally coming on through the person recalling to mind, or hearing the relation of, a case of true hydrophobia, and the duration of the dysphagia over four days without any more urgent symptom

* Dr. Trousseau relates the two following examples of this pseudo-hydrophobia. "In the spring of 1828, I was engaged with my colleague at the Academy, M. Leblanc (veterinary surgeon, Paris), and Dr. Ramon, in investigating the rot disease which was rife among the sheep of the Sologne. He had just inoculated with the disease three hundred sheep, belonging to M. Joupitre, mayor of the department. Whilst talking of virulent diseases in general, this gentleman told us that he had been affected with hydrophobia. A farm dog had tried to bite his arm, and about the same time it had bitten a good many beasts, which died of rabies. A few months afterwards, on Easter Sunday, after service, and at a breakfast at which every one had done his best to make up for the rigid abstinence of the past Lent, M. Joupitre exclaimed suddenly that he was seized with hydrophobia. He could not eat or drink any more, and was already beginning to rave, when his wife, who only believed that he had eaten too much, persuaded him to tickle his throat with his fingers. The advice was good, for copious sickness was brought on by the manœuvre, and nothing more was said about hydrophobia. That same year I happened to relate M. Joupitre's case to a presiding judge in chambers, who, in his turn, told me that he also had once believed himself to be seized with hydrophobia. He used to go out riding frequently, and a sporting dog, which generally accompanied him, often jumped to lick the hand with which he held his whip. During one of these rides they met a flock of sheep, after which the dog ran, biting all those he could catch. The animal still heard and obeyed his call, but it had a strange aspect. Again it ran after, and bit dogs, cows, and oxen, and lastly swam across a river; a few hours later it died. A short time after this, the judge heard that many of the beasts that had been bitten by his dog had perished of rabies. This news alarmed him, because he recalled to mind that on the same day the dog had licked his right hand several times. On examining this hand, he found several small scars on it, and, seized with terror, he no longer dared touch water to shave himself, and fully believed he had hydrophobia. A medical man, who was sent for from Orleans, tried in vain to calm his fears; for several days he was excited and delirious. At last, being told over and over again that persons seized with the disease died very rapidly, and that he could not, therefore, be hydrophobic, since his dread of water dated already ten days back; and after reading in books about the duration of confirmed hydrophobia, he allowed himself to be persuaded, and his dread of water vanished as soon as he became convinced that he would have died long ago if he had been infected."

appearing, are amply sufficient to characterise the affection, and to enable the patient's medical adviser or friends to persuade him that he is suffering from mere nervous symptoms, which will vanish as soon as he ceases to fear.

Cases have been recorded of what were believed to be outbreaks of spontaneous hydrophobia in man, and which, certainly, so far as the description of the symptoms goes, and the fatal results, appear to have resembled very closely the transmitted disease. But inoculation sometimes takes place in such an obscure manner, that one would almost doubt whether these instances were not due to the introduction of the contagious element. At any rate, we have no proof that a virus was generated in these outbreaks, and cannot accept them as belonging to the malady we are now considering; which is due to inoculation with the poison of a rabid animal, and which ought to be distinguished from the spontaneous malady by some such name as *toxico-rabies*—a designation proposed by Baumes,—or *virulent hydrophobia.*

Maniacs also sometimes evince a dread of liquids, and refuse to drink, according to Trousseau. Like all persons suffering from hydrophobia in the second stage, they are exceedingly agitated and loquacious, and have hallucinations; but they never have general rigors and spasmodic convulsions. They are, besides, delirious on all subjects, whilst a rabid individual retains all his reason, although he may occasionally have transient hallucinations. He is anxious to get well, and, believing that his complaint is merely due to his inability to drink, he submits to any treatment; and once the paroxysm of excitement is over, he allows a strait-jacket to be put on him without offering the least resistance. A maniac has lost his reason; in hydrophobia, on the contrary, as Boerhaave stated long ago, even in the last stage of the disease, the patient retains his firmness and common sense, and requests the persons about him to keep some distance from him, because he dreads lest he should communicate his complaint to them.

Indeed, it is not possible to mistake hydrophobia for any other malady, or to doubt its existence when it is present; for if, during the stage of incubation, doubts and fears may exist, all uncertainty comes to an end when the disease really appears. The muscular debility complained of in many cases, the restless sleep out of which the patient starts up, his continual fidgetiness, his suspicious breathing, his sadness and search after pleasure, and then his love of solitude, must awaken terrible fears in the physician: especially if there be no moral causes or organic lesions to satisfactorily account for these symptoms. The intense thirst, and general muscular pains and rigors, which might at first be ascribed to some grave febrile affection, are followed by a symptom that is almost pathognomonic of hydrophobia—namely, a sudden difficulty in swallowing liquids, water in particular. When there is complete inability to drink, and when this dysphagia is immediately succeeded by tremor on the patient carrying some liquid to his lips, all illusion is dispelled, and it becomes clear that he is under the fatal influence of the virus of rabies.

Symptoms in the Horse.

However much the symptoms of rabies may vary in the animals not naturally liable to it, but to which it has been transmitted by wounds inflicted by the dog, cat, fox, or wolf, the same nervous derangement and excitability are nevertheless predominant, and many of the symptoms are analogous and referable to the same morbid changes.

The commencement of rabies in the horse is marked by restlessness; biting at the seat of injury, as if it itched; changing its position frequently; starting suddenly as if frightened; much more susceptible to external influences than usual, and very irascible; the eye is more sensitive to light, the gaze is fixed; the pupil, in the majority of cases, is dilated; the ears are moved as if the animal heard strange sounds, and it appears to be the victim of mental hallucinations. Venereal desires in the mare and stallion are generally considerably augmented. The latter has priapism frequently, and neighs in a harsh tone, while the former stands with its hind legs wide apart, and shows signs of "horsing." As the disease progresses, cutaneous quivering is observed, which is soon followed by convulsions; loss of appetite and difficulty in swallowing are frequently noticed. During the paroxysms, the animal kicks viciously, and bites so furiously at any objects in its way, that sometimes its teeth, and even jaws, are broken. It will even bite its own body. The respiration becomes accelerated, and the voice hoarse and unpleasant. There is rarely much salivation.

The duration of the paroxysms, which are generally excited by the presence of a dog, is variable, and in the remissions the animal more or less regains its faculties, but is weak and exhausted. The succeeding fits are usually more intense, and the intervals shorter. The horse rapidly becomes enervated and sinks; towards the close, paralysis of the hinder extremities ensues, and it then ordinarily maintains the recumbent position. From the second to the fourth or sixth day after the appearance of the first symptoms, it perishes in a convulsive paroxysm.*

* The following interesting cases are here noted as examples of rabies in the horse. "On the 31st May, 1869, a heavy draught horse, fourteen years old, was admitted to the clinic of the Lyons Veterinary School. On the 25th of the previous March, while drawing a light cart, it was attacked in the street by a bulldog, which sprang at its face, and inflicted two bites—one on the inner, the other at the outer surface of the upper lip. The dog, which appeared to be a wanderer without a master, was immediately killed, and its body conveyed to the school, when it was found to have been suffering from rabies. The horse itself was conducted to the school, and the two wounds made by the fangs of the dog were cauterised deeply by a red-hot iron, *an hour and a half after their infliction.* Two months passed away without anything unusual being observed, and the animal worked as usual until the 30th of May, when all at once, and without any assignable cause, it became irritable. It was then remarked that its mouth was foamy, the eyes brilliant and a little haggard-looking, and that at times it was so restless as to give rise to the idea that it was suffering from *colic.* It was therefore led to its stable, in the hope that these colicky symptoms would disappear; for no one thought of the accident on the 25th March. The next day, however, the symptoms, instead of disappearing, were aggravated, and fearing a brain affection, it was now sent to the school to be treated. On its arrival there, it was in

In November, 1870, a case occurred at Huddersfield, Yorkshire, in which the symptoms were unusual liveliness when in

---

an extreme state of excitement, as if it had been terribly frightened; the eyes were sparkling, restless, and haggard, and the ears continually in motion. It was never quiet for a moment; everything around it appeared to disturb or frighten it, and it snorted loudly. The mouth was filled with a frothy saliva that escaped by the commissures of the lips; the jaws were moved incessantly in a champing fashion. At intervals it widely opened its mouth, as if to yawn, when it made a dull, hoarse, guttural sound. Then it shook its head from side to side, as if it had something unpleasant in its throat; at the same time it pawed violently with its fore feet. Placed in a stall and secured, it at first sprang back, as if startled by something before it, then opened its mouth and emitted the peculiar sound already mentioned, and struck the ground violently with its fore feet, but without tearing it up. It soon appeared to recover from its fear, approached the part to which it was attached, on which it placed its nose, and then commenced to rub this region of its head energetically, as if it experienced there—the seat of the injury—a violent itching. A handful of forage offered to it was seized with convulsive haste, and masticated and swallowed without any apparent difficulty. On a pailful of water being presented, it approached it with fear, snorting and snuffing in a very loud manner. After a few moments' hesitation, it plunged its nose in it and swallowed some mouthfuls without manifesting any pain or difficulty. Then it sprang back, widely opening its mouth and pawing with its foot. A stick being held before it was seized in its teeth and crushed. The sight of a dog placed in front of it did not cause much disturbance; it smelled energetically at it, but without attempting to do it any harm. The skin was covered with perspiration; the pulse frequent and hard (fifty per minute); the respiration accelerated (thirty per minute); the loins were insensible to pressure by the fingers. After a short period, the symptoms became momentarily exaggerated, either spontaneously, or through the influence of some external excitation; these exacerbations were separated by intervals of relative calmness. It was remarked, however, that these intervals became more and more brief, while the paroxysms became more frequent and serious. During their existence, the patient at times seized, with a kind of fury, the border of the *tourniquet* to which it was tied between its incisor teeth, and rubbed it so viciously as to make a deep groove.

These symptoms persisted during the night, and the next morning it was found that the horse, biting constantly in the same place, had made a large irregular cavity in the tourniquet. At five o'clock in the morning (1st June), the animal, completely exhausted by suffering, fell down, struggled and plunged violently for two hours, and died in the midst of frightful convulsions at seven A.M.

This case is noteworthy from the period of incubation—sixty-five days—being accurately ascertained; from the fact that cauterisation of the wounds within a short period after their infliction did not prevent the appearance of the malady,—showing that, to be safe, not an instant must be lost in destroying the virus; the prominent symptoms were those of cerebral excitation, with fear or fright, a tendency to bite or gnaw, and the manifestation of intense pruritis in the seat of the injury. The horse had neither a horror of liquids, nor was it impossible for it to swallow them: though there was a certain degree of fear on offering it the pail, and perhaps pain in deglutition, as evidenced by the harness, soon succeeded by violent trembling, and fury, during which it knocked the stable window out. When the breast or flanks were touched, the animal screamed. It seized the groom

---

movements of the head, which took place as soon as it had drank, but which, nevertheless, were also produced at other times. The animal was irritable, so far as mankind was concerned, but not vicious; as it did not kick or bite when any one was examining it. The course of the disease was very rapid, the animal succumbing through nervous exhaustion, and perhaps also by asphyxia, in forty-eight hours after the appearance of the first symptoms.—*Journal de Méd. Vétérinaire de Lyon*, 1869, p. 541.

The cases reported by Zahn, of the Vienna Veterinary School, are perhaps still more interesting, so far as the symptomatology is concerned.

A dog belonging to a carman, after biting several pigs and another dog, entered its owner's stable during the night of the 29—30 September, 1867, where it was captured the following day, and conveyed in a carriage to the hospital of the Veterinary School. It was there recognised as affected with rabies, from which malady it soon died. On his return, the owner remarked that one of his horses was wounded on the right thigh. This horse—a gelding, seven years old—was immediately sent to be taken care of at the Veterinary School. A minute examination of the wounds showed that they were produced by dog bites; their depth extended to the cellular tissue, and the surface was covered with coagulated blood. After being well cleaned, they were at once cauterised with quick-lime. The following day, some superficial wounds, covered with blood, were discovered in the right nostril; these were treated like the others. The carman, having inspected all his horses, sent three more to the school on the 1st of October. One of these had a superficial wound on the right shoulder, covered with coagulated blood; but it could not be asserted that this had been caused by the dog; it was therefore dressed with the quick-lime, and the horse was sent back to the proprietor. The second animal—a mare, twelve years old—had a deep, partly-torn wound on the right lip of the vulva, and was kept at the school. The third was a gelding aged six years; it had also a deep wound on the heel of the left hind foot. These two animals were submitted to the same treatment as the first two. The cauterisations with the quick-lime were repeated whenever the eschar fell off; this was also carried out in the horse that had been sent back to the proprietor; on the 8th October, the three horses received into the hospital were, by permission of the police, returned to the owner, on the understanding that they should be kept in a separate stable and exclusively employed for short journeys.

On the 15th of November, forty-seven days after the bits, the mare was again brought to the hospital of the school. According to the proprietor, this animal fell in draught the previous evening, and since then she walked unsteadily. On inspection, feebleness was only manifest in the lumbar region, and on the 16th in the joints of the posterior limbs. On the 17th it could no longer stand, the posterior extremities being paralysed, and it was necessary to remove the fæces and urine. The pulse was raised to fifty-six pulsations per minute; one-half the ration of forage was eaten, and nothing abnormal was noticed in drinking. The pulse was the same on the 18th; the animal was tranquil, though it ground its teeth, and on several occasions tried to bite the student who was ministering to it. It died on the 20th. The blood was black, thick, and not coagulated; the

by the shoulder with its teeth, and would not release him until beaten off by another man. In the paroxysm, it tore its clothing, which was removed with difficulty and danger. No sooner

---

spinal cord was greatly softened, and the spleen offered characters of an acute inflammation.

On the 14th December, seventy-six days after the bite, the horse that had been wounded on the right thigh was brought to the hospital. The driver said that it was quite well until the 13th December, when it began to show loss of appetite. On the morning of the 14th, it also refused a portion of its ration, and, contrary to its habits, snapped at the neighbouring horses; on which it was led to the school at eight A.M. It was put in a strong loose-box. At the seat of the bites in the thigh and nostril were dry cicatrices; the pulse was fifty-six, and the respirations irregular and numbering twenty-four per minute. Percussion of the chest did not reveal anything abnormal, but auscultation discovered a crepitant sound. The mucous membrane of the mouth was foul, and that cavity was filled with foam. The animal often ground its teeth, flexed its knees several times, and fell down in a quarter of an hour after being put into the box; it made some struggles, and after some difficulty it got up again. While standing, it appeared to be very attentive, moved its ears frequently, and passed much urine, but with regularity. When the box door was opened, it neighed with unaltered voice; at the approach of any one it prepared to kick, put back its ears, and tried to bite. From time to time it pawed the ground with the right fore leg, and rested sometimes on one, sometimes on the other posterior limb; then it bent its knees, and at last fell on the left side. The increasing weakness of its hind quarters prevented its rising; while it lay, and during its efforts to rise, its teeth continued to be ground; it pushed with its head against the floor on which its mouth rested, and bit at the soil and litter; at length it rose again. The falls became more frequent, and were repeated at closer intervals, while rising became more difficult. While it was standing, the respiration was quicker and more irregular than during the decubitus; sweat covered the body; the bread that was offered to it was seized with avidity, but mastication was slow and swallowing difficult. It would not drink the water put before it, but amused itself by laving its mouth in it. The difficulty in moving the hind quarters increased, and the animal stood stretched out; the eye was haggard, the conjunctiva greatly injected, and the cornea slightly opaque. The grinding of the teeth persisted, as well as the flexing of the knees. At ten o'clock, the horse fell for the fifth time, attempted several times to roll and to rise, but in vain. It seized the skin of the right knee with its teeth, folding it up and holding it; at a later period, it grasped the right fore arm between its jaws and held it so for half an hour. The respiration became irregular, very quick, and jerking; all the body was covered with an abundant perspiration, and a large quantity of foam ran from the mouth. At half-past ten, the animal sprang up, remained tranquil, but went down in a few minutes on the right side. It tried again to roll and get up, and continued to bite the ground and its fore legs. It remained in this condition until mid-day, when a calm supervened—the foam came from its mouth in streams, it appeared quite paralysed, the respiration became stertorous, and at length it succumbed at half-past one.

On the 15th December, seventy-seven days after the bite from the mad dog, at three in the afternoon, the third horse, which had been bitten in the heel, was

was this taken away than it commenced to tear its own body, striking violently with its fore legs against a manger. After a while it seized this manger, which was a strong one, with its teeth, tore it away from its fixtures, and shook it "as a dog would shake a rat;" then rushed into the next stall, where it

taken to the hospital, and put in a strong loose-box. This animal, since it was bitten, although in good health, was not so familiar as before. On this day a great weakness was manifested in the hind quarters, and while being shod it fell. On admission to the hospital, the respirations were from sixteen to twenty per minute, and the pulse forty-four to forty-eight. The membrane of the mouth was pale, hot, and dry. The animal rapidly devoured one-half of the ration put before it, drank regularly, was very sensitive to the touch, especially about the throat, often flexed the knees, relieved alternately the posterior members, manifested pain on pressure to the loins, and the hind quarters swayed from side to side in walking. The next day, the 16th, there was no change. The sensibility in the cicatrix of the wound in the hind leg was very great; the animal often essayed to micturate, but only a small quantity was voided. It ate and drank regularly. On the 17th, however, it did not eat all its food, and the respirations were thirty-six and the pulsations fifty-six per minute. The horse was very attentive and its ears kept moving in a very lively manner. Mastication was slow, and deglutition difficult. On the 18th, at eight o'clock, the patient lay down for the first time, but soon arose again after several attempts. The weakness of the hind quarters had increased, the fæces and urine were often expelled with difficulty, and always in small quantities. The eye was sometimes haggard, the conjunctiva injected, and the horse ground its teeth while eating, and towards the evening it tried to bite those who, having attended it, were leaving it. On the 19th, the paralysis of the hind quarters was diminished, and it would allow none to approach it; it reared against the wall of the box, and when hay was put in the manger by means of a shovel, it darted suddenly at this instrument and held it between its incisor teeth; in the same manner, with its ears back, it endeavoured to seize any one who approached it. The pieces of bread that were thrown to it from a distance were snatched up with avidity, masticated, and swallowed. It refused water, and fiercely gnawed the bucket. Restlessness came on towards midnight, and the body was soaked in perspiration. At four o'clock in the morning, it fell down for the last time, and expired. The fourth horse remained healthy.—*Œsterreichische Vierteljahresschrift für Wissenschaftliche Veterinærkunde*, vol. xxx.

In 1871, a horse which had been bitten some time before by a dog supposed to be mad, was brought to the hospital of the Royal Veterinary College at Berlin. It had been suffering from an uncontrollable propensity to bite not only men and other animals, but any hard substance it encountered, and even its own body; by which it had severely injured its mouth and broken several of its teeth. After its admission to the hospital, this propensity was manifested in the most violent manner in fits, preceded by remarkable convulsive movements; after which it would fall suddenly, and remain for a time perfectly motionless, becoming gradually weaker after each attack. It had refused food for two days, and died without a struggle on the evening of the day on which it was admitted.—*Zeitschrift für Parasitenkunde.*

demolished the manger in the same manner. "Then he knocked the boarding down which separated the two stalls, and rushed about the stable worrying everything he came near, every now and then stopping to paw with his fore leg, and tearing at it with his teeth."*

Diagnosis in the Horse.

The history of the case will, in this animal, as in others, prove of service in establishing a diagnosis. The only disease with which it might be confounded by the inexperienced is inflammation of the brain (phrenitis) and paralysis. The furious symptoms occurring in paroxysms, with no loss of consciousness; as well as the methodical manner with which the animal commits its depredations, and its antipathy to dogs, will distinguish this from the first-named disease, while the same symptoms will distinguish it from paralysis.

Symptoms in the Cow.

The symptoms of rabies in the cow are analogous to those observed in the horse. Loss of, or depraved appetite; prostration; great restlessness; increased excitability; muscular tremblings; a flow of saliva nearly constantly from the mouth; exaltation of the sexual desires, especially in the bull; difficulty in swallowing; and the manifestation of disagreeable sensations in the seat of the wound, as well as hallucinations, are the first signs; though sometimes the commencement is very insidious. During the paroxysms, the eyes are staring, brilliant, haggard-looking, and injected; the pupils are dilated; the mouth hot and foamy; and the voice is changed to a dull hoarse sound. The animals are very excited, bellow frequently, agitate their jaws, paw with the fore feet, throw behind them the earth or their litter; they fall down, roll about, or try to get away from their fastenings. There are tremblings and twitchings of the

* The *Veterinarian*, vol. xliii. p. 918.

muscles; in the cow, the secretion of milk is suspended; and frequently there is a disposition to attack other animals and people. They strike with their horns—or their forehead if they have no horns—at obstacles in their way; and with such fury that the horns are often fractured, and the forehead a mass of extravasated blood. They do not always, however, seek to strike with their horns, and very rarely attempt to bite. They sometimes jump on other cattle in a frenzy, if at large. The appetite is nearly always lost, and rumination entirely ceases; the appetite, when present, is often depraved; the fæces, at first expelled at long intervals and in small quantity, become at a later period liquid, and are often passed involuntarily. At other times the expulsive efforts are so great that the rectum is protruded.

Emaciation becomes extreme, and, finally, paralysis of the posterior extremities ensues. The cattle then lie, are incapable of getting up, and perish in a profound coma.*

* The Austrian Military Veterinary Surgeon, Fiala, reports that on the 18th July, 1868, Josef Mescevic, of Josefthal, observed one of his cows, aged five years, refusing its food and drink, frequently bellowing, and discovered that the lacteal secretion had diminished, while the animal had become very irritable. On the 21st, when visited by the veterinary surgeon, it was extremely restless; the ocular globes, protruding from the orbits, were slightly injected, the nostrils dilated, the ears in constant motion, and the flanks retracted; a viscid saliva flowed from the mouth; no appetite; the lacteal secretion suppressed; the vulva tumified; the excretion of fæces and urine frequently made, but in small quantity; the excrements were hard and slimy; at the sight of the house-dog it was very agitated, bellowed in a hoarse voice, and sprang at it. There was no wound or cicatrix visible on its body, and no one knew how or when the cow had been bitten. On the 23rd July, it was lying, the eyes sparkling and haggard, the conjunctiva injected, the hair erect, an abundant salivation, and the general condition had become one of emaciation. The animal tried to avoid the light, refused food, but drank plenty of water, though it swallowed with difficulty; it arose several times, but only to fall down again, and trembled all over. The presence of the house-dog excited its fury, and made it bellow in a jerking, hoarse tone; but it did not seek to bite or strike. It was killed.—*Œsterreich. Vierteljahres. für Veterinærkunde*, vol. xxx.

A rabid dog had been caught by a groom, who was ignorant of its condition, and who imperfectly secured it by a chain to the ring of a manger in a building where a number of calves and sheep were confined. During the night it broke loose, and repeatedly bit several of the animals. A goat among the number escaped by jumping upon some empty packages, at a considerable height beyond

The duration of the disease in the bovine species seldom exceeds from four to seven days; and, as in other creatures, the termination is always fatal (Röll).

Diagnosis in the Cow.

The nervous disturbance that sometimes marks the commencement of "cattle plague" (rinderpest) in cattle offers a

---

the reach of the dog, and a small calf was protected by creeping beneath the manger. Of the number, four calves and two sheep were bitten; but as one of the former had sustained a compound fracture of the fore leg, it was destroyed. The others were kept under observation. Twenty-three days afterwards, a calf exhibited an inordinate desire for water, but experienced a difficulty in swallowing. The appetite and rumination were suspended, and diarrhœa set in. Saliva flowed profusely from the mouth, and the animal regarded the movements of a stick or piece of paper held towards it with the most intense watchfulness, and after a time would rush violently at it. Twenty-five days after being bitten, a second calf became affected, and about the same time one of the sheep—a ewe; in a few more days the third calf and the second sheep—a ram. The first calf exhibited the most perfect quietude when any person stood near it; but when left alone it bellowed furiously, and, as far as the chain would allow, it mounted the manger or stall partition, or would sometimes jump with all feet at once from the ground to a considerable height, and fall helplessly on the ground, lying a few seconds upon one side, and rising with difficulty after several ineffectual attempts. The second and third animals were considerably more vicious; they would kick and run at all persons who approached them. Their loud bellowing became constant and annoying, and, in the end, differed little from the braying of an ass. . . . . It is to be particularly remarked that the wounds inflicted by the rabid dog had in every case healed up; but, contemporaneously with the first signs of rabies, loss of appetite and difficulty in swallowing, &c., there arose such an intolerable itching or irritation in the parts, that the animals commenced to rub them violently against the nearest object, until they were raw and bleeding. (Armatage, "Clater's Cattle Doctor," p. 453.) During the epizoöty of rabies in Lancashire in 1869, Mr. Worthington, veterinary surgeon, of Wigan, reported four cases of the disease transmitted to cattle. On Sunday, November 28th, he was called to inspect a heifer, two years old, and in calf, which had been observed to be dull and to separate from the herd in the field on the preceding Thursday. On the Friday, the owner's attention was again attracted to it by observing its face and horns covered with soil; it was then labouring under great excitement, had a wild and startled look, bellowed frequently, and occasionally charged furiously at its companions; a great change was also observed in the abdomen, which presented an extremely hollow—almost emaciated—appearance, as if it had been starved. It was placed in a loose-box, and the excitement and restlessness were almost continuous. The creature was ever on the alert, and would instantly charge at any one who entered. A large quantity of frothy saliva hung from the lips, and the bellowing was almost incessant. All food was refused, but the thirst was great, and when gruel or water was supplied eager

certain analogy to the symptoms of rabies in that animal. The fits of delirium that now and again appear in that disease, as well as the great depression and apathy, and the unsteady gait, have

---

attempts were made to drink, but swallowing was impossible. On Monday, the wild excitement had almost completely subsided, and was succeeded by comparative quietude and extreme exhaustion. The eyes had a peculiarly anxious, but watchful, look; the pulse was slow and feeble; and the debility was so great that the cow could scarcely walk, though it manifested much anxiety to escape from confinement. The thirst continued undiminished, and on a bucket of gruel being presented, the poor beast eagerly plunged its nose in it, and made repeated, but vain, efforts to drink, the liquid at each attempt returning by the nostrils. It rapidly sank during the day, and died early next morning; but its restlessness only diminished with the fast-failing strength, and was observable to the last. Throughout the disease there was little or no action of the bowels, and everything except fluids was persistently refused from the commencement.

The second case was a two-year-old heifer, in calf. The owner had noticed it first from its strange appearance and conduct in the field; it looked remarkably hollow, and instead of grazing with the other cows, stood with head erect, looking wildly towards various parts of the meadow, apparently intently watching some imaginary object. It would stand in this way until its companions had grazed some distance, when it would walk up amongst them, and again resume its attitude of suspicious watchfulness. As yet there was no desire to do mischief, and throughout the disease it would permit any of its companions to approach; but on the following day it made a fierce attack on some young calves, and became perfectly furious on seeing a dog which was kept at the farm for the purpose of driving cattle to and from pasture, and towards which it had never before displayed any indication of animosity. At length it manifested such alarming symptoms of violence that it had to be secured. Before entering the place where it was, the owner advised Mr. Worthington to be cautious in approaching it, as any attempt to do so strangely excited it; and this precaution was necessary, for they were almost deafened with the bellowings that greeted them as they opened the door. Their entrance had thrown it into a state of the wildest excitement, which, however, subsided after their quietly watching it for a few minutes; but the slightest movement, or even an attempt at conversation, instantly brought on a paroxysm of bellowing. The eyelids were widely dilated, and the eyes bright and prominent, giving the cow an extremely wild and startled expression; a quantity of frothy saliva adhered to the lips, and with head erect and ears pointed forward, it stood keenly sensitive to everything around. In its struggle to liberate itself, one of its horns had become fractured, and the blood streaming over the face considerably increased its startling appearance. There was no disturbance of the pulse; and both bowels and kidneys were acting naturally. From the commencement all food had been refused, and there was also an indifference to fluids. The paroxyms increased in intensity, and the remissions were of short duration; the bellowing could be distinctly heard at a distance of two or three miles. The animal was destroyed three days after the appearance of the first symptoms.

A fortnight afterwards, this veterinary surgeon was called to see another cow, older than the others. It had been unwell for two days, and had not eaten any-a resemblance to those present in a certain stage of rabies. But this resemblance is very superficial; the existence of the "plague" in the district, the appearance of the visible mucous membranes,

thing. The principal symptoms were extreme coldness of the whole body, a small, quick, feeble pulse, drowsiness, and great nervous depression, and a strange desire to eat its clothing. Although food of every description was persistently refused, this cow had deliberately masticated and swallowed a large portion of the horse rug and some sacks that had been placed upon it. Two days afterwards it was seen again, but it was then dying. The pulse was almost imperceptible, very quick, and irregular; the breathing slow and slightly stertorous; the whole surface of the body icy cold; a copious flow of saliva from the mouth, and intense depression. Though evidently fast sinking, there was still the same depraved appetite and unnatural desire to eat the clothing. It died a few hours afterwards. Five weeks before its death this animal, whilst being driven to a neighbouring field, was attacked by a large dog that was passing along the road with a half-worried cat in its mouth, and bitten rather severely on one ear. The wound did well, but two days before the cow was seen by Mr. Worthington it was observed to be chasing a number of sheep, and bellowing in a strange, unnatural manner. From this time till death ensued, paroxysms of bellowing, accompanied by great restlessness and excitement, would come on at intervals. These periods were succeeded by the greatest depression.

The fourth case was a bull calf, nine months old, on a farm near where the other cases occurred, and to which Mr. Worthington was called the day after the death of the last case. Since the Monday—three days previously—it had exhibited unusual symptoms. The Croston harriers had on that day passed through the field in which the calf was grazing along with about a dozen other calves, and shortly afterwards it was found bellowing and rambling over the field in a state of the greatest excitement. It was supposed at the time that this had arisen in consequence of having been alarmed by the hounds, and would subside in a short period; not being a valuable calf, it was neglected until the arrival of the veterinary surgeon, three days afterwards. It had then separated from its companions, and could not be found until diligent search was made, when it was discovered lying dead on the bank of a small pit, with its nose just immersed in the water, having apparently expired in the act of drinking. Since the Monday it had been in a state of the wildest excitement, incessantly bellowing and rambling round the field, and charging furiously at any one who approached it. Shortly before daybreak on the 8th November, the shepherd, on going his morning rounds, had observed a large black dog, which he described as looking "fearfully hollow and hungry," in a field adjoining the Hall, and which, after attacking his own dog, crossed the fence into the contiguous field where the calves were grazing, and ran in among them. It was not sufficiently light to observe whether it attacked any of them, but he thought it probable it might have done so, as he could distinctly observe all the calves running from it in a state of alarm. About the same time this dog also severely wounded a sheep-dog at a farm about a mile off; the owner, apprehensive of rabies, tied this animal up, and two or three weeks afterwards it died, presenting unmistakable symptoms of rabies.

This black dog, which had been seen with a cat in its mouth, had bitten case

and other definite symptoms during life, as well as the pathological alterations found after death, are sufficient to establish a distinction. We will hereafter refer to the diagnosis of rabies from the various forms of "Anthrax" in this and other animals.

Symptoms in the Sheep.

In sheep, the early symptoms of rabies are,—diminution of the appetite, cessation of rumination, itching of the skin, and exaltation of the sexual desires. There soon ensues agitation; the voice is modified, the eyes staring, with dilated pupils and reddened conjunctivæ; and the nasal secretion is augmented. During the paroxysm, the sheep make unusual jumps, paw with their fore feet, grind the teeth, and butt with their horns or forehead at other sheep, people, dogs, or any objects within their reach, and bite utensils when they can get hold of them. It is not at all unusual for them to show a disposition to bite people and animals, and the disease has been transmitted by them in this way. The presence or the bark of a dog will often make them furious, and they are not at all afraid of attacking that animal. At intervals they emit a kind of dull bellowing. The exacerbations alternate with intervals of quiet; emaciation sets in, and feebleness with paralysis ensues. The animals are then most frequently lying; saliva usually flows from the mouth, large quantities of mucus are discharged from the nostrils, and death usually occurs in a convulsive paroxysm in from the fifth to the eighth day.* Rabid sheep have been known to drink blood (Haubner).

---

three; and several dogs, a pig, and other animals were afterwards attacked by it in different parts of the country (the whole of the bitten ones were immediately destroyed), and it was ultimately killed, three days afterwards, by a labourer who was fencing, and upon whom it made a fierce and unprovoked assault; but the man being fortunately armed with a hedging hook, was enabled quickly to despatch it.—*The Veterinarian*, vol. xliii. p. 195.

* In the sheep affected with rabies, observed by Mr. Armatage, there was quietness, the head being generally elevated and held to one side; one ear and the eyelid of the same side drooping—the latter nearly closed. Any sudden

Symptoms in the Goat.

The symptoms of rabies in the goat are analogous to, if not absolutely identical with, those observed in the sheep. The only difference observed is in the desire to bite, which is always more marked in the former than the latter.

Symptoms in the Pig.

It appears to be no very great flattery to the "lord of the creation" to say that, with regard to diseases and the general action of medicine, no creature is so closely related to him as the pig. In fact, they have several maladies in common, which are scarcely, if at all, known to other species, and drugs, as a

---

movement or unusually sharp noise would cause them to drop awkwardly, as the calves were described to do, and rise in a similar manner. There was no viciousness, diarrhœa, or slavering. Temperature before death 107°. The ewe gave birth to two fine lambs about one week before the attack; but the milk rapidly diminishing, they had to be fed from a bottle. They were fattened, and after some months went to the butcher, without having shown any sign of the malady being inherited.

Mr. Worthington saw a rabid sheep at Parbold Hall in April, 1870. It will be remembered that rabies had appeared there in November among the cattle. This sheep was supposed to have been bitten at the same time. Throughout the disease the animal evinced great restlessness, by frequently stamping and scraping the ground with the fore feet, and riding on its companions' backs; with wildly glaring eyes it would go back several paces, and then butt furiously at any one who approached it; even a stone thrown towards it on the ground was sufficient to bring on a paroxysm of fury. In three days after the appearance of these symptoms it was destroyed.—*The Veterinarian*, vol. xliii. p. 607.

On June 5, 1841, Eckel inoculated a sheep at the nose, lip, and tail with the warm saliva from a he-goat suffering from rabies induced by the bite of a mad dog; this goat immediately afterwards died. On July 1, the sheep had partially lost its appetite, rumination was suspended, the urine was scanty, and there was constipation. On the 2nd, the animal greedily seized a mouthful of hay; it was restless and afraid of the slightest noise; the eyes were haggard-looking; the visible mucous membranes were injected; there was a discharge from the nostrils, and the mouth was foamy. It must have been very uneasy on the following night, for on the morning of the 3rd tufts of wool were adhering to the woodwork of its stall. It was then lying on its right side; the pupils of the eyes were widely dilated, and these organs were dull, haggard, and deeply retracted within their orbits; an abundant viscid discharge flowed from the nostrils and mouth; the respiration was accelerated; paralysis had set in, and the circulation was inexplorable. The animal died at eleven o'clock that morning, without convulsions. The *rigor mortis* appeared instantaneously.

rule, in almost the same quantities, have similar physiological effects. The same is the case with the disease now under consideration, particularly with respect to the exaltation of the senses, and more especially the morbid sensibility of the skin. Pigs are not so much exposed to the disease, from their being usually confined in enclosures, and when they are affected it is due to the bite of a rabid dog or cat.

When the pig is about to be attacked with rabies, the already cicatrised wound usually becomes more sensitive, and the animal rubs or gnaws it until it is raw. When the disease appears, the pig seems to be suffering from *malaise;* it becomes savage, frightened, and restless; the gaze is fixed, and the pupils widely dilated; the respiration is very accelerated; an abundance of saliva streams constantly from the mouth, and the voice is husky and emitted in frequently repeated grunts or groans, though sometimes the animal is mute. During the paroxysms the foamy saliva increases; the desire to bite is sometimes intense, and the unfortunate creature not only attacks inanimate bodies, but also animals,—even its own species, and mankind. It burrows and hides its head beneath the litter, jumps about in a fantastic manner, or tries to tear up the ground in order to conceal itself. These fits are followed by a sensible diminution of all the morbid phenomena; and during the remission the animal, if a sow, will suckle and caress its young even more affectionately than in health. At a later period, the mouth and snout become dry; the animal rapidly wastes, and paraplegia (paralysis) supervenes. It is not uncommon to see the lower jaw more or less paralysed, and though there may be hunger and thirst manifested, yet the poor creature cannot swallow. Sometimes the taste is depraved, and the animal eats all kinds of unusual substances, some of which it has previously torn or gnawed in its access of fury. The senses of hearing and seeing are more acute, and the sensitive function of the skin is strangely exalted.

Death ordinarily takes place in from the second to the fourth day (Röll). Bénion says it never exceeds eight days, that paralysis ensues ordinarily towards the fifth or sixth days, and death about the eighth day.*

* "Traité des Maladies du Porc.," Paris, 1872, p. 270.

No better illustration of rabies in the pig could be given than the cases witnessed by Gillman, in 1811. On June 22nd, a yard-dog belonging to a gentleman at Highgate, killed, the previous day, one of his fowls, which it carried into its kennel. Its master, when he saw it, put his hand into the kennel, took it out, and beat the dog, which did not attempt to bite him. The dog was not observed to be out of health, and, as was the usual practice at night, was unchained and suffered to run about the stable yard in which its kennel stood; on the following morning it was found in the pig-sty, worrying an old sow and her two store pigs, about ten weeks old, which were much bitten, particularly about the ears. The dog afterwards died rabid, though it lapped milk until shortly before death. One of the young pigs, which had been bitten least, and that only about the ears, on the morning of the tenth day after the bite, refused its food. When offered to it as usual by placing it in the trough, after smelling it, it ran back, pointed its nose in the air, and was much agitated; in the evening it had a convulsive movement and twitching of the limbs. The eleventh day—the second of the attack—when Gillman saw it, there was a considerable quantity of frothy saliva about the mouth; it started and threw itself about in a most extraordinary manner; sometimes it sprang at least three feet from the ground; then beat itself forcibly against the wall; and sometimes ran round on its hind legs, as dogs do when playing with their tails. This it continued to do till exhausted, when it would fall down and pant; but soon again it became convulsed, and leaped from the ground as before, falling with considerable violence on its back or sides. About noon, the person who fed it gave it a slight blow on the head and killed it. The head had suffered such injury from the violence of the convulsions that no dissection could be made, and the skull and lower jaw were fractured.

The other pig was seized on the noon of the fourteenth day after the bite. This animal was considerably torn by the teeth of the dog, and had a deep wound on the back, between the shoulders. It was first seized with rigors and stood shivering besides its trough, rubbing the bitten parts, which Gillman had observed it to do on the previous day. It refused its food and appeared debilitated, moving languidly and feebly. On the second day it became paralysed in the hind legs, and after crawling in the morning from the sty, in a few hours was so much worse as to be unable to return. It lay on its side, foaming at the mouth, rubbing its nose on the ground, pulling the straw about and breaking it with its fore feet and teeth the whole day: it made frequent attempts to swallow some of the bits of straw, in which it very seldom succeeded. The eyelids were much separated, which gave it a staring appearance; the conjunctiva was much inflamed. When the old sow went near, it made the same familiar noise or grunt; it did not appear to have the least inclination to bite at anything, and in this it was repeatedly tried. The pupils of the eyes appeared to be dilated, but it could see very well, and was alarmed at the motion of a stick within two yards of it. On the third day, it lay the whole time on its side, and, except occasional slight twitchings in the legs, it remained perfectly still

Diagnosis in the Pig.

With regard to the diagnosis of rabies in the pig, we may apply the same remarks as we did to the disease in the other animals already referred to.

Symptoms in Poultry.

As has been mentioned, rabies is developed in poultry as a consequence of bites received by them from other rabid creatures.

---

and unable to rise, having lost all power in its extremities; it shrieked when touched, as if the skin were more than usually sensitive, and particularly when the mother went near or touched it. Towards evening the breathing was scarcely discernible, and the conjunctivæ of the eyes were so turgid as to project beyond the palpebræ. It died late that evening. Two rabbits were unsuccessfully inoculated with its saliva.

Twenty-seven days after the bite, the old sow was observed taking up in its mouth the dirty straw and filth that lay about the sty, which at once gave rise to a suspicion that this particular disease was approaching. The following morning it refused food, but was perfectly quiet and harmless; came from its bed when called, and was seen to rub the wounded part upon its ears very frequently during the day. In the evening, as it had not eaten its usual food, a few ripe gooseberries were offered, which it took, but had much difficulty in swallowing them. The next morning there was nothing else noted, except that the pig was dull and there was some inflammation about the parts which had been wounded by the dog's teeth, especially about the ears. Milk was offered, but though eager attempts were made, it could not drink; there was a peculiar convulsive motion of the head and twitching of the lower jaw, but no dread of fluids, as it took up with its teeth, apparently observing much caution, some small pieces of cabbage leaf that swam on the top of the food; though after moving them two or three times between its teeth they were suddenly dropped, as they could not be masticated or swallowed. It walked steadily but very slowly. In the evening the disease had made much progress; the convulsive twitchings of the head were much increased, and the animal was extremely restless; for when this peculiar motion of the head from side to side had increased, it was busily employed in grubbing up the earth with its nose, as if in search of food. When the spasmodic fit returned—which it did once in a quarter of an hour or twenty minutes—it became alarmed, and screamed when any one approached. On the fourth morning all the symptoms were aggravated, and every hour the paroxysms returned more frequently and with more violence. The poor pig frequently jumped up suddenly on its hind legs, and threw itself back with considerable violence; it was affected by the slightest noise, and when any one stamped his foot it was thrown into the most violent convulsive state and shrieked horribly. To such a degree, in short, did the morbid excitability of the nervous system arrive, that the distressed creature was affected by the least touch, which seemed to be torture. In the evening the symptoms were still more aggravated; the animal beat itself against the walls, and sprung up against the roof of the sty.

When the disease has manifested itself, the birds appear to be influenced by the same nervous excitability and restlessness shown in other animals. They seem to labour under similar mental hallucinations; they perform all kind of frenzied movements, avoid the light if they can find shelter; their voice is husky, and at times they also appear to be moved by the same mischievous impulse to bite which generally marks the course of the malady in the lower animals, and forms one of its characteristic features. A staggering gait, and ultimately paralysis, indicate the approach of death.

These attacks continued and were repeated about once every ten minutes, till about two o'clock in the morning, when it was found dead.—*A Dissertation on the Bite of a Rabid Animal* (London, 1812, p. 28).

Schliepe describes a case of rabies in the pig, in which the first symptoms showed themselves twenty-eight days after being bitten by a mad dog. It refused all food, was dull, and champed the straw. Two or three days after this it became very weak in the loins, and when seen by Schliepe it was standing with its hind legs widely apart to prevent its falling. The feebleness in the loins was so great that it could scarcely move; it had no appetite; and from time to time it gave out a grunt or moan resembling the voice of a dog whining during its sleep. It showed no disposition to bite, and it died on the eighth day.—*Magazin für die Gesammte Thierheilkunde*, 1866.

In October, 1861, M. Dubois of Châtre saw a pig which had become rabid from the bite of a mad dog. The animal was lying with its nose buried in the straw, and made an incessant, but peculiar, grunting. It could scarcely be made to move, even by beating, but if any white body was placed before it, such as a piece of paper tied to a long stick, it immediately sprang up in a furious state, and ran about its sty, grunting loudly, and appearing to be very agitated. Every time the experiment was made the same effect was produced, until at last it became so mad that those persons who were looking on became afraid. It was paralysed on the sixth day and died on the seventh.—*Benion, op. cit.*

MORBID APPEARANCES AFTER DEATH.

As in most other nervous affections, the pathological changes observed in animals and persons who have died of rabies and hydrophobia are not generally at all in proportion to the severity of the symptoms manifested during life; and, indeed, it may be said that in very many cases it would be difficult to express an opinion as to the existence or non-existence of the disease in the lifetime of an animal, if the morbid appearances displayed by it after decease were alone to be relied upon. There is often nothing to be found in the dead body that will account for the strange behaviour and the peculiar symptoms that were present during the paroxysms of the disease.

The following may be accepted as the principal lesions noted in necroscopial examinations of the bodies of dogs which have died of rabies; though it must be mentioned that some of the alterations are less frequent and less marked than others, and a few are but rarely observed.

There is congestion of the brain, particularly at the base, as well as the spinal cord, and sometimes a serous effusion into these organs. Eckel reports that, in his examinations, the cerebral œdema occurred most frequently in the months of August, September, and October. The muscular system shows congestion (*hyperæmia*), as well as the cellular tissue, the liver, and the kidneys. The lungs are not unfrequently greatly gorged with blood, as in animals that die of asphyxia. The spleen is also more or less congested and frequently enlarged, and it is sometimes completely black and pulpy from extravasation of blood; at times, black salient patches stud its surface and give it a tuberculous aspect, and these, when incised, are found to contain a black grumous blood. The blood in the vessels is black and pitch-like, and furnishes little or no clot.

The mucous membranes exhibit, perhaps, the most constant alterations; these are—redness of more or less intensity; extreme congestion of the vessels; thickening of the membrane, and hæmorrhagic effusion to a greater or less extent on its surface. These hæmorrhagic patches are met with in the mucous membrane of the digestive organs, particularly in the stomach, where they are most numerous on the duplicatures of the membrane; in this situation they are veritable extravasations of blood, frequently accompanied by erosions (*hæmorrhagic erosions*). This condition is, in some instances, very conspicuous, and cannot fail to attract attention. It is delineated in a drawing carefully made from nature by my friend, Mr. H. Coates, M.R.C.V.S., and represented in Plate II. fig. 2 (*b b*), which exhibits the inflamed and congested state of the lining membrane of the stomach and bowels so often observed in rabies. A still more extraordinary illustration of this condition is given by Gillman, who discovered the alteration in the dog already referred to as having bitten the pigs. He says: "The stomach contained a chocolate-coloured, gelatinous-like fluid; the villous coat was very generally inflamed, and several of the rugæ were livid and of a chocolate colour; there were a great number of mortified spots, some having the appearance of flattened black currants; some were raised like pustules; and in some parts the villous coat was ulcerated and destroyed" (p. 31). The appearance was so striking that he gave a drawing of it. No foreign substances were found in this animal's stomach. In the pharynx this hæmorrhagic condition is not so conspicuous. These appearances have been more especially remarked in dogs that have died of "dumb-madness." The tongue is not unfrequently observed to be wounded by the teeth; it is deeply congested or inflamed, especially its papillæ; as are also the tonsils and the salivary glands (Plate I., Frontispiece, *a c*). The mucous membrane of the air passages, commencing with the larynx, and passing to the trachea and bronchia, is in a similar condition; the latter often contain a frothy mucus. In "dumb-madness," the upper air passages are found to be most seriously implicated, particularly the rim of the glottis, and the vocal cords. The tongue, fauces, and larynx are also coated with a considerable quantity of tenacious mucus, and the follicles are enlarged.

The pneumogastric nerve, the lingual or hypoglossal nerve, and the cervical and thoracic ganglia of the sympathetic nerve, have been stated by certain authors to be in a congested condition. Others, however, have not remarked this.

The contents of the stomach, and also sometimes of the small intestines, are usually abnormal, and this is very noteworthy. We have seen that, in the dog and some other animals, the appetite during the course of the malady, and particularly at its commencement, is very depraved, and the animal devours all kinds of substances which it does not seek to do in health, and which are not at all necessary as food. These are straw, hay, hair, wood, excrement, string, nails, earth, stones, sand, grass, glass, with the remains of food, &c. (Plate II., fig. 1). If such-like matters are met with in the stomach of a dog, it may almost be affirmed without hesitation that it has been rabid; for it is only the depraved taste which characterises this disease that would cause an animal to swallow matters so foreign to its nature. Bouley appears to attribute the condition of the lining membrane of the stomach to the contact of these substances, and adds that these may have been rejected by vomiting. "In such a case, the interior of the stomach preserves traces of their passage; it is greatly injected with blood, so as to be almost black, and it contains blood mixed with bile." It must be remarked, however, that this appearance of the stomach has been seen in other animals than the dog, and which have not swallowed any matters likely to injure the mucous membrane of that organ.

The liver and spleen, as already mentioned, are generally

full of blood, and the surface of the latter is not unfrequently studded with hæmorrhagic tumours.

Reynal has insisted upon the value of the vacuity of the bladder as a sign of rabies. In fifty-three cases noted by Lafosse, there was only one exception. The lining membrane of this organ is also very often studded with hæmorrhagic spots.

The able veterinarian, Dupuy, examined innumerable dogs, horses, cows, and sheep that had perished from rabies, and usually found the following lesions: The lungs and almost every part of the brain gorged with blood; traces more or less marked of inflammation on the mucous surface of the bronchi, œsophagus, stomach, and sometimes even on that of the intestines, vagina, uterus, and bladder; the air-passages were filled with a foamy mucosity; there was a more or less abundant quantity of serum in the ventricles of the brain, and sometimes between the membranes of the spinal cord; frequently there was an extraordinary redness in the covering of the pneumogastric and splanchnic nerves for a portion of their extent, but more particularly at their entrance into the chest; there was also an infiltration as of blood into the cellular tissue surrounding these nerves, whose pulpy substance was of a bluish colour.

Another very constant sign is the presence of a brownish coating on the tongue, which gives it an altogether peculiar appearance, and this nearly always coincides with a violet colour of the membrane of the mouth.

With regard to the presence of the "lysses" insisted upon by Marochetti, they have been sought for in vain by the veterinarians Bouley, Barthelmy, Renault, Colin, Leblanc, Delafond, Rey, Lafosse, Haubner, Pillwax, Röll, Eckel, and other careful comparative pathologists. Even when they, or similar appearances, do exist, no value, it would appear, can be placed upon them; as, according to other veterinarians,—among them Prinz,—they may be observed in healthy dogs; and Spinola says he has found them in dogs affected with anthrax.

Saint-Cyr mentions having found, in a horse that died rabid, the sublingual glands congested, and a patch of ecchymosis the size of a twenty centime piece at the base of each sublingual duct. Bruckmüller found a deep ulcer at the root of the tongue of a mad dog; in another he observed the lymphatic glands of the throat very red and swollen. And Peuch examined very carefully a dog that had perished from rabies, and found the laryngeal mucous membrane slightly inflamed and covered with mucus. On the right side of the tongue, and a little behind the base of the organ, beneath the epithelium, were two pustules of a white colour and different in size—one was of the volume of a grain of millet, the other smaller. They were surrounded by a slight inflammatory areola, and both showed in the centre a minute opening visible to the naked eye; inspected with a lens the opening appeared to be that of the lingual gland. Anteriorly, there were four pustules—two on the frænum of the tongue. They were about the size of a grain of millet; each had an inflammatory circle surrounding it, and when they were compressed a few drops of liquid escaped that looked like pus. On the frænum of the tongue on the left side was a seventh pustule, quite isolated, and the most developed and conspicuous. It was as big as a large millet seed, appeared to be perfectly closed, and was circumscribed by the inflamed ring like the others. The epithelium covering it was thin and slightly raised by a purulent fluid, which was not in sufficient quantity to practice an inoculation with.

In twenty-seven examinations of dogs that had died from rabies, Peuch found lesions of the tongue in fourteen—twelve as ulcerations, and two with pustules. The ulcerations were in dogs that had been affected with furious rabies, and were most frequently situated on one or other of the sides of the tongue—sometimes on both; at other times they were near the frænum, and nearly always occupied a region where the teeth could not reach them. In diameter from three to five millimetres, they either had irregular or perfectly circular borders; they were always superficial, and did not extend beyond the mucous membrane; there was no induration of the neighbouring parts, and the sublingual glands did not exhibit any alteration. The pustules had an opaline hue, and were situated in the same parts of the tongue as the ulcerations; they were about the size of a millet seed, did not project manifestly beyond the surface of the organ, and were always surrounded by a reddish areola.

It must not be forgotten that Marochetti did not contend for the existence of the lyssi after death, but only asserted that they were to be searched for during the incubation of the malady—a circumstance that appears to have been overlooked by those who have contended for and against the presence of these vesicles.

According to Röll, the cadaveric lesions observed in the rabies of the dog offer a certain analogy to those which, in this animal, are the consequence of anthrax, or acute poisoning by narcotic substances—Prussic acid, nux vomica, nicotine, &c. Pillwax, following Heusinger, admits a resemblance, or a certain degree of identity, between spontaneous rabies and "typhus" (*anthrax* or *febris carbunculosa*). In the examinations he made of thirty-two bodies of dogs, he found one in which the most characteristic lesions of this disease were present—redness and enlargement of the solitary and aggregate glands of the intestines, &c.; and he remarks that "it is perhaps only in those cases in which the symptoms of rabies noted during life have typhus for their point of departure, that a contagium, transmissible to man and animals, is developed; while in other cases where typhus does not appear, the rabific virus may not be produced." We shall again allude to this subject presently.

Dr. Bruckmüller, of the Veterinary Institute of Vienna, an excellent authority on the pathological anatomy of the domestic animals, has, in a recent work,* entered at some length into

* "Lehrbuch der Pathologischen Zootomie der Hausthiere." Vienna, 1869, 2nd part, p. 274.

the alterations that occur in this disease, particularly in the dog. Referring to the fact that many veterinary authorities believe in a similarity, if not an actual identity, between "milzbrand," or typhus, and rabies, he states that a very large proportion of mad dogs do not show any alterations characteristic of the first-named malady; but, on the contrary, that dogs dying of typhus have during life exhibited no symptoms of rabies. He also states that in different epizoöties or outbreaks, varying pathological changes are observed. In the Vienna epizoöty of 1868, to which we have already alluded, there was scarcely a case in which extreme congestion of the capillaries of the stomach and the presence of foreign substances therein was not noted; whereas in other years this had not been particularly observed. For a long time enlargement of the spleen had not been observed in mad animals, but in later years it had become somewhat common. In some outbreaks œdema of the brain and inflammation of the bowels were the chief alterations noticed; in others one or other of these features would be absent.

The result of the careful examination of 375 mad dogs, carried on for a period of twenty years, were tabulated by Bruckmüller as follows:—

1. Injury to the roof of the skull, with superficial hæmorrhage into the membranes of the brain 2
2. Hæmorrhage into the brain substance without indications of mechanical agency 3
3. Hyperæmia (congestion) of the brain 26
4. Œdema of the brain, usually accompanied by great softening (*starker durchfeuchtung*) of the membranes 74
5. Acute hydrocephalus, with inflammation of the membranes . . . 27
6. Chronic hydrocephalus, with great distention of the ventricles . . 10

From an examination of this table it will be perceived that alterations in the brain were observed in about 46 per cent. of the rabid dogs:—

7. Typhus, with enlargement of the spleen and hypertrophy of the mesenteric and Peyerian glands 36
8. Pyæmia, evidenced by metatastic formations 3
9. Cancer cachexia, marked by deposition of sarcomatous matter in the chest and parenchymatous organs 4

stances in the stomach, it will be seen that this organ was found to be involved in disease in 254 cases, or nearly 70 per cent. Indigestible or foreign matters were observed in it in 199 instances, or 55 per cent., and inflammation of the organ was noted in 125 cases, or 33 per cent.

Bruckmüller had not witnessed the congestion of the salivary glands and surrounding nerves so frequently alluded to by other authorities, and especially in this country, as present in rabid dogs.

None of the alterations above specified are absolutely characteristic of rabies, as they are found in other diseases of the dog; yet the most important circumstance to be indicated with reference to this malady was, he states, the condition of the stomach, and the finding in it all kinds of unusual matter, such as, in country dogs, leaves, grass, and grass-roots, and in others leather, rags, &c.; but the presence of these, he adds, is no certain criterion of rabies, as they are met with, though very rarely indeed, in other than rabid dogs.

During epizoötic rabies it has been observed that other diseased dogs have foreign substances, such as fragments of straw, in their bowels. Rarely these matters—hair and straw—pass into the intestines; but when they do so they are usually found mixed up with the fæces in the large intestines (*dickdarme*). The hair-tufts are very peculiar, being composed of closely-felted masses of hair with straw intermixed, sometimes half-a-foot long, and are found in the duodenum.

It is generally stated that no food is found in the stomach; but this, Bruckmüller states, is incorrect, as in six cases pieces of meat in considerable quantities were observed. Generally, however, no food is found; but no reliance can be placed upon this indication.

Another alteration, independent of the presence of foreign substances in the stomach, is the high degree of congestion of its lining membrane; this is apparent externally, through the serous covering, by the filling of the vessels, which appear as bluish-red streaks and extensive arborisations. This is shown in Plate II., fig. 2, *b*. The congestion of the mucous membrane of the intestines is not generally so marked, but appears in a more regular or patchy manner.

The more intense the congestion, the more frequent is the presence of the hæmorrhagic erosions, which appear as ecchymosed or blood-covered spots, most numerous at the pylorus. The mucous membrane is thickened, and covered with tenacious mucus, with parenchymatous inflammation. Not at all unfrequently this membrane offers the same appearances as in poisoning with phosphorus.

The alterations in the mucous membrane of the intestines appear simultaneously with those of this same membrane in the stomach, though occasionally alone, and consist in the accretion of a thick, tough, often blood-tinged mucus, which forms either one continuous adherent mass, or more frequently a covering about a line in thickness. The membrane itself is inflamed in patches and thickened, and the villi appear as small threads. At the commencement of the intestine these alterations are very marked, but they disappear towards the ileum; the inflammation attains a very high degree of intensity and diffusion when numerous tape-worms are present.

The most frequent alterations in the brain are due to œdema. The upper surface of the membranes (*hirnhaut*) is particularly shining, as if covered with dew. The pia mater (*weiche hirnhaut*) is very soft and sodden, the brain substance throughout soft and friable, and the cut surface is shiny and often streaked with effusion, the consistence of the brain being something like soup. Rarely there is congestion, and, as a rule, the brain is pale and bloodless. On the other hand, the vessels of the pia mater are sometimes much injected, and then the grey substance of the brain is somewhat darker coloured. In a comparatively few cases, this condition goes on to inflammation of the investing membranes, with an accumulation of serous effusion in the pia mater and choroid plexus, as well as in the lateral ventricles. These changes, however, are chiefly found in dogs that have died of "dumb madness," and which during life had dropping of the lower jaw; but they are more frequently found in dogs which were not rabid, and especially in those which had suffered from epilepsy consequent on distemper. Very rarely, comparatively speaking, and only in dogs that have been affected with the violent form of rabies, is there strong congestion of the membranes of the brain, and the brain itself.

The alterations or appearances of the blood in rabies are more varied than in any other disease. It is as frequently of a bright red colour, with a trace of coagulum, as it is a very thick dull-coloured fluid, rich in white corpuscles, and forming clots on the valves of the vessels. In by far the greater number of instances, as is usual among dogs, it forms a soft, spongy clot; and only in those cases in which the other signs of typhus were present did it appear dark-coloured, sticky, though not clotty, and without the presence of the characteristic bacteria. When the animals have been in great pain, as from an accumulation of *tænia echinococcus* or hair-tufts in the stomach, though also when these have been absent, the appearance of the blood is similar to that which it offers in narcotic poisoning. It is thin, fluid, very sticky, of a dark red colour, without any tendency to coagulation; rarely is it cherry-red, as in poisoning by an alkaloid. The appearance of the blood is most constant in those animals in which rabies has been induced by inoculation or the bite of a rabid creature. So far as Bruckmüller's experience went, he was able to state that it was in the same condition as in tetanus and other painful nervous disorders.

The alterations in the mucous membrane lining the mouth and larynx were mainly due to a highly congested state of the blood-vessels, but which rarely extended to a blue-red colour. Enlargement of the follicles and tonsils was rarely seen by him.

Swelling or enlargement of the spleen, is not common

among dogs; but when the other alterations are similar to those of typhus, it is always present, though it is rare in mad animals. The same may be said with regard to the enlarged lymphatic glands, which are more frequently found among non-rabid than rabid dogs. Hence, in rabies, this increase in the volume of the spleen is only of minor importance.

Bruckmüller had not much experience of the pathological alterations induced in other animals; as, during the twenty years, he had only dissected one cat, one fox, one cow, and four horses which had died of rabies. One of these showed the change in the blood peculiar to animals that have died of painful nervous diseases. In a horse there was found a more considerable enlargement of the spleen than had been seen, even in splenic apoplexy; in other two there was intense congestion of the membranes of the mouth, with swelling of the neighbouring lymphatic glands.

The conclusion Bruckmüller arrived at, after his long and attentive examinations of the bodies of rabid dogs, was that the evidence furnished by dissection alone proves of no value in defining or distinguishing the disease, and that all theories founded thereon can have no weight. By the diversity in the *post-mortem* appearances, it must always be a most difficult matter to decide whether an animal was really rabid; and this difficulty is increased from the circumstance that all suspected animals are killed at an early stage of the disease. Only is there certainty when the history of the animal is known, and when the symptoms during life have been noted. "In practice, however, I hold it certain that a dog which has not been under observation during life, and about which nothing is known, even though it may have bitten other creatures, has yet not been rabid if the stomach is well filled with food, or the small intestines contain a considerable quantity of chyme; and, on the other hand, it may be asserted, independent of other evidence, that if indigestible or foreign substances are found in the stomach, and the coats of that organ are highly congested and exhibit erosions, that the animal was rabid. With stray dogs, I consider the presence of rabies as established if the appearances of typhus, or a highly inflamed state of the bowels, accompanied with numerous worms in the intestinal canal, be noted. In the other domesticated animals the necroscopic appearances alone are not reliable."

In other animals the morbid alterations, according to some authorities, are similar to those observed in the dog, with the exception of the foreign substances in the stomach, which are much less frequently found, except in the cat, fox, and wolf. In cattle constipation has been noted; and in a sheep that died rabid, Armatage observed erosions on the lining membrane of the fourth compartment of the stomach; the spleen was also disorganised, and resembled a mass of jelly; the heart contained small clots of blood, and there was an accumulation of gas under the skin over the body.

In man the most careful examinations have been made of those who have perished from hydrophobia, but nothing has been found which could satisfactorily determine the nature of the disease. Not unfrequently, according to Dr. Wood, the brain and spinal cord are both perfectly sound. In a case examined by Dr. Sidey, of Edinburgh, the brain and its membranes were found quite healthy, as were also the medulla oblongata, the spinal cord, and the eighth pair of nerves at their origin and in their course; these were inspected with great care both microscopically and by the naked eye.* And more recently, several microscopical examinations of the cerebrum, cerebellum, and medulla oblongata have been made, but beyond intense congestion nothing could be noted. It is true that turgescence of the vessels, and injection of the spinal and cerebral membranes, have often been observed, and, in some rare cases, softening of the spinal marrow. But the congestion, in man as in the lower animals, might well be a mere consequence of the terrible disturbance in the nervous centres, without of itself

* *Edinburgh Monthly Journal of Medical Science*, 1850.

contributing in any way to the disease, and the admissible signs of inflammation are too seldom seen to warrant the belief that this process has any very essential connection with the phenomena.

The mucous membrane of the fauces, trachea, and œsophagus is in some instances reddened or very congested, in others pale, and in either case is likely to be covered with a tenacious mucus. The papillæ on the back part of the tongue are sometimes very much enlarged. The dark-coloured fluid that is ejected during the disease, or flows from the mouth after death, contains blood discs in every stage of disintegration, columnar epithelium from the stomach, and pavement epithelium from the mouth and œsophagus. Signs of inflammation of the inner coat of the stomach have also been noticed. As in the dog, it often contains a viscid, blackish-brown mucus, composed chiefly of disintegrated blood; its lining membrane is extremely congested, and speckled with many capillary extravasations or erosions. The trachea and bronchi are filled with mucus in many cases; the lungs, too, have been frequently found gorged with blood; indeed, Trolliet was of opinion that engorgement of the lungs and the accumulation of nearly all the blood in the arteries alone—phenomena pointed out previously by Haller, Boerhaave, and Magendie—were the only certain criteria of the disease.

The spleen and liver are usually healthy, but the kidneys are, in some instances, extremely congested, and show rupture of the Malpighian tufts and the renal tubes choked with blood and exfoliated epithelium. In these cases, the urine, when boiled with nitric acid, has the appearances of turbid port wine, and gives an abundant deposit of albumen; it generally contains numerous casts of the uriniferous tubes.*

Wood says the body is strongly disposed to putrefaction, and

* In the urine of a man who died of hydrophobia in King's College Hospital, and in whom the majority of the above symptoms were very marked, four kinds of renal casts were distinguishable: 1. Small transparent, waxy casts, few

quickly becomes offensive.* This peculiarity, if it does exist, has not been very often observed in animals.

Trousseau states that "the pathological changes found after death are only those dependent on the asphyxia which occurs in the last stage . . . Hyperæmia of all the parenchymatous organs is alone met with, as a consequence of the final convulsion."

In the case mentioned by M. Malherbe, and which has been alluded to, there was marked congestion of the veins of the convolution of the brain and injection of the pia mater; the grey substance of the brain itself was redder than in a natural condition, but was otherwise healthy looking. The lungs were considerably congested, though crepitant. The mucous membrane lining the trachea and bronchi was so congested as to look like a vast ecchymosis. The tongue showed a very curious alteration at its root, in the presence of a number of greyish-coloured glands, which projected beyond the surface of the membrane; they were as large as a hemp-seed, and their excretory ducts, when squeezed, yielded a puriform liquid. The tonsils presented almost the same appearance.

This glandular hypertrophy resembled, externally, the alteration observed in Peyer's glands in typhoid fever.

---

in number, evidently moulded in several tubuli still lined with epithelium. 2. A small number of similar but much larger casts, which had been moulded in tubes denuded of epithelium. 3. An abundance of epithelial casts, whose cells were small and opaque. 4. The same, containing also blood corpuscles.

In addition, the urine also contained free epithelial cells, crystals of lithic acid, lithates of soda and ammonia, triple phosphate, chloride of sodium, and oxalate of lime.

* "Practice of Medicine," vol. ii. p. 800.

ANALOGIES AND DISSIMILARITIES BETWEEN RABIES AND ANTHRAX.

Having described the symptoms and pathological alterations observed in rabies, as well as indicated, in a brief manner, the maladies with which it and hydrophobia might be confounded; this is, perhaps, the most appropriate place for referring to another disorder which has been frequently mentioned in the preceding pages, and whose importance in connection with the one now under consideration cannot be overlooked. For it must be admitted, that perhaps of all the diseases which might be mistaken for rabies, the most striking and prominent is "anthrax"—a special malady which assumes several forms, and attacks all creatures, though it only arises directly or primarily in herbivorous animals and the pig—they, apparently, having a particular predisposition to this mode of development. Its spontaneous production in carnivorous creatures has not been observed, though its transmissibility to them and to mankind is an indisputable fact; it appears in all climates, though rarely in a sporadic form, being either present as an enzoötic or epizoötic disease, and in several respects it bears a resemblance to maladies of miasmatic origin. In some situations, and at certain outbreaks, it has so many features in common with rabies that observers of no slight experience have not unfrequently been baffled and undecided in their diognosis, and may have even mistaken the one disease for the other.* More especially has this been the case in that

* For the analogies in the pathological anatomy of rabies and anthrax, see, in addition to the authorities already quoted and referred to: Locher, "Dissertatio inauguralis exhibens magnum lienis in Hydrophobia momentum." Gottingen, 1822. Prinz, "Die Wuth der Hunde als Seuche." Leipzig, 1832.

form which has been designated "anthrax fever," "inflammatio of the spleen," "splenic fever," or "typhus," in the horse; and the course of the affection is attended with such marked symptoms of fury, and even hydrophobia, that some German authorities have designated this special type as "anthrax madness" (*milzbrand wuth*); and several writers, as Von Heim* and Adolphi,† have even declared it to be identical with rabies. Gerold speaks of a kind of hydrophobia being present in anthrax fever (*milzbrand*) in man; he had observed it in the *milzbrand* district of Magdeburg.‡

Waldinger speaks of cattle presenting symptoms not unlike those of rabies;§ and Hurtrel d'Arboval writes: "We have seen animals in which the anthrax tumours, especially when they formed in the throat, pharynx, or larynx, give rise, some time before death, to symptoms of frenzy and hydrophobia."‖ Chabert has witnessed horses affected with anthrax in the hind-quarter biting the ground, the manger, and everything around them, and acting in a frenzied manner; so that any one unacquainted with the nature of their disease might have decided they had been bitten by rabid dogs.¶

Heusinger relates an outbreak of anthrax fever among horses which occurred at Saarbrück in 1831, and in which some of the prominent symptoms of rabies were noted.** Segretain, describing anthrax among the herds of Guadaloupe, alludes to this form and its furious symptoms.†† Hamont has mentioned the same peculiarities in this disease in the pig.‡‡ They have also been observed on several occasions in sheep, as in the

* "Vermischte Schriften," p. 30.
† "Magazin für die Gesammte Thierheilkunde," 1844.
‡ "Die Contagiöse Lungenseuche des Rindveihs," &c. Magdeburg, 1848.
§ "Specielle Pathologie und Therapie," 3rd edit. Part II., p. 156.
‖ "Dict. de Med. Vétérinaire, vol. i. p. 411.
¶ "Instructions et Observations," vol. i. p. 144.
** "Die Milzbrandkrankheiten," p. 517.
†† "La Clinique Vétérinaire," vol. xv. p. 490.
‡‡ "Recueil de Med. Vétérinaire," vol. xxiii.

anthrax year in England.* Deer have also manifested rabid symptoms when suffering from anthrax, even in this country.†

Heusinger observes that there is undoubtedly a type of intermittent fever (*wechselfieber*) in man (which he fancies has some relation to anthrax), in which not only hydrophobia and aphagia, but also, as happened in the case of Puccinotti, all the symptoms of rabies are present.‡ This is named "febres hydrophobicæ" by many surgeons, and, as the same authority remarks, Faber § is reminded, perhaps not without reason, of the epidemy which broke out among the German soldiers after the conquest of Rome in A.D. 553. Certain observations of this kind are communicated by Torti, and especially by Notarianni, Dumas, Puccinotti,‖ and Rasso.¶

Many of the older writers believed that rabies had broken out among dogs from eating the flesh of animals that had died of anthrax. In 1690-91 anthrax appears to have been very prevalent in Italy, according to Ramazzini, and dogs went mad; but whether Prinz ** is correct in ascribing this madness to the anthracoid affection, is doubtful. Ramazzini only says that so hot a summer (in 1691) occurred as had never been known before; the Etesian winds brought no alleviation of the continual heat, and on this account many animals, especially dogs, were driven to madness."†† In Transylvania and elsewhere anthrax was very prevalent, and we are told that in the former country, "dogs especially were driven to madness; they made a noise with their mouths, and were gasping with the heat like owls. They were marked on the body with carbuncles.‡‡ And a strange outbreak is recorded for us by Gensel in 1712, which we have already alluded to in our History (p. 29). In Hungary, "August being excessively wet, the mortality (from anthrax) among cattle increased, and they

* The *Veterinarian*, vol. viii. † Ibid., vol. vii. ‡ *Op. cit.*, p. 793.
§ "Wuthkrankheit," p. 511.
‖ "Di Una Epizoozia Contagiosa." Bologna, 1824.
¶ "Febbri della Calabria," p. 23. ** *Op. cit.*
†† "Animal Plagues," p. 164. ‡‡ "Animal Plagues," p. 182.

were attacked with a white pustular eruption, attended with difficulty of breathing. . . . Wild beasts of all kinds perished in large numbers at Somogy; and in the woods the country people found dogs which had been driven there by madness after feeding on these beasts; and men bitten by them were quickly seized with frenzy and hydrophobia, imitating the barking and the madness of dogs, and attacking those near by biting at them."* The same coincidence was noted in 1726 in Silesia, where dogs became mad after eating anthrax flesh.† In South America, in 1750, eating the infected carcases of dead cattle was supposed to have caused madness in dogs (see p. 30). In 1778, when anthrax (*milzbrand*) was frequent in North Germany, rabies prevailed at Berlin. (We have omitted this notice in our History). Heim thought the diseases were identical.‡ In the epizoöty of rabies at Vienna in 1814-15, Waldinger traced some resemblances between the disease and anthrax; and in the outbreak at Copenhagen and the neighbourhood in 1815-16, Viborg came to the conclusion that the malady was not rabies, but a malignant inflammation. The symptoms he enumerates, however, are certainly those of rabies, and he admits that this disease prevailed simultaneously with the other. Franque,§ with several other amateurs, imagined the epizoöty of rabies among foxes that was raging on the Continent at this period to be of an anthracoid nature, and different from the former malady; at a later period, however, he altered his opinion. Nevertheless, it is to be remarked that the advent of this singular epizoöty was in 1803, in a region (Waadt) where anthrax is very frequent, and at a time when it was more than usually common. It will be remembered, also, that it was in this year that the terrible outbreak of rabies occurred in the notorious anthrax districts of Peru.

* "Animal Plagues," p. 190. † Ibid., p. 239.

‡ *Op. cit.* We have already noted (p. 74) that in Roumania and El Hejaz flesh in a particular condition is popularly believed to produce rabies.

§ "Geschichte der Hausthierseuchen," &c.

In 1822, anthrax was very general and destructive throughout Europe, and rabies prevailed in Holland; and in 1823 pigs suffered most severely from the first-named malady in Central Europe, while, according to Barthelemy, madness was exceptionally frequent among dogs. In this year also, according to Brooke,* anthracoid disease was extremely common and fatal in Scandinavia, especially in North Sweden, among all animals, but particularly the reindeer; it assumed the phrenetic form. In 1824 rabies raged and spread to an extraordinary degree in Russia, Sweden, Norway, Denmark, and England. The Swedish outbreak was described at Stockholm, and appears to have presented some peculiar features; but the description is not satisfactory. Anthrax was general in 1826, especially in Russia and Sweden, and in 1827 rabies developed itself in a very virulent form, and continued until 1828. Prinz described it as the yellow fever among dogs.† The same madness was widely spread through France and Germany in 1828. Böhme states that anthrax was prevalent among dogs at Leipzig at the same time, and continued to 1831. Wagner, in Schlieben, says that madness in dogs had never been so frequent within the memory of man, as in 1831, during the epidemy of ergotism (*Kriebel krankheit*). This is an anthrax district, however; and Professor Prinz, after a careful study of the disease, concluded that it was not common rabies, but rather a form of anthrax. It appears, nevertheless, that he was in error.

Adolphi, in 1844 (p. 45), describes a disease among cattle which he thought was spontaneous rabies, but which may have been the furious form of anthrax. In 1861, during the epizoöty at Vienna, Pillwax notes the prevalence of the characteristic lesions of anthrax or "typhus" among the rabid dogs; and other observers have traced similarities between the two maladies.

Seeing the analogies between the two diseases, it has been

* "Travels in Lapland and Sweden."

† *Op. cit.*, p. 24.

attempted to establish their closer identity by referring to their particular localities, anthrax being usually looked upon as of malarial origin; so that if rabies is due to malaria, we should expect it to prevail in anthrax regions. But the attempt has only been partially successful, from the paucity of available materials, though some observations would appear to affirm the question.

For instance, Sicily was noted in ancient times for the frequency of rabies, and its prevalence in Apulia was not only remarked upon by Baglivi, but also by later writers.* In Rome it has been very common, according to the testimony of many observers. In Sondrio, where there is no malaria, it is extremely rare; but in Como, rich in fever, it largely prevails; it is the same at Lyons. Its frequency in Hungary and in the military frontiers of that country, has been indicated by Siebers; and Berlin, when compared with other places, appears to furnish a large number of cases of rabies. In the malarious countries of Ceylon and Bengal the disease is common, though in Egypt it is comparatively rare; and in Peru and the West Indian islands it has appeared, at times, as a terrible epizoöty.

But in other regions where anthracoid or malarious maladies prevail, rabies is either unknown or extremely rare—as in South and West Africa. At the Cape of Good Hope we have the fatal "horse-sickness" and anthrax fever, sometimes in a general and very deadly form, and yet there is no positive proof that rabies attacks dogs there. Other regions might be cited where one disease is absent or seldom seen, and the other of almost every-day occurrence; but, as with the outbreaks of the two diseases at the same periods, sufficient has been said to show that their simultaneous occurrence in any place at a certain period is, in all likelihood, nothing more than a mere coincidence.

* Baglivi, Opp. ed. Lips., vol. ii. p. 332. Michel Angelo. "Fisica Appula," vol. iv. p. 146.

The pathological changes observed in both diseases have at times lent some support to the idea that they were identical, or at least resembled each other. For instance, the alteration in the quality of the blood, the congestion of the vessels of the skin, the blackness and softness of the spleen and liver, and the effusion of blood in the mucous membrane of the stomach and bowels in some cases, or even in epizoöties, of rabies, indicate an approximation to anthrax; but then, again, in the latter affection the pathological lesions are constant and marked, while in rabies they are more or less inconstant and unreliable, and in a large majority of cases, at least in this country, the signs of anthrax are absent or rare. The result of careful investigation and comparison leads to the conclusion that at present we cannot be certain as to the exact relations existing between the two blood disorders, though the subject is one worthy of attention.

It is to be noted that none of the many forms of anthrax appear primarily or spontaneously in the dog—at least so far as observation has hitherto gone; it seems to be much less susceptible to the action of the contagium than most other animals, and it would appear that it is only liable to become infected through direct inoculation, or when it has devoured the flesh of creatures which have perished from the disease. After eating this poisonous flesh, its bite has been known to produce anthrax in sheep and swine, without itself becoming affected; and the milder forms of the malady are as readily amenable to treatment in this as in other animals. Nevertheless, through some special morbid susceptibility, or a more than usual potency of the contagium, dogs become infected, sicken, and frequently die very suddenly. The flesh of one dead animal has been known to induce disease in several dogs, and even packs of hounds have been infected; dogs eating this kind of flesh and biting each other, will, of course, produce inoculation. Numerous instances are recorded in continental veterinary literature in which dogs so infected have perished quickly, and have offered no marked traces of disease. Grev Gerlach, and Haubner have given some striking exampl Lüpke mentions an instance in which a dog became so infect by eating the blood of an animal that had died of intern anthrax (*innern milzbrandablagerungen*); an hour afterwar he found it lying on the straw vomiting, and in seven hou it died in convulsions. On examining its body, he found h conjectures as to the nature of the disease verified; the splee was very large and black, the stomach empty and inflame and the blood-vessels were filled with dark-coloured treacl blood.* In another instance a dog ate a portion of th intestines of a goat that had suffered from anthrax before was killed; within two hours it was attacked with sever symptoms of colic, vomited the remains of food mixed wit black blood, purged blood, and in ten hours after eating th goat's intestines it died. On examination, it exhibited all th alterations noted in acute carbuncular disease of the intestine even to the presence of the yellow effusion in the mesenteri glands.†

Mouth anthrax has also been observed in the dog throug infection; and, among others, Vix has given us example The latter veterinarian refers especially to his having made *post-mortem* examination of an ox that had died of spleni apoplexy, when his dog licked up some of the effused bloo that lay on the ground; in twelve hours there were anthra vesicles (*brandblasen*) in its mouth, and its head became s swollen that it was with great difficulty its life could be saved.‡ Other instances have been given of throat anthrax. Gerlac gives an account of a deer-hound that ate the flesh of a shee that had perished from the blood disease; soon after it wa sick, its throat became swollen, and it was some days befor it was well again.§ The disease also attacks the head, an

* "Zeitschrift für Thierheilkunde."

† Ibid., vol. iv. p. 130. ‡ Ibid., vol. ix. p. 209.

§ "Magazin für Thierheilkunde," vol. ix.

Wirtgen mentions an outbreak among a herd of swine and two dogs through their being fed on the flesh of a diseased ox.* Walch also alludes to a shepherd's dog that was affected in this way, and had a large carbuncle on its back through feeding on a piece of diseased sheep.† But the most remarkable instance, perhaps, is that recorded by Rougieux as occurring in a lot of English hounds, one hundred and fifty in number, forming the pack of Baron Von Schikler, at Morfontaine, near Paris, in 1827. Through the carelessness of those in charge of this pack, the flesh of a horse that had died of anthrax was given them all, except four or five, as food; on the following day the disease appeared; in four days a hundred were attacked, and on the arrival of the veterinary surgeon twenty had succumbed, and forty were in a hopeless condition. The remainder were in the early stages of the malady. "When the disease first showed itself, there was observed, as a precursory sign, swelling of the parotids; then a small round tumour, without any change in the colour of the skin, increase of temperature, or sensibility to the touch, formed on some part of the head—generally about the lips, forehead, parotideal region, or lower jaw, and sometimes, though rarely, on the body or limbs, accompanied by tension of the skin. In a few hours this tumour acquired a considerable development, occupying all the region in which it was situated, when it appeared on the head; then it gave the animal a hideous appearance, the swelling completely closing the eyes, extending down the neck along the trachea, and rendering the respiration so difficult and stertorous as to induce prompt suffocation. When the tumour had acquired considerable dimensions, the skin covering it showed numbers of circular ecchymotic spots of a reddish-violet colour, having a gangrenous appearance, and the largest of which corresponded to the point where the swelling had first appeared. Soon all the skin of the swollen part assumed this hue; the membrane

* "Journal d'Agriculture des Pays-Bas," vol. xviii. p. 343.
† "Zeitschrift für Thierheilkunde," vol. xvi. p. 186.

lining the mouth also showed the same tint, and a large quantity of viscid saliva flowed from this aperture. The appetite was in abeyance, fæces were rarely passed, and were mixed with blood. The animals lay continuously, in a great state of prostration, and insensible to the call of those persons who attended to them; they preferred cold, damp places in their kennels, to the excellent beds of straw prepared for them. . . . . The symptoms succeeded each other in some cases with terrible rapidity. In the morning, for instance, a small tumour would appear on the head, and in the evening the swelling of this part had attained its extreme limits. This state continued until the next day; then the suffocative *râle* was heard, and this was the prelude of death in the majority of cases, if therapeutical measures were not promptly adopted. The duration of the disease, whether the issue was favourable or unfavourable, was not beyond five days; death often occurred on the third day, and recovery about the same interval."

A necroscopic examination made in a great number of cases immediately after death, in consequence of the rapidity with which putrefaction set it, proved the pathological alterations to be identical in all. The black patches on the skin were coincident with infiltration of the subjacent cellular tissue with a considerable quantity of serum which extended beneath, and, in fact, constituted the swellings; it also penetrated between the muscles. When the disease occupied the head, this infiltration spread to the lower jaw, the laryngeal region, the neck, and the trachea; while the parotia glands were frequently of considerable size, were infiltrated with reddish serum, their cellular tissue congested, and here and there small ecchymoses. The blood contained in the heart and the large vessels was very black and pitch-like. The heart and lungs did not offer any remarkable alteration; in some animals the mucous membrane of the small intestines was reddened on its surface through the exudation of blood. With regard to the contagiousness of this disease, M. Rougieux one night introduced a small street dog into one of the kennels most severely visited by the affection; it was taken out in the morning, and during several subsequent days it did not manifest any abnormal signs. This was not, however, a conclusive experiment, and another fact adduced by this writer shows that this form of anthrax is contagious. Five dogs kept in a house a short distance from the kennels, and which had not been fed on the anthrax flesh, were allowed to run among the diseased animals on only one occasion, and some of them became affected.*

As has been said, in anthrax fever in the lower animals, and more particularly in the horse, there are symptoms of vertigo, a disposition to fury and destruction manifested by biting, kicking, &c., accompanied by cries, neighing, and other signs of excitement; but it is scarcely possible that a practised observer can mistake these signs for those of rabies. In the majority of cases the history of the animals can be relied upon to aid in establishing a diagnosis, and the differential signs should go a long way towards completing it. The rapidity with which anthrax—especially the internal form—runs its course, and the marked tendency to pass quickly into a state of putrefaction; the yellow tint of the visible mucous membranes, and the frequent presence of submucous and subcuticular infiltration and hæmorrhage, with at times sanguinary emissions, are scarcely to be overlooked. The pathological anatomy of the two diseases will also serve to distinguish between them, though it must be remembered that there has, in some epizoöties of rabies, been a strange similarity in the alterations found after death; but while in rabies the alterations are far from constant, in anthrax fever they are rarely, if ever, absent, and are characteristic. They consist of an accumulation of *black*, thick, pitchy blood; splenic tumours, frequently of enormous size; infiltration of the mesenteric glands; hæmorrhage into the intestines, cellular tissue, serous cavities, and the interstices of the muscles; oftentimes there are yellow gelatinous

* "Recueil de Médecine Vétérinaire Pratique," 1847, p. 757.

NATURE OF RABIES AND HYDROPHOBIA.

The pathological anatomy of the disease, as we have seen, enlightens us but little as to its nature. Indeed, this obscurity as to the essence of the disorder has for years placed it as a kind of debatable land between the neurist and humorist partisans, who have each looked upon it from their own point of view and classified it accordingly. But, strangest of all, there have been those who denied its existence altogether, or asserted that it was a mere aberration of the mind produced by fear, and that no such thing as contagion was present. Of course, these men must have been ignorant of the malady altogether, or of the incontrovertible facts which have been observed from the earliest up to the latest periods; or perhaps they were so mentally purblind as not to be able to distinguish the existence of a well-defined disease which is not only transmissible by the accidental bite of a rabid animal, but is also capable of being produced at will, in healthy creatures, by inoculation. The experiments of Renault of Alfort, Hertwig of Berlin, Eckel of Vienna, and a crowd of other distinguished veterinarians, abundantly and conclusively demonstrate, unfortunately, that it is no imaginary affection, but as definite and marked in all its characteristics as tetanus, hooping-cough, or any other well-known disease. Young children, dogs, sheep, cattle, pigs, horses, foxes, jackals, and wolves cannot be credited with that high development of imaginative power which would enable them to ponder over the effects of a bite, scratch, or trifling injury for weeks or months, until they came to believe themselves the victims of a malady which would all at once manifest itself in them by the same group of symptoms, and cause their death in a few hours. The idea is perfectly absurd, and would certainly not find mention here, were it not one of those fallacies which have done, and might yet do, an incalculable amount of mischief.

It is generally considered and classed as a nervous disease; but analogy would almost warrant its being grouped with such a malady as hooping-cough, which depends on a specific contagion, though it is at first a nervous disorder. It might be defined as a specific disease, in which a contagium or infecting element is generated, which, when transmitted to other creatures by means of a bite or inoculation, is capable of producing the same pathological disturbance and alterations. In this it differs from tetanus and other purely nervous maladies, a circumstance which would induce us to rank it rather as a humoral than a neural disease.

An analysis of the symptoms exhibited during life, with the appearances discovered on dissection, would lead us to look upon it as essentially a functional disturbance—sometimes excitation, sometimes paralysis—of the spinal cord and adjacent parts, which is denoted externally by abnormal phenomena in movement, sensibility, and intellect. Its etiology, and the character of the symptoms, mark it to be a virulent disease. The blood would seem to be primarily affected, both in spontaneous and transmitted rabies. The experiments of Eckel, already referred to, prove that this fluid contains the virus, and those of Hertwig that it does not reside in the nerves only. The manner in which the disease can be communicated, the results arising from the preservative measures timeously adopted, and the way in which the poison, if it is not promptly destroyed, is supposed to be taken up into the circulation and there produce its effects, differ in no particular from other virulent diseases due to blood alterations by the introduction of an infecting principle.

The contagium of rabies, then, produces its specific effects through the medium of the blood, and these effects are manifested by disorders of a nervous character—the brain and spinal cord being more particularly involved, and the poison in all probability being thrown chiefly off by means of the salivary glands.

The principal or characteristic symptoms would appear to indicate the parts of the nervous system for which this poison had a special predilection, and which are consequently most disordered in their function. The most striking of these symptoms, as has been remarked, consists in a terribly violent convulsion of the muscles of the pharynx and larynx, causing difficulty in swallowing, and obstructing, more or less, the entrance of air to the lungs; these two symptoms, combined with an unutterable anxiety and restlessness, are features peculiar to the malady, and are of an essentially nervous character.

This leads to the inference that the eighth pair of nerves—which really consist of three nerves, the glosso-pharyngeal, pneumogastric, and spinal accessory nerves—are chiefly involved, as they supply these parts with sensation and motion. The spasms or convulsions of the respiratory muscles, as well as those of deglutition, are due, there is every reason to believe, to disturbance of the function of this eighth pair; and the alteration in the voice of the rabid dog and other animals, or its entire suppression in "dumb madness," indicates a derangement in the branch of this nerve which is concerned in the production of the voice; though the congested or inflamed condition of the laryngeal region might also be invoked as the cause.

And death, as we have seen, is, in very many instances, due to asphyxia or suspension of respiration, just as when these branches are divided experimentally. This pair of nerves arises, it may be said, in the medulla oblongata and upper portion of the spinal cord.

But other nerves arising from this portion of the nervous mass, are, to all appearance, likewise involved. The seventh pair of nerves, for example, gives filaments to the stylo-hyoid and digastric muscles, which are concerned in swallowing.

The effect of a bright light on rabid or hydrophobic patients is due to abnormal sensibility of the retina, and the nerve which endows it with this property is a branch of the fifth pair. The depraved taste and peculiar sensation in the tongue may also arise from a change in the condition of the lingual branch of this pair of nerves. The inability to close the jaws in "dumb madness" is, in all likelihood, owing to impaired function of the motor branch of this pair also, whose office it is to produce closure of the mouth. The glosso-pharyngeal nerve, an efferent of the eighth pair, should also be implicated either as a nerve of motion, by its connection with the facial or spinal nerve, as a nerve of sensation, or through the influence attributed to it in the production of the abundant follicular secretion that takes place at the base of the tongue.

It may, therefore, be concluded that the part of the nervous system more particularly affected in rabies and hydrophobia and the part to which the most characteristic symptoms are due, is the medulla oblongata, and the cervical portion of the spinal cord in which the spinal nerve takes its origin. The nerves of special sense participate more or less, and the functions of the cerebrum are deranged; while the great sympathetic system of nerves shares in a commensurate degree in the production of the other morbid phenomena that distinguish this disease. The condition of the digestive and other organs would indicate an alteration in the constitution of the blood, and consequent impairment of nutrition in the tissues of which they are composed, with derangement of function. This condition is particularly marked in the digestive apparatus, especially in the dog.

MEDICAL TREATMENT.

WHEN rabies or hydrophobia have become fully developed, or even when they are only commencing, it may truly be said that there is but very little hope indeed of rescuing the unfortunate patient from an agonising death; for it may be asserted, in general terms, that nothing yet proposed has ever succeeded in arresting the fatal progress of this fearful complaint. Every known remedy has been tried, and all have failed. In the early and Middle Ages, magic, invocations, exorcisms, appeals to supernatural powers, and charlatanism of the grossest character, had to give way to the terrible fatality of the disease.* And the resources of modern times have not been more successfully employed in combating it.

* We have already, in our History, alluded to some of these strange, absurd prophylactic and curative measures, and particularly to the utilisation of portions of the mad animal therein, during the Anglo-Saxon period. It is curious to find that the roasted liver of the rabid dog is yet, according to Heusinger, in vogue as a remedy in Germany, where it has been employed from the earliest times for the prevention and cure of rabies. For instance, in a manuscript of the fourteenth century, published by Hofman ("Fundgruben," book i. p. 324), there is a description of the malady, its prevention, and a recommendation to employ this strange remedy. "Wiltu einen wutenden hunt erkennen, so merke wenn er loufet mit ofenen munde, unde mit uzgehangener zungen, Swenne er sich anseifert unde den zagel under die bein smuget unde sins selbes schin an billet, Swenne er ander hunde vluhet. Wiltu wizzen wen ein wutender hunt gebizzen hat, so nim des blutes, daz uz der wunden gêt, unde strich daz an ein brot unde wirf ez einem hunde; vluhet ez der hunt, so ist jener hunt wutende gewesen, der da gebizzen hat. Swen ein wutender bizet, dem troumet grewlichen, unde zurnet ane schulde, unde sihet alles hinter sich unde mac nicht erliden daz man in an sihet, unde wrchtet daz wazzer, unde swenne er ez an sihet, so billet er als ein hunt. Wiltu im zu helfe kumen, so tu im di wunden uf mit ysen oder mit fuer, daz daz eiter uz vlieze mit dem blute. Setze im egeln an di wunden di daz eiter uz zihen. . . Ein gebrante hundes leber gip im zezzen. . . . Gegen dez menschen biz vrumet kelber bein, so si gebrant werden unde gepulvert und mit honige getempirt, so sal man si legen uf den biz."

The whole magazine of therapeutics has been exhauste and vainly exhausted, in the treatment of hydrophobi Remedies the most violent have been used unsparingly; an practitioners have not been deterred by the apparent inert ness of any medicament from giving it a full trial. Bleedin in every degree, mercury, opium and other cerebral stimulant chloroform, tobacco, lobelia, and all other nervous sedative the acids and alkalies, oil of turpentine, cantharides, tar, whit hellebore, ceradilla, the salts of lead and those of iron, nitrou oxide inhalations, the injection of warm water and narcotic into the veins, electricity and galvanism, the hot vapour an hot air bath, even the poison of the viper, have all been trie and with the same sad result. Cases of cure are recorded a rare intervals, but when the same treatment employed in ther has been tried in undoubted cases of hydrophobia, it has uni formly failed. Some of these cases of recovery may have merel simulated hydrophobia, and not have been the virulent malady Veterinary-Surgeon Decroix,* Youatt, and Professor Rey men tion instances in the lower animals in which a spontaneou recovery took place; and Lafosse has also seen dogs which pre sented some symptoms analogous to those of rabies, recove An enumeration of all the medicinal agents that have bee tried, and all the methods of treatment resorted to, from th days of Celsus up to the present time, would be of little use i a treatise like the present. It only remains for us to hope, tha for this malady, as for so many others, a successful remedy o method of treatment may yet be discovered.

When the lower animals are affected with confirmed rabies it is most judicious to kill them as speedily and painlessly a possible; as not only is their recovery all but impossible, whil their sufferings are very great, but there may be grave dange to the creatures they come in contact with. All experiment with rabid animals should be conducted in proper establish

* "De la Rage: Curability—Traitement." Paris, 1868.

ments, such as veterinary schools, and under competent supervision.

The time has not long gone by, since, because of the inevitable death of the patient, and the horrible sufferings undergone before that event took place, human beings were destroyed by stifling and other means.

But though no faith is now put in the measures which used to be vaunted for the cure of hydrophobia, and the absolute inutility of the treatment hitherto adopted has been proved, alas! only too frequently, the malady is allowed to run its course until it terminates the life of the sufferer; and it is felt that if a cure cannot be effected, at least attempts must be made to palliate the most urgent and distressing symptoms.

We cannot abandon to their fate and to despair, those who exhibit indications of the disease; neither dare we conclude that it is infallibly mortal. In presence of a malady which constantly terminates in death, Trousseau says the practitioner's duty consists in boldly trying everything. The few instances of recovery recorded in the annals of medicine afford a glimmer of hope that others may be noted in the future, and that our increasing knowledge of physiology and pathology may enable us to contend more successfully with this very fatal disease than hitherto. Dr. Elliotson states that two little girls were bitten in the face by the same dog, and she who was last injured subseqently died of hydrophobia; at the same time exactly, the other experienced precisely identical premonitory symptoms—heaviness and general indisposition—but they all passed off.

It is scarcely necessary to say that the hydrophob should not be alarmed by those around him; but, on the contrary, soothed by kind, encouraging words. Quietude is above all things necessary, seeing that external influences induce more frequent and severe paroxysms. All useless interference or attention should be avoided. Like other nervous affections, such as tetanus, this demands absolute tranquillity, and everything at all likely to excite the patient should be rigidly abstained from, if possible; his questions should only be replied to, and n other talking ought to be permitted. Whatever he asks fo should, if believed to be proper for him, be allowed; an nothing should be forced upon him. In proportion as he tormented by nursing, visitors, inquisitive spectators, or the ad ministration of food, drink, or medicines, so the more frequen and harassing are the fits.

Seeing the evil effects of bright light in exciting the patien and well knowing the beneficial influence of darkness in curin or relieving tetanus in the lower animals, the apartment i which he is located should be darkened. Perfect quietude an tranquillity should, above all things, be rigidly enjoined, as th exacerbations of the malady—the return of the spasms an agonising symptoms—are frequent and severe in proportion a the patient is disturbed and excited. When left to himself h suffers less; and this fact, together with the soothing influenc of a darkened chamber, was no doubt chiefly in view with th Arabs whom Burton mentions. The mind should, at a hazards, be dispossessed of the idea that hydrophobia is pre sent; the patient might be told that it is fever, sore throat, c any other simple malady; and as all the senses are generall morbidly and painfully acute, everything likely to affect the should be abstained from. The great object to be attained the prevention of the recurrence of the paroxysms, and th allow the vital powers of the sufferer to overcome the effects the disease.

All allusion to the disease must be studiously avoided, an no mention should be made of the cause of it; "dogs," an "bites," and "water," or other fluid, ought not to be spoken o If the patient is an adult, precautions will be necessary again the recurrence of the furious paroxysms; means for restraint mu be at hand, and suitable attendants in readiness; but even whe force has to be employed, gentleness must not be overlooked, an the wishes of the unfortunate creature ought to be complied wit as far as may be consistent with safety. The irresistible desi to bite should even be gratified, as this will have a greater tendency to abbreviate a fit of fury than contention and opposition to thwart it, for the desire is soon satisfied. A napkin or a handkerchief, moistened in acidulated water and rolled up, may be placed between the teeth at this time, and removed as soon as the paroxysm is over. This will afford relief; whereas the opposite treatment would only aggravate the frenzy. It is well known from daily observation, as Decroix observes, that the rabid dog does not usually have a regular fight with every other dog it meets, but that it rather snaps here and there at those in its way, its passion for biting being instantly, and for the moment, satisfied; while if restrained and roused the eagerness to do harm is always dominant, and a fatal issue more prompt. In these fits of fury, and indeed when they are not present, those who are in attendance on the patient should be careful to avoid inoculation with the saliva; for though this secretion may not be so virulent in man as in the dog, yet it is an indisputable fact that it is potent enough to produce the malady.

In the more tranquil form of the disorder, or during the intervals between the paroxysms, a parent or acquaintance should be present to talk to the patient when necessary, to read or write, or do anything else likely to draw his attention from his own condition, and to watch what passes. This person should never be the first to speak, and when the sufferer seeks to talk about his malady, other subjects for conversation should be adroitly introduced. If he is thoroughly convinced that his disease is hydrophobia, and will persist in speaking of it, and especially if he believes that his case is hopeless, it will be best not to oppose him so far as to maintain that he is suffering from some other affection, but to admit that such is the nature of the malady, though there is not the least cause for despair, as cases of recovery are by no means unfrequent, and the worst cases have been cured. Every symptom should be described to him as a favourable omen in the progress towards recovery, and every means should be adopted to palliate the serious ment disturbance.*

From the supposed anatomical seat of the disorder in th upper part of the spinal cord, towards the base of the brai it is reasonable to infer that the modifying agents employed a medicine should be those which have most influence on thi disturbed region. These agents, it might also be indicate should be such as have a soothing, narcotic, or sedative effect and of these belladonna, datura, hyoscyamine, morphine, an digitaline, have been recommended. Atropine has been, b some, preferred to morphine. The hydrate of chloral, from it remarkable hypnotic properties, and its powerful influence i subduing the paroxysms, might be advantageously employe either in the form of an enema or hypodermic injection. Soothing or sleep-producing remedies should more especiall be resorted to when the paroxysm is about to appear. Chloro form has been used for this purpose, but its effect has not bee satisfactory on the whole. If resorted to, the inhalations shoul commence whenever an access of fury is setting in. Whil under the influence of this or any other hypnotic, attempt should be made to give the patient sustenance, and the grea thirst might be assuaged by frequent and copious enemas o water or gruel.

* Decroix, *op. cit.*

† Since the above was written, I observe that in the *Lancet* for August 12, 1871 there is an account of two cases of hydrophobia which occurred at Doncaster, o the 18th and 19th of April of the same year. One was that of a boy, aged eleve years, bitten in the face by a stray dog about three weeks previously. The othe was that of a girl, five years old, who was bitten at the same time in variou parts of the face. Mr. Ellis, in whose charge they were, treated them wit the hydrate of chloral, with the object of mitigating the distressing symptoms In this he appears to have been quite successful, the excitement and violenc being controlled by the remedy to a remarkable extent. It did not, however check the progress of the disease in the slightest degree, and both patients die on the third day. Mr. Ellis was quite satisfied that the agonising suffering were considerably alleviated. The dose was a teaspoonful of the syrup, dilute with a little water, every two hours or hour. In the *British Medical Journal* fo December 2, 1871 (p. 642), there is also a record of three cases at Nottingham which were much benefited by comparatively large doses of this drug.

Seeing the difficulty in swallowing, as little as possible should be attempted to be given by the mouth, and drugs should always, when practicable, be administered hypodermically or endermically.

It must also be remembered that the tolerance for narcotic remedies is extreme, and, in addition to their being given in larger doses, they should also be administered at short intervals.

Hot water or vapour baths should more particularly be resorted to during the incubatory period; as they are likely to increase the excitement, dyspnœa, and cerebro-spinal congestion when the malady has actually declared itself or made some progress.

As a rule, the medical treatment should be mainly directed to soothing the nervous derangement, and the less complicated it is the better. The recoveries which have been recorded as occurring in the canine species have taken place when the animals were left to Nature's restorative measures, and have not been at all due to the usual classical treatment.

Brown-Séquard, basing his treatment on the opinion he had formed as to the nature of the disease, and which we have already alluded to, recommends the division and excision of a portion of the nerve or nerves distributed to the bitten part. But it is obvious that if hydrophobia is a disease in which the blood is primarily affected, and through it the brain and spinal cord, this operation can have no possible result on the course of the malady. Other writers have proposed excision of the cicatrix, and even amputatoin has been resorted to without avail.

As asphyxia is usually the immediate cause of death in hydrophobia, tracheotomy has been recommended to counteract the urgent symptoms of spasm of the larynx; but it will readily be perceived that this operation cannot be productive of any positive or permanent benefit.

PRESERVATIVE TREATMENT.

Value of Preservative and Preventive Treatment.

In such a terribly fearful and mortal disease—one in which t resources of science are impotent to cure, and almost powerl to alleviate, when once the symptoms have fairly manifest themselves—the greatest interest and importance attaches those measures of a prophylactic or preservative kind, by whi dangerous results may be averted, and the disease kept check.

In a malady like this,—and indeed in every disease th entails suffering, either upon mankind or the lower animals, the great value of preservation and prevention can never be t much insisted upon; and more especially should this be the ca when attempts at a cure must be futile or uncertain in thi results. But, unfortunately, there are people whose evil influen tends to annul the benefits to be derived from the suppressi of contagious maladies—and especially those maladies who effects are most destructive—by bringing forward moral, sen mental, or religious reasons why these scourges should not interfered with: such as their being sent by Providence for t chastisement of sinful man, and its being wrong to attempt interfere with the infliction of this punishment; that in o attempts to suppress these contagions, we are resorting to me sures which offend the moral sense; that we should humb submit to the prevalence of the most deadly and disgustin maladies, merely because they are imagined to be a mark of th Divine wrath; or that the way in which the infection can on be thoroughly stamped-out is repugnant to the mind.

Such cant is nothing less than blasphemy, false sentimen or superstition worthy of the "dark ages," and those who reso to it must be looked upon as the uncompromising enemies of their species. Their religion is surely a mockery and a delusion, and their sentiment vicious in the highest degree.

The prevention of maladies which make life a burden and a curse; which curtail its duration; or which terminate it after a period of the most terrible suffering, whether in man or beast, must ever be the most sacred duty of the medical philosopher and legislator, and the fervent wish of the real Christian and true humanitarian,—no matter what fancied religious or sentimental feelings are supposed to be involved in the methods which must be resorted to. Man is most godlike when he relieves his fellow-man, or the creatures beneath him, from suffering; and he approaches nearest to the foul fiend that exults in torture, when, from hypocritical or unworthy motives, he permits a deadly, but easily suppressed, contagion to revel unchecked.

When we have discovered the cause of a disease—when we have acquired a knowledge of those laws on which its propagation and maintenance depend—then we are bound by every sacred and humane impulse to leave no effort untried, no measure unproved, either to abolish or ameliorate it.

The terrible consequences which, under certain circumstances, are produced among human beings and the lower animals by rabies, and our inability to cure the malady, render it absolutely imperative that the State, to which is entrusted the responsibility of protecting its people and the public interest, should aid science in checking or suppressing the malady.

True, the great affection that mankind has for the dog is rather a bar to the enforcement of statutes that may in any way militate against this kindly sentiment. Nevertheless, it must be obvious that in introducing laws to limit or suppress the outbreaks of rabies, we are not attempting to benefit the human species only, but are also endeavouring to save our canine and other companions from the dreadful effects of a deadly scourge. But let us see first what can be effected by preservative treatment.

Knowing that rabies and hydrophobia are propagated b virus or contagium usually introduced through the medium the saliva deposited in the wound made by the teeth of a ra creature, and that this infecting agent is organic matter, a therefore as easily destroyed by chemical and other means organic matter generally is, the grand object to be attain when a bite has been inflicted, is at once to prevent the abso tion of the poison by its immediate removal or destruction.

And though, as our statistics prove, only a certain proporti of those who are bitten by rabid animals become affected wi the disease, and therefore if every one so injured has to subn to painful preservative measures many will suffer needl torture; yet, as must be evident, there can be no selecti made of those who are likely to become diseased and those w are not: the most trifling scratch or wound may be as certain fatal as the largest and most complicated mutilation possib So that, to avoid calamitous consequences, the most insignifica contusion or abrasion demands as great attention as the deep and most lacerated wound. Besides, the moral effect of th attention in mankind far more than outweighs the pain, troub or inconvenience it may occasion.

We have also seen that rabies in the dog is, in its early stag not very well defined by symptoms such as would attract t attention of any one not cognisant of the malady in its differe phases; and it also frequently happens that a person is sudden wounded by a strange dog whose previous habits he kno nothing of, and of whose subsequent history he is likely to l uninformed. A large amount of uncertainty must, therefor prevail as to whether or not the animal is rabid; and it will l obvious that great danger is incurred if it is really mad, an no precautions are adopted to destroy the virus; whereas, if it not rabid, no harm will ensue from the precautionary measur adopted, and the wounded person may be saved from long da and weeks—nay, even months—of agonising suspense, by th knowledge that, even if the creature were diseased, he is safe.

It is, therefore, a wise precaution to adopt those measures which can do no possible harm should the bite not be poisonous, and which may, when carefully carried out, be the means of saving human life or that of valuable animals, and tend to prevent the spread of the malady, should it be present. All injuries, then, inflicted by canine or feline animals should not be neglected, but at once attended to; and the means which may ensure safety, if quickly brought into operation, are so simple and easily available, that every one who has attained the age of reason can at once apply them.

Object to be effected.—As has been said, the primary and all-important object to be effected, and to be strenuously insisted upon, with a view to prevent the occurrence of this fatal disease after the poison has been deposited in, or on, some part where it may be absorbed into the blood, is the immediate and thorough removal or destruction of this poison. The motives for, and the means to effect, this object were as well known in the days of Celsus as they are at present, and much—very much—of their success depends upon the promptitude and celerity with which the simple means necessary for this purpose are carried into effect.

It is wrong and cruel to teach that the virus of rabies may remain for a long time confined to the wound on or in which it has been deposited, and that its specific effects are only produced when the local injury begins to cause irritation. This teaching is in direct opposition to our experience of the disease, and to well-ascertained facts furnished by physiology and pathology, and may give rise to a fatal security, by causing the neglect of proper measures.

Rapidity of Absorption.—Nothing appears to be so clearly established as the rapidity with which the absorption of a fluid or solid in solution takes place from a living absorbent surface, and passes into the circulation. The ferrocyanide of potassium, for instance, takes no longer than a minute to pass from the inner surface of the intestines to that of the bladder in an animal that has been fasting for eleven hours; and t Veterinary Professor, Hering, has demonstrated that the sa compound has only required from twenty-five to thirty secon to pass from one jugular vein to the other. The rapidity wi which the poison of the viper and snake is taken up into t circulation, is also a well-marked instance of the activity absorption. These, of course, are somewhat exceptional exa ples; for if it were known that the virus of rabies could absorbed so rapidly, we might well despair of being able prevent its disastrous consequences.* All substances are not readily taken up into the circulation as those just mentione and even the repletion of the stomach appears to be not witho influence in this respect; for Hertwig found that, after feedi the animal, the period required for the transmission of t chemical compound just mentioned, to the urine, was fr thirty to forty minutes. Magendie ascertained that about s minutes elapsed between the deposition of the upas pois beneath the skin of the thigh and the first appearance of i effects; while Demarquay ascertained the presence in t saliva, of the iodide of potassium that he had applied in sol tion to a recent wound from fifteen minutes to an hour and half before.

The late Professor Renault made a series of experiments wi regard to the absorption of animal poisons by raw surface

* Though the prompt removal or destruction of the rabific virus must insisted upon, in order to ensure safety, yet we dare not despair of success ev when it has been deposited in a wound for some time; as we have already sho that there are reasons for believing that in some instances, if not in all, t poison is localised for a variable period at the seat of injury. This localisati of an animal poison is curious and interesting; and that it may remain for almost indefinite time in what may be termed an "encysted" or "imprisone condition, would appear to be proved by some very rare examples in oth diseases than that now under consideration. Perhaps one of the most remarka of these is that recorded in the *Monthly Journal of Medical Science* for Novemb 1853. A girl, aged fourteen years, was affected with influenza. She a complained of pain in each arm at the spots where, as an infant, she had be vaccinated. In fact, in these localities, vaccine vesicles soon became perfect developed, and an elder sister being revaccinated with the lymph obtained fr them, "beautiful vesicles formed, and ran a normal course."

from the results of which he concluded that the minimum period was about five minutes.

In the immense majority of cases, then, there is sufficient time between the deposition of the virus and its probable absorption, for the injured individual, or those around him, if presence of mind be brought to bear, to have recourse to preservative measures with the greatest possibility of their being fully successful: especially when we reflect that the wounds are generally bleeding; that the wounded surface may not be particularly active in absorbing; that the rabific saliva is always viscid, and therefore requires a longer time to be taken up; and also the chance that digestion may be active at the moment of the reception of the poison. But after twenty-four hours, according to Renault, preservative measures—at least those of a local nature—are useless; Lafosse says they can only be successfully resorted to within five minutes of the contact of the saliva, though there is still hope to be derived from their application within a quarter, and even half an hour. We would be inclined to add, within some hours after the receipt of the poison; for when everything, it may be said, depends upon the application of local measures, we are justified in resorting to them almost at so late a period as the cicatrisation of the wound.

Prognosis.

Our opinion as to the risk incurred will depend to some, indeed to a great, extent, upon the above considerations; but other circumstances will also have to be included in framing a prognostication as to the likelihood of immunity.

Seasons, &c.—For example, the season in which the wound has been inflicted has been, by some, thought to have an influence upon the virulency of the contagium; also the time and manner in which the injury is effected, both with regard to the recipient and the aggressor, and the situation, extent, and complicated nature of the wound.

We have already alluded to the seasons which appear to be most favourable to the development of rabies. The most dangerous period would appear to be when the disease is in its advanced stage, and during its paroxysms; especially if the creature has remained some time without biting and there is a quantity of saliva about the teeth, and if the recipient is in a condition to permit of the ready absorption of the poison. We have also alluded to the animals whose bites are most frequently followed by rabies: these are the wolf, dog, cat, and fox.

Nature of Wounds.—It may truly be said that all wounds made by a rabid animal are dangerous; but their gravity, leaving the other circumstances out of consideration, varies according to their situation, number, extent, and depth, as well as the nature of the parts involved. Those made in textures rich in lymphatic vessels, and very vascular,—as the face, head, neck, lips, eyes,—especially if uncovered, are most serious; if clothing, wool, hair, or harness intervene between the skin and the teeth, there is less reason for apprehension.

Though the smallest wounds, abrasions, or even contusions, may be extremely serious if not treated with the greatest care; yet a superficial injury that only involves the skin is less to be feared than one that penetrates it and the subjacent tissues, as the treatment is more easy and certain. But bites inflicted where blood vessels or nervous branches of any size are situated, or which involve the lining membrane of a joint, or such essential organs as the eye, are very doubtful with regard to consequences; as there is all the greater difficulty in employing efficacious means for neutralising the poison.

It has been remarked that the wounds made by rabid animals whose teeth are long and sharp are most frequently followed by symptoms of the disease: the bottom of the wound is less easily reached to destroy the poison it contains, and it is the last to heal. A wide open wound is, therefore, less formidable than a narrow deep one.

Local Treatment.

Local preservative treatment being that which is alone most assuredly efficacious, must, to be so, be resorted to before the absorption of the virus; and the simplest means to adopt, should no skilful person be available the moment any one is bitten, are the removal of the poison by suction, squeezing, washing, and cauterisation. It frequently happens that, because proper materials or instruments are not at hand, or because the person injured, or those who are with him at the time, do not know what is proper to do, the wound is left untouched, perhaps for hours after, when treatment can confer but questionable benefit.

Suction.—Suction, energetically employed, may either entirely or partially remove the poisonous saliva. The bitten individual, when the situation of the injury will permit, or a bystander, if it is not accessible to him, should at once apply the mouth to the wound and suck it vigorously, making pressure at the same time on its margin with his teeth. The blood that flows will carry with it the poison that may not yet have been absorbed, and the prolonged and repeated aspiration made by the lips, and the squeezing with the teeth, will in all probability induce a copious hæmorrhage that may still further ensure its entire removal. It may be objected to this practice, however, that the absorption that does not take place by the wound may occur by the mouth, if there chance to be any abrasion in that cavity or on the lips. But this risk may be largely averted if care is taken to spit freely after each aspiration. At any rate, though such an accident is possible, yet it is so unlikely, that the wounded person should have no hesitation whatever in at once adopting this means; for assuredly the chances of absorption of the poison in this way are infinitely smaller than they are if it is left in contact with the fresh wound. And though to the bystander there may be a certain degree of danger in performing this operation, yet when we reflect that we thereby, in all likelihood, rescue a fellow creature from the risk of a terrible death—more dreadful by far than drowning—surely the small amount of risk that might attend it would never deter any one from attempting such a noble and devoted act.* Rinsing the mouth with cold water, oil, milk, vinegar, claret, beer, or alcohol in the form of whisky, gin, brandy, &c., will still further diminish the chances of absorption.

Expression, Washing.—Squeezing or expression of the wounds should always be resorted to, in conjunction with suction, if possible, in order to increase bleeding. Washing the wound with cold or tepid water, or any other fluid, is also a sage measure, especially if it is poured with some force into the cavity for a good while—as from a water-tap, the spout of a kettle held at some distance from the wound, or a syringe; continuing also to squeeze it actively. Lime water, alcohol, chlorine water, &c., if convenient, may likewise be employed. Great benefit has been frequently derived from merely laving the bites with water.† Cold water is sometimes preferred to

* The efficacy of sucking poisoned wounds, and the comparative immunity of the operator, as already remarked, have been known from the earliest times and among nearly every people. We have previously alluded to the Psylli mentioned by Celsus, and we know that the suction of poison from wounds was resorted to in the days of Cleopatra. The practice was rendered famous in England in the thirteenth century, according to Rapin and Baker, by the heroic exploit of the affectionate Eleanor, who safely and successfully abstracted the poison from the wound of King Edward the First, which had been introduced by an arrow. According to Tennant, it was a common practice in the Highlands of Scotland. Berkenhout, who published "An Essay on the Bite of a Mad Dog," in 1783, strongly advises recourse to it: "The person bit must immediately apply his mouth to the wound, and continue to suck it during ten minutes or a quarter of an hour, frequently spitting out, and washing his mouth after each time with water, warm or cold, no matter which. If the wound be in a part of his body which he cannot reach with his mouth, possibly he may prevail on some rational friend to do him this kind office—especially when I assure him, positively assure him, that it may be done without the least danger. My own son, then about eight years old, in returning from school, was bit by a dog in the thigh. My eldest daughter, being informed of the accident, without the least hesitation immediately sucked the wound. She had heard me say it might be done with safety. The dog was certainly not mad; but I relate the story in justice to her affectionate intrepidity, which, in a young girl, was somewhat extraordinary."—(P. 73.)

† In the historical portion of this treatise, reference was made to several persons who escaped the effects of inoculation after being bitten by a rabid bear,

that which is warm or tepid, from its constringing effect on the blood-vessels. Whether it be hot or cold, the parts in the vicinity of the wound should always be well washed immediately.

Compression.—In addition to these means, there are others which are also of easy application, and likely to prove of great service. The first is compression between the injured part and the heart, so as to prevent the virus from entering the circulation by retarding the flow of blood; and accelerating the hæmorrhage. This can only be carried effectively into practice on the limbs or the appendages of the body, as the ears, &c. A handkerchief, bandage, leather strap, or other likely article may be employed; or when the formation of the parts prohibits their use, the fingers may suffice to exert a strong degree of pressure between the wound and the body, but always around a limb, if possible, if that be wounded. This compression is a most essential adjunct of suction, washing, cauterisation, and other local treatment at the time of the accident, and ought to be at once resorted to, and kept up until there is a certainty that the poison has been removed or destroyed. It is only necessary to add, that when straps and bandages are employed, care must be taken that they are not retained too long a time to produce mortification of the parts.

Cupping.—Cupping with any ordinary glass or deep vessel wider than the largest diameter of the wound, is also to be commended after compression, suction, and washing, or until other measures can be available. This operation is so simple that any one may practice it at once.

Cauterisation.

The above means, excellent in themselves when promptly and energetically resorted to, ought to be supplemented as quickly

through having to swim a river, the water of which washed the poison from their wounds. There is another instance on record in which several people were bitten by a mad wolf; some of these escaped across a river by a bridge, while others had to take to the water and swim. The latter escaped the disease, while the others perished from hydrophobia.

as possible by cauterisation of the injured parts, either by powerful heat or chemical compounds, which will destr the poison that may have already impregnated the tissues, eluded the attempts to remove it. Washing the wound as we as the neighbouring parts with plenty of cold water—acidu lated or alkaline, if convenient—throwing or injecting it wit force on the wounded surface, and suction, cupping, and com pression, must be looked upon merely as tentatives employe until more potent and certain measures can be available.

The Hot Iron.—Undoubtedly the most convenient, an perhaps, one of the most effective agents that can be employe to destroy the saliva and the tissues tainted by it, and th prevent its absorption, is the actual cautery in the form of piece of hot iron. There is no great skill needed to apply thi so long as the wounds are superficial; or should they be dee if they are confined to fleshy parts of the body. Neither the shape of the instrument of any great moment; indee from the domestic articles to be found in every dwelling, an sometimes even in one's pockets, a judicious selection can b made—a bodkin, skewer, key, curtain-rod, small poker—any thing, in fact, of a likely shape, rather round and pointed tha blunt and flat. The more it resembles the dog's tooth in shap of course it will the better adapt itself to the wound. The iro should be heated to a bright red or white heat, and applie with a firm and unsparing hand thoroughly to every part; fo it is a thousand times better to burn freely than hesitatingly imperfectly.

The pain of this operation is only of secondary importanc and not nearly so acute as many persons would be inclined t believe, especially if the iron is very hot and compression employed, as it ought to be, at the same time. Indeed, we ca say with Bouley that it is easily borne, particularly when th parts in immediate contact with the iron are carbonised; an there must be a particular satisfaction in enduring this pai when those who are operated upon know the nature of th disease, and that this operation is their only safeguard against its invasion. But should the injuries be very severe and the pain dreaded, general anæsthesia by chloroform or nitrous oxide, or local anæsthesia by the ether spray, may be induced, and particularly when excision of the bitten parts has to be performed. I would give the preference to the ether spray in many cases, from its peculiarly favourable action on a living surface,—its checking absorption, and reducing the parts exposed to it to nearly the condition of dead tissue; while depriving them, at the same time, of all sensation.

To make assurance doubly sure, and especially if the iron has been thin and incapable of retaining the proper degree of heat sufficiently long, it may be advisible to re-heat and again apply it. Or a brush dipped in the muriate of antimony or any powerful caustic solution should be inserted into the wound, which may then be dressed as a simple injury, and attended to for several successive days. When the eschar is coming away, its removal should be expedited; and if it is deemed necessary, the hot iron or the caustic may be again applied. If this is not considered quite reassuring, the wound may be kept open for five or six weeks, and dressed with some stimulating ointment. During this time, some authorities have recommended that mercurial frictions be made around the wound, in case any portion of the virus may have escaped the destructive action of the iron or caustic.

Substitutes for the Hot Iron.—On occasions it may not be possible to obtain the cautery sufficiently soon, and one's wits may have to devise a substitute. In these circumstances, a lighted lucifer match or fusee thrust into the wound may be very serviceable; and filling the cavity with gunpowder and exploding it, appears to have proved an excellent method of cauterising dog-bites. According to M. Manière, who resided for fifteen years in Hayti, rabies is very frequent there, and appears in all seasons; but the accidents arising from it are not at all in proportion to the number of persons bitten, as

deep, or in regions such as those of the mouth or nose, where solid or fluid caustics might prove dangerous. And it must also be noted that Constantinescu states that the nitrate of silver, alcohol, and ammonia, applied to wounds some moments even after they were inflicted, have not prevented the development of hydrophobia.

Solid Caustics.—Of the solid caustics, the nitrate of silver has been highly vaunted by Blaine and Youatt. It should be applied immediately after receiving the wound, and unsparingly. But the caustic potass, or "potassa fusa," as it is sometimes called, is more prompt and destructive in its action on organic matter, and therefore more likely to be efficient. It is also more diffusive: dissolving the parts with which it comes into contact, and penetrating beyond the surface to which it is actually applied. The best mode of preparing it for this purpose is as follows: Melt it in a silver or platina spoon, and when dissolved dip into it the ends of different sized probes. Each will take up a certain amount of the caustic, which will appear like a thin layer of varnish; when dry, dip in again and again, until a sufficient quantity has been accumulated on the extremity of the probe. With this the injury made by the dog's tooth may be penetrated almost to the bottom, and the subsequent liquefaction of the potass will ensure its reaching as far as the wound extends.

Fluid Caustics.—The fluid caustics have been, perhaps, more resorted to than those of a solid nature, chiefly because their fluidity insures their penetrating all the sinuosities of the wounds and coming in contact with every part of them. Of these the nitrate of mercury, perchloride of iron, and muriate of antimony have been most favourably recommended. Sabatier speaks highly of the nitrate of antimony. The neutralising or disorganising effects of carbolic acid, and the benefits which have been derived from its application in malignant pustule and in snake bites, should make it a useful local application in injuries from dogs or other rabid creatures. The pure acid would be too powerful, and likely to induce much sloughing; but two parts of acid one of alcohol, or equal proportions of both, would be efficien A strong tincture of iodine has also been prescribed.

Fluidity, and prompt and powerful action, are the speci features of these fluid caustics. A good way of applying the is the following: Dry the wound with care; make sever incisions if necessary and possible, in order to open the bitte part well up, and then touch it with a brush or a shred of li or tow dipped in the caustic, and afterwards introduce a pledg of lint well impregnated with it. The whole is then to b covered with a dry piece of lint or tow, and a plaster or band age placed over all. Some hours afterwards the dressings a removed, and if it is noticed that any part has escaped th action of the caustic, this is touched, and a blister larger tha the wound is applied; this hastens the sloughing of the escha and favours suppuration. In order that a fluid caustic b thoroughly efficient in destroying every part of the surface of wound, it is of course necessary that the wound be a dependin one, in order that the liquid may gravitate to its furthermos recesses. If it is not so, and the position of the bitten individua cannot be temporarily altered to permit of the escharotic actin in this manner, the actual cautery or solid caustic must b employed.

Modification of Treatment.—This treatment must, of course be modified according to circumstances. When a bite is no extensive, and only involves the skin, it is always most con venient, before cauterising it, to remove the margin of th wound by excision with a sharp knife, circumscribing it by tw semi-elliptical incisions. If narrow, deep, and angular, it mus necessarily be enlarged by incisions, so as to allow the cautery to touch its every part. If some shreds of flesh are hanging loose, it is better to cut them away altogether than to cauterise them; the object is to present a regular surface to the action of the cautery or caustic, so that no particle of the poison may escape. If a portion of a member, such as an ear, an eyelid, or a tendon, has been torn, it is most prudent to remove it when possible; if impracticable, the wound should be enlarged, and either the iron or caustic thoroughly applied. It should then be dressed with a stimulating ointment, as that of turpentine or cantharides. After some weeks' treatment allow the wound to heal, and if an animal, separate it from others for a certain period. Some authorities think it best to heal up the wound as quickly as possible.

Excision.

In excising wounds caused by the teeth of rabid animals, the greatest care should be taken that every portion likely to have been in contact with the saliva is removed, and particularly that the knife itself is not instrumental in its diffusion. To avoid this grave mishap, all around the wound should first be well washed, in order to clean away any saliva lying on the surface; then the excision should be carried on beyond the injured part, and the knife frequently dipped in a solution of carbolic acid. If this is not done, in making the incisions on each side of the wound, the sound parts through which they are made will likely become tainted with the virus. In general, two incisions should be made,—one on each side of the wound,—forming an ellipsis in such as will admit of it, which ought to be carried sufficiently deep as completely to remove the part, if possible. It must then be closely examined to discover if there is any portion in the piece excised through which the dog's tooth appears to have passed; if there is, the excision must be carried deeper. In making the incisions, great attention should be paid to the direction the tooth has taken; should the knife enter the wound made by the tooth, if carbolic acid or any other caustic is not employed, the operation must be recommenced with a clean knife; as the painful task may be rendered useless by the sound textures becoming soiled with the poison. Mr. Abernethy recommended the following plan, which may be adopted in certain cases: the cell into which a

lower animals, though the removal of such appendages as the ears or tail may be practised when it is deemed necessary; but to be useful a long period must not be suffered to elapse—Lafosse says no more than five minutes.*

It must ever be remembered, and cannot be too much insisted upon, that whatever method of procedure is adopted, the object to be obtained is the removal or destruction of the poison thoroughly and immediately after its deposition, as upon this depends the safety of the wounded.

The value of these preservative measures has been so often and strikingly manifested—even before the time of Celsus—that it appears almost superfluous to insist upon their employment nowadays, were it not that all kinds of silly quack nostrums are yet commended as specifics against the disease, and a belief in their efficacy by ignorant people is very likely to cause the only certain treatment to be overlooked or neglected. For it cannot be said of these proposed specific medicines that if they do no good, they cannot at any rate do harm. On the contrary, they are likely to cause great mischief, by inducing the wounded persons and those around them to place implicit trust in their efficacy, and indulge in a fatal security without resorting to the proper method of treatment.

Results of Cauterisation.—We have but little means of ascertaining to what extent caüterisation of the wounds inflicted by rabid animals has been really successful in a large number of instances—our experience in this country being limited to individuals here and there whose cases have chanced to be reported. But M. Bouley, impressed with the great interest that belongs to this question, has endeavoured to make the most of the statistics available to him, and has given the result in the following terms: If we compare, with regard to their consequences, the bites from rabid animals which have been cauterised,

* Faber gives an instance of an ox whose tail was bitten by a rabid dog, and though the appendage was amputated within two hours, yet the animal afterwards took the disease.—*Die Wuthkrankeit*, p. 295.

in thirty-six hours. The following table gives the details of the 16 cases:—

Immunity after immediate cauterisation with the hot iron	7
" " " " by cones of gunpowder	1
" " " " with late application of the hot iron	1
" " " " after at least 24 hours	3
" " " " " 36 "	1
" " " " with muriate of antimony after 3 hours	1
" without adopting precautions	2

Thus it will be seen that one half the cases of immunity might be supposed to be due to immediate cauterisation, three-eighths to tardy cauterisation, and one-eighth escaped without any treatment.

Of the 47 deaths tabulated by Roucher as occurring in Algeria, we find that their relations with preventive or preservative measures are as follows:—

Died without wounds having been cauterised	25
" " indications of precautions	10
" after tardy and incomplete cauterisation with the hot iron	2
" " cauterisation with the hot iron	5
" " cauterisation with the nitrate of silver	1
" after immediate cauterisation with ammonia, supplemented by the hot iron an hour and a half subsequently	1
" " immediate cauterisation with ammonia	2
" " " " " the hot iron	1

In the 47 deaths only one occurred after immediate cauterisation with the hot iron; 12 were preceded by delayed or insufficient cauterisation, and 35 had not been submitted to any preventive treatment; for it is very probable that in the 10 cases which afford no indication of precautions having been adopted, none were resorted to.

So that of the 37 cases allowed to take their natural course, there were 2 of immunity and 35 deaths, or a mortality of 94·6 per cent. Of the 9 in which cauterisation with the hot iron was immediately employed, there was only one fatal case, or a mortality of 11 per cent.; and of the 16 cauterised after some delay, or in a manner more or less imperfect, there were 10 deaths, or a mortality of 62·5.

This interesting information shows to what an extent the prompt intervention of surgical measures is useful in preventing the development of the disease.

Among the fatal cases whose history was more or less known, there was only one in which the wounds had been at once treated with the actual cautery, and another in which ammonia was applied first and the hot iron some time afterwards. In three instances there was a delay of nine and twelve hours, and in other three of some hours. In three more of the 47 cases, cauterisation was incompletely effected by ammonia or nitrate of silver; in one case cauterisation was only resorted to after two days; and twice the wounds were dressed immediately with liquid ammonia.

The only patient who died after having his wounds immediately cauterised with the hot iron, was believed to have been saved; as he enjoyed excellent health for six and a-half months, and in that time had taken part in the expedition against the Kabyles in 1851, and returned quite well.

In the two which had the wounds dressed immediately with liquid ammonia, the period of incubation extended to 116 and 130 days: a circumstance which might give rise to the supposition that caustics have a retarding influence on the development of the disease.

Three persons mentioned by Toussaint of Algeria, who had been bitten and had their wounds cauterised—two immediately and one the next day—escaped the consequences; while a fourth person, who did not have his wounds attended to, died of hydrophobia. Hugo speaks of seven persons who were bitten by a rabid dog; three had their injuries cauterised twenty-four hours afterwards, and the other four cauterised themselves with two pieces of iron heated in the fire; all escaped. The same dog attacked a child twelve years old, and, its wounds not being attended to, it died of hydrophobia.

Results of Excision and Caustics.—We have no statistics to guide us in forming an opinion as to the value of excision; but so much depends upon the completeness of this operation, as well as upon the interval that has elapsed between its adoption and the infliction of the injury, that even if we possessed these figures there would still remain some uncertainty, as with cauterisation. The same may be said as to the benefits derived from the employment of caustics. Youatt, who trusted to them, and who had himself been bitten seven times, says that he had used caustic for the wounds of more than four hundred persons who were bitten by dogs, of whose disease there could be no doubt, and that not one of these became affected. And a surgeon of St. George's Hospital told him that ten times that number had undergone the operation of excision there, after having been bitten by rabid or suspected dogs, and it was not known that any of these persons had become diseased.

Ingestion of Fluids.—Aware of the influence that plenitude of the circulatory system exercises on absorption, Lafosse, basing his recommendation on the physiological experiments made by Ericksen, thinks that great utility may be derived from the prompt ingestion of any fluid by the wounded person. Absorption by this means may be so delayed, that a substance which, under ordinary circumstances, would be taken up in a minute, will, perhaps, not enter the circulation until after thirty or forty minutes. Who knows, he continues, if this period might not be so prolonged by swallowing fluids at brief intervals, as to absolutely interdict the penetration of the virus until it has become decomposed or rejected by the eliminatory inflammation which is not slow in appearing? He gives the preference to alcohol, ammonia, and the acetates, carbonates, and hydrochlorates of this base, in large quantities of water.

The Moral Influence of Local Treatment.

It is obvious that, when the injury has been inflicted for many days, or even hours, cauterisation or other local treatment having been employed a number of times with people who would not have been attacked by hydrophobia.*

Mental Treatment.

When everything has been done to destroy the germ of the disease before its absorption may take place, it may be affirmed that nothing more that is likely to be materially efficacious can be devised to obviate danger; the means that have been adopted may be productive of the strongest feeling of security in the mind of the injured individual; or, apprehending the worst results, he may pass days, and even months, harassed by all the perplexities, anguish, and moral torture of one condemned to death—having them ever before him like an implacable spectre which, though a phantom to-day, may to-morrow be a possible reality.

It is in the latter circumstances that moral treatment may

* "Frequent immunity from the disease in persons who have been bitten has tended to confer reputation upon so many vaunted methods of prevention. Ignorant persons, and knavish persons, have not failed to take advantage of this. They announce that they are in possession of some secret remedy which will prevent the virus from operating: they persuade the friends of those who die that the remedy was not rightly employed, or not resorted to sufficiently early; and they persuade those who escape that they escape by virtue of the preventive remedy. If the plunder they reap from the foolish and the frightened were all, this would be of less consequence; but, unfortunately, the hope of security without undergoing a painful operation leads many to neglect the only sure mode of obtaining safety. . . . Some of the specifics are great secrets; and they who possess them—whether they believe in them or not is another matter—sell them at no cheap rate to those who, having been bitten by the dog, are weak enough to be bitten again by the quack."—*Watson*, "Principles and Practice of Physic," vol. i. pp. 616, 628. Perhaps one of the most vaunted of these impositions is that known as the "Birling (Kent) remedy," and attempts have been frequently made to raise a sum (£500, I think) sufficient to purchase it from the countryman who holds it as an heirloom. In these attempts to obtain subscriptions, it has been stated that the "remedy" was never known to fail in preventing the disease; and this statement coming from people of position—though unacquainted with medicine—may have frequently, and indeed has, had very pernicious results, for it is not correct. Out of some cases of failure at hand, I may mention that related by Mr. Weeks, surgeon, of Rochester, as occurring in 1793. The patient—a man-servant—would not have the bitten parts excised, but preferred the Birling remedy. In ten days he was attacked with hydrophobia, and in two days was dead.—See "A Plan for preventing the fatal Effects from the Bite of a Mad Dog." By Jesse Foot. London, 1793.

General Preservative Treatment.

Various preservative agents have been prescribed from time to time, but all have proved unreliable. An enumeration of them would prove of no possible utility; but it may be remarked that those medicaments which act more especially upon the absorbent system and the salivary glands have been much in vogue. Preparations of mercury * and iodine, particularly the former, have been recommended by high authorities. Vapour baths at a high temperature and purgatives have also been commended. Herbst, of Gottingen, recommended as a preservative, and also a specific method of treatment, the administration of tartar emetic and the sulphates of copper and zinc in large dozes, dissolved in water. He founded his faith in this remedy from having given it to nine dogs which had been bitten, and were not attacked by the disease. But Leisering, of the Dresden Veterinary School, has not found it to succeed in the instances in which he tried it.

Blaine fancied that belladonna was beneficial; associated with *scutellaria lateriflora*, he was positive that it was an almost certain prophylactic. Recent trials do not appear to have verified his anticipations, however, and we hear but little now of preservative remedies. For my own part, I would be inclined to suggest the long-continued use of the sulphite or hyposulphite of soda or magnesia, or some preparation of carbolic acid.

* A favourite method of using the mercury has been locally in the form of ointment—rubbing a drachm upon the wounded part every day for about ten days. Sometimes mercurial pills have also been given, in addition. Salivation was not frequently produced, though when it occurred it was not looked upon as injurious. When a period of two or three weeks had elapsed from the receipt of the injury, the mercury was more freely used. Another method, also said to have been attended with success, even when the disease had appeared, was mercurial fumigation:—placing the patient, entirely undressed, on a cane-bottomed chair, enveloped in blankets; then throwing several grains of mercury on live charcoal, placed beneath the chair. In a short time salivation was produced and the urgent symptoms allayed until recovery took place. Turpith's mineral has been long a favourite preservative, and even curative, medicament with the old farriers and cowleeches.

Though it is discouraging to reflect that we can only rely upon prompt and energetic local treatment, and that when this has not been adopted in time all other measures are comparatively hopeless, yet we must not give up in despair the idea of discovering, eventually, some means by which the action of the virus may be completely annulled, and the dreaded disease placed in the list of those which are preventible when their contagium has been absorbed, or curable when the symptoms have manifested themselves.*

With regard to the preservative measures in general, another important matter must not be overlooked. If a person has been bitten by a dog, or if animals have been wounded by it, and the creature at the time does not exhibit any distinct symptom of rabies, it is well, in order to tranquillise the minds of those chiefly concerned, and who are apprehensive of danger, to secure it properly for a number of days—say a fortnight or three weeks—before allowing it to go at large again. If it was really rabid when it inflicted the injury, it will soon exhibit unmistakable signs of the disease, and die; or it may then be killed, and every precaution taken accordingly.

If the above-mentioned period passes without any manifestation of rabies, then the possibility of future disaster ensuing from the wounds is happily disposed of, and great anxiety abolished. But if the dog is destroyed without any evidence that it was

* Lafosse is as hopeful as other sanguine individuals in this respect. He thinks that, owing to the terror inspired by the disease, the experiments have been few and not always properly conducted; and having devised a special form cage and apparatus by which he could, without danger, carry out researches with regard to the effects of medicines on those animals affected with rabies whose teeth renders them so formidable. This contrivance consists of a cage or den with a grille door, on the sides of which are two openings large enough to allow the mad animal's head, and which are closed by means of doors or shutters that are moved by a toothed wheel and rack. The head being drawn outside the cage by one of the chains employed to tie the animal, the neck is tied in such a fashion as to keep the head fixed without inducing strangulation or cerebral congestion. The mouth may then be easily opened by means of a speculum provided with a long handle, and an iron tube, having a funnel at one end, is inserted; medicines poured into the funnel and pass through the tube and readily find their way into the pharynx.

suffering from the disease, then months of the most painful suspense, and even anguish, may perhaps elapse before the result can be known. In these circumstances, all that can be done is carefully to inquire into the aggressive animal's history, ascertain all the symptoms exhibited by it, and its behaviour immediately before and after inflicting the wound.

In any case, however, there should be no hesitation or delay in adopting the precautions just indicated, to preserve those bitten from after consequences.

M. Desjardins fully recognises the value of this measure. As soon, he says, as any person has been bitten by a suspected animal, hasten to secure it, so that it can do no more damage; and watch it closely instead of killing it at once, as is the custom. Give it several drops of syrup of buckthorn, and afterwards a dose of phosphorus (fifteen centigrammes) reduced to powder, and mixed in a sufficient quantity of water. If the animal lives, its healthy condition should be made known to the injured person; for the mind exercises so great an influence that it seems at times and in certain conditions, according to the idiosyncrasy of the individual, to constitute the sole and unique cause of this terrible affection. But if, on the contrary, the dog dies, its death must be carefully concealed, or another must be substituted in order to make the person believe that the animal was healthy, and that the treatment to which he was submitted was merely adopted to dispel the fear and alarm he experienced at the receipt of the injury.*

Treatment of Lyssi.

We need do no more than refer in this place to the destruction of the lyssi under the tongue, already alluded to as appearing in the interval between the inoculation and the appearance of the malady. This, the method of Salvatori and Marochetti, consists in opening the pustules that show themselves in this part, removing their contents—which is

* "L'Indépendance Scientifique et Litteraire," 1869.

believed to be the virus—washing the mouth with salt and water, and administering a decoction of *genista tinctoria* internally.

Resume of Preservative Treatment.

The most important measures to remember in connection with the preservative treatment, by which dangers may be averted and life saved, are :—

To destroy or remove the poison at once from the wound, immediately on receiving a bite from a diseased or suspected dog or cat. As it is not always known whether these animals are in health when they inflict injuries, it is best to act as if they were diseased by adopting prompt and effectual precautions, which consist in :—

A. *Suction* by the mouth, carried on persistently and energetically for some time, spitting out very frequently, and, if possible, rinsing the mouth with water, &c.

B. *Expression*, or squeezing the wound, in conjunction with the above.

C. *Washing* with cold or tepid water, poured from a vessel held at some distance above the wound. A syringe or the ordinary water tap may be most advantageously employed to force the water to the bottom of the wound.

D. *Compression* above the wound, *i.e.*, between it and the heart, but close to the wound. This may be effected by the hand while the previous measures are employed ; or, if a limb be wounded, a handkerchief, piece of rope, strap, &c., may be fastened tightly around it.

E. *Cupping* with an ordinary glass larger than the diameter of the wound.

F. *Cauterisation*, when immediate, is at once the promptest and safest treatment. The best instrument is a piece of iron heated to a white heat, in shape pointed, round, or the figure of an olive. Iron instruments of a suitable shape are at hand in every dwelling, and, while being heated, suction, washing, and compression should be resorted to. Gunpowder, a fusee, or a lucifer match may be ignited in the wound when the iron is not immediately accessible.

G. *Caustics*—solid or fluid—may also be employed with the same success, or they may be preferable or supplementary to the actual cautery.

H. *Excision* and *scarification* should be practised when necessary, though they demand more skill.

I. The wounds should be kept open for some time, and made to suppurate freely.

J. The wounded individual should be made to drink large quantities of fluid to hinder the absorption of the poison.

K. The mind of the injured person must be kept as calm as possible. All anxiety should be allayed by every means, and no reference made to the injury at any time. Mental treatment is by no means to be neglected.

L. *General preservative treatment* must be directed to keeping the health in a sound condition, as on it depends a cheerful state of the mind. Medicines which act on the salivary glands may be prescribed for a certain period; antiputrescent medicaments may also be prescribed; or those which have a soothing effect may be used to allay apprehension.

M. A dog which has bitten a person should not be destroyed until it is positively known to be affected with rabies. It should be well secured and kept under observation, as a few days only are required to discover whether it is diseased or not. The wounded person should be convinced that it was quite healthy if it survives; should it prove to be rabid, he ought not to be informed of it.

PREVENTIVE MEASURES.

We have seen that the resources of art in this, as in so many maladies affecting man and beast, are but limited, and in several respects unsatisfactory, so far as preservative and curative measures are concerned. But in rabies, as in other contagious diseases, all countries that are so humane and enlightened as to place any value upon the lives and welfare of men and animals, institute legislative enactments which supplement the efforts of art, and bring to bear measures that compensate more or less for the deficiencies in our scientific knowledge. In many respects they are even more valuable, inasmuch as they aim at suppressing diseases entirely, by preventing the diffusion of the virulent elements on which their maintenance and vitality depend. These enactments, based on the teachings of science and scrupulously enforced by legal authority, are largely destined to rid humanity of many of the greatest inflictions that have scourged the world; for sanitary science, though but of modern date, has become one of the most important branches of human knowledge and research, and receives the earnest attention of every nation that lays claim to be civilised.

The measures dictated by Veterinary Sanitary Authorities would in this, as in other contagious maladies of the lower animals, prove perfectly effectual in at least confining the disease to the narrowest limits, if they did not tend to suppress it altogether, were they carried into operation with energy and circumspection.

These measures should have for their object not only the prevention of disastrous consequences to mankind from the presence of rabid dogs; but should also be based on humane and utilitarian principles, so far as dogs and other animals are concerned.

It may be said that the Veterinary Police Measures to be applied to this disease are founded on the consideration that, though it may be developed spontaneously in the canine and feline species, and though this spontaneous development may be more or less averted by proper hygienic treatment of these animals in a domesticated state, yet that perhaps 999 in 1,000 cases are due to contagion alone, and that therefore the destruction of the contagious source or sources is of primary importance; also, that rabies is not peculiar to any season, but may, and does, appear at all times of the year in a sporadic or epizoötic form.

These measures, in the general interest of the community, should be adopted and rigorously enforced, and owners of dogs or other domestic animals should be compelled to use every precaution.

Hygienic Treatment of Dogs.

There can be no doubt whatever, that if we wish to preserve animals from disease, we must carefully attend to their health, and remove them from those conditions which militate against their enjoyment of life to a degree compatible with their nature. As rabies may attack dogs in all seasons, the best precautions to adopt against its development in them are those which relate to their hygienic treatment; and to secure them from such a terrible disease and its results, surely no amount of reasonable care can be considered superfluous.

It is to be recommended, therefore, that they be provided with a sufficient quantity of solid and liquid aliment of good quality, and by no means putrid, particularly in summer. Heating or spiced food, and that which is naturally improper for them, should be withheld. Bones should constitute an integral portion of their aliment. Dogs should always be properly kept, and carefully brushed and washed; and, when possible, those which have long hair ought, according to some authorities, to be clipped at least twice a year. In summer it is good to take them frequently to the water. Their kennels should be regularly cleaned out and provided with fresh straw, fine shavings, or sawdust. In winter, they ought not to be submitted to the rigours of the weather—cold, bitter winds, and damp—but be kept in well-littered dwellings, and provided with pure water; it is necessary to see that the latter is not frozen during frost. It is not good for dogs to lie near a hot fire for too long a time, or to be directly exposed to the sun's rays in warm weather. During the summer, it is indispensable that fresh and pure water be supplied to them in sufficient quantity. Above all things, dogs should not be needlessly excited, abused, or deprived of water. If it should happen that an excited dog bites any one, the person who excited it should be held guilty of a legal offence.* Röll recommends that dogs in rut should be permitted to couple at favourable times.

Dogs ought never to be allowed to run about at large for a long time without being watched, as they are liable to fight with strange dogs, become quarrelsome and vicious, and, driven by hunger and thirst, eat and drink all kinds of unhealthy food and impure water; besides, rambling dogs cannot be properly looked after by their owners, and may become a source of annoyance and danger to other creatures and to mankind.

Quarrelsome and vicious dogs should, if circumstances render

* By the Austrian laws relating to contagious animal diseases and veterinary police (392), every one who, by excitation or any other intentional means, causes an animal to inflict a wound, shall be liable to eight days' imprisonment, or more, according to aggravating circumstances. The jurisprudence of our ancestors in this country, the Celts, included compensation for the diseases or unsoundness of, and damage done by, various of the domestic animals, but indemnification for the injury caused by mad dogs was not allowed. According to the Dimetian, or "South Wales Code" (in force in the tenth century), it is specified that for the damage done by a rabid dog there shall be no indemnity. And the laws of Wales (same period) say: "If the owner of a dog which has been killed denies that it was rabid, then he who killed it should prove that he had seen it attack people and dogs, and that it had bitten its tongue."

it necessary, be confined and chained up, and taken care of, so that they cannot do injury to any person or animal. To neglect this precaution should bring the offender within the penal code.*

The cruel custom of pampering and overfeeding dogs, giving food which is unnatural to them, or in too great quantity, should be particularly guarded against; and all dogs ought to have a sufficient amount of exercise. Nothing can be more reprehensible than keeping dogs confined to houses for days together, or chaining them up for weeks and months to a kennel, without once allowing them their liberty. This treatment is very pernicious to their temper and health, and quite opposed to the animals' natural instincts.

The maltreatment of dogs, however brought about, should be repressed.

Diminish the Number of Useless Dogs.

One of the first, as it is one of the most beneficial and humane measures, is the diminution of the number of useless dogs, whose existence is certainly not profitable to mankind, and whose presence, if sometimes a source of pleasure to a few, may yet be a cause of danger or annoyance to the many. It is also evident that the smaller the number of these animals, the less risk there is of rabies.

The dogs owned by poor people, without the slightest pretext of utility, should be more particularly the object of this measure, inasmuch as they are badly kept, and allowed to run about dirty and diseased, without any efficient surveillance being exercised over them. How often have we seen numbers of such currish brutes in the most squalid parts of large towns,

* The Austrian Penal Code (391) says: "Every owner of an animal—no matter to what species it may belong—which he knows to be vicious, ought, in or out of doors, to watch and take care of it, so that it may not wound any one. Any damage caused by the neglect of this precaution is punishable by a fine of from five to twenty-five florins, if there has been no wound inflicted; but when this is the case, the penalty may be increased to from ten to fifty florins." The French Civil Code contains a similar enactment.

living with their owners in the miserable and badly-ventilated dwellings that compose such regions, consuming a portion of the food that their owners were so much in need of themselves, and contributing to make these dwellings still more insalubrious by absorbing their share of the oxygen that was already far too insufficient in quantity to maintain health, and largely aiding in poisoning the atmosphere by their filthiness. Even without their tendency to become rabid, these parasites are a nuisance, and a source of waste and insalubrity.

The dogs kept solely for pleasure by those who can afford to feed and attend to them properly are scarcely less a source of danger and extravagance; for they appear to be very predisposed to be affected with rabies, while the food they consume forms no inconsiderable item of expense, and might maintain many people. Indeed, the waste of food due to the maintenance of useless dogs, whether they belong to rich or poor, must amount to a very great sum; though it is somewhat difficult to estimate it, from the fact that we have no statistics of the number of what we would distinguish as useful animals in contradistinction to those kept merely for pleasure, or allowed to live an idle, vagabond life.

The licences issued in this country do not give us the exact number of dogs maintained; for besides the exceptions to the taxation, there can be no doubt whatever that a large percentage escapes the impost, either through their being ownerless, or their owners not complying with the law. Nevertheless, through the courtesy of Mr. Cockell, of the Inland Revenue Office, I find that the number of licenses issued in England in 1870 was 944;496, and in Scotland 119,471—making a total of 1,063,967; and in the half-year ending 30th June, 1871, the number for England was 951,501, and Scotland 119,671—or a total of 1,071,172. There can scarcely be a doubt that the unlicensed dogs will amount to something like one-half the number of those for which duty is paid; and if we estimate the value of the food consumed by each of these animals at only one penny a day, it will be seen that an enormous sum is expended annually in keeping dogs of which we may presume not one-fourth could be classed as useful.

In France, in 1855, during the discussion on the dog tax, it was computed that in that country there were no fewer than three millions of dogs, and the cost of keeping them, at an average of from seven to eight centimes a day each, was calculated to be eighty million francs annually. According to M. Lavallée ("Encyclopédie de l'Agriculture"), however, the daily expense is heavier than in this estimate; for the food of a large dog he reckons to weigh a kilogramme.

In Austria the number of pleasure dogs (*Luxus Hunden*) is said to be one million, and the expense of their keep three million gulden; and in Denmark there are a hundred thousand dogs, nearly all of which are useless, and whose cost of living has been put down at a million thalers.

Boudin has estimated the number of dogs in Europe at more than twelve millions, and the price of their food at least five hundred millions (a demi-milliard) of francs.

Though many of these dogs may be fed on chance food and garbage, yet it cannot be denied that a very considerable quantity of aliment must be purchased specially to maintain the dog tribe, in addition to that which might be applied to the rearing of fowls, pigs, and other useful creatures.

In an economical point of view, therefore, the diminution of the number of useless dogs is most desirable; inasmuch as a proportionate quantity of food must be saved for the alimentation of people or useful animals. But from a sanitary point of view, the decrease in these creatures, as has been said, is even more essential. This decrease may be effected in several ways, the chief of which are "taxation," and the "capture," and if need be "destruction," of all vagabond or stray dogs.

A. The imposition of a *tax* upon dogs is generally very effective in diminishing their numbers, and the higher the tax and the more strictly it is imposed, so will the useless dogs become fewer. Dogs kept for pleasure only should be most heavily taxed.

The influence of this measure on the number of dogs has been well shown in the cases of Baden and Copenhagen. In the first-named kingdom, in 1832, the duty was 3 florins, and the number of dogs 26,000. On reducing the tax to 1½ florins in 1844, there were 45,000 dogs, and when raised to 4 florins the number again sank to 26,000.

In Copenhagen, with a duty on each dog of 2 thalers, from 1839 to 1852 the number of dogs rose from 2,468 to 5,673; then on raising the tax to 5 thalers, up to 1862 they were diminished to 2,121.

In France the effect has not been so marked, probably owing to the low rate of taxation, and to the carelessness with which, as would appear by Lafosse's statement, the law is carried out. But if there is no proof that the proportion of dogs has diminished, it would nevertheless seem that the cases of hydrophobia were fewer after than before the imposition of the tax in 1855. This is shown in the subjoined table:—

Before the Tax.		After the Tax.	
In 1850	27 cases.	In 1856	20 cases
1851	12 ,,	1857	12 ,,
1852	46 ,,	1858	17 ,,
1853	37 ,,	1859	19 ,,
1854	21 ,,	1860	14 ,,
1855	21 ,,	1861	21 ,,
Totals	164	Totals	103

In the two periods of six years each, it will be seen that there is a difference in favour of the second of 61 cases. But objections have been made to these figures which, if well founded, would somewhat detract from their value. For instance, the high figure in 1852 is due to an exceptional circumstance—a mad dog in one of the French departments caused the death of no less than ten persons from hydrophobia. And after the tax was imposed, the number of dogs was pretty fairly ascertained (in 1858 it was 1,696,104 dogs); but for the years previous to 1856 it was not possible to obtain any reliable information on the subject. Many French veterinary surgeons are inclined to attribute the fewer number of cases of hydrophobia to the greater restraint imposed upon the liberty of the canine species after the tax was decreed, while others imagine the diminution to be merely accidental.

We have no reason, however, to come to any other conclusion than that a measure of this kind must be most efficacious in ridding the country that energetically resorts to it, of a vast number of miserable and dangerous brutes; but, to be really efficient, the tax should be general and high, exception being only made in favour of dogs which are useful, or whose services can be proved to be absolutely necessary,—such as house and yard dogs, or those employed to lead the blind about. With regard to pleasure and sporting dogs, the tax should be highest, for whoever can afford to indulge in keeping such animals can also afford to pay a high tax. If, however, it can be shown that sporting dogs are necessary, then the impost might be reduced to that levied for useful animals.

When one person possesses more than one pleasure dog, then the tax should be proportionately increased.

Dogs and bitches should be equally taxed; at least the latter should not be less, as has been proposed by some authorities, but if anything more, as the fewer they are, the smaller the number of dogs.

Puppies should be sold, not given away; and all that are not purchased should be destroyed. It is cruel to breed puppies that they may grow up into half-starved, dangerous, vagrant dogs. As soon as they are weaned, the tax should be demanded; and with all dogs this tax had better be paid half-yearly.

Every dog should wear a collar with a brass plate, on which is inscribed the name and address of its owner, as well as a particular mark stamped thereon by the Police or Inland Revenue Authorities, as a guarantee that the tax is paid, and also for purposes of identification.* It would be well if in all towns and villages there was a dog census, or list of the dogs kept therein.

B. All stray dogs without the collar, or which have not the mark or their owner's name thereon, should be *captured*, and *sold* or *destroyed* immediately, or after a certain period. This period might be extended to three days, and if the animal was claimed by its owner, a fine should be imposed and expenses paid.†

Straying dogs, when furnished with the proper collar, may, when circumstances render it necessary—as when rabies prevails—be seized by the police, and conveyed to their owners, who should be compelled to pay a fine or expenses. This addressed and numbered collar is also useful in the case of damage done by dogs, as every one should be held responsible for the damage done by his dog, due to his negligence or imprudence.‡ Bitches in rut should not be allowed to wander

* A badge of this kind appears to be in use in Holland, according to the statement of Max Du Camp, who writes: "At Harlingen, in Friesland, I saw a dog pass which had a wooden cross hanging at its neck; then a second dog, and a third; and finally I observed that every dog in the town was decorated with a similar ornament. Making inquiry respecting this matter, I was informed that all dogs not wearing the cross were, in the canton of Harlingen, immediately apprehended, and led by the ears to the pound; for the crosses are issued by the municipality, and their possession proves that the tax imposed upon such animals has been paid."—*En Hollande*, Paris, 1859, p. 163.

† At Strasbourg, the law relating to dogs appears to be very efficacious and reasonable. Every owner must notify his possessing a dog to the police, who furnish him with a license duly numbered and registered. This number, with the address of the owner, is inscribed on the collar which every dog has to wear.

A covered conveyance, driven by two men, is constantly travelling about the town, and into this all the wandering dogs which do not wear a collar, or which do not carry thereon their owner's name, address, and registered number, are put, and conveyed to a building which is divided into three compartments. There these dogs are kept for three days, passing successively each day from the first to the second, and finally to the third compartment. On the evening of the third day, if not claimed, they are destroyed. During the three days, the proprietor may claim and take away his dog by paying a sum amounting to fifteen francs. The result is most satisfactory, so far as wandering dogs are concerned.

‡ The French Civil Code ordains that "the proprietor of an animal, or he who [illegible]

about at any time, whether with or without the collar; as they excite dogs, and lead to quarrels which may have some direct or indirect influence in the production or spread of rabies.

It has been proposed—and the proposal has frequently been carried into effect—to destroy dogs which are allowed to wander about, notwithstanding orders to the contrary, by scattering *poison* at certain periods in the places frequented by them. But this measure, though effective enough in this respect, is severe and cruel as regards the dogs, and even dangerous to the human species, as it may destroy other than wandering dogs, and cause much torture, in all probability, from the nature of the poison employed; it may also be a source of irreparable accidents to man as well as animals, and might even furnish the means of realising criminal intentions.*

Emasculation.

If it were clearly demonstrated that rabies was spontaneously developed only in male dogs, and that its development was due to the privation or excitement of the generative function, then *castration* must necessarily be practised upon all dogs, with the exception of those destined for reproduction. But neither experience nor observation at present justify recourse to this measure; and though certain advantages are to be derived from the castration of male as well as of female dogs, yet the owners of these animals should, in the absence

---

employs it, while it is in his employment, is responsible for the damage that it causes, either while in his charge, or when it is straying or escaped."

* At Lyons, in 1865, the preventive measures were certainly very severe. Whenever a case of rabies was reported, note was taken of the locality, and on the following night poison was laid down in profusion in every place accessible to dogs. A pitiless war was also carried on against stray dogs, all being considered as such which did not wear a muzzle or were not led by a cord.

These measures appear to have been most effective, however. They were only adopted in March, and in the first five months of the year there were sixty-one cases of rabies admitted to the Veterinary School,—being an average of more than twelve per month; in the three succeeding months there were only twenty entries—less than seven a month; and for the last four months of the year only six cases, or one and a half per month. Some of the animals, rabid in May or June, may have been bitten in February, or even in January.

of better proof as to the influence of the generative faculty in the production of rabies, be left to choose whether or not it may be practised.

Blunting the Teeth.

It has been proposed to *extract* or *blunt* the *canine teeth*, or fangs, of all dogs, and even the incisive teeth of those which are yet young; or to cause them to wear a metal shield or cap over the fangs, to prevent their wounding, should the animal attempt to bite. These operations have been proposed with the view of reducing the dog's jaws to the same condition as that of herbivorous creatures, whose bites are not so dangerous as those of the carnivoræ,—so far, at least, as the inoculation of the rabid virus is concerned. But it will be at once perceived that these proposals, if carried into effect, would to some extent interfere with the utility of many of the useful dogs; so that they could not be efficiently or thoroughly enforced, and even if they were, they would only have a partial influence, so far as concerns the suppression of the disease. Nevertheless, there are occasions which might justify the blunting of the sharp teeth of the domestic carnivorous creatures, and the proposal comes from one who has had a long experience of dogs and rabies. Bourrel proposes, as a preventive measure, the blunting of the front teeth in the upper and lower jaws. These are sixteen in number: twelve incisors and four canine teeth. This operation, as he truly says, makes it impossible for the dog to inflict wounds on men or animals which might lead to inoculation with the virus of rabies; and it is therefore the best preventive, as it imposes no restraint upon the animal. Bourrel's experiments in this direction commenced in 1862, and were conducted upon thirty dogs. When the permanent teeth are well grown, he states that the dog may be so disarmed. The operation occupies about eight minutes; there is no subsequent derangement of health, and the creature eats as well as before; the teeth are no more exposed to caries than they were previously;

the lips conceal them, except in aggression or defence; and the beauty of the dog is not impaired.

In general, says M. Bourrel, it is a sharp pinching produced by the front teeth that causes inoculation; the skin is torn, or the bite draws blood. By blunting or resection, sixteen obtuse surfaces are substituted for sixteen sharp points.

Sporting dogs in the habit of tearing the game, have been prevented doing so by this measure; while the ferocious disposition of some dogs—such as watch-dogs—which renders them dangerous to every one, was softened; and brutes which would have to be destroyed, were consequently allowed to live. Terriers have not ceased to kill rats after this blunting; they have only lost their power to kill cats, which is a happy result. The same operation disarms those bull-dogs that certain individuals have the discreditable passion of exciting to fight. Pet dogs have been operated upon without any inconvenience.

The only exceptions to the measure occur in those dogs whose services largely depend upon their teeth being sharp. These are dogs which hunt wild animals, and watch-dogs: though the latter rarely seize people, and their bark is more useful than their teeth. An inconvenience is noted in the fact that the operation removes one of the signs by which the age is known; but this is not serious, for it is always easy, by an external inspection and the bright aspect of the teeth, to classify dogs according to their age. Besides, it must be remembered that the value of the dog's teeth as a guide to a knowledge of its age is not always very trustworthy, as their wear is seldom regular.

The muzzle cannot always be kept on dogs, and few or no rabid ones have ever been seen wearing muzzles; and this article is more or less of an annoyance to them at all times. The blunting of the teeth obviates the necessity for resorting to its employment.

Bourrel attempted some experiments with animals whose mouths had been deprived of their inoculating power. Two mad dogs with rounded teeth were brought into contact with four other dogs, and at once attacked them fiercely, and tried to bite them, but no wounds were inflicted. Bourrel's gloved hand was seized by one of the poor creatures, but the glove was not torn, and the hand was only squeezed. Repeated experiments with healthy dogs to which he had given his uncovered hand to bite, proved that the blunted tooth cannot, notwithstanding the contraction of the muscles of the jaw, penetrate the tissues. "Nature, which created the dog in a savage condition, armed it for this condition. Man, who has domesticated and made a friend of this animal, should take care that the prejudice that its weapons of defence may cause him is removed."

Manner of performing the Operation.

The operation is a simple one. For a large dog two assistants are necessary; for a small animal only one. The creature is seated on a table; a gag, as in the figure, is fixed in the mouth between the molar teeth, by a band tied behind the neck; another band or piece of wide tape, fastened around the muzzle at the back of the gag, prevents any movement of the jaws. To blunt the incisor teeth a file is used, and, to expedite the operation, the longer canine teeth or fangs are shortened by sharp nippers, and then smoothly rounded by the file. The gag, of course, must be proportioned in thickness and length to the size of the animal. The subjoined figures will show the difference in the aspect of the teeth before and after the operation has been properly performed.

Bourrel's proposal has never been carried into general practice, so far as I know; but it will be seen that it is by no means an unreasonable one, and in countries where dogs are particularly susceptible to rabies, or during an epizoöty of the disease, it might, and indeed must, prove of the greatest

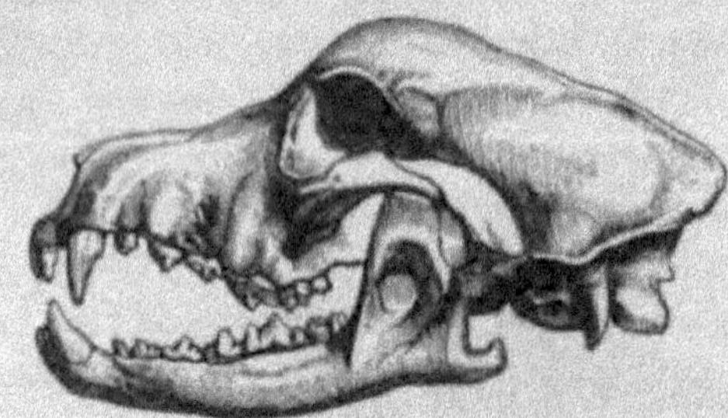

The Dog's Teeth in their Natural State.

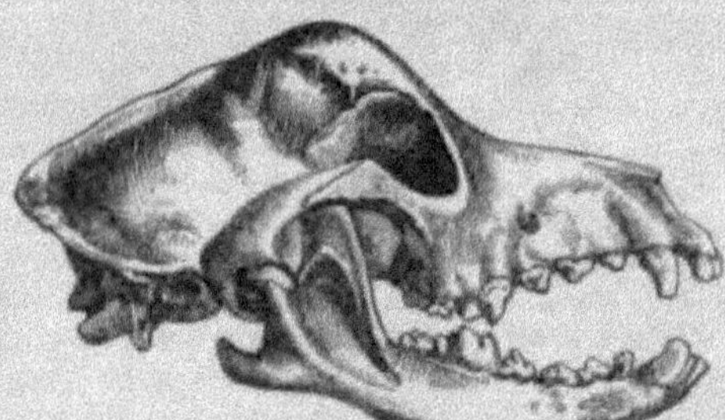

The Dog's Teeth after the Operation.

utility. Even in ordinary circumstances, with vicious dogs it would be most judicious to resort to it, to prevent their doing mischief.

Muzzling.

The use of the muzzle has become such a popular institution in nearly every country in which legislative measures for the prevention of injuries from dogs have been adopted, that any question as to the benefits conferred by it, might be deemed superfluous, and even impertinent, by those who have not paid any attention to the subject; and consequently believe in the reputed efficacy of this contrivance in preventing dangerous accidents.*

But to those who have carefully investigated the circumstances attending the development of rabies, and observed the results arising from the employment of the muzzle, there can be no doubt whatever that a large amount of discomfort—nay, sometimes even positive cruelty—has been imposed upon the dog species. Who has not witnessed the sufferings of dogs during the "dog-days," when the police regulations doomed them to have their jaws held close together and their heads and throats tightly bound by hard leathern straps, at the very time of all others when the poor brutes should have been spared torture and excitement, and when an open mouth and every

* The following is the only regulation existing with regard to dogs in the metropolis. It forms part of "An Act for regulating the Traffic in the Metropolis, and for making Provision for the greater Security of Persons passing through the Streets, and for other purposes" (20th August, 1867. 30 & 31 Vict., cap 134):—"18. The Police may take possession of any Dog found in any Street within the Metropolis, and not under the Control of any Person, and may detain such Dog until the Owner has claimed the same, and paid all Expenses incurred by reason of such Detention. The Commissioner of Police, if he see fit, may issue a Notice requiring any Dog while in the Streets, and not led by some Person, to be muzzled in such a manner as will admit of the Animal breathing and drinking without Obstruction; and the Police may take possession of any Dog found loose in the Streets without such Muzzle during the Currency of the Order, and may detain such Dog until the Owner has claimed it, has provided a proper Muzzle, and has paid all Expenses connected with such Detention. Where any Dog taken possession of by the Police wears a Collar with the Address of any Person inscribed thereon, a Letter, stating the Fact of such Dog having been taken possession of, shall be sent by Post to the Address inscribed on the Collar. The Commissioner of Police may cause any Dog which has remained in the Possession of the Police for Three clear Days without the Owner claiming the same, and paying all Expenses incurred by its Detention, to be sold or destroyed. Any Monies arising from the Sale of any Dogs, in pursuance of this Section, shall be applied in the Manner in which Penalties under this Act are applicable. When, upon Complaint that any Dog has bitten or attempted to bite any person within the Metropolis, it appears to the Magistrates having cognisance of such Complaint that any such Dog ought to be destroyed, the Magistrate may direct the Dog to be destroyed, and any Police Constable may destroy the same accordingly, and all Dogs detained by the Police under this Section shall be properly fed and maintained."

facility for lapping water should have been afforded them? No doubt this hardship has been greatly exaggerated by the pernicious and stupid shape of the muzzle employed, and the season in which it was ordered to be worn. But it has been questioned whether the use of this article is really calculated to meet the end proposed; and whether it is not likely that its employment at the hottest season of the year might aid in the production of the disease it is supposed to prevent. By some it has been pronounced superfluous and useless, or worse; while others are satisfied that, by the adoption and use of a properly constructed muzzle, the danger resulting from rabies may be averted. The principal recent French authorities incline to the former opinion; while the German veterinarians appear to favour the second. The question is a somewhat delicate one, and we cannot do better than examine it from both points of view.

The chief evidence in favour of the muzzle is that brought forward from the experience of its use in Berlin. From 1845 to 1853, 278 cases of rabies were reported; from March, 1852, to the same month in 1853, no fewer than 82 mad dogs were sent to the Veterinary School, and up to the end of July 37 more. On the 20th July it was ordained that the use of the muzzle should become general, and up to the close of the year only 6 cases were admitted. In 1854-5 the number was 1, and from that time up to 1863 there were no cases. In 1863, however, 11 cases were reported, and the following year 4. For the subsequent years exact returns are wanting, though an increase is noted: in 1867-8 there were 21 cases.

The exempt period of eight years is that which has been more particularly held to demonstrate the benefit to be derived from the muzzle. The veterinary authorities at Berlin laid most stress upon this measure in saying that the different administrative expedients taken against the propagation of rabies, *and notably the muzzling of dogs*, have not counted for nothing in causing the disappearance of this redoubtable scourge for a number of years in Prussia.* They were of opinion that rabies is an epizoöty which, starting from a primary centre, becomes developed under the influence of spontaneous generating causes; gradually extends itself among certain animals particularly predisposed; and, arriving at its culminating point, maintains itself for some time; then commences to diminish and suddenly disappears; only showing itself again at long intervals. But it must be observed that such periods of exemption have been noted before this period and since, when this constraint was not resorted to. We may refer to the number of cases reported by Lafosse as admitted to the Veterinary School at Toulouse, for a number of years, as a proof of this:—

1843	0	1851	3
1844	3	1852	6
1845	4	1853	4
1846	0	1854	5
1847	1	1855	2
1848	0	1856	3
1849	2	1857	1
1850	5	1858	5

If at Toulouse, without the use of the muzzle being made obligatory, years have passed without any cases of rabies being registered, we might be justified in concluding that the absence of epizoötic influences had at least as large a share in the non-production of the disease as the muzzle, were it not for the immediate and important diminution that took place when it was applied in Berlin. And it must be remembered that this article was only worn in the city, and not in the country; and that Hertwig accounts for the reappearance of the disease in 1863, by saying that in May of that year two rabid dogs showed themselves in the rural districts, and eventually found their way into Berlin, where their advent was followed by several cases of the disease. During 1864, and up to the middle of

* It must not be forgotten that Prussia, like Austria and some other countries, has occasionally a large mortality from hydrophobia, and consequently is compelled to resort to severe measures to limit the accidents from rabies. For instance, for the period between 1810 and 1819, the official documents show that no fewer than 1,666 persons died of this disease.

1865, between twenty and thirty cases occurred, in spite of the fact that all dogs in the city, without exception, were wearing muzzles permanently. In the autumn of 1864, within a period of eight weeks, three children died of hydrophobia from the bites of dogs, and this notwithstanding muzzles being worn.

Haubner, alluding to the decrease and increase in the number of cases at Berlin during this period, says that the same result has been observed elsewhere. When the increase took place eight years afterwards, the law relating to dogs might have become relaxed and the muzzle less resorted to. This supposition may have had a great influence with the German veterinary authorities; for Haubner, one of the most recent writers on veterinary sanitary police, says that muzzles should be constantly worn out of doors, especially in large towns, as he is convinced it is the best protection against the bite of dogs if well constructed. And he also justly remarks that biting horses have to wear muzzles, and the vicious bull or steer to carry a ring through its nose, to prevent their causing injury. Only the dog must not be inconvenienced by a constraint to prevent its biting, say the admirers of this animal, though it is naturally inclined to bite. He likewise asserts that the use of the muzzle in large towns is a real benefit to mankind, though in the open country it need not be used when rabies is not prevalent. Lovers of the dog, he adds, say that the muzzle induces rabies, or does not prevent its extension; but there is no proof that it causes the disease, though with regard to its not hindering its spread there is every reason to believe there is some foundation, owing to the faulty construction of the ordinary muzzle, which a dog may pull off or contrive to bite with; and also through the owner taking it off when he should not do so, as in walking out, &c. He also admits that leading dogs by a leash is no substitute for the muzzle, as powerful animals break away, even from grown-up persons.

And M. Renault, looking at the evidence furnished by the

Berlin authorities, was also in favour of this restraint; for in a communication to the Academy of Sciences, he says that if such results as followed the application of the muzzle from 1854 to 1861 be continued for some years, it might be concluded that, 1. Spontaneous rabies is vary rare; 2. Permanent muzzling is an efficacious measure in preventing the propagation of the disease; 3. The opinion of several authorities regarding the constraint resulting from the application of the muzzle as a cause of the development of rabies in the dog is erroneous. But M. Bouley, in a discourse delivered before the Imperial Academy of Medicine at a *séance* held in 1863, does not agree with Renault in his conclusions. He says: "The document that has been laid before you by M. Tardieu, and which came from the French Ambassador at Berlin, now proves that M. Renault was in error, owing to untrustworthy information. From it I can no longer see any reason why the muzzling of dogs, which is only a vexatious measure without any utility, should be maintained; and in this respect I willingly assent to the opinion of M. Vernois, and believe that, if it were adopted, it would have the three really advantageous consequences of delivering the administration from one of its cares, the administrators from one of their obligations, and lastly our poor brutes from the torments caused by the application of an apparatus which, if rigorously adopted—and to be efficacious it must be so—would condemn them to a slow asphyxia by obstructing the respiration and the buccal transpiration. One of the reasons given by M. Vernois for proscribing the muzzle is that, supposing a dog affected with rabies to have its head so garnished during the furious period of the malady, it would get rid of it immediately, because it is endowed at that moment with excessive strength, and being so highly excited, it would at once break every restraint. On this point, however, I do not agree with M. Vernois. The mad dog is not what he has painted it. On the contrary, it is much less able than a healthy animal to co-ordinate the movements of the paws to rid its head of the apparatus that confines its head, and when it is muzzled it remains so. The *surcanine* force with which he supposes it to be endowed is therefore a fiction. Do you wish for a proof of this? Here it is. It often happens that a suspected or really mad dog is brought to us muzzled, and is introduced, its head, still garnished with the muzzle, into the kennel where it is to remain. Well, under these conditions we do not see it give any demonstration of excessive force, in virtue of which it breaks all its bonds, as M. Vernois admits. Far from it; for it keeps the apparatus fixed around its head without any attempt to remove it; and if, in order to study the symptoms better, or for purposes of experiment, it is decided to take off the muzzle, this is done with great difficulty, and not without danger. In fact, it is a very fortunate circumstance that a dog is muzzled at the moment it has a paroxysm of madness, when it has a tendency to bite; for then the muzzle, by keeping the jaws closely together, is a very efficacious apparatus, and may serve as a protection against the dangerous attacks of the animal. If, then, the police ordinances which impose the obligation to muzzle, should produce the result that every dog was always muzzled at the moment when the dangerous period of rabies was manifested, they would be most valuable, and the administration should faithfully insist upon their being observed with the utmost rigour. But there is only one means by which the result might be attained. By the authority of the police, and by its direct intervention, the muzzle should be riveted to the dog's neck as the manacle is to the foot of the galley-slave, and that, night and day, the animal should wear it indoors as well as out of doors. Without this rigorous condition—and it only requires to formulate it, to show how impracticable it is—the muzzling of dogs cannot be in any way efficacious as a prophylactic measure against rabies. This is not difficult to demonstrate. Rabies is not a sudden disease, appearing all at once, like apoplexy; it does not instantly carry the dog it attacks from the most flourishing state of health to a condition of furious delirium, which impels it to bite every animal it meets. Far from it; for canine rabies has its premonitory signs. Several days before the manifestation of the furious symptoms, the mad dog testifies by a change of habit that it is not in its normal state; it is restless, agitated, retires into dark places—beneath furniture in rooms, beneath the manger in stables; and if it is a watch-dog, to the bottom of its kennel. These early signs, which have not yet a very precise signification, are manifested in the interior of houses, where dogs are always relieved from their muzzles. At this period they have no tendency to fly—to escape. On the contrary, their attachment for their owner having increased, they are more sedentary, and abstain from their habitual peregrinations. It is not until later,—at the moment when the malady has obtained absolute sway over them,—that they escape from their masters' domicile. Once outside, the excitement they experience, especially when they see other dogs, is not long before it increases the disease to its highest paroxysm. Then their destructiveness commences, and continues in proportion to the opportunities that offer.

"Thus, as has been remarked, it is in the dwellings where the dogs reside that rabies is prepared, and so long as everything is not ready for its last explosion the animals remain there, and do not decide to run away until the desire to bite imperiously dominates them. Then they escape, but *always unmuzzled*—for in their dwellings the muzzle is never used—and give themselves up to their redoubtable savageness.

"This is the order in which the phenomena most frequently succeed each other; and it follows from the *exposé* that, however rigorous the prescriptions of the police may be with regard to the muzzle imposed upon dogs in the public streets, it is evident that they cannot produce the useful effects expected from them; inasmuch as the majority of the accidents from rabäic bites, outside habitations, are caused by escaped dogs which, at a given moment in their as yet *unrecognised*, or even *suspected* malady, steal away from the surveillance of their masters, and run abroad, of course without their muzzles.

"Therefore it is that the muzzling, considered as a means of preventing the propagation of rabies from the canine to the human species, is a perfectly useless measure; because, in the ordinary course of things, it is only applied, and can only be applied, to inoffensive dogs."

The same distinguished veterinarian, when speaking of the disease at a later period (1869), and of the benefit to be derived from a rigid application of articles 1382, 1383, and 1385 of the civil code already noticed, says: "For my part, I have much greater confidence in the *salutary menaces* of these articles than in the muzzling of all the dogs which the prefectorial decrees pretend to render obligatory everywhere, but which is nowhere carried out properly. It might even be said that, with regard to preservation from rabies, it is altogether useless, for it is never applied to the dogs which are susceptible of causing injury by being actually rabid. Some words of explanation will prove this. What are the dogs which, in the streets and on the roads, show themselves to be mad, and bite the men and animals they meet? Had they been in perfect health immediately before, and suddenly, without any premonitory sign, became rabid? Certainly not. These dogs were already affected with madness for some days when with their owners; and if they are now wandering on the roads, it is because they have escaped from their homes, obeying the instinct which compels them to fly from those who are dear to them. In very many instances, it is not known to every one that they have escaped, and consequently it is always unmuzzled they make their flight; for it is not usual to wear a muzzle at home. Of what use, then, in a prophylactic point of view, is this muzzling which we would render obligatory for all dogs, when, by the force of circumstances, it is really mad dogs that, in the majority of instances, are exempted from this obligation, which is most frequently imposed on those that are in perfect health?"*

* "La Rage," p. 79.

The veterinary authorities in Brussels, in an excellent report on rabies drawn up in 1868, when the disease was causing some alarm in Belgium, also refer to this subject. They disagree with the Berlin authorities in their conclusions as to the value of the muzzle, especially while the disease exists in an epizoötic form; as this is precisely the time when dogs should not be subjected to any annoyance and excitement arising from such a constraint. Besides, they say, what usually happens? The muzzle is nearly always taken off in the house; whereas, to be completely efficacious as a preventive measure, it should happen that rabies develops itself at the moment when this apparatus is applied, and this is precisely what never takes place.

And Professor Lafosse, of Toulouse, no mean authority on such a subject, says: "As it is very rare that this disease appears in the dog that is always under the eye and obeying the command of its master, or which roams around the building confided to its care, without the symptoms that betray the invasion of the malady being perceived, and consequently the necessity for taking the proper measures being indicated; to make every owner of a dog keep it constantly muzzled, tied up, or led about in a leash would be to deprive him almost entirely of the companionship and the real services that are to be derived from the most devoted of our domestic animals; and, in addition, the too absolute constraint might multiply the cases of spontaneous rabies, if this condition could exercise any influence on the production of the disease. At the utmost, the application of these severe measures might be reserved for the seasons most propitious for engendering spontaneous rabies, when it is notorious that mad dogs are wandering about the neighbourhood, or when rabies prevails in an epizoötic form." *

On the whole, we are inclined to agree with the last-quoted opinion with regard to the general and everyday use of the

* "Traité de Pathologie Vétérinaire," vol. iii. p. 866.

muzzle, which should only be worn on special occasions: as when rabies is prevalent in a locality, when it has a tendency to assume an epizoötic character, or in the case of vicious dogs.

When the disease threatens to become prevalent, or indeed when there is reason to believe that a mad dog has bitten several others, and these cannot be discovered, the use of the muzzle should be resorted to, and all dogs seen in the streets of towns or in the country without a muzzle should be seized by the police as suspicious animals. This is one of the great advantages of employing the muzzle; for if it be correct that rabid dogs escape from their homes, and wander about without this safeguard, then surely a dog so unprovided ought to be at once captured. If muzzles were not worn, a rabid animal might cause a terrible amount of mischief without attracting the attention of the police, merely because it was like other dogs. On these grounds, I am certainly inclined to advocate recourse to the muzzle. Its use, when rigorously enforced, must be beneficial during an epizoöty of rabies; and that it is so is demonstrated by the veterinary professor, Fürstenberg, of Eldena, Prussia. He states that the disease was prevalent in his country, in different districts, for two, three, four, and five years; and no regulations, such as confining and chaining-up dogs, &c., could check it until muzzles were introduced, when it ceased. It is now an established rule in our country that, whenever and wherever the disease appears, all dogs which come into the streets must be provided with muzzles. Their use is not enforced on those dogs which are kept indoors. In the small island of Usedom, which is nearly cut off from all intercourse, rabies was prevalent during several years, and it was only by ordering that all dogs which came into the streets or highways should be provided with muzzles that it was possible to extirpate the disease. And Hering, Director of the Veterinary School at Stuttgart, mentions that in 1864 rabies occurred in Würtemberg during the first months of the year, the cases then being few; but in each month they became more numerous, until the use of the muzzle was enforced, not only in the towns, but throughout the whole country; after which, until the autumn of 1865, when this statement was made, not a case had been reported.

To be beneficial, it is obvious that the employment of the

muzzle must be universal; but, at the same time, should the disease be prevalent, the other necessary measures must not be relaxed, and the vigilance of dog-owners should not be diminished; for it must be remembered that if a dog wearing a muzzle runs about without any one in charge of it, it is possible that a mad dog may attack and bite it; the wounded animal then returns to its home, and the owner may know nothing of what has happened, until all at once rabies appears quite unexpectedly.

And it must also be borne in mind that a well-constructed muzzle is a protection against biting, so long as it is worn by the dog. But a bad muzzle is worse than useless, as it establishes a false security.

It is astonishing how soon dogs become accustomed to an easy-fitting, comfortable muzzle: that is one in which they can always breathe and drink without hindrance. The nostrils of the dog are very narrow, and even under ordinary circumstances it cannot breathe so comfortably as many other animals when its mouth is forcibly closed; when distressed by running it always respires with open mouth, and in warm weather the transpiration that takes place in this cavity from the throat, tongue, and inside the cheeks, tends to keep the creature cool, and compensates for the almost total absence of this process from the skin. Therefore the front portion of the muzzle should be sufficiently accommodating as to allow the dog wearing it to open its mouth freely and widely.

The muzzle patented by Grauhan, and sold in this country

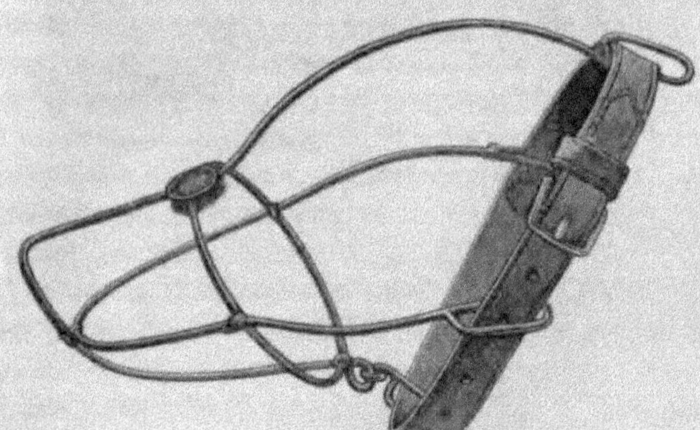

(manufactured by Butterfield of Bradford), is a good though not a very safe muzzle in its present form. (See figure on opposite page.) To make it perfectly secure at the mouth, there should be intermediate wires from the circular transverse wire, near the eyes, to the vertical nose-wire. (See figure above.)

The muzzle should fit the head properly, and above all things it should be securely fastened around the neck. The neck-strap should be strong, and as tight as may be compatible with the dog's comfort.

At ordinary times, making people at all times responsible for the damage their dogs may inflict, and giving them every opportunity for acquiring a knowledge of the law, and also the best means for complying with it—which would, of course, in this instance be a knowledge of the earliest symptoms of rabies and the measures necessary for preventing dangerous consequences—would be, perhaps, less onerous than compelling dogs to wear an apparatus which, when there is no urgent cause for its employment, is certainly not to be commended. This principle of responsibility would make owners of dogs particularly attentive to the health and welfare of these animals; and would also, in addition to diminishing the number of vicious dogs, induce them to resort to these exceptional means of restraint without being ordered. Their pecuniary interests—so frequently much more powerful than those of a sanitary character—would guarantee their attending to the condition of their dogs; and they would learn that, in the words of M. Bouley, the fear of a diseased dog is not only the beginning of wisdom, but wisdom itself; the owner of every dog committing mischief being identified by means of the collar and impressed mark thereon, would tend to make rabies a comparatively rare disease, and hydrophobia nearly, if not altogether, unknown.

Quarantine.

The idea of completely extinguishing rabies by establishing a quarantine of several months' duration among dogs, was based on the assumption that the disease is only maintained by contagion, and never arises spontaneously; and that therefore if these animals could be confined for a certain period, without any intercourse or any chance of the contagium being transmitted from those that were affected at the commencement of the measure, the pestilence must inevitably die out. Bardsley, who proposed it, after saying that the opinion he held as to its purely contagious character was founded upon a fair induction from facts and close analysis, adds: "The plan is as simple as I trust it will prove efficacious. It consists merely in establishing an universal quarantine for dogs within the kingdom, and a total prohibition of the importation of these animals during the existence of such quarantine. The efficacy of this preventive scheme rests upon the validity of the following propositions: First, that the disease always originates in the canine species. Secondly, that it never arises in them spontaneously. Thirdly, that the contagion, when received by them, never remains latent more than a few months. If these propositions have been established, it clearly follows that, by destroying every dog in which the disease should break out during strict quarantine, the propagation of the malady would not only be prevented, but the absolute source of the poison entirely suppressed."

Quarantine would no doubt be as effectual in stamping out rabies as in stamping out any other purely contagious malady were these propositions absolutely correct, and the measure completely and permanently enforced. But, unfortunately, the disease originates in other than the canine species, and in other creatures of that species besides the dog; and, unfortunately, also, we are far from convinced that it never occurs spontaneously; on the contrary, though ready to admit that in the great majority of cases it is spread by contagion, there appears every reason to believe that it may arise without this influence.

Besides, this authority proposed only two months as the period which he considered long enough to afford every prospect of success; whereas it is well-established that the incubatory stage is frequently protracted to a much longer interval; indeed, he admits this when he adds, that "it would undoubtedly be erring on the safe side if the time of quarantine should be extended to the very unusual period of *eight months.*"

It will be seen at once, by those who know anything of veterinary sanitary matters, that a strict quarantine for dogs for such a period, or even for the comparatively short space of two months, is absolutely impossible at present, and perhaps will always be so; and also that, supposing the disease to be confined to the dog species, and the quarantine to be religiously observed or rigorously enforced, other countries might not think fit to submit to the serious inconveniences arising from this measure, and consequently we should, in all probability, have the contagion introduced into the country again in a very brief space.

Public Instructions.

Provide dog-owners, when they receive their tax-paper, with printed, easily-understood instructions as to the proper method of keeping their dogs healthy, and how to detect the symptoms of rabies; as well as information respecting the preservative and sanitary police measures which they should comply with in order to prevent the disease. All this might be printed on the back of the tax-paper, which could, in addition, be made a valuable means of arriving at certain important information, such as the sex, age, breed, &c., of the licensed dogs. The most serious accidents occur through the ignorance of the public on simple matters like this of rabies.

Such, then, are the general measures to be recommended with regard to the prevention of rabies at ordinary times and in all seasons; for our investigations have shown in the clearest and most positive manner that the disease is not peculiar to any particular period of the year, nor limited to any season, but may prevail at any time. Therefore, careful supervision should be extended to all dogs throughout the year, and not only during the "dog days;" and it is to this supervision, and the possession of a general knowledge of the symptoms of the malady by every one who keeps a dog, that we must look for success in keeping down the contagion, and preventing the sacrifice of human and animal life through the effects of such a dreadful disease.

Measures to be adopted when Rabies has appeared.

Suspected Animals.—If, notwithstanding these measures, *morbid* or *unusual symptoms* appear in a dog, and particularly if cases of rabies have occurred in the vicinity shortly before, it should be carefully observed, and every precaution taken; as they may be premonitory signs of madness, which is contagious from its commencement. The animal should therefore be constantly watched, and kept apart from mankind and other animals; and in feeding or attending to it, the greatest possible care should be taken that it does not bite any one at this time. No children should be permitted to approach it, and all neglect of these precautions ought to be visited with severe punishment.

If the *morbid symptoms* become *more marked* and *more suspicious*—if it is observed that the dog manifests any of the peculiarities already indicated—that it is dull and bad-tempered, moves languidly from place to place, and seeks to go away—and, particularly, that its ordinary habits have changed: that it is hostile to people or animals, that it attempts to bite everything—even if it does not refuse water—then it is time to chain it up securely, or confine it in such a way that no one can be injured by it. Up to this time, the owner may be permitted to keep the dog in his establishment on condition that every security can be, and is, adopted; but now, and even before this period, if the means for affording security are insufficient, the owner, or whoever knows of a dog or any other animal to be rabid or in a suspicious condition, must not neglect reporting the circumstance to the local police without assuming the gravest responsibility; and whoever does so should be held guilty of a criminal offence.* If made known to the authorities by an informer, the greater part of the fine imposed should go to him.

As, however, the earliest symptoms of rabies are not always recognised, and the disease shows itself sometimes apparently in a sudden manner; and as, besides, a dog or any other animal already rabid may escape from home or arrive in another locality, the local authorities should be compelled to give warning to the inhabitants, and make known the symptoms of the disease, both at its very commencement and when fully developed. Similar instructions should be given by medical men and veterinary surgeons.†

As the domesticated animals of every kind may have been bitten by a mad dog or other creature, or soiled with the saliva, without the owner knowing it, the latter should be obliged to notice carefully every one that becomes ill, and bear in mind the earliest symptoms of rabies—such as unusual excitement, bad temper, and unwonted sulkiness, peculiar hoarse voice, viciousness towards those about it, and desire to do them injury. If by these manifestations the animal's condition gives rise to suspicion, it ought to be sequestrated, and proper precautions adopted.

* The Austrian Penal Code (387) says: "Is guilty of infraction of the law and liable to imprisonment, whoever knows of a dog or any other animal showing the distinctive symptoms, or symptoms which warrant suspicion, of rabies, and who neglects to report the same to the police. In case of the appearance of the disease and the biting of men or of animals, the culprit shall be punished with from three days' to three months' imprisonment (*carcere duro*). If a serious wound or the death of a human being has been the consequence of this negligence, the infraction shall come under the application of 335, which says: Shall be punished with from one to six months' imprisonment, he who shall be guilty of this negligence, if its consequence has been a serious wound; the penalty is from six months' to a year's close imprisonment, if the death of a man has been the consequence. Otherwise, the proprietor is always responsible for the damage caused by mad animals."

† In this country, so far as I can learn, no attempt has been made to carry out such a recommendation as this. All the legislative enactments have been limited to such measures as causing dogs to be muzzled, or led about in the streets, or confined to their dwellings. Stray dogs have also usually been captured. These efforts are, of course, far from effective.

If more serious symptoms show themselves, the proprietor should immediately report the case to the local police, to avoid incurring a grave responsibility; and the animal ought to be at once sacrificed by him, after inspection by an expert or by order of the police authorities.

If the owner is aware that the sick or suspected creature has been bitten by a rabid animal, it is still more necessary at once to report the circumstance to the local authorities.

Mad Animals, or those wounded by them.—With regard to the measures to be taken in the case of *mad animals* or those *wounded* by them, the following should be rigorously enforced:—

1. A *dog suspected of or attacked by rabies*, or one *that has been bitten by a rabid animal*, should not be killed at once and buried, unless there is reason to suppose that no person has been wounded by it.

2. If a person has been bitten by an animal really affected with rabies, or suspected to be affected with that disease, it should only be killed if the malady is unmistakably present; if it is only a suspicious case, it is well not to kill it immediately, but keep it securely confined and under close surveillance, so as to be able to verify whether the suspicions are confirmed, which will not be long; if they are affirmed, then the creature must be killed and buried.

3. If an animal suspected or affected with the disease escapes from its owner or from a locality, or if an animal of this description is seen in a locality, it is the urgent duty of every one to warn the police immediately. The latter should then, in their turn, warn the people in the town or village, or its suburbs, so as to put them on their guard. This warning should not be given in such a manner as to cause alarm and fear, but only to induce the adoption of careful measures and ample precautions. In such circumstances, all children should be watched, and dogs and other animals ought to be confined or kept from strange dogs, or those whose state of health is not

well ascertained. All wandering dogs should be confined or killed.*

* The New English Dog Act, published on the 24th July, 1871, entitled "An Act to Provide Further Protection against Dogs," and applicable to all the country, is a slight improvement in the matter of legislation in this country, but is not likely to be so effective as is necessary to cope with a malady like rabies. It is in these terms :—

"Whereas it is expedient that further protection should be provided against dogs:

"Be it enacted by the Queen's most excellent Majesty, by and with the advice and consent of the Lords Spiritual and Temporal, and Commons, in this present Parliament assembled, and by the authority of the same, as follows:

"1. From and after the passing of this Act, any police officer or constable may take possession of any dog that he has reason to suppose to be savage or dangerous straying on any highway, and not under the control of any person, and may detain such dog until the owner has claimed the same, and paid all expenses incurred by reason of such detention.

"Where the owner of any dog taken possession of by any constable is known, a letter, stating the fact of such dog having been taken possession of, shall be sent by post or otherwise to the owner at his usual or last known place of abode.

"When any dog taken in pursuance of this Act has been detained for three clear days where the owner is not known, as aforesaid, or for five clear days where he is so known, without the owner claiming the same, and paying all expenses incurred by its detention, the chief officer of police of the district in which such dog was found may cause such dog to be sold or destroyed.

"Any moneys arising from the sale of any dogs in pursuance of this section shall be paid to the account of the local rate, and be applied to the purposes to which that rate is applicable.

"All dogs detained under this section shall be properly fed and maintained at the expense of the local rate.

"2. Any court of summary jurisdiction may take cognizance of a complaint that a dog is dangerous, and not kept under proper control, and if it appears to the court having cognizance of such complaint that such dog is dangerous, the court may make an order in a summary way, directing the dog to be kept by the owner under proper control or destroyed; and any person failing to comply with such order shall be liable to a penalty not exceeding twenty shillings for every day during which he fails to comply with such order.

"3. The local authorities may, if a mad dog or a dog suspected of being mad is found within their jurisdiction, make, and when made vary or revoke, an order placing such restrictions as they think expedient on all dogs not under the control of any person during such period as may be prescribed in such order throughout the whole of their jurisdiction, or such part thereof as may be prescribed in such order.

"Any person who acts in contravention of any order made in pursuance of this section shall be liable to a penalty not exceeding twenty shillings.

"Due notice of such order shall be published at the expense of the local rate.

"The provisions in this Act contained as to the detention and sale or destruc-

Every means must be adopted, and all precautions duly observed, to capture the mad or suspected animal. If *really rabid* it should be killed; if only *suspected*, its life may be spared, adopting every precaution in the meantime in order to ascertain its condition. This measure, as we have already noticed, is all the more necessary if we do not know whether it has wounded people or animals. Even if it is ascertained that it has not done so, it is yet most prudent to keep it under observation until its diseased or healthy condition is assured. The reasons for this step have been given.

The period during which it should be kept under observation should certainly not be less than four months. Hertwig gives an instance in which a suspected dog was so kept for twelve weeks, when, showing no signs of rabies, it was discharged. In the thirteenth week the disease made its appearance. And the examples we have given, when speaking of the period of incubation, will show the necessity for extending the sequestration to something like six months.

In every case, and under all circumstances, the local authority should take exact note of these occurrences, and particularly endeavour to discover the domicile and the owner of the animal, and learn whether any person or animal has been attacked or wounded by it in the locality or elsewhere, &c. When a mad dog appears, the regulations and restrictions should be applied over a wide extent of country, and neighbouring districts should be warned; as it frequently happens that in this disease a dog will run great distances, especially at night: for it appears to choose this time for its wanderings—returning home in the morning after having, perhaps, inflicted injuries on other animals far and near. Besides, the owner might some-

tion of dogs found straying on the highway shall apply to dogs found at large in contravention of any order made in pursuance of this section.

"4. In England and Ireland any penalty under this Act may be recovered in manner provided by the Summary Jurisdiction Act, and in Scotland all such penalties shall be prosecuted and recovered before a court of Summary Jurisdiction, under the provisions of the Summary Jurisdiction Act, 1864."

times, not unnaturally, seek to save his favourite from the operation of the law, and remove it to another district where there are no restrictions. Hence the necessity for extending the preventive measures over a large expanse of country; for it must be remembered that strange dogs cause most cases of rabies and hydrophobia.

Hertwig is of opinion that the introduction of preventive measures should not be limited to towns, but must be extended to the open country. "During a period of forty years, whenever rabies has spread as an epizoöty, I have always observed that dogs belonging to peasants or other persons living in the country, and running at large, without supervision, into the towns, were the chief instruments in the extension of the scourge." In addition to this, in the announcement made to the inhabitants of the surrounding districts, the country towards which the animal is proceeding, or the direction from which it came, should be made known; as well as a description of the creature with regard to breed, size, colour, and other distinctive characteristics, in order that all necessary information be procured, so as to avert evil consequences as speedily as possible.

These measures are more particularly applicable to the occurrence of isolated or sporadic cases; but in times of special danger, as when the disease assumes a more than usual virulency, or when it becomes widespread or epizoötic, they are also beneficial, and must then be enforced with the greatest vigour and exactitude.

In addition, every possessor of a dog or dogs should be made to give due notice to the authorities of all changes taking place, either with regard to the sale, transfer, exchange, or death of animals, or on each new acquisition, in order that the same be duly noted in the register of dogs kept for each district. This register might be of a temporary kind, or be made every year. It should contain the names of all owners of dogs, with the number of the animals they keep, their sex, and purpose for which they are kept; these dogs should be identified by their license number.

It may be necessary at this time to have recourse to the muzzle for every dog out of doors, except useful dogs when employed, as the muzzle might then be objectionable. In populous towns, in addition to the muzzle, but not as a substitute for it, it might be necessary to ordain that dogs be led by a chain or thong.

It is above all things necessary that the muzzle should fit the dog's head in such a manner that it cannot bite through it, or slip it off. A muzzle too small is most objectionable, as it may irritate the animal and cause it great discomfort; while one too large may allow the dog to inflict wounds. If it is ordered that muzzles are to be worn, the police should see that every dog has one of a proper size, and any wilful infraction of this most essential regulation should be punishable by a fine.*

The destruction of dogs must be carried out assiduously. No dogs should be allowed to be at large, and all stray dogs should be caught and killed immediately, if without a muzzle; but, if at large with a muzzle on, they might be kept for three days; if wearing a collar with the owner's address, they might be returned, and a fine imposed. In all cases, neglect of the sanitary orders should be severely punished. All dogs bitten by those which are mad, or suspected, or which have been in immediate contact with them, ought also to be destroyed or sequestrated for a proper period; it is more particularly desirable, however, that those bitten should be killed, as, though our statistics show that only some 50 per cent. of the dogs

* In corroboration of these remarks, the following extract from the *Leeds Mercury* for June 7th, 1871, may be quoted:—"MUZZLING DOGS.—In numerous instances, the patent muzzle for the canine race proves to be little protection to the public. It is frequently noticed that the muzzles, when placed on the heads of the animals, are so large that they can not only drink water, but eat with the wire cage on their nose, and it not unfrequently happens the dogs are observed carrying or gnawing large bones with the wire protection still fastened on the head. In some instances, so large are the muzzles, the animal slips its head through the frame. On Tuesday, in Brighouse, a gentleman was walking along the road, when a dog—the muzzle being much too large—rushed at him and bit him on the leg. The wound, only skin-deep, was attended to by a medical man."

wounded by mad dogs become rabid, yet the value of the dog is too small and the danger too great to admit of any exception being made.

It must always be remembered, that dogs which have been in contact with those that are mad may have been wounded, though the wounds cannot always be easily discovered; and as the smallest scratch is sufficient to produce the malady, so all animals which have been in contact with the diseased, to ensure safety, should be considered suspected. The contumacy of the owner should not be allowed to interfere, as fatal experience has shown that there is no security save in these severe but effective measures. It is certainly a painful proceeding to kill all suspected dogs, and one which our better feelings and admiration for the most devoted and affectionate of animals would not readily allow us to resort to; but when we know the dreadful character of rabies, and the great danger to which the human species and other creatures are exposed, we can no longer hesitate in prescribing the measure, which is, if we look at results, a humane one.

If there was any possibility of suspected dogs being kept closely confined and under observation for a period equal to the extreme duration of the incubatory stage of the malady, then we would gladly recommend that this course should be adopted; and for this purpose our veterinary schools, if they were at all adapted for such an office, might be used as conservative hospitals, should the dogs be considered worth keeping for so long a period.

And if we insist on the immediate destruction of all suspected dogs, including those which have been attacked or bitten by rabid ones, or on a close detention of four, five, or six months in some secure place, it is because there are no certain limits to the period of incubation, which, as we have seen from Renault's statistics, may vary from five to a hundred and eighteen days. The only exception that might possibly be made in favour of sparing the lives of dogs wounded by others which were rabid, would be in those cases where the wounds had been thoroughly cauterised within five minutes after being received; though even then the most careful supervision would have to be exercised on the chance of a slight wound having escaped observation.

Lafosse indicates, as suspected of rabies, all animals which are found in the following conditions:—

1. Those which have been bitten by rabid animals.

2. Those which have been inoculated in any way with the saliva of rabid animals.

3. Those which have eaten the flesh, drunk the blood or the milk of animals affected with rabies, or which have been soiled by the simple contact of these or other matters, particularly the saliva.

4. Those which have had sexual connection with suspected animals that shortly afterwards have really become mad.

5. Those which have been bitten by dogs or other animals found dead, and at the examination of whose body there have been found indications of the presence of rabies.

6. Those which have been bitten by animals whose furious condition has caused them to be killed, and which on examination present these signs, independently of those caused by the violent death.

7. The dogs affected by some vague disease, accompanied by a threatening demeanour, modified voice, desire to bite, refusal of food and drink, and abundant salivation.

He also adds that all the animals suspected of communicated rabies should, as quickly as possible, receive those attentions which are recognised as the most proper to destroy the rabid virus or to prevent its absorption. If these cares are not bestowed within twenty-four hours at the latest, after the injuries have been inflicted or the inoculations effected, the animals should be killed. Every suspected dog should be sequestrated for three months, and rigorously muzzled for another three months.

Much care is required in capturing mad, suspected, or stray

dogs, as they might inflict wounds. In general, it will be found that a lasso of wire, catgut, or raw hide attached to the end of a walking stick, is, with a little practice, very effective; but the poor animals should be gently dealt with, and all cruelty should be studiously avoided. When captured, they ought not to be led or dragged along, but put in a covered cart or waggon with separate compartments for each animal, to prevent fighting and subsequent danger; for, if put altogether in one place, it might happen that a rabid dog would be among the number and wound the others, some of which might be claimed by their owners, and set at liberty again. The same observation is applicable to the building in which stray dogs are kept.

In destroying dogs, experienced men ought to be employed, and life should be extinguished as promptly as possible, the avoidance of pain being studiously inculcated. The use of instruments is not, as a rule, to be commended, and poison is generally preferable. Nothing can be more effective and humane than the administration of a sufficient quantity of strong, newly-prepared Prussic acid, poured into the throat.

M. Bouley's remarks with regard to the destruction of dogs bitten by those which are rabid, or by mad wolves, and the risks the population incur through mad dogs, are particularly valuable. In the documents which had been forwarded to him for inspection, he found that the number of dogs bitten was 785, and that out of this number 527 had been killed. Of the 258 remaining, the fate of only 25 was reported; these had been sequestrated, and 13 of them became rabid. These figures are far from giving an exact estimate of the animals belonging to the canine species which received virulent bites. They only show the number of animals about which the local authorities have received and given information. Such as they are, however, they have a signification which it is very important to indicate. Establish this first fact, that out of the number of dogs which are stated to have been contaminated by a rabific bite, there is nearly one-third—29 per cent.—that appears to have escaped the sanitary measures of sequestration or slaughter, in consequence, probably, of carelessness, ignorance, or the too great complaisance of the authorities charged to apply these measures: in consequence, also, of the indifference of the threatened populations, who ought to be always the first, if they rightly understood their own interests, to demand the application of those measures which are for the public good. Their necessity, too imperfectly understood, is demonstrated by the facts which are about to be related. Of the 25 dogs whose sequestration had been reported and history traced, one-half contracted rabies. Admitting that the same result was produced in the group of 233 dogs allowed to go at large, notwithstanding their contamination, it happens that 116 would have become in their turn the propagators of this terrible malady; and there is no exaggeration in stating that each of these might make a dozen victims in its own species, each again destined to furnish a new legion of propagating agents, and so on. In this way the rabies of the canine species maintains itself, and its increase goes on at a redoubtable rate; while, if the authorities were vigilant, and, more especially, if the people were more anxious about their own preservation, and knew how to protect themselves, we might soon be able, without any very great difficulty, to reduce to very minimum proportions the disasters caused by this disease, and the irreparable misfortunes that it only too often brings about when man himself is attacked. For it is excessively rare that canine rabies is spontaneous. In the immense majority of cases this malady only proceeds from contagion; in 1,000 rabid dogs there are at least 999 which owe their disease to the inoculation from a bite.

The contagion is, therefore, the great cause that must be extinguished, or at least whose action must be circumscribed within the narrowest limits possible. It is evident that this result would be obtained if, every time a mad dog has passed through a locality, we knew exactly the animals it had bitten, and these were put beyond the power to do evil by a real sequestration prolonged to eight months at the least; or by immediate slaughter, which is undoubtedly the most efficacious measure, because the germ of the disease is then destroyed before it has time to fructify. I do not conceal from myself that numerous difficulties oppose themselves to the application of one or other of these measures; but they are nevertheless absolutely necessary, and if applied with vigour would ultimately bring about the total extinction of the rabific contagion. In a very great number of cases, in fact, the dog is for man more than an animal—it is a creature to which he is attached by a sentiment of affection frequently of the strongest kind; to many, it is one of the family, the favourite of the children, and often a cherished *souvenir*. It will readily be conceived, therefore, that in such conditions it must be difficult to obtain the acquiescence of its master to its arrest or death. There only remains sequestration; but, unless this is maintained in a special establishment, there are many obstacles to its being carried out with all the necessary severity. During the first days, when every one is filled with the dread of the event that has occurred, the dog that has been bitten is submitted to a rigid surveillance; it is securely tied or shut up, and promises are made that it will be carefully kept in quarantine for the whole period necessary; but, as time passes, the fears entertained as to the future disappear, and on some fine day the suspected animal is set at liberty, just at the moment when it is most to be dreaded—at the period when the incubation of the disease is approaching its termination, and the outbreak of rabies is imminent. No one is disturbed by this premature liberty being allowed to the inoculated animal—its master, because he no longer believes in the danger; the inhabitants of the locality, because they have forgotten all about it; and the authorities, through ignorance of what may happen, neglect of their duty, or through fear of doing it. And in this way may be realised the fatal condition as to the propagation of rabies by this animal to which a bite has transmitted the germ. Let us remember that of the 25 dogs whose sequestration is mentioned in Bowley's inquiry, 13 became rabid. What a number! and how powerfully it testifies to the absolute necessity for taking vigorous measures against all dogs that have been bitten, so as to put them beyond the pale of causing mischief! And because sequestration is only too frequently an uncertain measure, while immediate slaughter of suspected animals is, for the people, a condition of absolute security, I believe that in such a case humanity points out the course to be adopted. It is better that dogs should die than mankind. Otherwise, if the sentiment of humanity does not speak loud enough to inspire, and cause to be followed by every one, the line of conduct above indicated as the best, and which must be resorted to after all, there is, it must be admitted, an excellent means for determining the owners of suspected dogs to sacrifice them; that is, to make the responsibility for the damage and disasters their animals may cause weigh heavily upon them.

The medical treatment of rabid animals is not to be countenanced, as a rule, except under the conditions already specified. The instances in which they are reported to have recovered are exceedingly rare; and they either have occurred under extraordinary circumstances, or are not sufficiently well authenticated to warrant any one in incurring all the risks attendant upon keeping such dangerous creatures alive on the slender hope of curing them.

Disinfection.

All the slaughtered dogs should be buried in a place set apart for the purpose, and at a good depth; the skins should not be removed from their bodies, but should have large cuts made crossways in them; and they ought never to be thrown into ditches, ponds, or streams, as is so frequently done. Quick-lime should be thrown over them.

If the animal has been kept in a kennel, all the wood-work, straw, shavings, &c., everything in fact that may have been soiled by the saliva, should be consigned to the flames, or thoroughly soaked with carbolic acid, chloralum, Condy's fluid, or any other powerful disinfectant. The floor of the kennel, stable, or place in which the animal has been kept, should be well scrubbed with boiling water, and covered with quick-lime, or any agent noted for its power in destroying contagious matters. The same should be done with the walls of the place as high as the dog could reach.* The chain that attached the animal, and other ironwork which may have been in contact with it, should be heated in the fire, and all necessary precautions adopted as in diseases which are communicable by a fixed, or even volatile, contagium.

With reference to disinfection, it may be worth referring to Hertwig's experiments. After giving a number of dogs the saliva and blood of rabid animals for a certain time without result, he put five of them into kennels where mad dogs had been, put the collars of these upon their necks, attached them by the same chains, made them lie upon the same straw, &c., but yet none of them became rabid.

* Mr. Trevalyan, in his correspondence with Dr. Bardsley, stated that, after losing one pack of hounds from rabies, he not only removed the straw, but had the benches scalded with boiling water, and afterwards all the joints, cracks, &c., painted over, and filled up with hot tar; the walls were then whitewashed, and the pavement cleaned with hot water. Thus secure, as he thought, he collected another pack; yet rabies broke out year after year. In consequence, the pavement tainted with the secretions was removed, and the earth in which it was imbedded thrown into the river; the kennels were then new painted and whitewashed, and ever afterwards the pack was free from infection.

It may be mentioned that, not long ago, it was the fashion among fox-hunters to keep a flock of geese in the kennels where mad dogs had been, and it has been asserted that this practice was found far superior to frequent ablutions.—*James'* "Treatise on Canine Madness," p. 19. This idea is about as absurd as the notion which the ancient Romans had, according to Pliny. They believed that a dog which had lapped or tasted the milk of a woman who had a male child would never become mad.—Hist. Nat., book xxviii. chap. vii.

Duration of Police Regulations.

With regard to the length of the time during which the police regulations should remain in force, there is no definite rule. Knowing the limit of the period of incubation, it might be inferred that the sequestration of dogs should extend to that period. In Saxony, where the dog laws have been rigidly carried out, it has been found that three months was generally an effective interval; though if new cases occurred during this time, the period was dated from them. Notwithstanding the inconvenience and annoyance oftentimes occasioned by the restrictions imposed for so long a period, yet those who suffer most from them should bear in mind the great interests that are at stake, and cheerfully aid the authorities in their endeavours to suppress a contagion which causes such terrible destruction and alarm; the more strictly judiciously-framed veterinary police regulations are obeyed, the sooner will the course of the pestilence be terminated, and the less will its ravages be felt.

The same police regulations are applicable to rabid or suspected cats. They ought to be at once killed, and all other cats and dogs bitten by them should be destroyed.

Measures to be adopted with other Animals than Dogs.

We have already made some allusion to the measures to be adopted with the other domesticated animals, and we have now to complete our observations.

In the last century, and perhaps even now—for in this country there are no veterinary police regulations for this disease—the same severe measures were sometimes applied to the other domesticated animals as to the suspected dog, through ignorance of the disease as it affects them, as well as indiscrimination; and they were generally killed at once or left to chance, as the case might be. In dealing with them it must be remembered that they are not like the dog,—our constant companion, and that their natural weapons of attack are different; so that they very rarely extend the contagion; and, in reality, veterinary police regulations with nearly all of them should only be secondary to medical police laws—those which have to do with the flesh, milk, &c., derived from them. The veterinary regulations should have chiefly for their object the health of the animal while alive, and its destruction when diseased.

When these animals have been in contact with, or been bitten by, a rabid or suspected dog, the circumstance should be reported; they should be visited by an expert as quickly as possible, and their bodies carefully examined, particularly the ears, mouth and nose, and limbs and tail, in order to discover if there are any wounds, even of the most trivial description. Those discovered to be wounded should be at once isolated, and carefully watched. Preservative treatment may be recommended, but of course cannot be ordered. Haubner states that the isolation of wounded animals is unnecessary, as nothing is to be feared from them should they become mad. Röll says separation and medical treatment is necessary, unless the proprietor decides to kill them. But, as will be seen from our previous description of the symptoms, all rabid animals — excluding the dog, cat, fox, and wolf, of course—are more or less dangerous to others or to mankind, and particularly the horse; even the sheep may become so at times. It is better, therefore, to separate the wounded or suspected from the uncontaminated, and to place them under veterinary or police observation. Such animals as horses, oxen, and other beasts of labour, should be permitted to work in the immediate vicinity of their home; but they ought not to be allowed to travel far beyond this on any pretext. If a mad dog has been among a herd of cattle or flock of sheep, the whole herd or flock should be placed under surveillance.

None of the domesticated animals, other than those referred

to, if bitten or suspected, should be sold, bartered, or removed within a period equal to the limits of their several periods of incubation. Röll gives four months at the least for the sale of horses and cattle; but for other animals used as food the minimum may be three months.

Haubner gives the period of supervision as two months for sheep, three months for pigs and horses, and six months for cattle, and we should prefer this as a basis for regulating the restriction to that of Röll. At any rate, it is a great mistake to make the quarantine time the same for all animals; this should be regulated by the average duration of the incubatory period in the different species.

The immediate slaughter of all the bitten animals is unjustifiable, as only about 50 per cent. take the disease; and, when compared with dogs, the danger is very trifling, even when rabies manifests itself. It is, therefore, time enough to resort to slaughter when the disease shows itself, unless the owner is desirous of avoiding the risk of loss and wishes to sell the carcase for food.

As soon as the disease manifests itself, notice ought to be given to the authorities, and an examination made by a veterinary surgeon; when, if it be ascertained that rabies is really present, and the owner does not object, the animal may be killed. All animals in which rabies is confirmed should be slaughtered, and no attempts at treatment permitted, except under the restrictions before mentioned.

The carcase must be buried intact, with the skin slashed profusely. Haubner admits that if, with the *rigor mortis*, the virulence of the contagium is extinct, then skinning might be allowed, if conducted with care, and the skins utilised.

Should the carcase chance to be dug up and eaten by animals, there is no danger to be apprehended, according to Haubner; but Lafosse says the dead bodies should be covered by at least four feet of earth, and the burial-places guarded from carnivorous creatures.

Disinfection.—Everything used with rabid animals was at one time destroyed; but neither observation nor experiment, as we have shown, warrant such a measure. The same means of purification may be resorted to as have been prescribed for the dog.

The Flesh as Food.

Haubner says that the slaughter of animals for food may be permittted within twenty-four hours after the bite of a rabid creature, but the injured portion must be cut out and destroyed; even after this time, killing an animal for the sake of its flesh may also be permissible, provided the flesh be consumed by the owner, and not offered for public sale; as the sentiment of the consumers must be consulted. He grants this permission on the plea, that before the outbreak of the disease no contagion is manifest; and that it has been positively ascertained that before the third day after the inoculation, the flesh of animals that afterwards became rabid was eaten with impunity.

Milk.

According to the same high authority, forbidding the use of milk derived from bitten animals is wrong until the disease appears. It may be given to other animals, and the owner of the cattle might use it. Butter and cheese might also be made from it, and kept until it was ascertained whether or not the animal had been successfully inoculated with the rabid virus.

People have remained healthy even when using the milk at the commencement of the disease; but our researches prove that both flesh and milk are dangerous when the malady is developed.

Resume of Preventive Measures.

The measures to be recommended for the prevention of rabies and its extension to the human species, may be comprised under the following heads:—

A. The owners of dogs and other animals should be made to understand the responsibility that rests upon them with regard to the health of their animals, and particularly when contagious diseases appear among them. To maintain them in health they should be properly cared for, and their food, water, cleanliness, and general hygienic treatment should be scrupulously attended to, more especially when rabies is prevalent.

B. The number of useless dogs should be diminished as much as possible, and a tax should be levied on all dogs.

C. Every dog should wear a collar with its owner's name and address engraved thereon, as well as a particular mark impressed by the licensing or police authorities for the proper registration and identification of the animal.

D. All stray dogs without the collar or the owner's name and address thereon should be captured, and if not claimed within a limited period, sold or destroyed; and dogs straying with the proper collar on, may, when circumstances render it necessary, be seized and confined, or returned to the owner, who pays expenses, and is fined, if need be. Bitches in rut should not be allowed to go at large at any time.

E. Unless under special circumstances, as when rabies is prevalent, or when certain animals are vicious, the muzzle should not be worn.

F. The owners of dogs should be held responsible for the damage done by them.

G. Diseased dogs, or those which show the slightest symptoms of disease, altered habits, &c., should be carefully watched, and precautions adopted. If the symptoms of rabies appear, the circumstance should be reported to the police by the owner or attendant on the dog, or other person who knows of its condition. Neglect of this should be estimated as a criminal offence. The police should know the early symptoms of the disease.

H. If other animals which have been in contact with, or bitten by, a rabid dog become unwell afterwards, the symptoms ought to be noted, and should they lead to a suspicion of rabies, the creatures must be isolated, and their condition reported to the police.

I. Suspected animals should not be killed at once if they have bitten any person, but only destroyed when the disease is unmistakably present. In the meantime, they should be well secured and confined.

J. A mad or suspected dog escaping from its owner, or appearing in a district, should be the signal for alertness, and those who know of the circumstance ought to warn the police at once. Children should be guarded, and animals confined or kept from strange dogs. All wandering dogs should be confined or killed.

K. Rabid dogs should be killed; if only suspected, they may be kept until their condition is ascertained.

L. The police authorities should endeavour to obtain every information about any rabid or suspected dog, and to discover the name and address of its owner, learning also what damage it may have done. Regulations and restrictions should be extended over a wide space of country, and neighbouring districts should be warned; all information necessary to put the inhabitants on the alert ought also to be given.

M. When the disease appears in a virulent or epizoötic form, all measures ought to be rigorously enforced. Owners of dogs should give due notice of all changes occurring among their animals. Muzzling may be necessary; but the muzzle for each dog should be properly and securely constructed, and sufficient in size, without being too large. It must have appliances for attaching it firmly to the head.

N. The destruction and confinement of dogs must be assiduously carried out, and heavy fines or imprisonment should be imposed upon those who attempt to evade or neglect the regulations.

O. Dogs should be slaughtered with as little cruelty as possible. They ought to be buried deeply in the ground.

P. Disinfection should be carried out, as with other contagious diseases.

Q. The police regulations and restrictions should be continued for some months beyond the appearance of the last case of rabies. This period should be dependent upon the limit of the incubatory stage of the disease in the dog.

R. With regard to other animals, when wounded by a suspected or rabid dog, the circumstances should be reported and steps taken to ensure safety. Horses, oxen, and other working animals may be employed in the immediate vicinity of their homes, but must not be sold, bartered, or removed within a certain period. The immediate slaughter of wounded or suspected animals is not necessary; but as soon as rabies manifests itself, notice should be given to the local authorities, and the necessary steps taken to prevent damage. The bodies should be buried intact; though under special circumstances skinning them may be allowed, in order to tan or dress these parts.

S. Disinfection to be resorted to as in the case of rabid dogs.

T. The flesh is not dangerous as food until the symptoms of the disease have appeared. If used before this period, certain precautious should be adopted.

U. The milk may also be utilised during the same period.

X. Competent veterinarians must co-operate in the execution of these measures.

PRECAUTIONS TO BE OBSERVED IN HANDLING DOGS AND OTHER CARNIVOROUS ANIMALS.

Though the dog, as a rule, is such a docile and gentle animal to those with which it is acquainted, yet to strangers frequently, and even to friends on occasions, it readily employs its teeth; and as its bite is not always without danger, it is best to be on one's guard by handling it with care. To those unaccustomed to manipulate the animal, these remarks are more particularly intended, as a little maladroitness may bring about serious consequences.

In administering medicine, either fluid or solid, precautions are very necessary, as the mouth must be opened to introduce the remedy well into the throat, and the animal generally struggles, when its teeth may cause injury. For those who are not practised in giving medicine, it would be as well to wear a pair of strong leather gloves, and the dog being firmly held by another person by the back of the neck, or between the knees of the operator, the mouth may be opened by inserting the fingers of one hand behind the fangs, and pressing down the lower jaw. A very good and safe plan is also to pass a wide piece of tape around the upper jaw behind the fangs, and another on the lower jaw in the same situation; by pulling these pieces of tape, one upwards, the other downwards, the mouth is drawn open, and can be so kept with safety for as long as may be necessary.

The only safe place to grip a dog is at the back of the neck, behind the head; there the skin is sufficiently loose to afford a good hold, while the hands cannot be touched by the animal's teeth so long as the grasp is maintained.

With savage or rabid animals, it only too frequently happens that blows will not prevent their biting and holding on. This is particularly noticeable in fighting dogs, which will endure any amount of punishment before they relax their grip, or desist from tearing. Serious accidents have over and over again arisen from people attempting to defend themselves, or rescue other persons or dogs from some infuriated or mad animal's fangs.* The simplest, safest, and by far the most effective plan is *choking*. If the animal wears a collar, this is easily done, as one has only

* The instances are numerous in which I have seen serious wounds inflicted on persons who have interfered to stop dogs fighting or biting other persons; but one of the most unfortunate cases is that related by Dr. Moseley in 1808, and alluded to by Lipscomb (p. 97), in which a man in Compton Street, Soho, was bitten in the right hand as he was humanely interfering to separate two dogs that were fighting with so much violence that one of them had an eye torn out. This person seized one of the dogs awkwardly, and two of the animal's teeth penetrated the outside of his right hand, and wounded the palm considerably. This was in July, 1807. On the 9th of November following he showed the first symptoms of hydrophobia, from which he perished in forty-six hours. The period of incubation was eighteen weeks.

to seize it firmly at the back and pull it tightly against the throat in front. The foot or other hand may most usefully aid in the operation, by pressing strongly against the back of the neck. As soon as the animal experiences the sensation of choking, it will, in attempting to breathe, let go its hold. It should by no means be released immediately, but ought to be still further choked until it is harmless for the time, when means may be had recourse to for securing it properly; indeed, it should be strangled to such a degree as to render it unconscious, or it may do damage to the operator.

When there is no collar on the neck, a strong handkerchief or piece of rope tied round it, and pulled in the same manner, or twisted with a stick, is a ready appliance. I have separated some scores of fighting dogs in this way with absolute impunity, and many of these were so large, and sometimes so ferocious, that it would have been most dangerous to have ventured to interfere with them in any other fashion. It only requires strong arms, and a little coolness and tact.

Should a wound or scratch be inflicted, suction, washing, and, if deemed necessary, cauterisation, ought at once to be employed.

It is scarcely necessary to remark that strange dogs should always be respected until their tempers and character are known, particularly in the streets, roads, or fields. Those suspected of rabies, or rabid, when at liberty, should be captured as speedily as possible, though with every precaution.

APPENDIX.

History (p. 68).

In *Land and Water* for January 27, 1872, there is an intimation that "dumb madness" had broken out in the Cheshire kennels. It is added, "We regret to say that Mr. Corbet has been obliged to destroy twenty-five couples of hounds. One hound was suspected of having "dumb madness" late in the autumn, and about two months ago it was deemed advisable to destroy nine couples, and last week those remaining of the mixed pack, which Mr. Corbet got for hunting the extra day (sixteen couples), were obliged to be killed."

This new outbreak, added to the others among the packs of foxhounds, makes this epizooty of rabies one of the most serious ever experienced in England.

In December and January the disease was also observed at Detroit, Michigan, United States. People and animals were bitten. Mr. Murray, M.R.C.V.S., describes a case of rabies in a horse, which died on December 26, having been bitten on November 25. There were no unusual symptoms beyond those already enumerated; the most marked were restlessness and fury, a savage tendency to tear everything with its teeth, and fly at people to bite them.—*The Veterinarian*, March, 1872. *Detroit Free Press*, January 11, 1872.

Geographical Extent of Rabies (p. 70).

In reply to my inquiry in the *Lancet*, as to whether rabies was really known in Australia or New Zealand, a correspondent, "Ahuriri," in the number of that journal for March 2, 1872, courteously states: "I lived there (in New Zealand) for eleven years, and neither saw nor heard of a case. The inhabitants often wondered at this, as dogs are there exposed to the same influences as in other countries. From its non-appearance, cannot we see that the numerous causes mentioned in standard works, viz., heat, deprivation of sexual indulgence, want of couch grass, etc., are wrong? New Zealanders are greatly afraid that imported dogs will convey the dread disease, which would entail most disastrous results, as the islands teem with dogs, tame and wild."

Symptoms in the Rabbit (p. 280).

The rabbit is so seldom exposed to the bites of mad animals, that I can find no instance in which the disease has been produced in it by accidental inoculation, though it has been induced experimentally. The symptoms in this animal, though of the usual nervous character, are nevertheless peculiar; and I have added a brief description of them in order to complete the list of the domesticated animals in which rabies has been observed. The following history is very interesting in more than one feature.

In 1839, fifty-six lambing ewes, about to yean, were attacked by a very small cur dog on a farm near Shrewsbury, and forty-seven were bitten in one night. The dog was killed by the shepherd in the field next morning, but there was no suspicion that it was mad. A fortnight afterwards several sheep became ill and died, and fifteen were lost before the nature of their malady was guessed, at which period others were ill. By this time a great many of the ewes had lambed, and the lambs of all those which brought forth before the symptoms appeared did well; but with those which manifested the disease before lambing, the young were born dead, or died very soon after birth. The lambs were allowed to suck until the parents died, which was generally in about three days; they were then put to other ewes, or reared by hand, and remained in health.

Mr. Simonds, on April 22, inoculated two rabbits with the saliva from one of the rabid sheep, by introducing setons saturated with that fluid behind their ears. On the 26th they were dull, hanging their heads, and inclining them to one side. They took their food when it was placed before them, but evinced little desire for it. Towards evening the respiration of one was considerably accelerated, and the stupor had increased. The other manifested a strange desire for jumping, which it did in an awkward manner, having apparently lost much power over the voluntary action of the muscles on one side. Occasionally, in these jumps, its head would come in contact with the wall of the box, but this did not deter it from attempting to accomplish the act. At midnight they were both evidently worse; and on taking them up and placing them on their sides, they would remain in that position for some few minutes, being evidently in a state of unconsciousness. On the morning of the 27th each was resting its head on the floor, and they could not be roused from their comatose state: being turned on their side, they struggled until they had resumed their first position. The appetite was gone; there were occasional spasmodic twitchings of the muscles. The stupor increased hourly, and about midday one died. The other at times attempted to jump, which it did still more awkwardly, alighting nearly on its head. If teased, it uttered a slight moan, expressive of its sufferings, and obstinately refused to change the position of its head, which it seemed quite incapable of supporting. Late in the evening it died; but immediately before death a dog and a cat were inoculated with its saliva; on May 8, these animals remained healthy.

The morbid appearances found on examination were: an unhealthy state of the inoculation wound; the coats of the stomach thickened towards the pyloric orifice, apparently from rigid contraction; traces of inflammation on its peritoneal surface, and the mucous membrane covered with a white matter resembling pus, with inflammation of the rugæ; the small intestines exhibited traces of increased vascular action; the vessels of the bladder were beautifully injected, and there was considerable inflammation of the uterus, both body and cornua; the dorsum of the tongue and epiglottis were inflamed; and a singular injection of vessels, distinctly marked, pervaded the whole course of the trachea; on its inner and upper side some frothy viscid mucus filled the larynx; the vessels ramifying on the pericardium were injected; the lungs were inflamed, and the thorax contained some effused fluid. The vessels in the right hemisphere of the cerebellum and on its external surface were injected; not so the left. The vessels ramifying on the medulla oblongata were also beautifully shown. In the second rabbit the larynx and trachea were more inflamed than in the first, and the stomach was less affected.

To make certain that the rabific virus produced the above-described symptoms, and not the irritation arising from the setons, two rabbits were setoned in a similar manner, and the tape allowed to remain in for the same time; but no disease was produced. Two other rabbits were inoculated in the same way with the saliva of a healthy sheep, and they also remained in health.

Morbid Appearances after Death (p. 296).

We have referred to the absence of any notable alteration in the minute structure of the brain and nerve tissues in this blood disease in man, notwithstanding most careful examinations; but it would appear that in some cases, at least, of hydrophobia there are marked and important alterations in these. At a meeting of the Pathological Society of London, held on January 2, 1872, Dr. Clifford Allbut exhibited a series of microscopic sections from the cerebro-spinal centres of two persons who died from this malady. The specimens were taken from the cerebral convolutions, and from the central ganglia, the medulla oblongata, and the spinal cord. Throughout all these centres were found the same morbid conditions, but in different degrees, and these were as follows: 1. Evidences of great vascular congestion with transudation into the surrounding tissues. In all the grey centres the vessels were seen in various degrees of distension, their walls in many cases being obviously thickened; and here and there were seen patches of nuclear proliferation. There was a diminished consistence of some of the parts, particularly of the medulla. This seemed to be due to serous infiltration and soddening, as has been observed in the dog. 2. Hæmorrhages of various size. In many places a refracting material was visible outside the vessels, due apparently to coagulated fibrinous exudate. 3. Little gaps caused by the disappearance of nerve strands which had passed through the granular disintegration of Clarke. In addition to these appearances in the nervous centres, an enlarged spleen had been found in both cases.

The parts appeared to be affected in the following order as regards severity: (1) Medulla, (2) the spinal cord, (3) cerebral convolutions, and (4) central ganglia.

This was in accordance with the symptoms presented during life—viz.: 1. Reflex irritability in the region of the medulla, with no tetanic spasms. 2. Increasing irritability throughout the cord, with semi-tetanus. 3. Delirium.

Killing Diseased or Suspected Animals (p. 388).

In destroying dogs, it was recommended that Prussic acid should be employed in sufficient quantity and newly prepared. But this poison usually loses its potency in a short time unless great care is taken to preserve it, and consequently the promptness of its destructive action cannot always be guaranteed.

Dr. Richardson, who has done so much for humanity in abolishing pain, has endeavoured to benefit the lower creatures in suggesting means and appliances by which, when necessary, they may be quickly deprived of life without experiencing any suffering. He proposes that animals doomed to be destroyed should be made to inhale certain narcotic vapours: one, a mixture of vapour of hydride of amyl and methylene bichloride; another, a mixture of carbon disulphide and methylene bichloride; and a third the vapour of chloroform or of methylene bichloride and pure coal gas. The effect of either of these vapours is rapidly produced; but the first and last are chiefly recommended. They are inhaled by the animal from a muzzle-shaped inhaler, and insensibility follows in a few seconds with the slightest manifestation of pain or distress.

The vapours are certainly not so readily procured as the Prussic acid, and an inhaler might be difficult to find when required to kill a mad dog or cat; but as all humane persons must be deeply interested in the matter, it is well to know that other and more certain, if less common and accessible, means are in existence to deprive small animals of existence without a pang.

THE END.

PRINTED BY VIRTUE AND CO., CITY ROAD, LONDON.